I0649383

Anonymus

Lucas Garcia and other stories

Original, translated, and selected

Anonymus

Lucas Garcia and other stories
Original, translated, and selected

ISBN/EAN: 9783741179143

Manufactured in Europe, USA, Canada, Australia, Japa

Cover: Foto ©Andreas Hilbeck / pixelio.de

Manufactured and distributed by brebook publishing software
(www.brebook.com)

Anonymus

Lucas Garcia and other stories

LUCAS GARCIA,

AND

OTHER STORIES.

ORIGINAL, TRANSLATED, AND SELECTED.

NEW YORK:
THE CATHOLIC PUBLICATION SOCIETY,

Copyright :

THE CATHOLIC PUBLICATION SOCIETY.

1876.

CONTENTS.

LUCAS GARCIA.

FROM THE SPANISH OF FERNAN CABALLERO.

' In an age when all impressions are effaced by the double hammer of civilization and incredulity, it is touching and beautiful to see a people preserve a stable character and immutable
beliefs."

I.

EASTWARD from Jerez, in the direction of the Sierra de Ronda, which
rises in a succession of terraces, as if
to form a suitable pedestal for the
rightly named San Cristóbal, lie the
extensive Llanos de Caulina. A bare
and uniform road drags itself for two
leagues through the palmettoes, and
makes a halt at the foot of the first
elevation, where a lazy rivulet widens
in the sun, and, stagnating in summer, changes its waters into mire.

On the right is seen the castle of
Malgarejo, one of the few Moorish
edifices that time and his faithful
auxiliary in the work of destruction,
ignorance, have left standing. Time
makes ruins, groups them, crowns
them with garlands, and adorns them
with verdure, as if he desired to have
them for places of recreation and
rest ; but the barbarian ignorance
gives no quarter—his only delight is
in dust ; his place of repose, the desert waste ; his end, nothingness.

The angles of the castle are flanked by four large towers. These, as
well as the walls of the whole enclo-
sure, are surmounted by well-formed
turrets, perfect still, and without
notch or break in their beautiful uni-
formity. The castle took its name
of Malgarejo from a knight of Jerez,
by whom its reduction was accomplished in a manner so curious, that
we cannot resist the inclination to
relate it, for the benefit of those who
are unacquainted with the tales of
partisan exploits that abound in the
annals of Jerez.

In the beginning of the thirteenth
century, a hundred and fifty Moors,
with their families, occupied the castle. They went clothed in white, according to the custom of their nation, and mounted gray horses. Shut
up as they were, they procured their
subsistence by foraging the country
at night, and carrying to their stronghold whatever booty they could seize.

Malgarejo resolved to get possession of this formidable place. It was
surrounded, at that time, by a wide
moat. This moat—opened by the
Moors for their protection, and afterward serving them for a sepulchre—
no longer exists.

The Christian cavalier had a slave
that was a most accomplished horse-
man, and to him he promised liberty
if he would swear to devote himself
to the proposed undertaking. The
slave, agreeing, was entrusted by his
master with a mare of singular agili-
ty, and was directed to train her to
leap a ditch, which was to be enlarged, by degrees, to the width of
the one that surrounded the Saracen
castle.

This being accomplished, Malgarejo called together his followers, dis-
guised them as Moors, caused them
to cover their horses with white
cloths, and, one night, when the gar-

5

rison had sallied out upon a raid, approached the fortress. Those within, taking his host for the one they were expecting, viewed its approach without suspicion. When the Christians came nearer, they saw their mistake, and would have raised the bridge, but the slave of Malgarejo had already leaped the moat, and cut the cords, so that it could not be lifted; and the *Jerezanos* made themselves masters of the castle.

The sight of this stronghold, over which the destroyer Time has passed leaving as little trace as would the footstep of a bird, transports the beholder to the past with such vividness of illusion, that he is surprised not to see the pennon of the half-moon fluttering above its towers, and misses a snowy turban from behind every one of its turrets. No fitter place could be found for the representation of a fight or of a tournament between Moors and Christians.

The road to Arcos leaves on its left the sleeping stream and the dead fortress, within whose precinct, like ants in a skeleton, laborers plying the tools of peaceful husbandry are moving.

Ascending this first step of the mountain, the traveller crosses other plains, covered as far as the eye can see with rich harvests, and, finding no nearer inn or stopping-place, takes his siesta at the grange of La Peñuela, formerly the property of the Carthusian fathers—an order so pious, so severe, so worthy and respected, that the country folk still ask each other, " And was there indeed a power that could, and a hand that would dare to touch such men and such things ?"

As the country rises, it covers itself with olive groves, as if it would shelter white and ancient Arcos in the pride with which she preserves her title of city, her venerable privileges, and her state parchments, in spite of decline, or, better said, in spite of her still life, in the midst of the progress that waits upon the march of time—a progress at once gentle, deliberate, and spontaneous.

True to the guerilla traits of her Moorish founders, Arcos appears to the traveller, wearied with the ascent, alternately advancing and retiring, until, passing between two high rocks, he enters unexpectedly into a city so beautiful for situation as to astonish and delight even those who are rarely moved by the charms of nature or the enchantments of the picturesque.

One afternoon, in the year 1840 or thereabout, a crowd of people might have been seen entering a poor-looking house in the barrier of San Francisco. From this house they had carried, on the previous day, the body of one who had been its mistress, and the neighbors were now uniting for the *condolement* required by the rigorous etiquette which is observed by the people, and which manifests the instinctive courtesy and dignity that distinguish them. For all etiquette and all ceremonial are founded upon these bases, and are not the ridiculous and superficial things, either in public or private life, that the revolutionary spirit of the age, and the anxiety to escape from every rein, material and moral, would make us believe. Ceremonial and etiquette, in the right acceptation of the words, are external conduct, disposed so as to give worship to things divine, consideration and respect to things human.

On entering the house, the women assembled in the parlor of the mourner's *habitation.** Opposite this room was another, which had been lent by

* A house sometimes contains two or three sults of apartments for distinct families. Each one forms a habitation.

a neighbor for the accommodation of the men.

Upon a mat in the middle of the apartment first mentioned was extended a handkerchief, into which each person, as he entered, threw one or two copper coins, destined for the stipend of the Mass of San Bernardino.' This custom is observed not only among the poor, but also among those who are well-to-do, for this Mass must be owed to charity. Let sceptics and rationalists explain this as best suits them. We look upon it as an act of humility, joined to the desire of uniting many suffrages. And although we may be more impressed with terrestrial honors, such as a splendid funeral, a showy catafalque, and a proud mausoleum, the fervent petition of the heart, the coin given in charity, the prayers of the church, are better suffrages for heaven. In a corner of the room, upon a low chair, was the principal mourner, a little girl of eight years. Wearied with weeping for her mother, and with remaining so long in one position, she had leaned her head against the back of the chair, and fallen asleep — for sleep is a lover of children, and hastens to their relief whenever they suffer in body or spirit.

"Poor Lucia," said one of the mourners, a kinswoman of the deceased, glancing at the child, "how she will miss her mother!"

"This was the thorn that poor Ana carried to the grave fastened in her heart," observed a neighbor.

"But," asked another, "of what did she die?"

"Only the ground that covers her knows what ailed her," answered the relative, "for Ana did not complain. If she had not been so thin, you might have drunk her; as yellow as a waxen flower, and so weak that a shadow could have knocked her

down, no one would have thought that she was on her way to Holy-field."

"She died of a broken heart!" exclaimed an energetic-looking young matron; "all the world knows it; and because we have an alcalde that is afraid to strap his breeches to the work and cast out of town with the devil's sling these trulls of strangers who come among us to set up drinking-houses, and chouse married men, to their perdition and the ruins of their families!"

"Yes, yes, the alcaldes·have eyes of fishes for all these things," said the relative of the deceased, "just as they have owls' eyes for some others. But they'll get their pay, woman; for though God consents, 'tis not for ever!"

"Yes," answered the first—"consents to the death of the good, and lets the bad live, and crow on. God reserves the justice of heaven for himself. The rod of earthly justice he puts into the hands of men; and a fine account they'll have to give of the way they use it! I'd like to break the one our alcalde carries upon his shoulders!"

"Neighbor," said an old woman, "you are more hasty than a spark from the forge; you attack like the bulls, with eyes shut. Think whom you are speaking of; and bear in mind that 'evil wounds heal, but evil fame kills.' Poor Ana was never well after her last confinement. Death does not come without a pretext: the summer pulled her down, and September finished her; for 'from friar to friar,* God be our guard!'"

"Of course, Aunt Maria," retorted the young woman, "it's quite proper for you, because you are aunt to Juan Garcia, and cousin to the al-

* 28th of August, St. Augustine; 4th of October, St. Francis.

calde, to say so ; for ' with reason or without it, aid us God and our kin.' But I tell you that my José is not to set his foot inside of *La Leona's* * gin-shop ; and I'll see that he don't ! A man may be as honest as Job, but in ' the house of the soap-maker he that doesn't fall slips.' And say what you please, you who are a widow, with the coolness of age in your veins, I shall not go back of what I have said. ' He that jumps straight, falls on his feet,' and I say, and resay it : they ought to flay alive the good-for-nothing calamary of a she-sergeant, with her sentry-box figure, and face darker than an oil-skin, so full of pock-marks that it looks as if she had fallen into a bed of chick-peas, and more hair on her lip than a grenadier ! Remember the proverb, ' Salute the bearded woman at a distance !' "

" And her children," said the mourner—" little imps that she keeps so greasy and neglected ! They look like a nest of calamaries."

" But she thinks them little suns," added another.

" Ya !" exclaimed the first who had spoken ; " said the black beetle to her young ones, ' Come hither, my flowers !' and the owl calls hers ' drops of gold.' Who ever saw such a thing, sirs," she continued, growing excited—" who ever saw anything so wicked as to dupe a married man, the father of children, ruin him, pull down his house, and murder his wife by inches ! And this is known and permitted ! I tell you, such a thing sinks deep !"

" Yes, it is worse than stabbing with a knife," exclaimed one woman.

" It cries to God !" added another.

" It is a scandal of the monstrous kind," proceeded the first. " Poor Ana, though I did not see much of

* *La Leona,* the lioness.

her, I loved her well. Almond-paste is not milder than she was, and as meek and free from malice as a sheep in the hands of the butcher. O men ! men ! There is a curse on them that pull their clothes on over their feet ; and that is the reason our dear Lord would not wear breeches, but always dressed in a tunic."

" Come, daughter," said Aunt Maria, " nothing is mended by malediction, nor by spitting out the quinine. Let us pray for the soul of the departed, for that is what will really benefit her."

These words were the signal for complete silence. Aunt Maria took her rosary, the rest following her example, and, after saying the act of contrition and a solemn credo, proceeded to recite the rosary of souls, repeating three times after the Paternoster, and instead of the Hail Mary,

" O Lord, by thy infinite mercy,"

the others answering in chorus,

"Grant to the souls of the faithful departed peace and glory."

Nothing was now heard in the mourning room of the women but the grave murmur of the prayers and suppressed sighs of pity and sorrow.

The other parlor presented a very different spectacle. The widower, serene as a glass of water, and cool as a fresh lettuce, now that the day of the burial had passed, considered himself dispensed from the attitude of mourning, and smoked, listening and talking to all, just as usual, as if death had entered his house and departed without leaving either trace or impression of his awful presence.

The indifferent ones followed his example, so that, had not all worn cloaks, no one would have supposed that this was a condolement, a tribute of love and respect to a life that had ended, and of sympathy with an overwhelming sorrow. The only figure that appeared to be in harmony with the object of the reunion was that of a boy thirteen years old, the son of the deceased, who sat near his father with his elbows resting on his knees, and his face buried in his hands, weeping inconsolably.

" What kind of day has it been ?" asked the widower.

" Unhealthy," answered one.

" And the sky ?"

" Patched; I think the rain is not far off. There was fog this morning, and ' fog is the rain's sponsor and the sun's neighbor.' "

" The wind will soon sweep the cobwebs from the sky," said a third, " for it blows from sunset side. The rain is shyer than sixpences."

" No matter," answered the first, " last year it did not rain till All Saints ; and a better year, or another of the same piece, hasn't been seen since the creation. Laborers, farmers, and tenants all got tired of gathering, and had more than enough— the barley, in particular, grew so thick that you couldn't set a spade between the blades."

" The month of January is the key of the year. If the sky does not open in January, there will be no harvest."

" Hola ! Uncle Bartolo !" all exclaimed, as a small, vigorous old man entered the apartment. " Where do you hail from ? where have you been ever since we missed you from here ? "

Uncle Bartolo, after offering to the mourner the usual condolences, seated himself, and, turning toward his interrogators, replied :

" Where do I come from ? The district of Doñana, without varying from the most direct line. Since the French war ended, and I took the road, I have been water-carrier* to the *You Sirs.*† They have them there in Doñana of all complexions—legitimate, grafted, cross-breed, and supposititious, even English. *Caballeros !* Deliver us; but those Swiss of the French are the ones ! Stout fellows; very white; very ruddy; very fair-haired, and very puffy. But as to spirit, they have no more than they drink ; and grace, they have not any. They carry their arms like the sleeves of a capote, and set their feet down like pestles. Whenever I saw those feet that resembled *jabeques*, ‡ I used to say to myself,

' A good foot and good ear
Signs of a good beast are.'

For talking, they make use of a kind of jargon that, in my opinion, they themselves don't understand. These parleys that I don't comprehend displease me, for I never know whether I am being bought or sold.

" There was one—the size of a tunny-fish—they called Don 'Turo.§ He fell to me. To see him blowing and sweating over those sands made one pity him, for a league finishes them ; the sun offends them ; the heat makes them weak, and dissolves them entirely. That platter-face would persist in doing everything contrariwise, as they do it in his country. Once he took it into his head to use my clasp-knife to eat with, and cut himself. With that he got out a medicine-chest as big as a surgeon's. ' Go along !' said I to myself, ' a spider bit me, and I bound the wound up in a sheet.' He was as hard-headed as a corner. Another time he made up his mind that he ought to shoot a partridge, and,

* *Asacan*, water-carrier, said of a servant or very laborious person.
† *Los Ustias*, the You Sirs. That is to say, grand folks that must be treated to the *Usted* (you), instead of the *tu* (thou) of common people.
‡ *Jabeque*, a clumsy three-masted vessel used in the Mediterranean.
§ Arturo.

though I told him it was against the law to shoot partridges at that season, he fired, and would have fired if his father had stood before the mouth of his gun. He fired and killed an urraca.* 'Sir,' said I, 'what has your honor done?' Says he to me, 'Killed the partridge.' 'Why, sir, it is n't a partridge, it's an urraca.' 'It's all right,' said the big bungler, quite composedly.. 'But it is not right,' answered I; 'the killing of urracas is prohibited.' 'And who prohibits it?' he asked, putting on his face of a lion. 'I have my license, that cost me three thousand reals.' 'But, sir, that is for large game—you understand? The urracas mustn't be killed. You comprehend?' Says he to me, 'In this country of *Santísima María*'—for, as I have told you already, he said everything reversed. as they do in his—'in this country there's no end of privileges, and do the very urracas have them?'

"That question was so foolish, or else meant to be ironical, that I did n't care to set him right; so I told him, 'Yes, privileges that were granted to them in very ancient times, by *Doña Urraca* herself.' He took out a blank-book and wrote that down. 'Let the ball roll,' said I in my jacket, 'it isn't my business to stop it.'"

"But, Uncle Bartolo, why may they not kill urracas in the district?" asked a young man.

"Because they are the ones that planted the pine woods," answered Uncle Bartolo.

"Oh! none of that! you are not talking to platter-face," replied the youth.

"So I perceive, since his swallow for novelties was too big; and you—for a blockhead of those who believe only what they see—haven't any. Nevertheless, sir, that the urracas do

plant the pines is a truth as evident as a house. They open the ripe cones, and pick out the seeds for food. Being very saving birds, they bury those that they can't eat; and, being very brainless ones, they forget all about it and never go back to look for them; and the seeds sprout. If it were not true, why would the dukes prohibit the killing of urracas, when they are thicker in the district than sparrows on a threshing-floor? Therefore, Alonso, no one may say, 'This camel can't enter the eye of my needle'; for, of two silly birds, the one that always keeps his bill shut is more silly than the one that has his always open. But you were a dunce from the beginning; and, as you grow older, you are gaining upon Blas, that ate horse-beans."

"And at night, uncle, what did those people do with themselves there in the province?" asked the listeners.

"The Englishmen ate and drank, for their honors are made hollow, in order that they may always be putting things into their mouths. That is the reason they are so fat and big. Platter-face told me one day—with an air as if God had just revealed it to him—that I was able to go so long without getting tired because I was lean; and that he would give a thousand dollars, or some such sum, to be as lean as I. I answered—shouting to make him understand better—'Your worship has only to eat *gazpacho* * to dry up your flesh, and raw onions and garlic to sharpen your senses.'"

"And the Spaniards—how did they pass the evenings, Uncle Bartolo?"

"The Spaniards? Talking through the very stitches of their garments; bawling till you would have thought they were echoes: and quarrelling

---

* Magpie.

* A common dish on the table of the country people.

about things of the government. For, nowadays, everybody wants to know everything himself, and to command: the very beetles set up their tails and complain of a cough. I tell you, sirs, there are no more such Spaniards as there were in the time of the French war. We were as one man then, and all of one mind. Now there are moderates and *extremists*. I, who am an *extremist* only when it concerns my gun, my wife, and my children, could wish the devil would fly away with so much gab. It made me want to say to them : 'Gentlemen, where there is less tongue, count on more judgment,' and 'so much grass chokes the wheat.'"

"One night one of the *You Sirs* called me, and wanted to know if I was in the war against Napoleon. 'Yes, sir,' I answered, 'I was a guerilla.' 'Well, then,' said he, 'you just come here, for I am going to read you the will he made.'"

"What! did that man make a will, Uncle Bartolo?" asked some of the oldest of the listeners.

"Yes, and before he died, it is supposed.

"'But, your worship,' I asked, 'what had that kingdom-thief to give away? Did they not then make him throw up everything he had taken?'

"The *You Sir* had an open book, and began to read. Gentlemen, that *soccarron*,* in his will, went on distributing everything, his goods, his arms, his body, and his heart. I was perplexed. 'Well, what do you think of it, uncle?' said his honor, when he had ended. 'Sir,' I answered, 'from what I can see, that unbeliever thought of everything; but neither in his life nor in his death did he remember his soul.'"

"Why did you join the guerillas,

Uncle Bartolo?" asked one of the company.

"What a question!" exclaimed the guerilla, looking at the one who had asked it, and weaving himself backwards and forwards with much composure.

"'He that asks does not err,' Uncle Bartolo."

"Yes, but this is a case of 'He that asks does not err, and I ask if they bury the dead with the deceased?'"

"What I mean is, when did you leave your house, and how did you happen to fall in with the *partida?*"*

"Ya! those are other questions, Lopez. Some French horsemen came here—they call them *colaseros* (cuirassiers) — my wife was more afraid of them than of a contagion, and every time she heard the clarionets, she would say to me, in a fright, 'They are sounding the charge.' 'No, wife,' I would tell her, 'they are sounding the *premonition.*' One day the cornet—they used to call him *Trompi*—came in tipsy, and insulted my wife. I, who was not afraid of any three that might come, and never stopped to think of consequences, said to him, 'Out of here, little soul of a pitcher, and Barabbas cut a slice from you!' With that he drew his sword, and would have cut me, but I snatched my knife, and finished him at once; and then, catching up mantle and blanket, took the wind for the mountains. I stopped in Benamahoma with the Padre Lovillo—and there you have it all."

"The Padre Lovillo was the captain of the partida?" questioned a youth.

"Yes, the Padre Lovillo. *Candela!* That was a man you could call a man! No talker—not he ; but the words he used were few and good..

---

* Offscouring.

* Partisans, or party.

If any one wanted to brag of his doings, he would say, ' Let them be seen, not heard. You understand, cackler ? Stabs with steel, not with the tongue; balls of lead, not of wind.' Sirs, that man was ready for everything, as you would have declared with two tongues if you had had them. When we were going to attack the French, he used to say, ' Listen, sons, our fathers died for their country, and we are not to be less than they.' Then, drawing his sword, he would shout, ' *Now* let us see who has pluck!' and charge like another Santiago,* and we after him, as if he had led us to Paris in France. We felt neither hunger nor weariness; it was a fight without drum or trumpet, but it made the Frenchmen shiver. They named us the ' *Briganes* † of the Black Mountain,' and were more afraid of us than of the trained soldiery.

" Don 'Turo, who knew that I had been a *brigan*, called me into the parlor one evening, and, when he had squeezed himself into a chair, told me to sit down. I began to wonder where all these Masses were going to end. ‡ Surely, I thought, he cannot want me to clean his gun ! But I waited for the mountain to bring forth, and presently he asked me to explain the *trafica* § of guerilla fighting. When I saw him come out with that ladder, I got angry, and told him, ' No ;' that my pronouncing was very bad, and his understanding worse. But all the others insisted, and, not to seem disobliging, I repeated a very good and well-versed poem, that was going the rounds then."

" And what was it about, Uncle Bartolo ? "

* The patron of Spain.
† Brigands.
‡ To have misgivings as to the result of anything.
§ *Tactica*, tactics.

" It relates a conversation between Malapart * and that Indian, *Munrô*, Duke of *Ver*." †

" Go on, uncle, say it," exclaimed all present.

The following romance, which the old guerilla recited, was very popular at that time among the people. It owes its humor to the fact that neither its unlettered composer, nor those who recited it, had any suspicion that they were giving a caricature. They considered it a simple and probable account of what would take place between Napoleon and Murat when they saw their last troops vanquished. Even the conclusion is in no way inconsistent with their ideas of the antecedents and characters of the personages.

Nap. How is this, friend *Munrô !*
Why are you here again ?
Why have you left your capital ?
What sent you out of Spain ?
Speak on, and don't delay ;
We have no time to spare ;
Tell me, in terms exact,
What has happened there.

Mur. Easy, sir, if you please ·
Sire, do not press me so ;
Only let me get breath,
I'll tell you what I know.
But, first, send for a chair,
That some rest we may take
While I tell you the tale,
For, indeed, my legs ache.

Nap. Right, for you have grown fat,
And glad am I to see
Proof that the airs of Spain
So well with you agree.

Mur. Sire, you are mistaken ;
But let the matter go,
For things of more account
Your majesty should know.
And, come to what must come,
Without any more ado—
For, believe me or not, sire,
All I tell you is true.

Nap. Why, what has happened now ?
Good Heavens, man, speak out !
What have you seen in Spain
To put you so about ?

Mur. Great Emperor of France,
Your force has been in vain ;
Nor did flatteries avail—
You cannot conquer Spain.

* *Mala*, bad ; *parte*, part ; name given by the Spanish soldiers to Bonaparte.
† Murat, Duke of Berg.

No notice will they take
Of your promises of pay,
And peace, and rank to all,
And bull-fights every day.

Nap. But, my soldiers, do not they
In the mountains still remain?

Mur. Yes, captives they remain
With their general, *Dupon,*
And the eagles of France;
And every sword and gun
Might as well be a distaff,
For Castaños and his men
Have settled their account.

Nap. Peste! Because you tell it,
The tale I must believe;
From another I would not
A word of it receive.
No doubt, in Zaragoza
Our cause has better speed,
In humbling them at last
We surely must succeed.

Mur. All your force is useless;
The knaves will not submit.
If you wish to lose France,
And make an end of it,
Send it to Zaragoza,
It will find a bloody tomb,
And remain there, buried,
Until the Day of Doom.

Nap. Can nothing, then, be done
With those troops of Arragon?

Mur. We have none that on them
Will venture to advance.

Nap. But Moncey's triumphant
In the kingdom of Valence?

Mur. Sire, he has dropped his ears,
And slunk away, ashamed;
Those Valencians have a way
Their enemies to tame.
They mount on swiftest steeds,
And, running a swift career,
Unhorse the astonished foe
Before he is aware.

Nap. It seems, then, that maxims,
And lying, and caution
Have failed in that country;
But who had a notion
That Spain would be equal
To France in a contest?
We now can do nothing
But send for Funest.[*]

Mur. And how can he get here,
When the Portuguese men,
With the Spaniards united,
Have him closely shut in,
With sentinels stationed?
No help can avail him,
For surrender he must,
When eatables fail him.
The best thing to do, is
To yield to their clamor,
And give back the king
That Spaniards all honor.

[*] *Funesto.* Nickname given by the Spanish soldiers to Junot.

Perhaps, sire, if—with him
Appeased and delighted—
They will let our troops go,
Your throne may be righted;
For upset it they will
At the rate they are making,
And cut off your head,
And from me be taking
My fine dukedom of *Ver;*
Or, if we escape, sire,
The fate I am dreading,
We'll have to sweep chimneys
Again for a living.
I've forgotten the trade,
And lost my dexterity;
But you, who were master,
Would mount with celerity.

Nap. Only a pitiful knave
Such memories would renew.

Mur. Well, sire, if that don't suit,
I've another thing in view;
We'll seek a brighter sphere,
And a foreign city find,
Where through the streets we'll rove,
Crying "Sci-i-issors to gri-ind."

"And which did he do, uncle?" asked one — "sweep chimneys or grind scissors?"

"*He sweep chimneys!*" exclaimed Uncle Bartolo. "Such people always fall into feather-beds! They carried him to St. Helena—beyond Gibraltar—where he had it quite comfortable till he died raving, after the devil had helped him to make that will."

"Here comes Uncle Cohete," said a man who sat by the window.

"Make him a sign to come in," said the person nearest him, in a low tone.

Uncle Cohete was a simple, good old man, who acted the merry-andrew for the purpose of obtaining alms for a religious house of which he was *demandante.*[*] He could mimic to perfection the songs of all birds; the near and distant barking of the dog, the mewing of the cat; and so excelled in imitating the peculiar hiss and crackling of a kite in the air, as to have obtained the nickname of *cohete* (kite), by which he was known. He had, besides, a stock of

[*] One who asks alms for charitable purposes.

simple verses, ballads, riddles, and odd scraps of humor, which he would repeat with inimitable expression and drollery. The sources from which he drew his supplies could not be told. This, he had learned in a town on the Llanura; that, in a village of the Sierra; another at the fireside of the manse. But, in his mimicry of the birds, they themselves had been the teachers, aided by unusual flexibility of organs, and great patience and perseverance on the part of the disciple. For, in all branches—whether important or insignificant—perseverance yields great results.

It having been intimated to Uncle Cohete that the company wished him to tell something diverting, he began by saying *The Commandments of the Rich Man and the Poor Man*—a collection of ironical precepts, which enjoyed great popularity at that time —as follows:

" The commandments of the rich man, nowadays, are five, namely:
" The first. Thou shalt have no end of money.
" The second. Thou shalt despise all the rest of the world.
" The third. Thou shalt eat good beef and good mutton.
" The fourth. Thou shalt eat flesh on Good Friday.
" The fifth. Thou shalt drink both white wine and red.

" These commandments are included in two:
Let all be for me, and nothing for you.

" The commandments of the poor man are five, namely:
" The first. Thou shalt never have any money.
" The second. Thou shalt be despised by all the world.
" The third. Thou shalt eat neither beef nor mutton.
" The fourth. Thou shalt fast, even if it be not Good Friday.
" The fifth. Thou shalt taste neither the white wine nor the red.

" These commandments are included in two:
Scratch thyself, and bear everything for the love of God."

" Uncle, did not the son of *Roba-Santos** who is heaping money, give you an alms?" asked one.
" No, he gave me nothing," answered Uncle Cohete.
" Like father, like son," said Uncle Bartolo.
" Next year, uncle, you will get a pile, for 'when the fields have, the saints have.'"
" Uncle Cohete, take these two coppers, and tell us *The Commandments of the New Law*," said the man who had called him in:

" The commandments of the new law are ten, namely:
" The first. Let there be no money in Spain.
" The second. Let the world turn upside-down.
" The third. Let every one play gentleman.
" The fourth. Let not a single copper come from America.
' The fifth. Let there be no end of drafting.
" The sixth. Let the new law come from abroad.
" The seventh. Let there be fewer people that are not wanted.
" The eighth. Let them distribute biscuits in Navarra.
" The ninth. Let every one look out for himself.
" The tenth. Let all be at variance.

" These commandments are included in two:
Some say yes, and others say no."

" Tell us a riddle, uncle."
" Fifty ladies and five gallants: the fifty ask fowl; the five ask bread," said the old man, of whom nature, and the kind of life he led, had made the personification of ready and good-humored odedience.
" The Rosary! I knew that," said a little boy. " Tell another."

* Rob the saints.

*The mantle of Lady Leonor
Sinks in the river, but covers the shore."

" We give it up, uncle."

" It is the snow, gentlemen."

At this moment they were interrupted by the ringing of the sunset
bell, and, and, all rising, stood with uncovered heads.

" Will you recite the prayer, Uncle
Bartolo," said the widower.

Uncle Bartolo repeated the Ange-
lus, adding a Paternoster for the
deceased. And now the grief of
the sobbing child in the corner broke
forth in bitter crying.

" Stop that, Lucas !" said his father. " You have been going on in
that way, hic ! hic ! like an old woman for two days. You ought to
have gone into the women's room.
Let me hear you crying again ! You
understand ?"

" Let me tell *you*, Juan Garcia,"
said Uncle Bartolo, "that you are
the first man I ever heard rebuke
the tears of a son for his mother !
You see me, with my years, my beard,
and my guerilla life ; well, I remember mine, and weep for her still !

" But, uncle, 'frown, and frown
again, of a bad son makes a good
one.' Lucas here is a regular *Mar-
cia Fernandes*,* brought up in the
folds of his mother's skirts. I must
teach him that men resist, and do
not allow themselves to be overcome
by tribulations."

Uncle Bartolo shook his head.
" Time and not ointment will cure
the patient. If you had died, his
mother would not have been the one
to rebuke your son for the tears he
shed over you."

Juan Garcia continued his former
life, abandoning himself with more
liberty to the wicked woman of whom
the friends of his dead wife had spok-

* A girl-boy.

en at the *condolement.* She was called *La Leona* in allusion to her native island of Leon, where she had
married a sergeant, who was afterward sent to serve in America. Like
all bad women, *La Leona* was much
worse than men of the same class,
inasmuch as, in the subtle organization of woman, the delicacy that
is given to her for good turns into a
refinement of evil, and her instinctive
penetration into malignant sagacity.
Not satisfied with having attracted
to herself Juan Garcia, who possessed a small patrimony, *La Leona*, impelled by the bitter envy which a
lost woman feels toward one who is
honest, undertook to render him indifferent to his wife, and succeeded
not only in this, but also in causing
him to ill-treat and abandon her.
Juan Garcia was a weak man, easily
subjugated by those who knew how
to obtain an influence over him, and,
by way of compensating himself for
this complaisance, very obstinate and
overbearing in his treatment of others. By degrees, it came to pass
that his mistress would not receive
him with favor unless he brought
her, as an offering, the relation of
some act of coldness or cruelty to
the victim whose only crime was
that of affording, by her right, and
by her silent and prudent endurance,
the most patent condemnation of
the conduct of these two, a condemnation all the more ignominious
because of the great purity of manners which prevails in country places.
And in order to gain our assertion
credit with those who are disposed
to accuse us of partiality for the
country people, we hasten to say
that this purity may naturally be attributed to the wholesome influence
of labor, which, in putting indolence
to flight, puts to flight with it the
vices it generates, and to the blessed
poverty, which, being without the

means of satisfying them, hinders their birth. Having convinced utilitarians with these reasons, we will add to them others of our own; namely, the salutary ideas of morality and rooted principles of honor that many centuries of Catholicism have fixed in the hearts of these people—principles renewed, in each successive generation, by the unchanging zeal that is the property of religion, and that never wearies or grow lukewarm.

Like all other general rules, the above has its exceptions. Juan Garcia furnished one. His unkindness, united with the grief and shame his conduct caused her, had certainly hastened the death of poor Ana, whose last act of affection as a wife, and duty as a Christian, had been to forgive him. Alas! the soul of the husband was so deeply mired that even this saintly death could awaken in it neither pity nor remorse. Not that he was utterly perverse, but his eyes, like those of many another in this world of error, were covered by one of those veils which must fall on the day of God's judgment, when the light of truth will be the first punishment that awaits the willingly blind.

His boy and girl remained orphaned and neglected, and would have been entirely forsaken but for that active charity which makes women constitute themselves fervent protectors of the helpless and severe judges of the wrong-doer. The wives of Juan's neighbors took care of the children, and obliged him to feed and clothe them, freely casting in his face his evil conduct, while, with imperturbable coolness, they prescribed to him his obligations.

Ah charity!—some proclaim and others comprehend thee; some would guide thee, and thou guidest others! Why art thou not found in the palaces that philanthropy builds for thee? Why dost thou appear in all thy brightness in the dwellings of the poor, delighting thyself with the widow's farthing? It is because thou wilt be queen and not a slave!

The children could not be consoled for the death of their mother. Isolated as they were, all the sentiments of their hearts became converted into love for each other, and sorrow for their loss.

Lucas, however, who was five years older than his sister, did his best to enliven and distract her.

" Don't cry so, Lucia," he said to her one night, not long after the *condolement.* " Mother will not come back for crying, and you make me cry. What shall I do to amuse you?"

The child made no answer.

"Shall I sing you a romance ?"

Lucia inclined her head in token of assent, and the boy sang in his clear, sweet voice the following ballad:

Holy Saviour of La Luz,
Teach a child's tongue how to tell
A thing that happened in Seville,
Right, and worthily, and well.
Of a mother who liv d there,
And two daughters that she had;
One was humble, mild, and good
The other one was proud and bad.
They marry with two brothers,
Who are brothers but in name—
Under the same roof nurtured,
But in nothing else the same.
The younger sells his portion,
And loses the whole in play ;
The elder follows the plough,
And works in his field all day.
Then the younger dies, and leaves
His wife, all alone and poor ;
Her children weep for bread,
And she seeks her sister's door,
Praying, "In God's name, sister,
And for his sweet Mother's sake,
Give my little children bread,
And his word in payment take."
"Go, Mary," cries the sister,
"Beggar, take yourself away !
Was my lot better than yours
Upon our wedding-day ?"
Weeping and broken-hearted,
The poor mother turns again ;
To know her cause of sorrow
The neighbors ask in vain.
Of the parlor of her house
She had made a room for prayer

To our Lady of the Beads:
And now she enters there,
And, with her little children,
Before the altar falls
Of our sweet princess Mary,
And on her name she calls.
  Now, homeward in the evening
The good brother turns his feet;
Finds table spread and waiting,
And he sits him down to eat.
He takes a loaf and breaks it,
But throws it away again,
For blood runs out of the bread,
On his hand he sees the stain.
Then he takes and breaks another,
But still the red blood falls—
"Oh! what is this?" astonished,
To his trembling wife he calls.
"Tell me, I say! what is it?"
For to tell she is afraid:
'In vain to me, this morning,
For bread my sister prayed!'
"And she that, without pity,
To a sister refuses bread,
To God's Mother doth refuse it,"
Then the angry husband said.
  Six loaves the young man gathered,
And in haste to the abode
Of his sister and her children
He straightway took the road.
The window-shutters were closed,
And locked were windows and doors;
But the gleam of many lights
Shone out through the apertures—
Shone on six angels of God,
All kneeling upon the floor
Round six bodies of mother and children
That would never hunger more.
  "Farewell, my soul's dear sister,
And sweet nephews of my heart!
Though gold I have, and plenty,
I would gladly give my part
For yours in the blessed country
Where sorrow is all forgot,
And the labor of life exchanged
For the eternal better lot!"

"And did she let her sister starve to death?" asked the child, her eyes refilling from her already surcharged heart.

"Yes, yes; she was a good-for-nothing; but don't cry, Lucia, a story isn't a thing that ever happened."

"If it had never happened, they would not have put it in the romance," said the little girl.

"They made it up," replied Lucas. "Don't you believe it, dear. When I am a man and can earn, the least piece of bread I may have, I must divide with my heart's little sister. You know that before mother died she put you in my care, and I made her a promise never to forsake you."

"And will you keep it?"

"So may God give me his glory!"

"And if you ever forget it, I am to sing you this romance, to put you in mind of what you say now."

"That is so; you must learn it.'"
And the boy set himself to teach his sister the romance.

II.

SEVEN years passed in this manner. Lucia was fifteen, and had blossomed into one of those exquisite and fragile creatures that, in hot climates, appear so rarely and vanish so soon. Lucas, who was twenty, had developed admirably. He was a youth of manly appearance, and so judicious and industrious that farmers and managers of haciendas employed him in preference to others. Both inherited their mother's type — the oval face, fine aquiline nose, large and expressive black eyes, small mouth, adorned with perfect teeth, broad high forehead, and the bearing of mingled grace and nobility that distinguish the Andalusian.

Their father had yielded completely to the influence of *La Leona*, who absorbed his living, and had made the more effectually. Too enervated and lazy to enter upon a new path, he went on selling his possessions to satisfy the woman's exactions, as an exhausted stream continues to flow in the channel it made when it was full and strong, without either the will or the force to open another. From the time that Lucas was able to work, he had maintained the house alone, with that mysterious day's wages of the laborer which God seems to bless, as he did the loaves and fishes destined to feed so many poor people. Else, how the *peseta*, sometimes two reals * a day can support husband, wife, generally half a dozen robust children; an old father or mother, or widowed mother-in-law, clothe them all and the head of the family in a very expensive manner,* pay house-rent and the costs of child-birth, sickness, and unemployed days; and still yield the copper they never refuse to *God's-namers*,† is a thing past comprehension, and belongs to the list of those in which, if we see not the finger of God or his immediate intervention, is because we are very thoughtless or voluntarily blind.

Lucas, who loved his sister above all things, seeing her entirely neglected by her father, had assumed over her the sort of tutelage, recognized and incontestable among the people, which belongs to the eldest brother —a tutelage which is annexed to the obligation of maintaining younger brothers and sisters if they are fatherless. This obligation and right instinctive do not constitute a law, nor are they laid down in any code, but are impressed by tradition on the heart, and have, no doubt, given rise to the institution of entails.‡ Lu-

cas presented, also, the uncultivated type of those chivalrous and poetical brothers that Calderon, Lope, and other contemporary writers have given us in their delightful pictures of Spanish manners as models of nobility, delicacy, and punctilious honor.

As for Lucia, she was, as her mother had been, loving, impressible, and yielding. She regarded her brother with the deepest affection, in which respect mingled, without lessening its tenderness.

One evening, when several neighbors, who tenanted Juan Garcia's house, were met together in the yard, one of them—it was the kinswoman of the departed Ana—said:

"Have you heard the news? It is reported that *La Leona's* husband is dead. What do you say to it?"

"That *La Leona* is just now singing:

'My spouse is dead, and to heaven has flown,
Wearing the thorns of a martyr's crown,'"

replied one of the neighbors.

"There will be talk enough, woman, if it is true," replied the first speaker.

"Well, what do you want me to say? I feel it for one."

"I feel it for *two*," added a third, laughing.

"That is what I feel most," continued the kinswoman. "It is reported already that Juan Garcia is going to marry with the rag of a widow."

"Woman! will you hold your tongue?"

"No; and I say more: I say that I don't doubt it; for the wretch has him down, and holds him from beneath, so that she can put him to the torture with "thou must swallow this, or I will lay on thee with that.'"

"True enough," observed the other, "she has made a fool of him with drink; and, not satisfied with giving him wine, which is natural

---

* We have thought it worth while to give the exact cost of the simplest dress—such a one as the poorest laborer is never without—of an Andalusian peasant:

		reals.
Cloak,	. . .	260 reals.
Cloth jacket,	. . .	60 "
Cloth breeches,	. .	60 "
Set of buttons (silver), .		60 "
Idem for jacket,	. .	36 "
Woollen sash, .	. .	50 "
Vest,	. . .	30 "
Linen shirt,	. .	20 "
Linen drawers,	. .	15 "
Calf-skin shoes,	. .	28 "
Gaiters, .	. . .	40 "
Stockings,	. .	14 "
Handkerchief,	. .	4 "
Hat, .	. . .	30 "
Total,	. . .	696 "

—without the making, which is done by the women of the household.

What will be said to this by those who are all for utility, economy, and savings-banks, when the Andalusian rustic might, without inconvenience, go clad in a frieze sack, a pair of hempen sandals, and a rush hat?—*Authoress.*

† *Pordioseros*, those who ask in God's name—that is to say, beggars. For this and other delicate and tender epithets that the Spanish poor apply to the unfortunate, our stern language has no equivalents.

‡ The actual organization of the family throughout the kingdom of Aragon, the Basque provinces, and the mountains of Santander. It is this that makes the mania for codification that at present exists in Spain so much to be dreaded.—*Spanish Ed.*

and the legitimate child of the soil, she poisons him with bad brandy."

"The kite will get everything away from him by degrees, till she leaves him stuck, like a star lizard, to the bare wall," added another; "for she is more covetous than greediness, that 'walks one hand along the ground, and the other in the sky, and, with its mouth wide open, that nothing may go by.'"

"She'll be Juan's third wife, and may die like the other two, and the four children he has under the sod. He must have some deadly exhalation about him, like a snake."

"Kill *La Leona!* As if that would be possible! It's my opinion that Death himself couldn't do it, with a century to help him. There was the cholera, that carried off so many good people; it never approached her door."

"The she-rake has no end of luck."

At this moment Lucas entered. It was Saturday evening, and he had come to spend the Sunday at home.

"Lucas," asked his kinswoman, "do you know that *La Leona* is a widow, and they say that your father is going to marry her?"

A thunder-bolt could not have hurt Lucas more suddenly than did these words; nevertheless, he maintained his composure while he answered:

"Either you are dreaming awake, Aunt Manuela, or age is getting the better of your understanding."

"Don't fling my age into my face, *Luquecillo*," * said the good woman, who was jocose. "I would rather you called me sly fox; it is permitted to say *old* only in the company of wines and parchments."

"Well, then, why were you born so long ago? But don't come to me with your troubles."

* Big Lucas.

"Publish your decrees in time, my son, for this one is in everybody's mouth."

"They may say what they please behind my back. Regiments can't capture tongues and thoughts, but no one is going to speak against my father when I am present."

"I'll lay you something, Lucas, that he'll marry!"

"That will do, Aunt Manuela; you know the saying, 'Stop jesting while jesting is pleasant.'"

Like all men of stern nature, Lucas, when in earnest, had in him a something that imposed respect: the women were silent, and he went into his own dwelling.

He did not speak to his sister of the matter that occupied his thoughts so painfully, but, after giving her the money he had brought, remained a while talking cheerfully and affectionately with her, and then went in search of his neighbor, Uncle Bartolo.

He knew that the guerilla, on account of his age and good judgment, and because he had been his grandfather's friend, exercised great influence over his father, and could think of no one so suitable to confide in, and implore to interfere in the matter, and dissuade Juan Garcia, if, indeed, he entertained it, from such an outrageous project.

"Hola! What brings *Luquillo* with the step of a Catalan and face of a blacksmith?" exclaimed the old man, as Lucas entered.

The youth told his errand.

Uncle Bartolo, having heard him to the end, shook his head, as he remarked:

"Lucas, the proverb says, 'Between two millstones one had best not put his thumbs;' but—well, for your sake and Lucia's, the pretty dove! I will do what you ask, even if I lose—and I shall, for certain—

your father's friendship. I tell you though, beforehand, that interference will do no good."

" But, uncle, that which is never attempted is never done."

" Have I not told you I would try ? You shall never say that you sought me and did not find me. I only want to remind you that counsels are thrown away upon the foolhardy, and perfumes upon swine. And to tell the truth, I would rather tackle one of those highwaymen of last year than your father ; notwithstanding that the she-bandit has taken and done for him as easily as a spider would vanquish a fly."

Our old warrior went, the next day, to see Juan Garcia, whom he found indisposed.

" Hola ! Juan," he cried, as he entered, " how are you ?"

" Not so well as I might be, uncle," responded the invalid. " And you ?"

" As well as can be, since I am a man of the old times, and not sorry for it : better suited beneath white hairs than white sheets. But," continued the guerilla, who in his long career had never studied diplomacy nor learned the art of preambling, " let us come to the point ; for one needn't go by the bush where there's a highroad ; they tell me, though I don't want to believe it, that you are going to marry."

Juan contracted his brows, and replied :

" And if I have never told any one so, how could they tell it to you ?"

" Answer one question with another, to avoid committing thyself," is a rule of rustic grammar that the people have at their fingers' ends. Uncle Bartolo proceeded :

" It's easy to see how ; you are thinking of it ; and people nowadays are so sharp that they divine the thoughts. So that we may as well be plain—it

is what you mean to do. Tell the truth, now."

" The truth !" responded Juan, availing himself of another subterfuge. " Then, though—because I was not prepared to tell it—I have not complied with the church this year, I am to tell it to you ! No, sir ! ' He that reveals his secret, remains without it.' "

" It is plain enough from your crafty answer that your mind is made up. So you needn't deny it, nor put me off with palaver."

" The thing is yet in the blade, and to be nibbled at," replied Juan.

" Do you know, Christian, what you are about ? For the beginning of a cure is a knowledge of the sickness."

" Yes, sir, I have my five senses counted."

" Yes, Juan, four of them useless, and one empty. But, my son, you know me well, is it not so ?"

" Yes, sir."

" You are sure that I am your friend ?"

" I don't say no to that, Uncle Bartolo."

" And you know the proverb says, ' An old ox draws a straight furrow ' ? "

" Agreed, Uncle Bartolo ; we know that kind of wisdom years give, for we are told that the devil is knowing not because of his devilship, but because he is the *old one.*"

" Well, that being so, you will heed what I say."

" That remains to be seen."

" And you will consider my advice ?"

" What is the meaning of all this advanced guard, Uncle Bartolo ? Why do you sift and sift without falling through the sieve ?"

" To fall with all my weight in saying this, and no more : ' Don't you marry, Juan Garcia ! ' "

" Why not ? if you would please tell me."

" Don't marry, Juan Garcia ! "

" Uncle Bartolo, don't leave your counsels like foundlings in the hospital, without father or mother. I must not marry—the reason ? "

" Juan, ' where there has been familiarity, let there be no contract.' "

" If it were as you intimate, I ought to marry ; for, if this woman has lost respect through me—"

" Stop, Juan ; that'll do ! Don't come to me with your ' *mea culpas.*' There is always a pretext for wrongdoing. But you know very well that the woman has not lost respect through you. Nobody loses what he never had."

" Uncle Bartolo, by what I shave off, but that you comb gray hairs, and were my father's friend—*Vive Dios !*—"

" Tut, tut, man ! Don't get excited, and talk nonsense ! I did not come here to poke you up, nor to pick a quarrel, but with a very good intention ; and, as the friend I am to you, to prevent your making an atrocious fool of yourself. Have you considered your children, and the kind of step-mother you are going to give them ? "

" If she will be a wife good enough for their father, it appears to me that she will be a good enough step-mother for them ; especially as, where they are concerned, what I do is right."

" Right ! Now you are like the Englishman, Don 'Turo, that killed an urraca for a partridge, and then said ' all right.' Take notice, Juan, that they are not likely to be willing to live under that woman's flag. You are going to alienate them from you, and, ' withdraw thyself from thine own, God will leave thee alone.' "

" They will not be willing to live under her ! What are you saying,

sir ? We shall see, however. ' Where the sea goes, the waves go.' "

" Well, Juan, we shall see that Lucas, who is high-minded, will not consent to let his sister live with a woman of evil note."

" The note I have put upon her, I will take from her. Do you comprehend ? And Lucas will be very careful not to set himself up to crow while I live. There cannot be two heads, and, ' in sight of the public stocks, street-criers keep their mouths shut.' "

" Think, Juan, that your son should be the staff of your old age. You may provoke him so far that he will leave you some day without warning."

" Let him go ; I have the means to maintain myself, and my wife and daughter."

" Ah ! Juan, what have you left ? Juice don't run out of a sucked orange. As if that woman had not swallowed your slice of field and olive-yard, leaving you nothing but the house ; and that will go the same way the field and orchard went. As for making a living—you have thrown yourself away ; your back is getting stiff already, and ' to old age comes no fairy godmother.' Where, then, are those ' means' to come from ? What you are going to do is get entangled in debts ; and, let a man be as honest as he will, ' if he owes and doesn't pay, all his credit flies away.' "

" *La Leona* has a gossip at the port that is a contrabandist ; he is going to take me for a partner."

" *Only this was wanting !* " exclaimed the old man indignantly. " *You ! you take to the path !** Does Barabbas tempt you, Juan Garcia ? Have you lost your senses entirely, or are you fooling me ? Sure enough,

* *Tomar la vereda*—Take another than the high or legalized way. Said of contrabandists.

'he that goes with wolves will learn to howl.' Don't you know that the devil takes honest gains and dishonest, and the gainer with them? But let us keep to the matter in hand. Juan, the woman has a bad name that neither you nor the king, if he tried, could take from her. She is bad of herself; and neither you nor the bishop, if he set his heart on doing it, could make her good. Moreover, 'a rotten apple spoils its company.'"

"Go on with the bad! 'Against evil-speaking there's nothing strong'; but, if she appears good to me, we are all paid."

"Juan, 'look before you leap.' You have not the excuse of youth for your indiscretion; you are more than forty years old."

"And have more than forty *arrobas** of patience, Uncle Bartolo. *Candela!* I have long sought and never found a friend that would offer me a sixpence, and have found, without seeking, one that gives me advice."

"Well, my son, your soul is in your palm," said Uncle Bartolo, rising. "Remember that there was not wanting a friend to give you good advice—a man of ripe brain, who warned you of the future—for this marriage is going to be the perdition of your house. And, remember what I tell you now, a day is coming when you will have eyes left you only that you may weep." With these words, Uncle Bartolo went his way.

"Son," said he to Lucas, who had waited for him in his house, "it was lost labor, as I foretold. But go, now, and mind what I say. Submit to what can't be helped, and don't be stiff-necked, for you'll surely come out loser. The rope breaks where it is slenderest. You are his son, and

* An arroba is twenty-five pounds.

the authority belongs to him. You will only be kicking against the goad."

Lucas went back to the country and to work with a heavy heart. When he returned home on the following Saturday, he learned that the bans of his father's marriage were to be published the next morning for the first time. Grief made him desperate, and he resolved, as a last recourse, to speak himself.

We have already hinted at the cool and formal relation that existed between these two—thanks to the neglect the abandoned man had shown his children. For some time past, the excellent character of Lucas and the good name it had gained him had inspired Juan Garcia with that bitter sentiment which rises in the heart of a man who possesses the legal and material superiority, against the subordinate to whom he feels himself morally inferior—a sentiment of hostility that is apt to manifest itself in despotism.

"Sir," said the son, speaking with firm moderation, "they have been telling me that you are going to marry."

"They have been telling you what is quite true."

"I hoped that it was not true."

"And why? if I might ask."

"On account of the woman they say you are going to have."

"She is not, then, to your taste; and you think, perhaps, that I ought to have advised with you?"

"No, sir, not with me—I am of small account; but with some one that has more knowledge and judgment than I."

"So, then, it appears to you," said Juan, with repressed ire, "that your father needs counsel?"

"Yes, sir," answered Lucas calmly, "when he has a young daughter, and is going to give her a step-mother."

" For fear he might give her one that would eat her up, like the *Cancon !* "*

" No, sir, no ; we understand now that people are not swallowed like sugared anises."

" Or make her work, being herself industrious, and not willing to. sit hand upon hand like a notary's wife ? "

" It is not that, sir ; Lucia is not afraid of work. She knows that work is the honor of the poor."

" Or, perhaps, keep her at home like a chained dog ? "

" No, sir ; I am not thinking of that ; for my sister, though brought up without a mother, is modest, and not a girl to be seen at the street door or with a hole in her stocking. She is used to the shade, but—"

" But what ? Have done ! "

" That which this woman will give her is evil, and may be her ruin."

Juan Garcia, who had with difficulty restrained himself, rushed upon his son, as the latter uttered these words, with his hand uplifted to strike. Lucas, perceiving the action, quickly inclined his head, and received upon it the blow that had been aimed at his face.

" God help me, father ! what have I done to be chastised ? Have I said anything wrong ? Have I been wanting in respect to you ? Father, just before my mother—heaven rest her !—died, she said to me, ' Lucas, watch over your sister.' I promised her that I would, and have kept my promise."

" She meant," replied Juan, somewhat softened by the memory of the mother evoked by her son, " she meant in case Lucia should be left without me. But, while I live, which is it that has the authority over my daughter ? "

A monster they frighten children with.

" Father, for the love of the Blessed Virgin, leave her to me ! I will support her."

" Are you in your senses ? "

" For God's sake, don't separate us ! I will work with all my might to maintain us both."

" Separate you ! Nobody has thought of doing it. You will come with her to my house."

" No, sir."

" How is that ? What do you mean by ' no, sir ' ? Do you think you have a right to call your father to account ? Is it not enough for you to know what his hands decide ? Perhaps you would like to have another proof of what they are able to do ? "

" My father may kill me, and I shall neither open my lips nor forget my duty ; but—make me live with that woman—never ! "

" We shall see about that, insolent upstart ! "

" Yes, we shall see," said Lucas, as he went sorrowfully out.

Lucas was gifted with one of those noble and delicate natures that humble themselves in victory, and grow firm in defeat ; that is alike incapable of noisy elation in triumph, or pusillanimous abjection when prostrate. But the determination of his character was degenerating into stubbornness, as it always happens when will forsakes the guidance of reason to follow the promptings of pride. Therefore, though he had not, in the slightest degree, failed in the strict respect that morality enforces, neither the threats of his father nor love for his sister could shake the resolution he had taken in that decisive interview. On leaving his father's presence, he went in search of Lucia, whom he found weeping. For a long while neither spoke : brother and sister mutually comprehending the cause of the profound depression of the one and the tears of the other.

"If mother could open her eyes!" at last exclaimed Lucia.

"They whose eyes God has closed have no wish to open them again in the world," replied Lucas; "but remember, that from heaven she always has hers fixed upon her daughter. I cannot help you; for, though I have tried my best to keep you under my flag, I have not succeeded: because, heart's dearest, there is no power in the world that can oppose a father's."

"But I am to do only what you tell me, Lucas, for my mother left me to you," sobbed the girl.

"Well, then, pay attention to what I am going to say.

"Bear your cross with patience; for that is the only way to make it lighter. Be a reed to all storms, but an oak to temptation. Never turn from the right path, though it be steep and sown with thorns. Always look straight before you, for he that does not do this never knows where he will stop. As for this woman who is going to be your father's wife, give her the wall; but remember that she is bad, and neither join yourself to her nor talk with her, except with reserve and when you must."

"Shall you do the same, Lucas?"

"I—I shall act as God gives me understanding."

Nothing was seen of Lucas on the day of Juan's marriage, and it was in vain that they looked for him: he had disappeared. Juan, who left no means untried to ascertain his son's whereabouts, learned some days later, from a muleteer who come from Tevilla, that he had enlisted. The father felt indignant at the contempt thus shown for his authority, and sorry to lose an assistant in his son: but found consolation in freedom from the immediate presence of an interested witness whose censure like the fog, without form, voice, or action, penetrated him with an uncomfortableness from which there was no escape.

Lucia went to live with her stepmother, and it is hardly necessary to relate what she had to endure; in particular from the daughters of the latter, who, being both foolish and ugly, naturally disliked one who was beautiful and wise; for she had commenced by playing with sweetness the role of Cinderella that her brother had recommended. But, little by little, the continual friction was wasting her patience, and indignation, repressed discontent, and rancor were beginning to find place in her heart. She wished, sometimes, to humiliate, by her advantages, those who were continually humiliating her, and grew presuming and fond of admiration. So it is that evil seeds spread and multiply with prodigious rapidity: one suffices to open the way and prepare the ground for the rest.

While these things were passing, a regiment of cavalry, commanded by one Colonel Gallardo, came, and took up its quarters in Arcos.

Gallardo was rich, well-born, had been good-looking, and a great coxcomb. He was still the latter; with the kind of conceit that is often the result of living in the atmosphere of adulation that surrounds the possessors of money and command—an atmosphere that intoxicates many, making them overbearing and insolent, and apt to do, with great impertinence, things that would not be tolerated in others. While authority is thus misunderstood, it is hardly to be wondered at that it has lost its ancient prestige, and is hated and set at naught. Authority should be consecrated to its mission, and, with its advantages, accept its responsibilities, the first of which is to give good example. Do those in place really think they owe the masses nothing?—that these are, at once, mothers to nourish, and incensories to deify them? Shall we ever go back, morally, to those remote times when men were both worthy and self-respecting, and neither admitted flattery nor refused to rule its reverence; for the latter was never so despised as it is at present; the former never so cringing.

But to return to Colonel Gallardo, who has given margin to those reflections.

This admirable person added to his other pretensions that of youth in its flower. His own having already gone to seed, the result was that, instead of appearing the young cock, he suggested the idea of a very old chicken. By grace of the peruke-maker, which, as everybody knows, consists in creating ringlets where there is no hair, he wore curled locks. He encased himself in a French corset, which gave him a slenderness a sylph might have envied. It was an article of his belief that amorous conquests were as creditable to a soldier as military ones; and he considered a little hare-brainedness in a man and a spice of coquetry in a woman the proper seasoning, for each respectively. These things, united with vanity enough to fill the space left vacant in his heart and brain by the absence of other qualities, made of Colonel Gallardo one of those characters that are detestable, without being malevolent and ridiculous, though they do not provoke mirth.

This cavalier, a bachelor, of course, like all of his stamp, had lodgings opposite the house of *La Leona*, whose daughters were not long in becoming acquainted with his attendants.

The preludes to acquaintanceship were couplets worded and sung with the evident intention of opening a flirtation. The soldiers took the initiative, singing to the music of their *guitarillos :* *

> " If your person can be won
> By valor in the field,
> Here's a man with sword in hand
> Will sooner die than yield."

Another followed :

> " If for a a rustic's love
> You slight a soldier bold,
> Base metal you will have
> Instead of shining gold."

To which the girls replied in a similar strain, declaring that they found it difficult to have patience with " these men of the fields," whom they describe as " persecutors of the ground " and "sepulchres of *gaspacho.*"

Neither was the colonel behindhand in becoming enamored of the beauty of Lucia; nor was he the man to dissimulate his sentiments. And, alas! Lucia herself had ceased to be the discreet and modest maiden, who would once have shrunk offended from demonstrations that could not fail to give occasion for scandal.

The hopes of our decorated aspirant, who soon learned the interior circumstances of this family, rose high in view of the antecedents of the step-mother and the unhappy lot of the young girl. But he deceived himself. For, though vanity had led Lucia beyond the limits of prudence, she receded from corruption with all the energy of the honorable blood she had inherited from her mother. This resistance exasperated the step-sisters, who, wishing both to be rid of Lucia and to see her undone, hoped that the colonel would take her away with him, and laid a plan to accomplish the result they

* Small guitars.

desired. Having previously concerted with the lover, they carried out their project in the following manner: One night, when Lucia had gone to her room, and sat combing down her beautiful hair, the door opened suddenly, and admitted the colonel, hidden to the eyes in cloak and slouched hat, and accompanied by the daughters of *La Leona* in giggling triumph. They had hardly introduced him into the chamber, when, with jests and bursts of laughter, they turned and ran out, closing the door behind them and drawing the bolt.

Too much overwhelmed with indignation, terror, and shame to think of any means of escape, the unfortunate girl covered her face with her hands and remained silent. The colonel, also, who had been led by *La Leona* to think that it would not be difficult to propitiate Lucia by tender and gallant speeches, found himself without words in the presence of grief so real and so mute. For, unless a man is totally base, no amount of daring will enable him wholly to overcome the respect that innocence inspires.

"Am I, then, so disagreeable to you," said Gallardo at last, drawing nearer to Lucia—"I who have no wish but to please you?"

"Lucas! Lucas! O my brother!" cried the girl, bursting into sobs.

"I will go! I am going!" said the colonel, half-offended, half-compassionate; and he approached the door, but it was locked.

"You see that I cannot get out," said he, turning again toward Lucia.

"I know it," she exclaimed. "They wanted to ruin me, and they have done it! Have locked me in here alone with you! How can I ever bear to have any one look me in the face again! What will Lucas say? Ah, my heart's brother!"

"You are not ruined, child!" said the colonel, irritated. "I am no friend to tragedies; heroic Lucretias frighten me. Believe me, I desire to go, and, to prove it, since I cannot leave by the door, I will get out by this window." With these words, the colonel wrapped himself again in his cloak, and, mounting the window-seat, sprang into the yard, which was enclosed only by a low paling.

Hardly had his feet touched the ground when he felt himself attacked by an infuriated man, who apostrophized him with the most violent insults. At the same moment, *La Leona* and her daughters ran shrieking from the house, while the unhappy Lucia called from the window in a voice of anguish: "Don't hurt him! It is my father!"

The man had drawn a knife but Gallardo, who was vigorous and wished to escape from the adventure without hurting Lucia's father and without being recognized, pushed the assailant from him with such force as to throw him upon his back; ran to the paling, leaped it, and disappeared.

Juan Garcia rose from the ground in that state of blind rage in which men of his uncultivated nature stop at no obstacle and hesitate at no crime. Violently repulsing his wife and step-daughters, who, alarmed at the result of their work, would have detained him, he hastened to the house, and was making directly for Lucia's room.

"Lucia! Lucia! jump from the window!" screamed *La Leona*, foreseeing a catastrophe. "Your father is going to kill you!"

Wild with terror, Lucia, who heard the enraged and drunken voice of her father approaching her chamber, precipitated herself into the yard.

"Run to the colonel's!" urged the step-mother, with no intention then but that of saving her life. "He is the last one your father will suspect. It is the nearest house, and you can be hidden there better than anywhere else."

Lucia obeyed mechanically, guided by the instinct of self-preservation, the only motive that rules weak natures in moments of supreme peril.

Gallardo was excitedly pacing his room when she rushed in, pale as death, covered with her long black hair, cold and helpless with fear and desperation, and, sinking upon a chair, exclaimed:

"You have been my ruin! At least save my life!"

It is to be supposed that even the dry and sterile heart of this man would find, in such circumstances, sentiments and words to soothe the wretched creature thus forced to seek his protection. It is certain that, at the vision of her youthful and innocent beauty, seen through the prism of her tears, he became more enamored than ever, and took advantage of the distress, of which he was the cause, to advance his suit.

And the poor child, bereft of affection and support, having nowhere to lay her head, lacking firmness to resist and energy to act, unsustained by principle duly and constantly inculcated, which would have made her prefer misery to shame, allowed herself to be persuaded and retained, drawn by a love that began with the promise and conviction that it was to be unchanging and eternal.

The colonel soon left, taking with him, secretly, Lucia, who had already begun to feel contented in the atmosphere of tenderness and luxury that surrounded her.

The fit of passion that Juan Garcia had experienced, united with grief, shame, and remorse, so affected his constitution, already spent and worn by the life he had been leading, that he fell into an inflammatory

fever, from which he never recovered. A little while before he died, he said to his old friend: "Uncle Bartolo, you hit the mark when you told me that the day would come when I should have eyes left only to weep. It has come, and—well, better to close them for ever."

Two years had passed since the events last narrated, and five since Lucas left home. His regiment was in Cordova, where a general recently arrived from Madrid was going to review the troops of the garrison. The evening before the parade, Lucas was in the quarters with several other soldiers from Arcos, one of whom, with the careless and constant gayety which characterizes the Spanish soldier, and proves, to the extreme scandal and disgust of the votaries of utility, the non-material genius of the nation, was alternately touching his guitar, and singing:

"Oh! 'tis gay to be a soldier,
    Standing guard with tired feet,
And head erect, in stiff cravat,
    And nothing at all to eat.

"And, for the bread of munition,
    He gets from the King of Spain,
To be 'Alert there, sentinel!'
    All night, and never complain.

"This is the life of a soldier,
    To march wherever he's led,
To sleep under alien shelter;
    And die in a hospital bed."

At this moment the picket-guard, which had just been relieved from duty at the general's quarters, came up.

"Oh!" said one of the newly-arrived, "if the general's wife isn't a fine one! In all my travels I have never seen her equal."

"She is not his wife," replied another, "so drop the 'fine.'"

"And why should I drop it? Good words neither add to beauty nor take from it; but what do you know?"

"What they tell me; and, besides, if she was his wife, he wouldn't keep her so grand; for that is the way with the *You-Sirs,* they spend more money upon their dears than they do upon their wives."

"Because they are afraid their mistresses will leave them for other lovers. What do you say, Lucas?"

"That it's like keeping a lead knife in a golden sheath," answered Lucas.

"The soul of this one may be of lead, or something cheaper, but her person—by the Moors of Barbary!"

"We hear enough," replied Lucas; "dress up a block, and it will look like a shopman. I tell you, these good-for-nothing she vagabonds appear to me more like bedraggled rags than women."

"Get away! If this Lucas hasn't always the rod of justice lifted! He has entered the uniform, but the uniform hasn't entered him. If you had been born king, they would have called you the *Justiciero.*"[*]

The next morning the troops were drawn up in splendid array, the bands were playing, and the general, magnificently mounted, came galloping upon the field, followed, at a little distance, by an elegant open carriage, in which was seated a beautiful and richly dressed woman.

The carriage stopped near where Lucas and his townsmen were formed at the end of a line.

"That is the general's mistress," said the man at Lucas's right in a low tone. "Did I not tell you she was a sun?"

Lucas raised his eyes, and fixed them upon the woman, at the same instant starting so perceptibly as to attract the notice of his companions.

"What ails you, Lucas?"

"Nothing," he answered calmly.

But the glances of the occupant

[*] The door of justice.

of the carriage had fallen upon the gallant-looking soldier who stood so near her, and a cry of delighted surprise burst from her lips.

"Lucas," said his other neighbor in line, "that lady is looking this way, and making signs to you."

Lucas, pale but perfectly composed, neither looked up nor replied.

"Lucas, who can it be? She knows you; she is waving her handkerchief, and seems as if she would spring out of the carriage. Look at her! Say! who is she?"

"I do not know her," answered Lucas.

"By the very cats!" exclaimed the first who had spoken, in an ecstasy, "may my end be a bad one if it isn't your sister Lucia! Look at her, man! it is she!"

"I have looked at her, and I tell you that I do not know her," responded Lucas.

"Look, now, look! the poor little thing is crying. She is not much changed, only handsomer. You must be blind not to see that it is your sister!"

"I do not know her," repeated the young man, with the same composure.

There are men who feel profoundly, but exercise such self-control that they succeed in covering with a mantle of indifference the most violent and agonizing emotions — moral Scævolas, who astonish without attracting us. We like neither the motive nor the effects of a stoicism that parades itself so disdainfully. For, if in order to judge of all things human, it is necessary to compare them with the example of the ideal of humanity — the God-Man — we cannot fail to be repelled by such arrogance when we reflect that the most holy passion would have lacked its tender and sublime sanctity, if in it bravado had taken the place of meekness.

The voice of the commanding officer was now heard prescribing the evolutions. When these were concluded, the troops marched to their quarters, where, gathered in groups, they made their comments upon the beautiful lady of the carriage, some of the soldiers from Arcos declaring that it was Lucia, others, who had not seen her so near, maintaining the contrary.

" Her brother will know," they exclaimed, running to find him.

" Lucas, is that grand, fine *You-Madam* your sister Lucia ? "

" I don't know the woman. And now, comrades, no more questions; for I am not a repeating-clock, and am tired of answering."

Before half an hour had passed, an orderly arrived from the géneral in search of a soldier named Lucas Garcia.

Interiorly shaken by the indignation which he would not allow his face to betray, Lucas followed the messenger to a house of good appearance, and was shown into an elegant and luxuriously furnished cabinet. As he entered, a fair young girl robed in silk rose from a sofa, and ran towards him with open arms.

" I do not know you, my lady," said Lucas, quickly repulsing her with his right hand.

" Lucas, my brother ! " she exclaimed, bursting into tears.

" I have no sister," he replied, in the same tone as before.

" Lucas, my own brother, listen, and I will tell you what happened ! "

At this moment, the colonel—that had been, and was now general—entered.

" Ah ! Lucia," said he, with ostentatious condescension, " so, then, you have already seen your brother."

" He will not know me," sobbed the girl.

" How is that ? " asked the general,

turning toward the soldier. " And why ? "

" Because it would be a deceit, my general," answered Lucas, lifting his open hand to his temple. " I am the only one left of my house, and have no sister."

" I sent for yoɪ " proceeded the general, " to make you one of my orderlies, to keep you near me, have you taught to write, and fit you for a career. You will mount rapidly. I know already that you are intelligent and brave."

" I do not wish to learn to write, my general."

" And why ? " asked the general, repressing his ill-humor, " since without knowing how to write, you cannot rise ? "

" I do not want to rise, my general."

" The reason is evident," said the general, with a mocking laugh. " It is not strange that the heir of such a house should disdain the service of the king."

" He that sees not the king is king to himself," answered Lucas.

" What is there that you want, brother ? " asked Lucia.

" I desire nothing but to serve my time out and return home."

" But who calls you there, if, as you say, you have no one ? " questioned she.

" Love for my native place," he answered. " God give me rest in the soil that gave me birth ! "

" Valiant goose ! " exclaimed the general.

Lucas neither opened his lips nor moved an eyelid.

" Dearest brother ! by our mother's memory, don't make as if you did not know me ! You break my heart ! Stay here."

" It would not suit me to be a stranger anywhere, madam."

" Enough ! " said the general. ' Let

the clown go, he will think better of it."

" I do not think twice of things," replied Lucas, saluting as he went out.

Lucia ran after him into the ante-room, caught his arm, and, pressing it against her bosom, cried in a voice of passionate and tender entreaty :

" Lucas ! my brother ! for God's sake stay ! The general has promised me that he will do all he can for you; and he can do a great deal."

" The sack is not big enough to hold both honor and profit," respond-ed Lucas, hurling his sister from him with all the loftiness of a proud nature and the brute force of an angry churl.

Lucia fell overwhelmed upon the nearest chair, and her brother went his way to the quarters with clinched fists and lips compressed—pale with lividness that ire stamps upon the faces of children of the south. Ire was suffocating him ; for he could neither express it nor follow its venge-ful impulses, which would not have been satisfied short of the commission of a crime; and of this he was inca-pable.

But, oh ! for a war. The private soldier would have given in it a hun-dred lives if he had had them for a pair of epaulets that would lift him to the rank required, in order to enable him to demand satisfaction of the villain who, after having seduced his sister, had insulted him so impudent-ly—epaulets that he would have thrown away the next hour, like flat-tened orange skins; for Lucas was not aspiring ; neither fortune nor show attracted him. He clung to his con-dition, loved the labors of the field ; was attached to his town and its cus-toms, and would not have renounced the things that suited his taste, and in which he excelled, for the sake of hoisting himself upon a platform where he must always have been an unwelcome stranger and intruder. The very words were antipathetic to his innate devotion, to his country, his province, the place where he was born, his lares, and his class.--And the effort of the age is to destroy this beautiful instinct of the heart, by con-tinually saying to the poor, " Rise, rise ! the summit is your goal: the heights are common to all," thus infusing a vain arrogance into the wholesome minds of those who are so worthy and respectable in the place they occupy.

LUCAS, who could neither do nor remedy anything, suffered fearfully from the presence of his sister so near him. Happily, in two days the general left for Sevilla.

But from the hour when she met her brother and he refused to recognize her, Lucia's existence was changed. To her, in the flowery butterfly life into which, at seventeen, she had been almost forced by circumstances, the encounter with Lucas had been like the striking of a bark indolently voyaging, without patron and without compass, to the breath of light and laughing breezes, against the first rock of firm land: the shock had been terrible. In perplexity she asked herself, " Where am I ? Whither am I going ? Who is this that flatters and shelters me ? Who he that rejects me ? " In terror she gazed around her: all seemed new and strange, all odious and reprehensible. In her memory—oh! that she had consulted it before!—she found the words her brother had said to her at parting: " Never turn from the right path, though it be steep and sown with thorns. Always look straight before you, for he that does not do this never knows where he will stop." Lucia's wretchedness was augmented by the seeming impossibility of escape from the position in which she found herself. Could she turn back without either encouragement and support, while, by continuing in sin, she would have both ? Her natural want of energy made it the more difficult for her to return to the right path, with no help but his

who never fails those who seek him with faith and without fear or faltering. The tears she shed tarnished her beauty, and the sorrow that preyed on her heart robbed her manners —hitherto so gay and caressing— of their charm. All this at first annoyed Gallardo, then offended, and finished by exasperating him. Violent scenes took place between the lovers; these introduced discord; and discord, when once it has burst its primitive embankments, filters through whatever others may be raised to contain it.

When the general was recalled to Madrid, expecting to be employed, and thinking that his stay would not be long, he resolved to leave Lucia in Sevilla. She allowed him to go without opposition, for so weary was she of the life she led that any change seemed preferable. She was, besides, very far from possessing the brazen and insolent courage that women of her condition are wont to acquire, and that causes so many of them, when they have ceased to be objects of passion, to be dreaded by the men around whom they have coiled themselves like horrible snakes; making miserable Laocoöns of the victims, who often marry them through fear, where before they would not do it for love, and thus render the latter part of their career as ridiculous as the beginning was scandalous.

A worthy manner, truly, in which to fill up a man's existence!

The stay at court, however, of the *young* general, as the papers styled Gallardo, was prolonged. He alternated in various combinations of second-class political intrigues, and allowed himself to be made the conceited tool of one of them, under the full persuasion that he had become the imposing leader of a party.

The general now began to think, with excellent reason, very sound judgment, and profound calculation, that it was time for him to be more considerate. The reader will pardon us the expression, which, in his case, meant to enter upon a life of usefulness and devotion to the interests of the country—without sacrificing his own, it will be understood. Influenced by these grave considerations, our young leader subscribed to newspapers, bought books and read some of them, though he soon forgot precisely which he had read and which not; wrote a memorial on river navigation, and another upon the *Renta del Excusado ;* * made short speeches as a preparation for longer ones, which succeeded very well and met with the entire approbation of his hearers; and, in the time it takes to say a devout *amen,* exchanged the rakish air of the young blood for the pompous tone of the prominent and influential citizen.

Our friend, as may be seen, had reached his apogee : in confirmation of which—among other sacrifices made to seriousness—he had procured a good cook, and loosened the lacings of his stays.

Nevertheless—since there is a difference between a serious man and a moral one—our hèro maintained a sort of toned-down dissoluteness behind the scenes, where he and his intimates entertained themselves in conversations tissued with a variety of subjects, such as the discourse *A* and the scandal *B ;* the concordat

and the theatre royal; the ministry and the *danseuse ;* the bishop and the prima donna ; the crown and cards ; erected a throne to Tauromaquia ; proposed an apotheosis of industry ; and passed a vote of censure upon the luxury of novenas.

" Look here, *little one !* " said to him just such another " *little one* " at a breakfast party—where champagne was made to represent the tone of good society that the greater part of the guests lacked—" what has become of *La Lucia ?* "

" She was not very well, and I left her in Sevilla," responded the hero.

" Doesn't it strike you that she is losing her varnish ? "

" At twenty-one, man ? "

" It is not singular," remarked the elegant son of a capitalist (the youth had been educated in France). " At that age, one who lives fast is *sur le retour.*" *

" The existence of *camellias* is like that of roses," quickly added another, whose Christian name of Bonifacio they were in the habit of contracting into *Boni.*

Having constituted himself an inseparable copy of the engrafted Parisian, and not wishing to fall behind his model in anything, *Boni* never allowed the capitalist to express an idea without instantly reproducing it in different words, always endeavoring to surpass the original in elegant Gallicisms ; in scepticism of the most material, and cynicism of the most approved kind, and in extreme affectation of the fashionable foreign mannerism.

" You ought to place this Lucia *dis*-lucent among the number of the thousand-and-one Didos," said the would-be Gaul.

" Lay her aside with last year's *modes fanées,*"† the copy hastened to add.

* Name given to the subsidy formerly levied by the King of Spain for carrying on wars against the infidels.

.* On the wane.   † Faded fashions.

"I cannot do that," said the general.

"'Stale Spanish morality!'" exclaimed the capitalist, bursting into a laugh. "Does the fair creature expect to find an Amadeus of Gaul in a general of the age of enlightenment?"

"Or a Pastor Fido in one who aspires to become a father to his country?" put in *Boni.*

"The fact is," replied our friend, "that in my connection with Lucia there have been exceptional circumstances."

"Tell them to us, little one," said his intimate. "The romantic tale will flavor the coffee."

The general related all the preliminaries and particulars of his relations with Lucia.

"Don't you see, general," said the imitator of the tone Parisian, "that it was all a farce, very well got up, by those *fourbes rustics* to set you on; alarm you; interest you in the girl, and oblige you to take her?"

"That it was all an intrigue of *las étage!*" added the copy of the copy.

"*Apropos* of impositions," said the capitalist, "I must tell you what happened to me yesterday. A fellow came into my office—"

"Don't omit," said *Boni,* "that you were counting an immense sum of money at the time, for that is what heightens the joke."

"He asked me," continued Creseus, "if I would lend him two doubloons. I told him that it cost me the greatest pain to be obliged to refuse, but that I had not sixpence by me."

"If I had not wished to give, I would have sought another reply," said an old general—uncle to ours—who had lost a leg in the battle of Bailen.

"General," replied the narrator, "among us, *I have not* is synonymous

with *I will not;* even sucking-babes understand it."

"A synonym which Huertas has omitted, but which is known in these days, even in the Batuecas," chimed the repeater.

"It could not have existed when he composed his work," said the general.

"The fellow," proceeded the narrator, "begged and implored, lowering his demand to the most insignificant sum. I was as inexorable as destiny." And the millionaire cast around him a look worthy of Cato.

"He was, then, in real need, and not an impostor?" questioned the old general.

"O sir!—general rule—every one that asks is an impostor."

"Unless he is an intimate friend," said *Boni,* speaking this time with un accustomed personality.

"*Ma foi,*"* answered the Gaul*isk* Spaniard, "I except no one. Seeing that he was not going to desist, and always with the amiability and delicacy that must be used in such cases—"

"*Sans doute,* the same as in affairs of honor," said the bad copy of a worse original.

"I told him that, since his necessity was so extreme, I would venture to lend him—not money, for I had none—but something that would be of more use to him in his circumstances. The imbecile thought, perhaps, that it was going to be my signature."

"Your signature! What one might call the only and unique *sanctum sanctorum* of the disciples of Mercury. A thing so sacred!"

"My dear *Boni,*" said his friend, "*veuillez ne pas m'interrompre!*† The fellow's countenance lighted up. I believe, upon my word, that he had not eaten in three days. Laughing

---

*In faith.
† "Will you please not interrupt me?"

within myself, although my face denoted the gravest sympathy for his situation, I led him to a closet, took out a case of pistols, which I opened, and, handing him a weapon, said, as I bowed his dismissal, ' Here is a remedy for all your troubles.' My mendicant turned upon his heel and left ; and you may be sure that I have rid myself of him, *une bonne fois pour toutes.*" *

Boni's mirth was overpowering.

Gallardo and the rest of the Spaniards were silent.

" You must positively put this joke into some paper," said the capitalist's admirer, between his paroxysms of laughter.

" *Mon cher, à quoi bon ?* " responded the hero of the anecdote, with an air of modesty.

" To show people how to get rid of impostors," answered Boni ; "to furnish a specimen of your humor— to let it be seen that you are as richly endowed by nature as by fortune— to give circulation to an entertaining item—and to—"

" And could a paper be found that would print such an iniquity as an entertaining item ! " shouted the old general, no longer able to contain his wrath. " Is it the mission of the press to propagate such ideas and sentiments ? God help us, sirs, if there is no one left in Spain capable of a blush ! Can the press parade infamy shamelessly, and no one be found to repudiate the impudence that relates such a scandal in terms of laudation ; or appeal from it to the noble and generous instincts, and sense of public decorum, of good and true Spaniards ? Have we become as positive as the written law ? In former times, gentlemen, not all gave, but the few that denied did not boast of their refusal. Charity made men

sorry to say no, even to impostors, and, having said it, they would have been silent about it for shame. Avarice was looked upon as one of the disgraceful vices which respect for public opinion required to be kept out of sight."

" Uncle, for God's sake ! " entreated Gallardo.

" For God's sake what, nephew ?"

" Speak with more moderation."

" When I do, look towards Antequera for sunrise."

" Don't feel apprehensive, general," said the capitalist, *Je sais vivre.* * I respect your family, and know how to make allowance for gray hairs and the ill-humor of advanced age."

" Yes," instantly added the speaking shadow, " *carte blanche* belongs to ladies, children, and—"

He was going to add *old men,* but a look from the general silenced him

" No, nephew, don't be apprehensive," said the latter. " The weapons of a gentleman are for nobler uses than the punishment of insults."

" Come, let us talk of something else," said Gallardo's intimate, anxious to change the subject, but glad in his heart, as were all the other guests, of the lesson the braggart had received from so worthy and authorized an antagonist.

" It is not possible, Gallardo, that you will allow Lucia to be an irredeemable lien upon you. Let me tell you, my boy, that it would be a pretty piece of folly on your part to create an obstacle to your future establishment.'

" I don't see that—in order to be a deputy, senator, or—"

" Oh ! you're on the wrong tack. Your political ideas absorb all your thoughts ; but I have been told—by one of her friends—that the daughter of Don Juan de Moneda,† the

---

* Once for all.   † What for, my dear ?
* I know how to behave.
† Don John made of Money.

banker, is quite smitten with your person."

Gallardo straightened himself, and caressed his curled locks.

"Her mother is completely taken with the title of Marquis de Monte Gallardo, which they say you are about to receive, and her father with your capacity."

"We are even there," said the general, "for I am as much impressed with his. To buy—"

"But," proceeded the friend, "he is equally so with your sash and rent-roll. Here, boy, is an opportunity to settle in life."

"Really, I hardly know the kind and amiable young lady who has been so condescending as to think of me!" drawled the extremely flattered Gallardo, privately resolving to tighten his stays again.

"She is very beautiful," affirmed his friend, "and you must know that she rides like a Cossack."

"Oh! Athenaïs la Moneda has the most elegant figure and complexion—so pale!—and the fiercest glances" (he meant haughtiest) "of all the belles of Madrid. She is delicious!" exclaimed the Parisian.

● "She has the neck of a swan, with such *serpentine undulating*," said Bonifacio, quite at a loss for another comparison.

"The most desirable *parte, ma foi!* Her father is worth forty millions, and she is the only daughter," continued the capitalist, who did not allow his appreciation of beauty to interfere with his devotion to dollars.

"You ought to improve your opportunity, and marry at once," advised the friend. "These girls with forty millions are more capricious than the wind. They change oftener than weather-cocks, and do just as they please; for millionaire fathers who know only the Castilian have the highest consideration for daugh-

ters who have learned French from Sue's novels, and Italian at the opera."

"An heiress's whim is like a flash of lightning. In losing time, you expose yourself to a—"

"To a deception," said the capitalist, concluding the sentence.

"To a *disabusement*," said the copy, thinking, with profound satisfaction, that he had, for once, surpassed the original.

"What is your opinion of all this?" asked Gallardo of his uncle, with a laugh, intended to appear jesting, but which betrayed his interior satisfaction.

"Yes, give us the benefit of your wisdom," said the capitalist, covering his ill-humor with a tone of light irony. "In matrimonial as well as martial councils, the Nestors should be heard.

'*La face des vieillards est pleine de majesti :
Leur voix sur l'existence a des secrets intimes.*' ' ●

"*Une vieux de la vieille*,"† confirmed *Boni*, "is a California of experience; a barometrical and chronometrical counsellor; a universal grammar bound in gold; a—"

"Hush, *Boni!*" whispered the capitalist in the ear of his friend, who, less accustomed to champagne than the others, began to feel its emancipating influence.

Meantime, the old officer stroked his gray moustache in silence.

"Well, what do you think, general!" questioned Gallardo.

"I think that you ought to marry."

"*C'est clair*," said the Parisian.

"It is clear," repeated *Boni*—"as clear as detestable water; and they think of bringing it into Madrid! Will spend millions to do it!"

● " The aspect of the old is full of majesty:
Their words are laden with the secrets of
existence."
† An old soldier of the olden time.

" *Taises vous, mon cher,*" entreated the model, in a low tone.

" I am not in the humor," replied the copy, in excellent Spanish.

" Of course he ought to marry," said all the rest.

" Let us understand each other, gentlemen," said the old general. " I think, Gallardo, that you ought to marry, not the mushroom of the millions, but Lucia."

These words were received with clamorous disapprobation.

" You take advantage of your *rôle* of Nestor, general," exclaimed the capitalist.

" The hero of former times dotes— I would say *radote.* I propose a vote of censure ! " hiccoughed the copy.

" S-s-s, Boni. *Le vous en prie !* * Do you want to get another broadside from the disabled old pontoon ? Don't provoke him, for the next time neither prudence nor contempt will enable me to keep my temper," murmured his patron.

" The general is jesting. A gentleman of his fine delicacy cannot mean to counsel one, in Gallardo's position, to marry a woman of light reputation," said Gallardo's friend.

" I do it because I have delicacy— a plant that strikes so deep when once it has taken root, that neither the silver plough nor the golden spade which cultivates the field of ideas of the present day can turn it out. I counsel a man who has done a wrong to repair it. I advise one who has been the ruin of an honest girl to become her defender. And the more public he has made her position, the more he is bound to set her right in the eyes of others. If the future looks smiling, I counsel it all the more earnestly, that the past may not reproach him. In my days, gentlemen, marriages were not dis-

cussed in semi-public meetings. The only counsellors were, according to the circumstances, the heart, the honor, and the conscience. But," added the old man, rising, " my sentiments are as much out of harmony with yours, as my person is out of place in a reunion of gay young men. Gentlemen, I salute you. Nephew, good-by. Do not ask me to your brilliant wedding if you marry with the million-heiress of the caprices. If with Lucia, I will be your groomsman."

With these words the noble veteran took his leave.

" Style of an epic poem," said the pseudo-Parisian.

" Tone of an *elegiac lyric,*" stammered the copy. " One would think the governor had been drinking some kind of palate-skinning Catalan wine, instead of the excellent, exquisite, delectable, delicious— "

" Enough, *Boni,*" interrupted his friend, indicating to him with his foot the urgent necessity of more discretion.

" The general has, so to speak, one foot in the grave, and, naturally, all looks to him *de profundis* color," observed Gallardo's intimate. " But we live in a positive age, and must conform to the step of its march ; to do otherwise would be to make ourselves antiquated and ridiculous."

Days followed days, each one bringing to our hero its business, novelty, interest, and forgetfulness of those that had preceded it. Lucia, in the meantime, saw her means of subsistence failing without informing him ; for, with the reawakened sentiments of duty and shame, came the comprehension of her guilty dependence, and sense of the double humiliation of soliciting and receiving. She had lived for some time by the sale of her valuables, but this resource was almost exhausted.

" What is to become of me ?" she questioned, with more of weakness than inquietude, more inertia than anguish, as she sat one day alone, her head drooping upon her breast. " In forgetting how to work, I have been like the sailor that forgets in a calm how to handle the ropes. What shall I do when all is gone? What can he who has brought me to this be thinking of ?"

Her questionings were interrupted by the entrance of the woman of the house with a letter.

" It is from Madrid," she said, with a fawning smile. " I'll bet that the general tells when he is coming, and confirms the report of his appointment as captain-general of this province."

Lucia opened and read the following epistle :

" DEAR LUCIA : Nothing can last for ever. Mature age brings serious ideas ; the life of a man, obligations, circumstances, compromises, and position, duties, which force us to make, in favor of reason and morality, sacrifices that are not the less painful because they are necessary.

" My family has undertaken to negotiate a marriage for me, which will assure me a certain and brilliant future ; and matters have proceeded so far that I cannot oppose myself to the arrangement without offending a powerful and respectable family, compromising my own, and causing grave inconveniences, inconveniences which you would be the first to deplore.

" I believe that you will understand the necessity of my establishing myself in life, and will feel neither surprised nor pained. I am equally persuaded, having noticed for a long time how unhappy you seemed at my side, and how little pleasure my presence gave you, that you will not miss me. It may be that another already occupies in your heart the place that once was mine. If you will be happier with him than you have been with me, I trust that I have enough philanthropy to rejoice in your good fortune.

" Adieu. It is likely that we may not meet again ; but, believe me, I shall never forget you ; and, if I can serve you in any way, command me."

" Well," asked the woman, eagerly, " does he say anything about coming ?"

" No," answered Lucia, with the tears raining down her cheeks, " he says that he is not coming."

Lucia did not feel for Gallardo that which can properly be called love ; but, during four years, her naturally affectionate heart had attached itself to him, and could not but be wounded by the cold insensibility with which he had abandoned her.

The harpy's face, manner, and tone changed at once ; for this grief confirmed her suspicions. Lucia's lover had cast her off.

" Madam," she said, " certain exigencies, in which I unfortunately find myself, have obliged me to introduce a rule into my house, requiring my boarders to pay in advance. All the rest have agreed to it, and I trust that you will do the same."

" No, madam," replied Lucia, " for I am going away to-morrow, and so shall have to give you only what is already due."

The poor forsaken girl went out that night and sold her wardrobe to a pawnbroker. After satisfying her creditor, she had enough left to pay some wine-carriers for a ride upon one of their mules as far as Jerez, and from there she meant to go to Arcos on foot. At dawn, on the following morning, she passed through the Carmona gate, casting a long, sad look upon the sleeping city — the city that the Bitis serves as a page ;

La Giralda for insignia, and the verdure of its orange groves for adornment; the city that is at once gay as a village maiden and imposing as a queen; beautiful as a young girl, and full of wisdom and memories as a matron; graceful as the Andalusian of to-day, and chaste and noble as the Castilian dame of olden time.

Lucia found herself in Jerez alone and without resource, but, by favor of her good angel, met Uncle Bartolo at the inn where she alighted. The visible presence of the former would not have rejoiced her more than did the sight of this old friend of her family, to whom she told the whole of her sad story, adding that now she knew not what to do, since she dared not seek even a servant's place.

" My daughter," said the old guerilla, " you grew vain in the fiend's own house of *Leona*, and forgot that wings were given to the ant for its destruction. If you had shown that wretch a repulsive face, he would not have ventured to do what he did. What motive, will you tell me, could a *You Sir* have for playing clucking fox to a little country girl, but to make of her a mark for shame ?

" However," he continued, seeing that Lucia's tears began to flow, " far be it from me to hack at the fallen tree, or double the burden of the ass that is down. The baptism of repentance opens the fold, and your repentance is sincere, because you return to poverty, when, if you had chosen otherwise, profligates would not have been wanting, in the great city, to complete your ruin. Come with me, and I will talk to Lucas. It is his duty to take care of you."

" He will never forgive me, Uncle Bartolo !" exclaimed Lucia sadly. " He has said that he had no sister, and no one can make him say the contrary."

" True," replied the guerilla, " the Garcia heads are harder than anvils. I learned that by experience when your father—Heaven rest him !—married *La Leona*. But this is another thing, for, notwithstanding that your father did so badly, Lucas has turned out well. And it is a great deal easier to yoke two that are united by blood than to unyoke two that the devil has united. We will see, God helping us, and, in the meantime, you shall come to my house ; there is no great abundance, but good-will is not wanting."

The next day saw Uncle Bartolo and Lucia travelling along the road which we described at the commencement of our story ; Lucia mounted upon a little ass, and the agile good old man following on foot. At nightfall they reached Arcos.

Alas ! for the one who, returning to his native place, instead of experiencing pure happiness, feels his heart torn by grief and shame ; finds his parents dead, the house where he was born the property of strangers, and sees, in the looks of neighbors, cold disdain instead of the joyful smile of recognition and welcome !

Uncle Bartolo took Lucia to his own house, and, while they were preparing supper, went himself to that of Lucas, who, on receiving his discharge, had returned to Arcos and to his post among the day-laborers, and had, by his aptness and diligence, won so much credit that several profitable jobs and positions had already been offered him. As will be supposed, he had found his father's house sold. But as his kinswoman still lived in it, he hired his former habitation, and she assisted him.

Uncle Bartolo entered, just as Lucas had finished his supper.

" Sit by, Uncle Bartolo," said the young man.

"No, thank you. May what you have taken profit you! Will you have a cigar?"

"It wouldn't come amiss."

Uncle Bartolo handed Lucas a paper cigar, lighted his own, and, with characteristic bluntness, plunged into his subject.

"Lucas, man, will you tell me why you never speak of your sister? Does it appear to you that a sister is a patch sewed on to be ripped at pleasure?"

Lucas, disagreeably surprised, contracted his brows as he answered:

"I have no sister, Uncle Bartolo."

"What! what do you say?"

"I have already said it. 'In my manse they bestow but one loaf.'"

"Go a-walking with your grand talk! I'd like to know what right you have to deny your sister, even though her life has not been what it ought to be?"

Lucas had turned pale, and his beard trembled with repressed indignation.

"Uncle Bartolo," he replied, affecting an air of indifference, "the saying is, 'He that goes away is not counted.' Let us drop this conversation."

"I don't feel disposed to; you may as well understand that. And now, let me tell you that this face of a judge, though it may be the correct one to show to a sinner, is not by any means the one to show to a penitent. Do you comprehend? Your poor little sister is penitent; and you know that

'He who sins and mends,
Himself to God commends.'"

"I have said that I had no sister."

"Don't be stubborn, for God's sake! Look here now, soul of an ape! How can you say you have no sister, if he has given you one? Lucas, I have come, and I shall not go away until you forgive Lucia."

"Uncle Bartolo, don't pledge yourself to what you cannot accomplish."

"You are your father's own son —the one and the other harder-headed than oxen. Juan Garcia and Lucas Garcia: there's a pair fit for a cart!"

"Why fall upon me, sir, in such a shower of sarcasms? Is it necessary to give so many punches to say that the bull is coming?"

"Because he comes with a purpose, and, 'when things come with a purpose, more than the ass may fall to the ground.' I tell you only the pure truth, and you, with your devil's motto of 'few words and bad ones,' what you say has neither form nor sense! But to come back to the subject, for I don't let go the handle this way when I am defending the right. As I was going to say, your stubbornness is worse than your father's; because it is not so bad to be determined upon marrying one's girl as to be determined not to forgive one's sister. It's better to do more than your duty than to do less. If your father lacked puncto, you have half a share too much. Your mother committed your sister to you; and you are disobeying the last will of her that bore you!"

"She committed my sister to me, but not the kept miss of a villain."

"You are soaring as the eagle, which is a royal bird; you pronounce your sentences like a judge of the Audiencia, and make yourself believe that you are wiser than the Regency. But you are greatly out of the way, my son. It ill becomes you to go before God in casting out your sister; your own mother's daughter, when her misfortune was partly your fault."

"Mine, sir?"

"Yes, yours; for you threw off the burden like an untamed colt; cast behind you the trust you received from your mother, and, without commending yourself either to God or the devil, shouldered your gun and made off; knowing that for six years, walled up in a uniform, you must lose sight of your charge; knowing, besides, that you were leaving her in a house where wickedness was well established. And so what happened, happened. The past is past, and can't be mended now; but after this, do you think it is right, Christian, that your sister should have no one to turn to when she leaves her sinful life ?"

"She ought to have remembered in time that every uphill has its down."

"But, my son, is not this to

'See the ulcer, see the woe: Shut the purse, and naught bestow'?

This is to have bowels of a pagan toward a poor creature that they pushed and pushed—a child that did not know what they were doing."

"Uncle Bartolo, ignorance does not take away sin."

"Do you think, if you had had your evil hour—suppose it for instance, only—and had robbed or done something that had dishonored you, and had gone to your sister, that she would refuse to own you? I'll be bound she wouldn't !"

"Well, I should have acted badly. But the case is impossible, for it would have been my care not to put myself in her way. 'He that touches his own with his leprosy, gives it to them, and does not cure himself.'"

"Lucas, my son, the sentence says, 'Act with good intention, and not with passion !'"

"And the proverb says that 'blood boils without fire,' Uncle Bartolo."

"Lucas, for the love of the Blessed Virgin ! How can he who shows no mercy hope for the mercy of God ? Do a good deed, and, when you lie down, though it be upon a mattress of rushes, you will sleep without bad dreams, and as sweetly as if it were a bed of feathers !"

"You are wasting words, Uncle Bartolo. Even if I am condemned for it, I will not hear that vile thing spoken of, and so—stop !"

"Go to, then, *Cain !*" exclaimed the good old man as he rose to leave, "and God set a mark on you as he did on the cruel brother that he cursed ! I'd rather have her, with her sin and her repentance, than you, with your virtue and your pride."

To paint the grief of the wretched Lucia when Uncle Bartolo informed her of the no-result of his mission, would be impossible.

"Holy God !" she exclaimed between her sobs, "only with thee shall I find mercy ! Ah! how I loved this brother in the days of my happy childhood, when I was innocent, and he was all my consolation! Then he could not do enough to please me, and used to swear never to abandon me !"

"Come, come, dry your tears, my daughter, said Uncle Bartolo. 'The frightened partridge is the first to get skewered.' What do you want of an unnatural, without bowels of compassion ? You have me, and the roof of my house is not so small that it cannot shelter you. What I have you shall share, and you can help my poor Josefa. She has become a potsherd, and don't get much rest, for 'woman's work is done and to be done again.'"

When the other inmates of the house slept, Lucia kept lonely vigil, and wept the things that had formerly made her happiness—her poverty, her innocence, and her brother's affection. Wandering in the vast field of her recollections, she found both affliction and consolation in recalling all the particulars of her simple life; every proof of tenderness that she had received from her brother; every hope, withered or dead. With the deepening silence and shadows of the night, her anguish increased. "What shall I do? What shall I do?" she cried, wringing her hands. "I cannot be a burden to this good old man! I cannot stay in this neighborhood, for my own brother's rejection of me will encourage others to outrage me! What shall I do? I must beg if I cannot find work! Where shall I go? Wherever God may lead me!"

Without waiting for daylight, and silently, in order that her departure might not be perceived by her protector, Lucia opened the door, and stepped into the street.

But she could not leave, for ever, a place so dear to her, without lingering for a moment before the adjacent house. It was the one in which her mother died; its roof had sheltered her tranquil infancy: in it she was leaving the brother that she still loved, in spite of her guilt and his inhumanity.

Lucas was not asleep. Exasperation, a disquieted conscience, and heavy heart had driven repose from him.

All at once, he was startled by the tones of a sweet and tremulous voice near to the street door, singing the romance that he had taught his sister when she was a child. He sprang from the bed, moved by an irresistible impulse, but instantly covered his ears with his hands as if to shut out the sound.

The voice sang:

"Praying in God's name, sister,
    And for his sweet mother's sake,
Give my little children bread,
    And his word in payment take."

Struggling with mingled emotions of rage and grief, Lucas seated himself upon his couch, and beat upon the ground with his feet.

The voice, becoming all the while more low and quivering, proceeded:

"He takes a loaf, and breaks it,
    But throws it down again,
For blood runs out of the bread."

The brother's heart was choking him, yet, still resisting, he covered his now tear-stained face with both hands. But when the voice, broken by sobs, continued,

"And she that, without pity,
    To a sister refuses bread,
To God's Mother doth refuse it "—

he rushed to the door, and, dashing it open, ran out; and Lucia, with a cry of joy, threw herself into his extended arms.

The next day, Uncle Bartolo remarked to his wife:

"When the devil enters into one, he locks all the doors behind him. But until the last hour, his divine Majesty keeps a postern open in the sinner's heart."

FORGET-ME-NOT;

OR, THE PICTURE THAT WAS NEVER SEEN.

THE lord chamberlain, who had just returned from Italy, had become the subject of the greatest attention with the brilliant but not extensive circle which the queen was accustomed to assemble around her, in the king's secluded summer residence.

The narratives of the count's travels served to shorten an unpleasant, stormy evening, which visited the shady park surrounding the castle with gusts of rain and hail, interspersed with streaks of lightning and heavy reëchoing claps of thunder. The imagination of the queen revelled in the recollections which the stories of the count awakened ; but the king, more interested in business of state, interrupted the speaker suddenly, with the question as to whether anything new had transpired in the capital city, which he had passed through on his return. The lord chamberlain praised the quiet and elegance of the city, not neglecting to extol the wisdom of the sovereign to whom all this prosperity must be attributed, and closed with the assurance that, excepting the exhibition of industry and art, the inhabitants of the city were occupying themselves, at present, with nothing but their own homes and amusements. The Princess Eliza inquired interestedly concerning the success of that institution which owed its existence to her suggestion, and the count, passing slowly from one thing to another, ran easily into the enumeration of the articles exhibited in the tasteful gallery. He left till the last what he considered the crowning glory of the collection—the paintings by native artists—and described with the versatility of a cicerone all the pictures of Madonnas, pictures from every-day life, historical pictures and portraits, which were worthy of attention. Having come to the end, he interrupted himself suddenly, as if rebuking himself, and said—

"I had almost forgotten to mention a picture, which, although anonymous, and very unfavorably placed, deserves to be named as the gem of the gallery, both in idea and execution. I have seen nothing more wonderful in my life, and even now, when I speak of it, all the details of the striking picture appear clear and decided before the mind, so that I can give them without omitting anything essential."

This preliminary was calculated to raise the greatest curiosity, and the queen, with the company, formed a narrow circle around the narrator.

"Imagine, your majesties, a medium-sized tablet divided into two parts, of which each represents a single picure," began the lord chamberlain ; "the conditions of space divide this picture in form : the character is one and the same. In the first, the principal figure is a maiden in the full blooming freshness of youth. The flowing drapery flutters lightly in the wind. One foot already rests upon the edge of the barge which wavers in suspended dance, and which the stream, curling up into foaming waves, seems about to drive from the shore, without rudder or anchor. The eyes of the maiden look longingly into the distance: in her features lies romantic enthusiasm. On the shore which the mariner leaves, stand sympathizing friends. An old man, with silver hair, waves a farewell: a group of maidens, blooming as she, and familiarly clinging to each other, wave handkerchiefs and ribbons after the departing: a youth, handsome and earnest, folds his hands together, and out of the clouds, a friendly, loving, sorrowful countenance looks down upon her. Luxuriant roses signal from the beautiful shore, and form a rare contrast to the lurking, green-haired water-fairies who swim under the mirror of the water in scarcely defined outlines, and seem to pull the frail boat forward. The maiden, it is plain, goes hence on a dangerous journey; but a tender, shimmering cloud-figure, doubtless the ever young Hegemone, hovers near her, and by solicitous glance and imploring gesture, seems to express admonition and prayer. Whether the mariner shall be saved by the grace of this guardian angel, or fall by the wiles of the waiting fairies, is the question with which the gazer unwillingly leaves the charming picture to turn to its companion piece.

"In the picture which we know consider, the principal figure is a young man with walking-staff and travelling-bag, who passes rapidly away from the narrow doorway of a house, and steps out boldly on the broad highway. He breathes freely, and an earnest satisfaction speaks from his eyes. Joyfully starting out to meet life, he takes notice neither of the noble matron who would hold him back, nor of the affectionate maiden who longingly extends her hands to him, nor of the faithful dog that, although fastened by the chain, nevertheless raises himself entreat-

ingly. From the windows of an inn may be seen a waiter, standing at a counting table and swinging his hat: a Jew stands in the way and holds out a paper, which the wanderer refuses: at the well in the foreground a thoughtless maid nods saucily and piquantly to the youth; and so far the picture represents a gay scene, a little saddened by the quiet grief in the background; but, before the wanderer, who looks carelessly around, gapes an abyss, which is suspended a frightful dead body, with a severe but honest countenance. Its eyes are shut, but it raises the right hand warningly toward the approaching youth, while the left rests on the breast in quiet consciousness.

"And so," continued the narrator, "the picture is finished."

A short silence reigned in the company. The king rested gloomily in his chair; while the queen, on whom the affectionate daughters were leaning, at length replied:

"The picture is finished, and we have an obscure allegory, to find the key to which will not be difficult. Man and woman going from the narrow home-circle to enter upon life, leaving behind them the sheltering paternal roof, and the innocent joys of childhood; the youthful desire to toss upon tempestuous waters, or to journey on the parched highway; these are—or my feeling must be very much at fault—the subjects which the poetical painter wishes to represent."

"Your majesty's penetration is equal to the solution of the most obscure enigma," replied the count; "but in the attractive double picture lies still more, if one leave not out of notice that it is surrounded by a wreath of forget-me-nots; that the mariner wears these flowers in her hair, and the wanderer on his bosom. The artist thought to give the signification of the harmless little flower, and how well he has succeeded in painting its characteristics. The departing is for those remaining behind a forget-me-not; but even these who remain on the spot which the loved one leaves, desire to impress their remembrance on the bird of passage just as firmly. 'Forget me not!' call after her the silver-haired father, the youthful friend, and the play companions of the maiden. 'Forget me not!' whispers the glorified mother out of the clouds, and the protecting spirit hovering over the waters. Well for the mariner if she fail not to hear the warning voice. Well for the youth, if the forget-me-not of the mother, the bride, and the creditor, cling long to his heart: he will return true and noble, scorning the temptations on the way of life, and remembering the paternal honor, which, through the dumb mouth of the dead body, calls to him 'Forget me not!'"

The queen rose hastily, nodded, as it seemed, overcome by tears, to the narrator, leaned upon the arm of her daughter, and apparently struggling to hide her emotion, left the room. The king threw a disapproving glance after her, which finally met that of the count, who stood transfixed in the middle of the hall, without knowing how or why so peculiar a circumstance had transpired.

The courtiers had fallen back and were whispering among themselves.

"Will your majesty condescend to point out to me whether any indiscretion of mine has caused the present event, or whether it may be attributed to an unfortunate coincidence," said the count timidly. Instead of answering, the ruler gave those standing around the signal of departure, and commanded the count to remain. Being called nearer, and permitted to sit opposite the king, he waited impatiently for the discourse which his commander should direct to him.

"Your ignorance is excused," commenced the latter, in his usual short manner of speaking, "but the queen is unpleasantly affected by the name Forget-me-not. It is an old wound that has to-day been opened afresh, and hence the strange scene. It is, perhaps, nineteen years since I undertook the rule of this state. The care of it called me into the field against the enemy formed by the exiled royal family. I was but just married. In order to acquaint my aged father-in-law with the fortunate result of a battle, I sent to the capital a young ordnance officer. He returned to the camp at the time designated, but at the same time came secret dispatches from my zealous agents, who noted the disposition of the people, and kept guard on the actions of the crown-princess, my wife. The ordnance officer, who had long loved my wife in secret, had, in special audience, received from her hands, a bouquet of forget-me-nots. My jealousy knew no bounds. In the next tournament, the officer found his death, and—as it is said—on his breast lay the fatal flowers. After I had returned as victor, it became clear that my wife had intended this present for me, and that she was unacquainted with the feelings of the unsafe messenger who had retained for himself the love-gift of a queen. But now it was too late. Mother and sister mourned on his grave, and the tender heart of my wife was so shocked by such a catastrophe that even to-day, after so many years, her grief has again been manifested." The king was silent, and leaned his head on his hand. The count, overcome by the unusual confidence of his sovereign, and feeling himself inadequate to console, did not venture to reply. The king, instead of dismissing him, remained in troubled thought, while a bitter smile played around his mouth. "Finally," he continued, "my position at that time was difficult. My zealous temperament was bent on vanquishing the obstacles in the way of my successful career. My motto was, 'Onward!' The people were dissatisfied that a man not of royal descent should have the audacity to claim the crown. I had, by force of arms, held the old king on his throne, banished the pretenders, and rescued the people, the property, and the church. I had shown that no one understood better how to readjust the disorganized affairs of state; but when the eyes of the old man closed, and I seized the sceptre, according to agreement, then arose a cry of consternation. The fools had believed that I would give the house which I had built up to the alienated Merovingians, and myself be satisfied with the position of major-domo. A conspiracy was formed. You remember that the flower forget-me-not passed for the symbol of rebellion. The faction of the refugees have not yet forgotten the day on which I gave the command which the times demanded. The first name which met me upon the list of those seized was Albo. The family of that officer bore this name. I knew that the baroness had hated me irreconcilably since the death of her son; that her daughter hated me not less, and that a determined ally of the exiles was about to offer his hand to the latter. Now burst the bombshell. In the house of Albo were said to have been held meetings. The baroness was said to have sworn to give her daughter to the one among her countless suitors who would take the most prominent part in my overthrow. My sternness passed the sentence of death upon the women; but the entreaties of my

wife—to whom it had been represented that the accusations which had been heaped upon the mother and daughter were only the work of envy and private hatred—disarmed my sentence. I banished the women, and confiscated their property. The bridegroom died in prison; and so the fate of that family was mournfully fulfilled." The king then continued in a monotonous tone: "I will not deny that later I have thought of these poor women who must wander in exile, with a certain unwilling pity, and that still later I made inquiries concerning them. No trace of them could be found. But I see that I have allowed myself to say more than is customary for me. We will pass to something else. Who is the painter who executed the picture of which you have spoken?"

"Sire," replied the count, "I do not know. He cannot, however, be unknown to the inspector of the gallery. I know only that he is not one of your majesty's subjects, and that he begged permission to exhibit the double picture for a few days. For the present he remains in the capital."

"Yes, yes," replied the king; "no one but Cremati can have created this picture; his power alone manifests itself in such allegorical compositions; and the allusion to the forget-me-not — yes, yes, watchful man we will make peace, and thy pride of art shall melt in the sunshine of my favor. I wish to see the painter, count. You will take pains to bring him here. He will not willingly obey, but an autographic command shall place all authority at your disposal. Depart as early as possible, and the day after to-morrow I shall expect to see the painter. Good night, count!"

The count departed, and the king retreated to his cabinet. After a few fruitless struggles, he overcame the melancholy which clouded his soul, and went to the table, on which lay in great numbers the reports and dispatches just brought in by the courier. He sought impatiently among the letters for one, which when found, he broke with anxiously suspended breath ; but after the first line, the restless expectation vanished from his features ; cheerfulness spread over them, and with a light " Good, good !" he took up the silver candlestick, impatient to share his satisfaction, and opened the tapestry door which led into the corridor connecting his rooms with the queen's. As he approached the door, he heard voices, and upon entering found the queen sitting in an arm-chair, and leaning, in pleasant resignation, upon Eliza's shoulder. At their feet, on an ottoman, sat Sophia, the younger princess, resting her smiling face on the mother's lap. The beautiful family picture charmed the king, and he commanded the ladies, who would have risen in his honor, to remain in their positions. The group remained, but the former spirit was gone; and the king himself, after a few moments' thought, broke the restraint.

" I forgot," he said, as he gave his daughters a sign to leave their places, " I forgot that my wish serves only to govern the *actions* of my family, but cannot charm away a grief. I cannot approve of the tears which I see in your eyes, madame. You have given to the court a spectacle, the cause of which is too antiquated to render it any longer excusable, and too unimportant to have been entrusted to your daughters, as I must imagine has been done."

" You err, sire !" replied the queen, drying the last traces of tears from her eyes ; " the tenderness, not the curiosity of my daughters has comforted me."

The princesses kissed the queen's hands caressingly, and the king replied :

" Right ; that I must commend ; and to prove that it pleases me to give pleasure, I will confide to you what gladdens my heart and somewhat lightens my paternal cares. This letter from my ambassador in a neighboring kingdom makes the heavens look joyful. The dissensions which have for so long a time threatened to separate that country and mine, are peacefully settled, and I hope to see soon at my court an ambassador with instructions to sue for Eliza's hand. So I have finally succeeded in entering fully into the band of sovereigns. The fortunate soldier is forgotten, and hereafter kings will speak to a king, and make room in their ranks for him whom fortune raised to their level. My name and the remembrance of my deeds will not pass away with my body. If I am blessed with no son, my grandchildren will wear my crown, and enjoy the fruits of my labors."

The queen gave him her hand softly, and spoke :

" May fortune still further attend you, gracious sire. Your wife willingly submits to your wisdom, and your daughters will fulfil the duties which your position imposes upon them."

" Have you not taught me early, beloved mother, that renunciation and offering is our destiny ?" said Eliza calmly, but sighing softly. " I will obey my royal father without objection, without complaint, if—"

" If the prince do not disappoint the ideal that a maiden's heart is accustomed to create," said the king. " Be without fear, my daughter ; the prince is renowned as a second Bayard, whose bravery goes hand in hand with the most pleasant courtesy. He is not remarkably beautiful, as I understand, but moderately so, and possesses all those brilliant accomplishments which pertain to a royal education. At least you will be able to boast of a better suitor than your mother, whom I, having neither the advantage of beauty nor of birth, and grown up in the rough customs of the camp, won by the power of my sword, to the astonishment of her father. The brazen age ruled in the land then, and my sword must cut out for your grandfather the royal robe that he had taken from his cousins, as the people demanded. But with your marriage, daughter Eliza, shall begin the golden age. I will give *fêtes*, and the world shall wonder before my splendor as it has before my renown. This old Frankish building shall put on a festival dress, and gleam with gay pictures as for a carnival. Cremato comes again, and his brush shall prove worthy of my generosity."

"Cremato!" repeated the queen wonderingly; "Cremato," cried the princesses together, as they recalled the wonderful, sprightly Italian, who had many times appeared at the court like a flying shadow, and as quickly disappeared; and who did not fear to express the strongest criticisms on the drawings of the royal children, but from whom the little students learned more in a quarter of an hour—when he sometimes condescended to instruct — than from their well-paid court teacher in months. The queen thought proper to send the curious princesses to their apartments, a command that was quietly obeyed.

"What will Cremato here?" she asked her husband who, sunken in plans for the brilliant future, walked silently back and forward. "His name wakes only sorrowful recollections. Is there a new conspiracy to denounce? Shall blood flow again? Shall the innocent again wander in misery? Speak, my husband! Why shall the terrible accuser, who has the misery of thousands on his soul, return?"

"Woman condemns as quickly and as thoughtlessly as she excuses," replied the king earnestly. "Cremato, having by accident become acquainted with the first threads of the conspiracy, fulfilled the duty of a brave citizen in disclosing them. Cremato owed this service to the land and the prince who then gave him protection and security. The most indifferent stranger would have been to that extent under moral obligations. Cremato rescued *thy* throne through his denunciation. Neither for this favor nor the disinterestedness which refused every reward does he deserve the unthankfulness which thy mouth has spoken against him. It is true that many persons fell, but the pressure of necessity absolutely demanded them. Therefore, no word more about it! For all I have done—except one— I will answer before Him who judges the most powerful."

"And must this one example of vengeance work on for ever? Thy suspicious jealousy drove poor Albo to a certain death; and still, after my innocence was manifest, must make his family the offering of an ever insatiate revenge. Cremato's accusation—"

"Not so," replied the king, with vexation. "The guilt of the women came to my ear from another source. A report was spread that Albo was sacrificed . . . . . enough; the mother breathed vengeance, and for this the law demanded her life. I was gracious still!"

"Fearful grace," cried the queen, "which drove the unfortunate from their home and the graves of their dead, to wander in poverty and misery in a strange land. That was not what I asked when I prayed for mercy for the innocent. That was not what they expected when they sent petitions to thy throne to recall the sentence, and to allow them to return to their native land, even if it must be in poverty and want."

"A ruler does not play with law and verdict like the conjurer with a snake," spoke the king sharply. "The women who were thirsting for revenge could not be allowed to come back at that time: they cannot now: nevermore. And you, madame, might better let the dead rest. Your feelings lead you to a false conclusion. The gift of a few flowers caused the death of the thoughtless Albo. Your tears for that are shed in vain. The youth's destiny and my passion bear all the blame. You are free from all responsibility. Do not disturb yourself longer with frightful fancies. Leave the burden to my conscience. Admonishing to repentance is of no use, and only embitters. Such attempts it was, madame, that drove from my side the painter Cremato, to whom I had given my confidence. He did not accuse Albo's family, as you falsely believe; he defended them only too boldly. He took the liberty to speak to my conscience—to play the Massillon to me. I am tolerant only to a certain extent, and for nine years he has avoided the court, at which he so often appeared and went like a bird of passage."

"I did not know the man as you have painted him to me, sire," said the queen, only half convinced. "My heart shudders before extreme punishment and severe retribution, therefore I trembled before the in-

former who called forth both at that time. You say he comes again? Where has he lived, and how, until now?"

"I must explain," replied the king, "that I have no correct account of this man's residence for some time. He was a person worthy to be the friend of a king. I am not a chief of police. I need to know nothing more. Had he any settled dwelling-place? I do not know. In my dominions he has only wandered back and forth since that time. But, so much as I desire to see him again, I do not know whether I should not rather dread the meeting, as for many years I preserve his remembrance in fear."

"Fear!" asked the queen, with wondering eyes; "does the hero, my husband, know the possibility of fear?"

"The heart of iron trembles before the Eternal Judge, even when he speaks through the fearless tongue of a human being," answered the king, with anxiety depicted on his countenance. "Cremato's last words might convince thee, my guileless wife! He pleaded with impetuous eloquence for Albo's sentenced family; painted their suffering, that they must die far from the land that bore them, and asked their recall in the name of humanity. I refused.

"'Well!' spoke then the peculiar man, coldly and threateningly to me. 'I desist from further attempts to move the cold heart of the conqueror. Fortune's son no longer recognizes the unfortunate. But, from now on, another shall speak to him in my stead. Albo's fall, and the accompanying circumstances, are no secret, and my brush shall immortalize the unfortunate. His picture, in the pale mask of death—his picture—the herald of bloody tyranny, be my next work, and the recollection that

I leave to you, sire. Take it as my legacy; and as often as an injustice or cruelty comes into your soul, or on your lips, so often may this pale face, swaying on black ground, stand before your eyes. May it serve to moderate your vengeance: may it be to presumption a reminder of annihilation: may it sharpen the penitence of your conscience.' He went, but the sting of his words remained with me from that hour. My self-consciousness turned, thousands and thousands of times, back to the terrible picture which he had left to torture me. Many times, as my dreaming thoughts wandered over my battle-fields, arose, from all the bodies only this one giant countenance, ghost-like, before me. Often, when overcome by the weariness of business, I rested upon a chair, I have seen on the wall the promised picture—like to the old countenances of Christ, which swung on a black ground without neck or robe —frightfully and threateningly coming nearer, as a phantasmagoric image."

"Stop!" cried the queen, in terror, for, in addition to the shock which the reference to Albo had given her, the countenance of her husband had, while he had been speaking, become like that of a ghost, and his voice had sunk to a hoarse whisper. "The dreadful Cremato," continued she, "has he kept his word? How long has the unholy gift been in your hands? and have you destroyed it?"

The king shook his head. "I have never seen the painting," he answered. "Cremato has not kept his word; but I feel—I know certainly—that the picture is ended; that it exists, and that, if it came into my hands, the strength to destroy it would fail me; but look upon it I could not, for my fancy has already created it to break my heart. Countless sentences has it mitigated, countless misfortunes arrested; for, whenever I have taken the pen or opened the mouth to decide over the life, happiness, or honor of any subject, I saw him—I saw Cremato's dreadful work opposite me."

The king stopped suddenly, took a few thoughtful steps through the room, and went out; but the overpowering feeling which the disclosure of the long-kept secret had aroused in him, prevented the monarch's enjoying his rest. He left his couch, opened the window, and looked out into the still, cool summer night. The trees of the grove whispered, while here and there a drop, condensed from the moist air, fell sounding from leaf to leaf, and from the distance came an indistinct harmony, disturbing the song of the nightingale. As the listener's ear became accustomed to the rustling of the forest, the distant sounds became more distinct and figured themselves into a song that the king recognized, while it recalled a sweet tide of youthful recollections. The past, lying far back behind the confusion of endless wars, behind the tumultuous years of ambition and seeking for glory, worked its nameless magic on his soul. He saw himself again a boy on the rocks of the Mediterranean sea; he heard again as then—with never-ending satisfaction, the melodious song of the fishermen as they rowed out in the golden gleaming of the morning red, or in the rosy shimmer of evening when returning into secure harbors and the peace of their homes.

O sanctissima,
O piissima
Dulcis Virgo Maria!
Mater amata,
Intemerata,
Ora pro nobis!

But now it was no longer the strong tenor voices of the south, but two sweet female voices, so low and melodious, that rest and peace came back to him, and turning to his couch, he murmured softly:

"Holy, blessed fatherland. The rolling fates have taken me from thy lap to fasten me in a strange land, with a strange crown, but with blessings I think of thee; and blessed, thrice blessed, may'st thou be, O my loved fatherland, my sweet home!"

.   .   .   .   .   .

"That is not Cremato," spoke the king, as the count, according to the command, presented the modest painter, a slender, handsome youth, scarcely arrived at manhood.

"I am called Guido, sire!" answered he fearlessly.

"Guido was always a fortunate name for one of your art," replied the king, as he dismissed the count. "I have heard good of you. Have you brought with you the picture of which the count has spoken?"

"No, sire," said the painter; "a iberal connoisseur had bought it and taken it away, before the command of your majesty reached me."

"What a misfortune!" said the king condescendingly. "I am a patron of art, and desire to employ your brush."

"I am sorry," replied Guido, "that I have no specimen of my poor talent to show to your majesty. But I have brought with me a work which I hope will obtain your favor, sire. I was on my way to your court, and have Cremato's masterpiece to give to your majesty."

The king became pale at these words. He looked at the painter piercingly, but as he received the glance without restraint, questioned him further.

"Cremato! His last work? You, sir; perhaps his son?"

"His student, gracious sire! his student who buried him a few months

ago at Naples, and promised the dying man to bring the picture to your majesty."

"Cremato dead!" sighed the king. "In him died a true artist, a peculiar but noble man. I have never inquired further concerning him. He was to me only a human being whom I could protect," added he slowly. "The last sign of his independence! You have brought it with you?"

"Yes, your majesty," replied Guido. "It stands in the anteroom. I hasten to bring it."

"Yet a word," began the king disturbedly to the artist. "The subject of the picture?"

"For me a secret," answered Guido. "The master worked on it with closed door—embellished it with his own hands, and locked it in the box. It stood long so, ready for departure. Cremato would entrust it only to me, and said to me, on his dying-bed, that only your majesty knew what that picture designated."

The king's countenance cleared, and he allowed that Guido should bring the box, in which the picture was locked, into the room. With a kind of grim horror, he refused to have it opened.

"Some other time," he said abruptly, "I will see if you are the student of your teacher. Did Cremato leave relatives to whom I can return the price of this masterpiece?"

"A mother and two daughters," replied Guido. "It is true, they are not pressed by want, but from a painter's inheritance is seldom left a surplus. Yet, do not pay for this gift in gold. Weighty grounds compel them to remain in a foreign land, and they wished to find a refuge in the kingdom that your majesty's wisdom makes happy."

"To take care of Cremato's daughters shall be my work, but perhaps his student has found his way to the heart of one of them ?"

Guido bowed blushingly and denied.

"I am already bound," said he, "but to take to them the hope of your majesty's grace will be my first duty. They will soon thank you in person." The king bowed and said :

"Let yourself be presented to the queen and look at the drawings of my two young daughters. Cremato's pupil has certainly inherited quickness in art from him. His spirit is in your eyes. You please me."

He dismissed the joyful painter and turned toward the secret picture. "It seems to me," he said to himself, "as if Albo's eyes looked through the wood in order to wound me. Angry friend! On thy death-bed, hast thou after so many years kept thy pledge and made the shade of the murdered one at home in my court? When will I obtain the strength to look at thy earnest work ? To look at it! Never! I think I should die from the glance. I will never see it. I know it already too well. Away with it !"

With his own hands he set the box away behind the heavy silken curtain that fell down in long folds before a window. Then he threw himself into an arm-chair and asked himself, "How is it possible that one single deed performed in unjust revenge must perpetually swing its whip over my wounded heart? The fields which my battles have enriched with blood, the scaffolds which have been erected in the course of time— these disappear when my eyes look into the past ; but Albo's grave lies ever open before them."

* * * * *

It had become late in the evening. Government cares occupied the king. He had worked with his counsellors.

The reception room was deserted ; but the tapers still burned in the rooms of the queen. The Princess Sophia, overcome by weariness, had gone to her room. The more beautiful sister kept her mother company. She endured impatiently the reading of the governess. An indescribable unrest spoke in every movement of the beautiful maid. Her eyes rambled from the ceiling to the walls, then looked fixedly down at the floor. The light work with which she employed herself did not increase in her hands, and dropped, finally, entirely from them. With growing unrest she changed her place a few times and started when the clock struck the departure of another hour.

The queen, a careful, loving mother, delayed not to notice this unusual behavior, and herself becoming anxious, took advantage of the first suitable pause which came in the reading, and released the lady from further duty for the evening. Mother and daughter remained alone.

"Please do me the favor to play something on the harp," said the mother to Eliza. "The instrument that I once played so readily will not do duty under my neglectful fingers. Quick young fingers succeed better in bringing feeling out of its strings. Play, my child ; I need the enlivening."

Eliza obeyed. Her tender fingers glided over the strings in prelude. But the affectionate performer could not long hold the measured run of the selected piece. The restless, trembling spirit betrayed itself in the rising and falling tones. Andante became presto, and presently broke out into a striking dissonance.

"Forgive me, mother," cried the princess, springing up. "I cannot play any longer. My heart will break that I have since morning kept something secret, and secrecy must not be between you and me."

"It shall not," replied the mother, calmly, "because thy own feelings lead thee to confide."

The princess came closer to the mother, and related that in the morning, in her sister's room, almost under the eyes of Aja, while the strange painter was looking over Sophia's crayon sketches, a paper was dropped into her hands, on which she, with astonishment, read the words, 'Most gracious princess! Doubtless your heart is what your lovely features speak, noble, tender, gracious, and charitable. Oh! will you plead for the unfortunates who are hidden by Hergereita in the forest, and wait for a gleam of hope? Hear their prayer. Interest your elevated mother in this work of love. Protect the most humble from the anger of your father.' These strange, entreating words," continued the princess, "took possession of my heart. The painter must have placed the paper in my hands. My searching glance read in his the answer, 'Yes.' I should, perhaps, have scorned the boldness; but his entreating glance disarmed me. I could not shame him before my sister and the instructress. I concealed the paper, and this afternoon my devoted maid has spoken to Hergereita, and found an old, troubled-looking woman and two beautiful young girls, and, at my command, requested them to be in my room at eleven o'clock to hear how I can be useful to them. I should have liked to hear what the grieving ones wanted before speaking to you of them, dearest mother, but my unrest has betrayed me, and so, if you allow, I will bring the petitioners immediately before you."

"Thou hast done rightly, my daughter," said the queen, kissing Eliza's brow. "Thy trust excuses the censurable indiscretion of taking a paper from a stranger's hand. We will together find out what the circumstances of the strangers are, and deal with the young artist according to the truthfulness of his representation."

"The maid of her royal highness waits in the ante-room," said a maid to the queen.

Eliza blushed.

"The pointer stands on the eleventh hour," whispered she. "The petitioners are certainly already in attendance, and, if you will allow it, I will command that they be conducted here."

The queen consented. The princess gave the necessary command, and in a short time a lady, dressed in mourning, entered the room. She seemed astonished at finding herself in the presence of the queen; but this circumstance failed to deprive her of the security of carriage which immediately betrayed her acquaintance with life of the highest stand, although her dress belonged to a time long past. Her noble, expressive countenance betrayed her great age, but the firm, erect gait almost denied the white hairs which spread out thinly under the black veil. With the usual bow, the matron approached the queen, kissed, before she could prevent it, the hem of her robe, then arose, and spoke with a voice filled with emotion:

"Your majesty sees before you a woman who has had the misfortune to become gray under sorrow, and older than her years would speak. Unjust fate has finally overcome my pride, and now when I have lost all except two hearts which love me, I pray only for the favor to be allowed to die within the borders of this kingdom. The making of a new throne could not so rejoice your illustrious husband as a grave in this land would rejoice me."

"Madame," replied the queen, as-tor.ished and overcome by the weary sadness in the suppliant's voice, "before you speak further, who are you? Your name?"

At this moment the tapestry door opened, through which the king was accustomed to enter, and the monarch appeared suddenly before the women. The queen and Eliza were silent in terror. The stranger looked him fearlessly in the eyes. His wrathful look fell only on her. With a curious mixture of hardness, astonishment, and anger, he finally broke out into the words :

"Whom do I see here? What is passing here? How did you come into this room, Frau von Albo?"

"Albo!" cried the queen, and threw herself upon the arm of her trembling daughter.

"You have not forgotten me, sire!" answered the lady, earnestly and firmly. "For many years I have been unaccustomed to this name, and just here where it is proscribed I hear it again. Your presence, sire, decides my fate, which I would have intrusted to friendly hands. Unjustly banished from your state, I know only too well that I stand before you now as a criminal. I have stepped over the ban, and death is my fate. Dispose of this gray head as you will, only protect my grand-daughters, my king ! Their mother has departed. They do not bear the hated name of Albo. Let them live in the home of their mother, to plant flowers on mine and their uncle's grave."

For a long time the king made no reply, but his expression was dark and menacing.

"I am no tyrant who thirsts for your blood," said he finally, "but guilty you are. I must know how all this has come about."

Eliza threw herself at her father's feet, and related to him what had happened.

"Guido !" replied the king, and pulled the bell, "this presumptuous stranger shall answer to me on the spot."

The servant, who had come, was ordered to bring the painter immediately into the royal presence. The lady appeared to hear nothing of all that was passing. Her eyes raised toward heaven and her lips moving as if in prayer, she stood there as if separated from her surroundings and belonging to another world. The queen spoke conciliatingly to her husband, but his features remained hard and dark.

"Must pictures of a miserable past swing for ever before me?" murmured he. "Must death resign the booty long due him in order to torment me? And what could have induced you, Frau von Albo, now that you are on the verge of the grave, and have lived so long away, to put yourself into such a position?"

"Age makes me a child again," replied the baroness quietly. "I was miserable in the strange land; I must, even at the price of my life, see once again the spot which bore me. It remains my fatherland, in whose bosom my bones would gladly rest near those of my son."

"O sanctissima !" sang the two angel voices through the forest, and the tones came through the open window, and the king thought again of his fatherland, and sighed deeply.

At that moment the painter Guido entered, quickly and boldly. "Your command, your majesty," said he. The baroness interrupted him with the words, "I have lost my play. most gracious prince, and I commend to you the orphans whom I must leave."

"That will God and the brave king's magnanimity not allow," replied the betrayed, and went reverently to the royal pair. "I am Prince

Julius," said he. "I wished to convince myself, without being recognized, whether the soul of the beautiful princess, whose hand I wish to gain, were like her rare charms. My hope has not deceived me, and my confidence in your majesty's grace will surely be justified to the favor of the two innocent suppliants whom I recommend to your mercy."

The queen bowed pleasantly to the prince. Eliza, overcome by delighted surprise, clung bashfully to her mother. The king reached his hand to the prince and spoke with light reproach. . . .

"The young hero, who is so welcome to my court, had no need of dissimulation in order to call out my justice. His word alone" . . . .

"Sire!" The prince interrupted him, "I flattered myself that the circumstances themselves would speak to the heart of the wisest of kings more than any word of the undistinguished man who would consider himself happy if the ruler whom he so admires would allow him to become his student and belong to his family."

The ambition of the king was so flattered by these words from a descendant of an old royal family that he, with joyful pride, led the exultant Julius to Eliza, with the words, "My prince, your bride." Turning toward the baroness, he spoke, "You have placed yourself under the protection of the queen. I will not have seen you, but a woman who conspires against me I will not endure in my kingdom. Go back. An amount sufficient to meet your expenses shall show that I do not allow private vengence to work against you—I cannot do more."

"Away from the home!" cried Frau von Albo sorrowfully; "no, no, never! Be merciful, your majesty! I have never plotted against you. The mother's heart commanded it-self. I have never cursed you. The calumniation of your dead chancellor ruined me and chased me into banishment, and still I have never cursed you. Therefore show mercy. Do not keep an old woman in doubt. My daughter found her grave in the waves. I cannot seek it out to die on it. The grave-mound of my son is in this land. I cannot leave it again. Keep the gift of your graciousness, sire! Keep the property which was unjustly taken from us. Take my life. Take the last treasure, the legacy of my son; only let me finish my days here where I was born." In the outburst of feeling, the baroness had pulled a letter from her bosom, and with trembling hands handed it to the king. A few withered forget-me-nots, sprinkled with drops of blood, fell out on the floor. The king and queen stood trembling, and "O sanctissima!" sounded anew, blessing and entreating, through the silent grove.

"Whence these wonderfully entrancing tones of home?" asked the king quickly.

"Cremato's daughters it is," answered Prince Julius, "and here stands his mother. Albo's sister was Cremato's wife, and, shortly before his death, perished on a pleasure excursion near the coast. Grief for her loss hastened his death, and his family, to whom your majesty to-day promised your protection, pray for a home in their fatherland. Shall they pray in vain?"

"Cremato the husband of your daughter?" asked the king, astonished. "Riddles multiply."

"In our humiliation and poverty in a foreign land, the strange man found us," answered the lady. "Less love than the warmest thankfulness which we owed gave him my daughter. God bless the noble man!"

"God bless him!" said Julius

quickly. " He was nobler than even his family knew. I was his student. To me he disclosed himself. His conscience had compelled him to discover that plot. His feelings tortured him when he discovered that Albo's innocent family had, through calumniation, become entangled in the terrible affair. Unable to disarm the anger of the insulted monarch, he sought untiringly the helpless family ; found them, and compelled himself to take the yoke of marriage in order to become the protector of those whom he had undesignedly and unknowingly driven into ruin. The noble man kept his relations secret from the king, and left his court after he had proved that the hatred against the name of Albo was ineradicable. The king had never discovered that Cremato was his countryman. On his deathbed he confided to me his family and that picture which I have never seen. A picture which I finished after Cremato's plan, and had exhibited, attracted the notice of the lord chamberlain, and brought me here more quickly. Cremato's remembrance ; that fatherland song that Cremato had taught his children ; the sight of this worthy matron, of the noble queen, and your angel daughter's entreaties, shall finally move the heart of the king ; and if I see rightly, if these be really tears which fill the eyes of the most noble-hearted monarch, then has my plan succeeded, and this night makes three happy."

The king was silent, struggling with his emotion. All eyes were fixed on him.

" Take up the flowers," said he. Then, deeply moved, to Albo's mother : " I am not able to give you anything more precious, even when I return to you all the property that you have lost. Albo's, Cremato's mother, be greeted ! forget as I forget.

The few days that remain to you shall be peaceful, and your granddaughters shall be my care."

" Most noble king !" cried Julius, and fell on his breast. Wife and daughter embraced him. The baroness folded her hands and prayed. . . " Oh ! see, my Albo, how he redeems the past ! Oh ! forgive him, the repentant, as I forgive him !"

As the king freed himself from this embrace, two beautiful maidens lay at his feet and moistened his hands with their tears. They were Cremato's daughters. " O sanctissima !" he sighed, and softly left the room to hide his tears.

The monarch kept his word, and peace reigned in his kingdom. But Cremato's picture he ventured not to look upon, and for long years it stood locked behind that curtain. The baroness had long since slept in her grave, and her granddaughters were happy mothers by their own firesides.

A host of blooming grandchildren, Eliza's and Sophia's sons, had made the king himself a grandfather. Then death came upon him slowly, and warned him to quit the stage of life. Joyfully he made himself ready, and willingly allowed the crown, so valueless to the dying, to glide from his hands. Satisfied with life, and resigned to death, he asked calmly to see Cremato's picture. "I am strong," he said to the weeping wife, the only one entrusted with that secret. " Myself in the arms of death, the countenance of the dead will no longer terrify me." The cover fell ; courageously the king threw his glance upon the glowing background, and the light of transfiguration came over his face. It was no ghastly figure of death. A cherub, beaming in heavenly light and glory, nodded from the clouds. Ethereally beautified, Albo's features smiled upon him ; the right hand of the angel pointed above, and the left reached out conciliatingly the wreath of forget-me-nots, taken from the golden hair.

The work of the noble painter, a sign of his love for man and his trust in God, transformed the last struggle of the monarch to the gentlest peace.

"Cremato ! Albo !" stammered he, going smilingly. "Wife ! Children ! My people ! farewell ! and thou, my fatherland, Forget me not !"

TRANSLATED FROM THE FRENCH.

SISTER ALOYSE'S BEQUEST.

I.

How delightful it is to sit under the grand old trees of the courtyard on this charming mid-summer evening ! The light breeze is redolent with the fragrance of the new-mown hay, and the leaves seem to quiver with joy in an atmosphere heavy with sunshine. The swallows pursue each other in play with short, wild cries, and in the foliage of the linden-tree that brown bird, the nightingale, tries her brilliant cadences, drowned at times by the shouts of the children at their sports answering her in the silences, whom without doubt they understood and admired. The children, happy as the birds, dance and whirl about, just like those motes one frequently sees rising up in a sunbeam. The nuns, sombre and silent figures, watch them, contemplating life in its flower and carelessness. This court-yard where the children play and the birds sing belonged formerly to a monastery of the order of St. Benoit; but now to a cloister built out of its ruins, where the virtues of ancient days flourish under the shelter of modern walls, which are hallowed by the memories of the past.

Some young girls, no less pleased with the gambols of the children, were walking in groups to and fro under the vaulted arches which encircled the court, talking and laughing merrily ; but whenever they approached a nun reclining in an easy chair, by an involuntary impulse they lowered their voices. She was a poor invalid, who had been brought out to enjoy the sweet odors and the pleasant warmth of the evening. She appeared to be nearing the end of life, though still young. For the paleness of her cheeks, the emaciation of her body, and the transparent whiteness of her hands, all proclaimed the ravages of a long and incurable illness. There was no more sand in the hour-glass, no more oil in the lamp, and her heart — like a timepiece about to stop — was slacking its pulsations. One could not help but see that Sister Aloyse retained a very powerful fascination in the beauty which her terrible illness had not been able to efface. Her dark blue eyes had not lost their almond-shape or sapphire hue. Her figure was still elegant, seen under the loose robe which wrapped her like a winding-sheet; and her voice was as sweet and agreeable as in former days.

At first she felt a little better upon being brought into the garden; but she still suffered, and neither the pure air nor the mildness of the beautiful evening had revived her. She sat in silence, absorbed, perhaps, in those last thoughts, which she did not confide even to herself, and which, to one who is about departing, seem to give a glimpse of those unknown shores which are yet so near to her who waits them.

What is she thinking of? Of her past without remorse; of her future without terror? Does she regret anything which she has renounced for her God? Does one last thread hold captive this celestial bird? I cannot say. She appears sad; yet her companions, always so affectionately attentive, do not seem to be surprised. For Sister Aloyse had always been characterized, even in the more beautiful days of her youth, by a kind of melancholy. She resembled an angel of peace, but yet an angel who weeps.

One young girl, who was walking under the arches, regarded her with great interest; and finally, leaving the group by whom she was surrounded, approached the nun, dropped on her knees in the grass before her, and, looking in her face, said earnestly:

"Well, my sister, are you better this evening?"

Sister Aloyse blushed slightly, just as porcelain is tinged with a faint rose-color when a flame is passed behind it, and answered in a voice sweet and low:

"Thank you, Camille, I am not well, and I shall never be any better till I come into the presence of our Lord. Look! does it not seem indeed as if the gates of heaven were opening yonder?"

She pointed to the west, then filled with the glory and splendor of purple and gold and flame colors.

"Yet one cannot go there," answered Camille in a caressing tone.

"Oh! yes; provided the great God will receive us. And something warns me that I shall shortly go to him."

Both now became silent, Camille sadly regarding her companion. Educated in this convent, she had always been accustomed to see Sister Aloyse there, where she was much beloved. She would like to have given her some pleasure, but what could she give, or what could she say, to a person so detached from earthly things, and whose aspirations were fixed on joys eternal?

The nun was still thinking, praying perhaps; and after a long silence she said,

"Camille, you must come and see me some time before I go away from here. But now good-night, dear!"

Two nuns now came forward to help the sister into the house, while Camille, who had gathered some white roses, carried them to Aloyse, saying,

"They are from my own little garden, my sister; therefore take them, I pray you."

"Willingly," said Aloyse, "and I will offer them to the Holy Virgin. And, Camille, do not forget to remember me in your prayers to-night."

II.

"Go, my child," said the old abbess to Camille, "go to the infirmary and see Sister Aloyse; she has something to say to you."

"Is she going to die?" asked Camille with tears in her eyes.

"She will go to her eternal home soon, but not to-day. Have no fear, child, but go and listen carefully to what she tells you."

Camille with agitated heart (for this poor heart is so quickly stirred at sixteen years !) ascended the staircase which led to the cells of the nuns. She passed through a long corridor out of which opened the little doors, all of which, instead of a number or design, bore some holy image or pious inscription. At the end of this corridor she found the infirmary, a large room, quiet and retired, whose windows opened upon the court and garden below. At this moment it was almost vacant; she found only one bed occupied, that of Sister Aloyse, who, as she had no fever, had been left by the infirmarian while she attended vespers in the chapel. Camille noiselessly approached the bed, the curtains of which were half drawn so that Aloyse could see out. She was sitting up supported by her pillows, and her hands were joined before her on the cross of her rosary. She smiled on the young girl, who timidly embraced her; and then Camille very earnestly asked her why she had sent for her, to come to her bedside instead of any other of the girls, or her friends or companions; for she was afraid, as one naturally dreads what is unknown. The nun fixed upon her those searching eyes which seemed to look through and beyond anything present, and said with much sweetness,

"Sit down, Camille; I have something to say to you." She hesitated, but finally said, "You have never heard any one of your family speak of me ?"

"Never," answered the child, somewhat surprised.

"I have known something of your family—your father," she said with an effort. "But it was a long time ago, a very long time—before you

were born. I was related to your grandmother, Madame Reville."

"I never saw her, but I have seen her great portrait," said Camille.

"Yes, it hangs in the red drawing-room, does it not ?" asked Sister Aloyse with a sad smile. "Ah! well. Madame Reville received me into her family as a lady's companion — a reader—for I was poor, and needed some home. Your father did not live at home with his mother, but he came there very frequently."

Here she paused, breathing with difficulty, but continued:

"He wished to marry me; Madame Reville was opposed to it; he insisted. I saw he would disobey his mother; I was afraid for him; I was afraid for myself. So I prayed to the good God. He did not reject my afflicted and desolate heart, but he —the Divine Consoler — called me into this home, and placed this holy veil as a barrier between the world and myself. Here I found peace, purchased sometimes with bitter suffering, but real; for it filled the depths of my heart; it was the price of my sacrifice. And I was able to see, in the clear light which streamed from the cross, how all joy is deceitful, and all pleasure empty and false. After two years had passed, I came to consecrate myself with irrevocable vows to God's service, when the friends who now and then came to see me, and public report, which in our day finds its way even into the cloister, told me of the only thing which had still power to afflict me. For, Camille, your father—but what can I say to you who bear his name! M. Reville, angry at my departure, and grieving for the loss of the poor creature that I am, sought forgetfulness in dissipation. Undoubtedly, he forgot me—I trust and hope he did —but he also forgot his God! Your father is not a Christian; nay, he is an enemy to Christianity! Ah! since the day when I first knew that our prayers did not meet in the pathway to heaven, how have I wept, how have I prayed, how have I done penance! Alas! my tears, my blood, my vigils, my sufferings—all have not prevailed, and I am pierced to the depths of my heart with the terrible reflection."

She was unable to continue; her voice died upon her lips, while tears, clear and burning, rolled down her cheeks. Camille, kneeling by her bedside, wept too; for she began to see what this self-denying heart had suffered.

" My, child," finally said the sister after a long silence, " I shall soon die, and there will then be no one to pray for. him, since your mother, who ought especially so to do, is dead. You love your father, don't you ?"

" Yes, with all my heart!"

" Well, then, promise me that you will unceasingly pray for his conversion—that you will offer for him your every action and your every pain; promise me that there shall always be a suppliant voice to take the place of poor Aloyse's, which will soon be hushed in death—to cry ' mercy!' Think of what it is to have a soul and an eternity, and that soul your father's !"

She had seized the hands of the child in both her own, and fixed upon her a look in which the last forces of her life were concentrated. " Promise !" said she. Camille thought a moment—her young face wore a grave and stern expression. Finally, raising one arm toward the crucifix, she said in a distinct voice: " I solemnly promise you, my sister, I will continue what you have commenced. I will pray, I will labor all my life for his conversion." A ray of heavenly light illumined Sister Aloyse's countenance, and she sank back upon

her pillows, murmuring, " I can die now."

Two days later she passed away, with a peace and serenity worthy of the blamelessness of her whole life, though in breathing her last she cried, " Have mercy !"

Was it of herself she thought ?

III.

Many years have passed away. The grass grows thick and green upon the bed of clay where sleeps Aloyse. Camille, grown into a fine young woman, keeps house for her father. She has travelled with him, she has seen the world, its balls and its routs, but she has never forgotten the promise made to Sister Aloyse. This promise has banished the strength of her limbs and of her youth. She has become serious all at once. She has given to her life but one aim, and that sublime and difficult, and from that moment when the struggle which had animated the life of Aloyse passed into her own all her actions, all her thoughts, had been devoted to the redemption of one soul. At first overflowing with the thoughtless and enthusiastic zeal of youth, she would talk to him of that religion whose arguments her heart found so natural, and which seemed to her so irresistible. Her father would laugh at her, and she would cry; she would persist, however, until he became so angry that she was frightened. Finally she decided to be more quiet in the future, and to leave to God the conduct of her cause. But with what vigils, with what prayers, what sighs, what agony of heart, and with what fervent desire did she ask God for that precious soul! And what vows did she make to the Blessed Mother! What flowers she offered upon her altar! What prayers, in which she thanked God for the kindness that had given mortals this all-powerful Mediatrix! Her father's guardian angel, what careful conversation did she hold with him! How she labored and prayed for that of which he never thought!

As years pass, Camille's piety becomes more rigid; self-denial joins itself to acts of earnest charity, in their turn supplemented by generous alms!

One would naturally ask why Camille, rich and young, charming and admired, should rise so early in the morning, should spend so many hours upon her knees in church? Why she went with the Sisters of Charity to visit the sick, why her attire was so plain and simple, why her room was so little ornamented, why she labored without any relaxation, and finally, why with so interesting an appearance and conversation she preferred so severe a life? No one upon earth could answer these questions except the guardian angel who writes down these noble acts to the account of their forgetful subject, her unrepentant father.

But she accomplished nothing, although the rigors were not for herself, though she maintained, for her father, this piety united with a tenderness which only made her more sweet and affectionate. His hard heart did not open to the rays of divine grace, nor to the timid smiles of his child. The taste for amusement, born of a desire for forgetfulness, had chased from his heart, at the same time with a pure love, the belief in holy things. The heavenly flame had been quickly extinguished beneath the ashes of pleasure; and, like many other children of his age, he had neglected to believe through fear of being compelled to be good. Bad society and bad literature had completed the work of headlong dissipation; and neither marriage nor

paternity had reclaimed him. His birth, fortune, and indisputable talents raised him to public offices. And, to be consistent with his principles, and congenial to his friends, he had to be inimical to all religion. The seminaries; the Brothers of the Christian Doctrine; the Sisters, hospitallers or teachers; the free establishments; the Carmelites, who ask nothing of a person; the Clarisses, who ask only a piece of bread; the Little Sisters of the Poor, who gathered food for their old men; the foreign missions; the sermons in Lent in the parish; the general indulgences granted by the pope; the cardinals in the senate; and the Capuchins who went barefooted—were all equally the objects of his strong aversion. He read continually the *Journal des Débats*, the *Revue des Deux Mondes*, and the liberal journal of his department—of that department in which he played a prominent part. Shall we say, in excuse for him, that his impiety had never been tried by adversity; and that he had found the world so delightful that he had wished to live for ever in it? In youth he had lived in the midst of noisy pleasures. In more advanced life he lived for comfort, for his house—cool in summer, warm in winter, splendid at all times—for his grand dinners, his good wine, his fine horses and elegant equipages. He enjoyed exquisitely those excellent things which the public generally esteem, but in which divine grace does not much appear. The memories of youth he did not often recall. He now scarcely recollected the name of that poor cousin whom he had once loved so passionately, but who had never forgotten him, who, even in the arms of death, had displayed an angelic love. One day Camille spoke of Sister Aloyse, and added,

"Was she not related to us, father?"

" Yes, yes — a romantic affair ! She threw herself into a convent; she became weary even there !"

He took several turns through the room with a preoccupied air, and finally stopping before the great picture of his mother—a withered and haughty figure—he said,

" My mother did not love, this poor Aloyse much ! Poor girl ! What a charming voice she had ! A voice which ought to astonish the convent when she chants the *Miserere !* She will sing no more ; she has a pain in her chest. Zounds ! The discipline of the convent ! What a pity for this pretty Aloyse to be buried alive ! On the stage she would equal Malibran !"

And this was all ! The remembrance of Aloyse was only that of a young girl who could sing charmingly, and who, perhaps, might have commanded a situation in a theatre !

He loved his daughter; but, for all that, she troubled him, and he was anxious that she should marry, so that he might be relieved from the care and responsibility. She did not oppose his wishes, for she did not feel that God appointed her to lead the life of a nun; but she wished her husband to be a Christian, and said so to her father. He only shrugged his shoulders and cried,

" Still these absurd ideas !"

The Christian, however, presented himself, and at twenty-two Camille Reville became Madame de Laval.

IV.

Camille is now no longer twenty. Her youth has passed on swift wings, and white is beginning to streak her dark hair; but her pleasant face preserves the repose of former days. She has been blessed with mixed and imperfect happiness, such as every one tastes in this world. For in this life

the black squares are never far distant from the white ones; and in its tangled skein the dark threads are woven in by the side of brighter colors. She had lived most happily with her husband. Together they had laughed over their little children's gambols, and together wept over them in sickness. They had brought them up with the labor and care which, in our day especially, accompanies all true Christian education. Their eldest daughter, Amelia, had been married about a year; and they were now very happy in expectation of her approaching maternity. The second daughter was finishing her education in the same convent of Benedictines where her mother had been in her youthful days. Their son André was in a polytechnic school, and their youngest, Maurice, was pursuing his Latin studies in his native village.

Through the disappointments and joy of her life, through days of rain and days of sunshine, Camille had pursued one thought faithfully—the grand aim which she had proposed to herself in early life, her father's conversion. As a young wife she had prayed with her husband, for his heart beat in unison with hers. As a young mother, she had taught her children to pray with her. And now, having reached the autumn of life, she still prayed—prayed constantly; but as yet her prayers had received no answer.

The old man lived with her; and every moment she surrounded him with care and tenderness. She watched him and brooded over him more like a mother than like a daughter. And it was hard indeed for her, that this old man of sixty-six years would not listen to any serious conversation, would only rail at holy things, and would learn no lesson from either life or death. And she was ever obliged to turn his words from their real meaning, and interpret his jeers and sarcasms so that they would not shock her innocent little children.

At this moment we find Camille in the drawing-room with her father, who is half asleep before a great fire, with the *Débats* at his feet. She is sewing on some linen for the coming baby; but twice stops to read two short letters received that morning from two of her absent children. After a thousand details about boarding, upon the compositions in history, upon the new piece of tapestry which Clotilde had just begun, upon the sermons delivered by a new father whose name she did not know, she went on to say: " I never forget, dear mother, to pray with you—you know why! It seems to me that the moment is approaching when the gentle God will answer us — as if grandpapa was going to be astonished that he had been able to live so long without thinking of God!"

The second letter was from André, and would have been unintelligible to any one who did not possess the key to a school-boy's language. But at the end there was a passage which Camille kissed again and again: " Dear mamma, I love you, and I always pray with you, just like you." A stick of wood which just now rolled down with a great noise awoke M. Reville, who, after rubbing his eyes, asked his daughter, " Where is Maurice?"

" He is skating. Do you wish me to take his place, and do anything to amuse you?"

" No, thank you. But stop, you may read instead; read this discussion in the Chambers upon the military law."

Camille took the paper and read slowly; and the old man's eyes were still closed when the violent ringing of the door-bell woke him up completely, and made Madame de Laval start.

" What is the matter with you?" asked her father.

" I do not know; only the sudden ringing frightened me."

She jumped up and ran into the hall, and at the same instant her husband entered from the street. She moved toward him, but suddenly stopped, frozen with an inexplicable horror. M. de Laval's face was of an ashy paleness; he tried to speak, he stammered—the words died upon his lips, and his wife, in one of those quick transitions which thought makes, believed he was going to fall dead at her feet.

" What ails you?" she cried, reaching out her arms toward him.

" Do not be frightened, Camille," said he; " but Maurice—"

He was unable to finish.

" Maurice!" she echoed. " Where is he? Why does he not come home? O great God! he is dead. He is drowned!"

M. de Laval had now somewhat recovered himself, and he explained: " He rescued a child who was drowning, and was wounded in the head. They are bringing him home. My dear Camille, keep up heart! He lives! God will restore him to us!"

She staggered and looked at her husband with fixed eyes.

" Have courage," he cried.

The servants, already called together by the sad news, had opened the gates to the relatives and the friends who were coming in every direction, and also to those who were bringing Maurice. They bore him on a litter, covered with a mattress, and his head, all bloody, with eyes wide open, rested upon a pillow made of the coats of the brave men; while behind the litter walked a man all covered with blood. He was the father of the child whom Maurice had saved at the price of his own life.

The boy was quickly placed upon

the bed, and the physicians were soon by his side, followed by the parish priest. Camille, kneeling beside him, saw, as in an evil dream, the surgeon dress the wound which Maurice had in the temple, and afterward talk in a serious manner to the other physicians behind the curtain. She saw the priest go up to Maurice, and, after talking to him in a low voice, bend over him and raise his hands in the benediction of the dying, and immediately after give him the holy oils. As in a dream she heard her husband's voice saying, " Dear wife, the good God wants him! Look at our Maurice."

She then looked at him. Maurice, aroused by the words of the priest, had regained complete consciousness, and knew that he was dying. He seemed more than tranquil—happy; and, looking around on all present, said,

" Good-by, papa; I only did what you taught me."

He then discovered the father of the rescued child, who had concealed himself behind M. de Laval. " Give my love to your little boy," said he.

His eyes then sought for his mother. She got up, and, bending over him, took him in her arms. " Dear mamma, make me an offering for dear grandpapa's conversion. Say to him—" He stopped. His mother saw the light fade from his eyes, and knew

that his breath was hushed in death. For a long time she remained holding him in her arms, like that more desolate of mothers, bathing him with her tears, and unable to listen to the comforting words of either husband or father, both of whom were overwhelmed with grief. At last, her piety, those religious sentiments which had always animated her life, prevailed, and she said aloud,

" Yes, my God! I accept the sacrifice, and I sacrifice him for my father. Save him, Lord, save him!"

Two days later they buried poor Maurice, the whole village attending his funeral.

The same evening the priest, who had been with him in his last moments, presented himself to Madame de Laval, and said:

" You are afflicted, but your prayers are heard. Divine grace has pursued your father, and this very morning, when the body of your child was yet in the house, he called me to him and made his confession. He could hold out no longer, he said to me. Rejoice then, madam, in the midst of your grief."

She did indeed rejoice, though she still wept.

" O Aloyse," said she, " and my dear Maurice! They are then taken away, but at what a price!"

" Thank God!" cried the priest. " He separates a family here only to reunite them in eternity!"

TRANSLATED FROM THE FRENCH.

AN UNCLE FROM AMERICA.

ALTHOUGH at the beginning of this century Dieppe had, as a city, lost much of its importance, its maritime expeditions were on a grander scale than its limited commerce to-day would lead us to suppose. The era of fabulous fortunes had not so long passed by but that occasionally there came from distant lands some of those unexpected millionaires whom the theatres have so much abused; so that, without being at all simple-minded, one might then easily believe in " uncles from America." In truth, many a merchant at Dieppe whose vessels crowded the port had, perhaps, departed thence, twenty years previous, a sailor in his simple jacket. Such examples encouraged the strong and afforded eternal hope to the penniless, who were always on the look-out for a miracle of fortune in their favor.

Such a miracle was apparently about to be performed for a poor family, of the small village of Omonville, some four leagues from Dieppe.

The widow Mauraire had experienced sad afflictions. Her eldest son, and the only support of the family, had been shipwrecked, leaving his four children to her care. This misfortune had likewise interfered with —perhaps rendered impossible—the marriage of her daughter Clémence. At the same time, it had entirely deranged the projects of her son Martin, who had been obliged to relinquish his studies, and reassume his part in the work of the farm.

But, in the midst of the uneasiness and dejection of the poor family, a ray of hope seemed to dawn for them. A letter from Dieppe announced the return of the brother-in-law of the widow, who had left there twenty years before, with, according to his own account, "some curiosities from the New World," and with the intention of establishing himself at Dieppe.

This letter, received the day before, now completely occupied them, and, although it contained nothing precise, the son Martin, who had some little learning, declared he recognized in it the style of a man so good-natured and liberal that he could not fail to have enriched himself. The sailor evidently was returning with some tons of crowns, and his relations would, of course, not be neglected.

Once started, imagination travels fast. Each one added his supposition to that of Martin; even Julienne herself, a god-daughter who had not been forgotten by the widow, and who lived at the farm less as a ser-vant than as an adopted relative, wondered what the uncle from America would bring her.

"I shall ask him for a cloth mantle and a gold cross," said she, after a new reading of the letter aloud by Martin.

"Ah!" said the widow, sighing, "if my poor son Didier had only lived till now. Who knows what his uncle would do for him!"

"But there are his children, godmother, and Miss Clémence, who will not refuse a legacy," said the young girl.

"What use have I for it?" said Clémence, hanging her head sadly.

"What use?" replied Julienne; "why, then the parents of M. Marc would have nothing to say. They would not have sent away their son to hinder the marriage if Uncle Bruno had then been here; or, at least, he would soon have come back again."

"Better consider first whether he would want to return," replied the young girl in a sad voice.

"Well, if he did not come, you could easily find another," said Martin, who thought only of the *marriage* of his sister, while she thought of the *husband*. "With an uncle from America, any one can make a good match. Who knows if he may not have with him some young millionaire he would like to make his nephew-in-law!"

"Oh! I hope not, indeed," cried Clémence, frightened. "There is no hurry about my marriage."

"What there is hurry about is a place for your brother Martin," said the widow, in a sad tone.

"Well, the Count gives me some hope," replied Martin.

"But he never decides," said the mother; "and, meanwhile, time passes and the corn is eaten. Great lords never think of that; their time is given to pleasure, and when they remember the morsel of bread they have promised, one is almost dead with hunger."

"Never mind; with Uncle Bruno's friendship we shall have no more to fear," said Martin. "He is not going to forget us. His letter says, 'I will arrive at Omonville to-morrow, with all that I possess.'"

"He should be on his way now," interrupted the widow; "he may arrive at any moment. Is everything made ready for him, Clémence?"

The young girl rose up and showed her mother the sideboard, loaded with unusual abundance. Near a leg of mutton, just taken from the oven, was an enormous quarter of smoked bacon, flanked by two plates of wheaten buns, and a porringer of sweet cream. Several jars of sweet cider completed the bill of fare. The children looked on with cries of covetousness and admiration. Julienne spoke, besides, of some apple-sauce and short-cake, which were before the fire.

From her linen closet the widow had chosen a table-cloth and napkins, which want of use had turned yellow. The young servant had placed on the waiter the plates that were the least notched, and had begun to set the table—the only silver spoon which the family possessed conspicuously exhibited at the end—when one of the children, keeping watch outside, rushed into the house, crying—

"Here he is! here he is!"

"Who is it?" cried they all in one voice.

"Why, it's Uncle Bruno," replied a strong and jovial voice.

The entire family approached the door. A sailor rested on the doorstep, and looked up at them. On his right hand he held a green parrot, on his left a little monkey.

The children, frightened at his appearance, took refuge at their grandmother's side, while she herself was unable to restrain a cry. Martin, Clémence, and the servant looked on as if stupefied.

"Why, what's the matter? Are you afraid of my menagerie?" said Bruno, laughing. "Take courage, my hearties, and let us embrace each other. I have come three thousand miles to see you."

Martin took courage first; then Clémence, the widow, and the largest of the grandchildren, but nothing could induce the little girl and the youngest one to approach.

Bruno made amends by kissing Julienne.

"Upon my word! I thought I never would get here," said he; "it is a good long cruise from Dieppe to this infernal place."

Martin noticed for the first time that the shoes of the sailor were covered with mud.

"Did you come on foot, Uncle Bruno?" asked he, with an air of astonishment.

"Why, man, did you expect me to come over your corn-fields in a canoe?" replied the sailor, gayly.

Martin turned to the door.

"But your baggage—" he hazarded.

"My baggage! it's on my back," said Bruno. "A sailor, my boy, has no need of other wardrobe than a pipe and a nightcap."

The widow and children looked at him.

"I beg your pardon," said the young man; "but, after reading uncle's letter, I had supposed—"

"Well, what? You thought I would arrive with a three-decker, did you?"

"No," replied Martin, trying to laugh agreeably; "but with your trunks—to stay some time; for you gave us to understand you would remain with us."

"Did I?"

" Yes! for you said you would come ' with all you possessed.' "

" Well! here is all I possess!" said Bruno; " my monkey and my parrot."

" What! is that all?" cried the family simultaneously.

" With my sailor's trunk, where you will find stockings without feet, and shirts without sleeves But, my hearties, such things need not make you sad. If your conscience and stomach are in good order, the rest is all a farce. Excuse me, sister-in-law; but I see here some cider, and the dozen miles I have walked have made my throat rather dry. Hallo, Rochambeau! salute my relations."

The monkey made three little jumps, then sat down before them, and scratched his nose.

The sailor, in the meantime, had helped himself to something to drink. The family looked on in consternation. As soon as the table was set, Bruno sat down without ceremony, declaring that he was almost dead with hunger. Whether they liked it or not, they had to serve the applesauce and the smoked bacon, because they had been seen; but the widow Mauraire contrived to shut up the rest in the sideboard.

The sailor, during dinner, being questioned by Martin, related how for twenty years he had sailed the Indian seas in different ships, receiving nothing but his scanty pay, which was spent as soon as earned; and so, at the end of an hour, it appeared that Uncle Bruno's only fortune was good humor and an excellent appetite.

The disappointment was general, but displayed itself differently according to the character of each one. While in Clémence it only awakened surprise mingled with sadness, Martin seemed spiteful and humbled, and the widow angry and mortified. So

changed a state of feeling soon manifested itself. The monkey having frightened the little girl by chasing her, her grandmother demanded its consignment to an old stable, and Martin declared he could not bear to see the parrot eat off the sailor's plate. Clémence said nothing, but left with Julienne to attend to household affairs, while the widow resumed her wheel outside the door.

Left alone with his nephew, Uncle Bruno quietly set down his glass, which he had emptied little by little; gave a sort of low, short whistle; and then, placing both elbows on the table, looked Martin steadily in the face.

" Do you know, my boy," said he quietly, " that the wind in this house appears to come from the north-east? Your looks are enough to freeze one, and as yet nobody in the house has spoken to me a single friendly word. This is not the way to receive a relative whom you have not seen for twenty years ?"

Martin replied brusquely that his reception had been as good as it could be, and that it did not depend upon them to offer him better cheer.

" But it depends upon you to offer me pleasanter faces," replied Bruno; " and I'll be hanged if you have not received me as you would a white squall. But we have said enough on the subject, my boy, and I don't like family quarrels. Only remember, some day you may be sorry for such behavior; that's all I have to say."

Then the sailor cut himself another slice of bacon, and commenced to eat again.

Martin, struck by his words, began to suspect that Uncle Bruno would not have spoken in this way if he possessed only a monkey and a parrot! We have been duped, thought he. He wanted to prove us, but the menace he has just made has betray ed him. Quick, let me repair our stupidity, and win him back again.

He ran to his mother and sister to make known his discovery. Both hastened to enter, and their faces, hitherto so frowning and dissatisfied, were now radiant with smiles. The widow excused herself by saying that the necessities of housekeeping had taken her away from her dear brother-in-law, and seemed astonished at the empty appearance of the table.

"Why! where is the short-cake?" said she; "where are the buns and the cream I put away for Bruno? Julienne, what are you thinking of, my dear? And you, Clémence, see if there are not some nuts in the sideboard—they sharpen the teeth, and help one to drink an extra glass."

Clémence obeyed, and when all was on the table, sat down smiling near the sailor. The latter regarded her with kind complacency.

"I am glad to see you," he said; "you are something like a relative—like the daughter of my poor George."

And then passing his hand under her chin—"This is not the first day I have known you, my little one," added he; "some one spoke to me long ago of you."

"Who was it?" said the young girl, astonished.

Before the sailor had time to reply, a sharp, quick voice called loudly, "Clémence!" The latter, surprised, turned, but saw no one.

"Ah! you can't tell who calls you!" said the sailor laughing.

"Clémence! Clémence!" repeated the voice.

"It's the parrot," said Martin.

"The parrot!" exclaimed the young girl; "why, who taught him my name?"

"One who has not forgotten it," said Bruno, twinkling his eye.

"Was it you, uncle?"

"No, child; but a young sailor from Omonville."

"Marc!"

"I believe that was his name."

"Have you seen him then, uncle?"

"Occasionally, as I returned on the same vessel with him."

"Has he returned?"

"With sufficient after his voyage to enable him to marry, without any need of his parents giving him a house-warming."

"And he has spoken to you—"

"Of you," said the sailor, "and so often that Jake has learned the name, as you see."

Clémence blushed deeply, and the widow could not restrain a gesture of satisfaction. The projected marriage between Marc and her daughter had greatly gratified her, and she had been sadly disappointed at the obstacles his parents had interposed to their union. Bruno informed her that Marc had only been detained at Dieppe by the formalities necessary for his landing, and that perhaps he would arrive the next day—more in love than ever.

Every one rejoiced at this news— but Clémence especially, who kissed her uncle in a transport of gratitude.

"Well, now you and I are the best of friends," said he, laughing; "but for fear you grow tired waiting for the sailor, I will give you the parrot. It will talk of him to you."

Again Clémence kissed her uncle, thanking him a thousand times, and held out her hands to the parrot. It perched on her arm, calling cut, "Good-morning, Clémence!"

They all burst out laughing, and the delighted young girl carried it off, kissing it as she went.

"You have made one happy, brother Bruno," said the widow, following Clémence with her eyes.

"I hope she will not be the only one," said the sailor, looking serious as he spoke. "To you also, sister, I would like to offer something; but I fear to awaken many sad remembrances."

"You would speak of my son Didier," replied the old woman, with the natural promptness of a mother.

"Yes, precisely," said Bruno. "We were not together, unfortunately, when he was shipwrecked. If we only had been, who knows? I swim like a porpoise, and perhaps I might have rescued him, as in that affair at Tréport."

"Oh! I remember you once saved his life," replied the widow, suddenly recalling this distant memory. "I ought never to have forgotten it, brother."

She had given her hand to the sailor. He pressed it in both of his.

"Oh! that's nothing," said he with simplicity; "only a neighborly turn. When our ship arrived in India, his had been there two weeks. All I could do was to find out where he was buried, and put over his grave a simple cross of bamboo."

"And you did that for him?" cried the widow, bathed in tears. "Oh! a thousand thanks, Bruno! a thousand thanks."

"I have not told you all," continued Bruno, who was affected in spite of himself. "Those beggarly Lascars stole everything belonging to him; but I managed to find his watch, which I have brought back to you, sister. Here it is."

While speaking, he showed her a large silver watch, suspended by a cord made of yarn. The widow seized it and kissed it over and over again. All the women wept, and even Martin seemed moved; Bruno coughed, and tried to drink to smother his emotion.

When the widow found words again, she pressed to her heart the worthy sailor, and thanked him again and

again. All her bad humor had disappeared, and the ideas which till then had occupied her mind vanished entirely. The precious gift which recalled a son, so cruelly snatched from her, had awakened all her gratitude. The conversation with Bruno became more free and friendly. They were soon undeceived as to his being wealthy. The "Uncle from America" had come back as poor as he went away. In telling his nephew that he and his might, some day, repent their unkindness, he had only had in mind the regret they would sooner or later experience for having misunderstood a good relative. The rest was Martin's own inference.

Although this discovery gave a final blow to the hopes of both mother and daughter, it changed in nothing their conduct toward Uncle Bruno. Their hearts warmed toward him, and the good-will which interest at first had prompted them to testify, they now accorded him from choice, and were ready to load him with affection and kindness.

The sailor, for whom they had exhausted the resources of their humble housekeeping, now rose from the table just as Martin, who had gone out but a moment before, suddenly returned to ask Bruno if he would be willing to sell his monkey.

"Rochambeau? Jove! I would not," said he. "I raised him, and he obeys me; he is my companion and servant. I would not take ten times his value for him. But who wants to buy him?"

"The Count," replied the young man. "He just passed by, saw the monkey, and was so taken with it that he asked me to sell it to him at my own price."

"Well! you may answer that we prefer keeping him," said Bruno, puffing away at his pipe.

Martin looked woful.

"This is an unlucky day," said he; "the Count told me he recollected his promise; and that if I would bring him the monkey he would see if he could let me have the appointment of receiver of rents."

"Alas! your fortune will never be any better," cried the widow in a distressed tone.

Bruno made him explain the whole affair.

"Then," said he, after a moment of reflection, "you hope, if the Count gets Rochambeau, to obtain the place you desire?"

"I am sure I shall get it," replied Martin.

"Well, then!" said the sailor, brusquely, "I won't sell the monkey, but I will give it to him. You will make him a present of it, and then he will be obliged to recognize your politeness."

A general concert of thanks arose around Bruno, which he could cut short only by despatching his nephew to the castle with Rochambeau. Martin was received most graciously by the Count, who talked with him a long time, assured him he could well fill the office which he had asked, and which he granted him.

The joy of the family may be imagined when he returned with this news. The widow, wishing to repair the wrong she had done, confessed to the sailor the interested hopes which his reappearance among them had excited. Bruno burst out laughing.

"By Neptune!" cried he, "I have played you a good trick. You hoped for millions, and I have only brought you two good-for-nothing animals."

"Oh! no, uncle," said Clémence gently; "you have brought us three priceless treasures. Thanks to you, my mother has now a souvenir, my brother employment, and I—I have hope!"

A RUINED LIFE.

It was the saddest, saddest face I ever saw.

She stood before the stove in my front office, on that dark December day, and the steam from her wet, heated garments almost concealed her from my sight. Yet the first glimpse I caught of her, through the partition door, excited my interest to an unusual degree; and, though I saw her not again for a half hour, that one glance fixed her features in my memory as indelibly as they are printed there to-day.

It was term time, and the second return-day of the term. For ten days my eyes and brain had both been crowded with all that varied detail of business which sessions aggregate upon the hands and conscience of a rising lawyer; and the musty retinue of *assumpsit, ejectment,* and *scire-facias* had nearly vexed and worn out the little life I had at the beginning. But the criminal week, which was my peculiar sphere, was close at hand, and I looked to its exciting, riskful cases as a relief from the dull, dreary current of civil forms and practice.

The little room I dignified with the name of "*front office*" was filled, as far as seats went, with rough backwoodsmen, witnesses on behalf of a gentleman who occupied with me the snugly carpeted "*sanctum*" in the rear. While we discussed together the points of strength or weakness to be tested at the impending trial, the voices of the rude laborers reached us brokenly, and more than once words fell upon my ear which made me tremble for the sensibilities of the

lonely woman who was with them.
They meant no harm, those bluff,
hearty men. A tear from her drooping eyes would have unmanned them.
But they were not well-bred, nor tender to the weakness of the other sex.
My poor client, as she afterward became, stood while they sat, kept silence while they laughed and jeered
each other. It was not their fault
that they never minded her. They
were not hypocrites, that's all.

At length I had the happiness to
see the door close on the last of
them, and, after arranging the maps
and diagrams which would be needed
on the morrow, I called to the stranger
to come in. She obeyed, hesitating-
ly, and then, for the first time, I saw
that she belonged to that most forlorn and pitiable of all the many
classes who throng around our mining
districts, the recent Irish emigrant.
The very clothes she wore were the
same with which she dressed herself
in the green isle far away, and her
voice and manner had not yet caught
that flippancy and pertness which pass
among the longer landed for tokens
of American independence and equal-
ity. She was certainly very poor, or
the rough, wintry winds would not
have been permitted to toss her long,
black hair in tangled masses around
her shoulders, or drop their melting
snowflakes on her uncovered head.
My chivalric interest died without
time to groan, and whatever thought
of profit or romance in assisting her
I might have had, at the first sight
of her, perished at the same instant.
But I saw poverty and sorrow, and I
determined in my heart, before she
told her errand, that my life of legal
labor should embrace at least one act
done thoroughly and for nothing.

Her story was a short one. Her
husband and herself had lived in a
neighboring village. Others of their
own people dwelt around them, and

among these was an old woman and
her son. No difficulty, that she knew
of, had ever risen between her family
and theirs. But, a few days before,
as her husband was gathering fuel by
the roadside, these two had rushed
out on him, and in cold blood murdered him. The son had fled, and
the murderer's mother, with barred
doors and windows, forbade the vici-
nage of friend or foe. The broken-
hearted wife, urged on to take such
vengeance as the law afforded, had
come to me and asked my counsel
and assistance.

It was of little use to question her.
Like most of her peculiar class, her
mind could entertain but one idea,
and that, in some form or other, re-
curred in answer to every inquiry I
could make. Satisfying myself, however, that a murder had really been
committed, and taking down such
names and dates as were necessary
for the initial steps of prosecution, I
sent her home, with the assurance
that justice should be done her, and
her dead husband's ghost avenged.

The warrant was issued, the arrest
made, the indictment found, the trial
finished. There was no doubt of
guilt. The murder was committed
in the broad light of day, and many
eyes had seen it. The counsel for
the defence had felt the untenability
of his position before a tithe of the evi-
dence was in, and slipped down from
innocence to justifiability, until his
last hope for the prisoner was in the
allegation of insanity, late suggested
and faintly urged. It was useless.
The twelve inexorable men brought
in their verdict of "wilful murder,"
and Bridget Davanagh was sentenced to be hanged by the neck till she
was dead.

It has never been my custom to
follow cases, on which the solemn
judgment of the law has been pronounced, beyond those immediate

consequences of that judgment which the connection between a lawyer and his client has compelled me to superintend. But there was something in this case which both attracted and disquieted me, and one day in vacation I found myself at the grated prison-door, seeking admission to the cell of the condemned. The old woman received me quietly. She seemed to have forgotten me, or, at least, how active a part I had taken in the proceedings which had ended in dooming her to a shameful death. She was taciturn and moody; and, the longer I remained, the more satisfied I became that her mind was now unsettled, if it had not been before. I went several times after that, and gradually, by kind words and the gift of such simple comforts as aged matrons most desire, I won her confidence so far that, in her faltering, disconnected way, she told me all that sad history of woe and wrong and suffering which had brought an untimely grave to Michael Herican, and a felon's fate to her. It was one of those tales of falsity and sorrow which we cannot hear too often, and whose moral none of us can learn too well.

The little village of Easky, in the County Sligo, was, when this present century was young, one of those lonesome, scanty-peopled hamlets whose very loneliness and isolation render them more dear and homelike to their few inhabitants. The waters of the Northern Ocean foamed about the rocks where its fisher-boats were moored. The feet of its rambling children trod the rough paths and crumpled the grey masses of the wild Slieve-Gamph hills. Thus hemmed in between the mountains and the sea, it was almost separated from the world. The white sails that now and then flitted across the far horizon, and the slow, lazy car

that twice a month brought over his majesty's mail-bags from Dromore, were all that Easky ever had to tell it that there were nations and kingdoms on the earth, or that its own precipices on the one side, and its weed-strewn rocks upon the other, did not embrace the whole of human joys and sorrows.

In this solitary village the forefathers of Patrick Carrol had dwelt for immemorial years. So far back as tradition went they had been fishermen, and the last remaining scion now followed the ancestral calling. He was a sort of hero among his fellow-villagers. True, he was as poor as the poorest of them all, and had no personal boast save of his vigorous arms and honest heart. But his father, contrary to the custom of his race, had refused to lay his bones within an ocean bed, and had died fighting in the bloody streets of Killala. All victims of '98 were canonized by those rude freemen, and the mantle of honor fell from the father upon the children, and gave to Patrick Carrol a deserved and well-maintained pre-eminence. And so, when Bridget Deery became his wife, the whole hamlet agreed that the village favorite had found her proper husband, and, when the little Mary saw the light, the christening holiday was kept by every neighbor, old or young.

Four years of perfect happiness flew by. Death or misfortune came to other families, but not to theirs. The little hoarded wealth, hid away in the dark corner, grew yearly greater. Health and affection dwelt unremittingly upon the hearthstone, and the hearts of the father and mother were as full of gratitude as the heart of the child was of merriment and glee. But the four years had an end, and carried with them, into the trackless past, the sunshine of their lives. One long, long summer day the wife sat among the rocks, watching for her husband's boat, and playing with the prattler at her side. The boat came not. The sun went down. The gathering clouds in the offing loomed up threateningly. The hoarse northwesters felt their way across the waters, and whistled in her ears, as she clasped the child to her bosom and hurried home out of the storm. As the gale strengthened with the darkness, she fell upon her knees, and all that wakeful night besought the Mother and the saints to keep her baby's father from the awful danger. In vain; for when the morning dawned, the waves washed up his oars and helm upon the beach, and an hour later his drowned corse was found beneath the broken crags of Anghris Head.

For the first few years after that fatal shock the widowed mother lived she knew not how. One by one the treasured silver pieces went, till destitution stared her in the face. The charity of her neighbors outdid their means, but even that could not keep her from actual suffering, and work for the lone woman there was absolutely none. What wonder was it, then, that, when the flowers had bloomed three times above the peaceful bed of Patrick Carrol, his widow, more for her child's sake than her own, consented to violate the sanctity of her broken heart, and become the wife of Bernard Davanagh?

Bernard was a bold, reckless, wilful man, and both the mother and the child soon felt the difference between the dead father and the living. As time passed on, and the boy Bernard was born, the passions of the man grew stronger, and cruel words, and still more cruel blows, became the daily portion of the helpless three. Oh! how often did the widow yearn to lie down with her children by her

dead husband's side, in the dreary churchyard, and be at peace for ever. But not *without* them. No, not even to be united with the lost, could she have left them, and so they clung together, closer and closer, as the years rolled on—knowing little of life except its dark page of sorrow.

There never yet was a life without some ray of joy, and, even in the midnight darkness which hung around the childhood of Mary Carrol, there were faint gleams of happiness. Next door but one to their poor cot lived James Herican. He too was a fisherman, and, in better days, had been Patrick Carrol's most intimate and faithful friend. He had remained such to the widow and the fatherless, and, but for him, the family of Bernard Davanagh also might sometimes have perished from want and cold. He was the father of one child, the boy Michael, older by two years than Mary, and doubly endeared to his heart by the mother's early death. The gossips of Easky had wondered, in their simple way, why James Herican and Bridget Carrol did not marry, but the memory of his dead wife and his dead friend forbade the one ever to entertain the thought, and the poor widow was as far from wishing it as he. They were happier as they were; he, by his kindness and true Christian charity, laying up heavenly treasures, which, as the second husband of a second wife, he never could accumulate; she, keeping ever fresh and pure the one love of her maiden's heart, the one hope of reunion in the skies. What, and how different, the end had been, if they had married, the eye of the Eternal can alone discern.

The friendship of these parents descended to the children. In all their sports, their rambles, their labors, (for in that toiling hamlet even tender childhood labored,) Michael

Herican and Mary Carrol were together. When her half-brother, eight years younger than herself, grew into boyhood, Michael was his champion against the impositions of larger boys, and taught him all those arts of wood and water craft which village youth so ardently aspire to, and so aptly learn. It could not happen otherwise than that these constantly recurring kindnesses should beget firm and fast affection, and knit together these young hearts in bonds difficult, if not impossible, to sunder.

It may have been the law of nature, it may have been the chastening of God, that Michael Herican and Mary Carrol should come, in later years, to love each other. It was simply fitting, to all human sight, that it should be so; and it was so. The father and the mother thanked God for it, day by day, and bestowed upon them such tokens of encouragement as the bashful lovers could comfortably receive. The boy Bernard, when he heard of it, (and there could be no secrets in Easky,) threw up his cap for joy, and the old village crones for once smiled on the prospects of a happiness they had never known. Only Davanagh appeared displeased, but his abuse of the poor girl had been so extreme for years that it could scarcely suffer any increase, and all the influence he exerted over her or them was by his ruthless fist and cursing tongue. This at last ceased; for ears less patient than her own received his stinging insults, and a blow, quicker than his drunken arm could parry, stretched him upon the ground to rise no more.

Mary Carrol reached her twentieth birthday. She was a frail, delicate girl, below the middle height, and with that beautiful but strange union of large blue eyes and pearly complexion with jet black hair and lashes

which tells at once of the pure Irish blood. We should not have called her handsome; perhaps no one would, except those who loved her, and in whose sight no disfigurement or disease could have made her homely. But she was one of those superior natures which solitude and suffering must unite with Christian culture to produce; and the whole neighborhood, for this, and not for her beauty, claimed her as its favorite and charm. Michael had grown to be a stalwart man, half a head taller than his sire, and his fellows said that none among them promised better for diligence and success than he. His devotion to Mary Carrol knew no bounds, and she, in turn, cherished scarcely a thought apart from him. Her mother had rapidly grown old and broken. Grief, and that yearning for the dead which is stronger than any sorrow, had made her an aged woman long before her time, and the fond daughter, between her and the one hope of her young life, had no third wish or joy. Her only trouble was for her brother. The wild elements of his father's nature became more apparent in him every day, and, though he loved his mother and half-sister with an almost inhuman passionateness, they frequently found it impossible to restrain his turbulent and curbless will. The stern control of a seafaring life seemed to be their only chance of saving him, and so, at little more than twelve years old, he was torn away from home and friends and sent out on a coasting merchantman to be subdued. This parting nearly broke his mother's heart, but her discipline of suffering had been borne too long and patiently for her to rebel now. It was only another drop to her full cup of bitterness, when, a few months later, news came, by word of mouth from a sailor in Dromore, that the merchantman had foundered in the stormy Irish Sea.

It would be beyond the power of human pen to describe how these lone women now clung to Michael Herican. His father went down to the grave in peace, and he had none but them, as they had none but him. Already the one looked on him as a husband and the other as a son. When a few more successful voyages were over, and when the humble necessaries, which even an Easky maid could not become a wife without providing, were completed, the benediction of the church was to fulfil the promise of their hearts, and give them irrevocably to each other in the sight of God and man.

It was an ill-starred day for Michael Herican and the Carrols when the Widow Moran and her daughter came to live in Easky. Pierre Moran, deceased, had been a small shopkeeper in Sligo, where he had amassed a little competence, and, now that he was dead, his widow returned to her native village to pass her remaining life among her former neighbors. There were few among them who had not known more or less about the reckless girl who ran away with the half-French half-Irish shopman, twenty years ago, and her name and memory was none of the best among those virtuous villagers. But she cared less for this because she had enough of filthy lucre to command exterior respect, and it was better, so she thought, to be highest among the lowly than to be low among the high. In coming to Easky she had had two ends in view: to queen it over her former associates, and to secure a steady and good husband for her daughter. Kitty Moran was like her mother, but without her mother's faults. She was a girl of dash

and spirit, and with a pride as quick and a nature as impressible as her mother was emotionless. She was a thorough brunette, with a brunette's violence and passion, with a brunette's power to love and power to hate. In actual beauty no maiden of the neighborhood could vie with her, and she had just enough of city polish and refinement to give her an appearance of superiority to those around her. Between her and Mary Carrol the angels would not have hesitated in choosing—unless, indeed, they were those ancient sons of God who took wives from among the daughters of men because they saw that they were fair, and then, like men, they would have chosen wrongly.

It was not many days before the Widow Moran heard of Michael Herican, or many weeks before she had decided that he should be the husband of her child. True, she knew of his betrothal, for his name was rarely spoken unconnected with the name of Mary Carrol, but this made no difference. The pale-faced step-daughter of the drunken Davanagh was of no consequence to her, and to the right or wrong of her designs she never gave a thought. Whatever she wished, she determined to have. Whatever she determined to have, she set herself industriously to secure. So when she marketed, it was Michael's boat from which she purchased. When there was a message to send to Sligo, or packages from thence to be brought home to her, it was Michael's boat that carried it. When she had work to be done around her cottage, it waited until Michael had an idle day, and then he was hired to do it. Well skilled, as every woman is, in arts like these, she used her knowledge and her chances all too well.

It is but just to say that Kitty

Moran had no share in her mother's wicked plans. She was young and gay. Michael Herican was the finest young man in the village. It was not disagreeable to her to watch him and to talk with him, as he worked by her directions in the little garden, or to sit beside him at their noontide meal. Unconsciously, she grew to miss him when he was away at sea, to have a welcome for him in her heart when he came home, to look for him with impatience when she knew that his vocation brought him back to her. Before she was aware of it, she loved him ; and when she realized her love, she threw herself into it, as her one absorbing passion, without a dream of its results or a suspicion of her error. She would not, for an empire, have deliberately wronged the patient girl whom, by the stern law of contraries, she had already learned to cherish, but to her love there was no limit, no moderation. She could not help loving Michael Herican, and no more could she mete out or restrain her love. So, when it mastered her, it *was* her master, and her reason and her conscience were whirled away before the rushing tide of passion like bubbles on the bosom of a cataract.

How Michael Herican came to love this new maiden not even he himself could tell. Rochefoucault says, " It is in man's power neither to love nor to refrain from loving." And false as this may be as a general law of life, there are cases in which it appears almost divinely true. It was so in his. He simply could not help it. When he compared the calm, deep, tried affection of the heart that had been his for years with the tumultuous outburst of this impetuous soul, his judgment taught him there ought to be no such comparison between them. He never had one doubt as to his duty. He fought nobly and manfully against the spell that seemed to be upon him. He would gladly have left Easky, and have stretched his voyages beyond the northern seas ; but he could not leave Mary and her mother there alone. He thought of hastening his marriage, thereby to put an end to all possibility of faithlessness, (and this is what he should have done,) but he had no reason for it that he dared to give. It was a fearful trial for him, and would have bred despair in stronger hearts than his, if such there be. He became lax and careless in his business, harsh and moody in his intercourse with others. A few tattling croakers, here and there, wiser than the rest, laid the evil at the Widow Moran's door ; but they could give no proof when asked for it, and the frowns and chidings of the neighborhood soon put them down.

In this way things went on for months. The day drew near when the wedding-feast should usher in a new life to the waiting pair. It was a drawing near of doom to him. The enchantment had not weakened by indulgence. The siren's song was as soft and seductive as when its first notes took possession of his soul. Feeling as he did toward Kathleen Moran, he would not marry Mary Carrol, although from his heart of hearts he could have sworn that his love for her had known no change or diminution. Nor did he dare to tell her that the fascinations of the stranger had enchained him ; for he knew that he was all she had, and all she loved. But it could not go on thus always, and he knew it. Something must be done. Had it been the mere sacrifice of himself, he would not have hesitated for a moment. As little did he hesitate between marrying where he did not love supremely, and not marrying at all. He had a conscience, and when his conscience decided between these, and told him that he must not marry Mary Carrol, it compelled him also to go to her and in plain words tell her so.

It almost killed her. The shock was so great, at the moment, mightily though she strove to command herself, that her life was in immediate danger. After a while she rallied again, a very ghost to what she had been, though little else before. Her mother bore the blow less calmly. She could not understand the powerlessness of the one to save himself, or the self-sacrifice of the other, which gave up her life's last greatest hope without a murmur. She felt the disappointment keenly, but the injury more. Dispositions, that through all her sorrows had never been apparent in her character, began to show themselves. She grew stern and vengeful in place of her old meekness and submission, and brooded over their cruel wrong until it became a second nature with her to impute to Michael Herican all her troubles, and curse him in her heart as the destroyer of her child.

Of course all Easky soon knew the grief that had come to Bridget Davanagh's household; and, not unnaturally, most of them sided with her in her condemnation of Michael Herican. They could not understand, they would not have believed, that he was under the dominion of a passion which he could neither escape nor resist. To them there was no fascination in the Widow Moran's daughter, and they loved the mother too little for them to suppose that any one could love the child. It was a hard lot for her, poor girl, to hear their cutting censures passed upon her as the cause of Mary Carrol's sufferings; for the people of that uncultivated neighborhood did not

care to conceal their bitterness beneath soft-spoken words, and did not hesitate to tell her to her face all that they felt concerning her. Nor spared they Michael Herican. Old men and young greeted him now with looks askance and cold, instead of the warm welcomes which every hearth had had for him a month before. And every woman in Easky, except the few old crones who grudgingly had wished him well when all was well with him, went by him on the other side, and prayed the saints to deliver their young maidens from such faithless lovers as he.

Intolerable as all this was to him, and unjust as it would have been, even in their sight who did it, could they have known how he had fought against his destiny, it still had its inevitable effect upon him. As there was but one house in Easky where he met a cordial greeting, that house became his continual resort. As there was but one heart into which he could look and find responsive love, he sought his consolation in that heart alone. To Mary Carrol he would have gladly have continued to be a friend and brother, but her mother would not suffer him to come inside the doors, and if the brokenhearted maiden could have received his kindnesses, they would have been to her a mockery worse than death. Thus Kathleen Moran's was sometimes the only voice he heard for days, her smile the only smile ever bestowed upon him, and she became, in time, as necessary to his existence as Eve to Adam. They were almost always together. He made longer voyages, and took longer rests; and, when on shore, rarely left the roof under which she dwelt. But he had no definite aim and purpose for which to earn, or to lay up his earnings. He never trusted himself to plan for, or look upon the future.

He never yet had dreamed of marrying Kitty Moran. The light had fallen out of his life as effectually as out of Mary Carrol's; and it would have seemed to him as bootless to have heaped together money as it would to her to have finished and arranged her bridal gear.

A year like this told terribly upon him. The indignation of the villagers did not abate with time, and more and more did Michael Herican become an outlaw. It was strange that an event which, in the swift whirl of our metropolitan career, we meet almost every day, should have made such an impression on the minds of sturdy men and women. But it was the first time, in the memory of man, that an Easky lover had proved faithless to an Easky maid, and these rude hearts were as honest in their hate as in their love. He bore it as long as he could, but he was only human; and when the Widow Moran, herself made most uncomfortable by the active hostility of her neighbors, determined to return to Sligo, he was only too willing to go with her. He sold the little cottage where his forefathers had lived and died for many generations, and bade farewell for ever to the home where he had known so many years of happiness, such months of weary suffering.

If Mary Carrol suffered less in conscience and in self-respect than Michael Herican, her suffering made far more fearful havoc with her bodily and mental health. The privations of her childhood had sown the seeds of premature decay; and, at her best and strongest, she was frail and weakly. The shock she had sustained when her life's hopes were shattered had partially unsettled her mind, and physical disease, now slowly developing, sank her into hopeless imbecility. She was not violent or peevish. She never needed any restraint, and, usu-

ally, but little care. She would sit all day in the sunlight, listening to the roaring of the sea, her hands folded in her lap, and her great blue eyes gazing out vacantly into the sky. She knew enough to keep herself from danger, and, at long intervals would go alone into the narrow street, and wander up and down, groping her way like a blind person, yet taking no notice of anything that passed around her. It was a sad sight, indeed, for any eyes to see, but far more so to those who knew her history, and could repeat the story of the cruel wound she bore. There was not among them a heart that did not bleed for her, and scarce a hand that could not have been nerved to vengeance, if the blood of her destroyer could have put away her doom.

The old woman—God knows how old in sorrows!—became more firm and resolute as her daughter grew more helpless. She never wearied in doing all that a mother's heart could prompt, but it was gall and bitterness to her that Mary suffered so uncomplainingly. If she could once have heard her say one hateful word of Michael Herican, it would have satisfied her, but she never did. She learned that Michael had left his home, and had gone with the Morans, and she felt as if she were robbed of her prey. Not that she ever purposed ill to him, but she did wish it, and the scoffs and denunciations of his neighbors seemed to her so many weapons in her hands against him. Alas! for her that this should be the lot of Patrick Carrol's bride.

It might have been a half year since the widow and her victim left Easky, and the midsummer days had come. Mary Carrol had been so long an invalid, and, in her many wanderings, had been so singularly free from harm, that her absence from the cottage caused her mother no surprise or fear. The village children, as they met her rambling in the fields, would sometimes lead her home, and the seaward-going fishermen would often watch her footsteps on the beach with fond solicitude; but they became accustomed to it by and by, and let her have her way.

One cloudless day in July she had strayed out at early dawn, while the dew was scarcely dry, and wandered off along the shore, beyond the furthest cottage. The matron of that house, as she went by, sent out her little boy to see that she came to no danger, but in a moment he returned to say that she was sitting on a broken rock out of the water's reach, and so for the time she was forgotten. The day wore on, and Bridget Davanagh grew lonely in her desolate home. A dread of coming evil fell upon her, and, though her cup already so ran over that she could hardly realize the possibility of further misfortune, she could not shake off the new shadow. Restless and uneasy, she started out to seek her child. She hurried past the village eastwardly along the sands. She peered into every crevice of the rocky coast that was large enough to hide a sea-gull's nest, and hunted behind every fallen fragment that might conceal the object of her quest. Slowly, for it was severest toil to her aged feet, she groped over one mile after another, until the lofty cap of Anghris Head rose up before her. She had never been so near it since that fearful day, long years ago, when she came out to see the mangled body of her young husband lying underneath its stormy crags. And now there came over her an impulse to go there once again; again to visit the place where the waves cast him in their murderous wrath; the place whither she went last to meet him when

he last came home to her. So she climbed over the huge boulders, one by one, in the declining sunlight, till she stood directly underneath that ragged spire which Anghris lifts aloft above the waves, and there she saw the spot where her beloved had lain in his sad hour of death. There, too, she found her daughter, lying on the same rocky couch where her father lay before her, one arm beneath her head, her face turned up to heaven in the unbreaking slumber of the dead.

This same midsummer's day brought news, from Sligo to Easky, that Michael Herican had married Kitty Moran, and that the widow's heartless schemes had been accomplished.

The house of Bridget Davanagh was now desolate indeed. Her son lost for ever in the unknown waters. Her daughter sleeping in the village churchyard, bearing the burden of her cross no more. There was no cheer for her in the well-meant gossip of her neighbors. There was no comfort for her in the promise of a land, beyond this mortal, of perpetual rest. If her religious instincts and principles were still alive, they remained dumb and dormant. She could not read. She loved not company. Her few personal necessities rendered much bodily toil superfluous, and, when her work was done, she had no other occupation than to sit down and brood over her sorrows. The range of her thought was narrow. She had no future to look forward to. Her eyes were only on the past, and the past held for her but two figures—her murdered Mary and her Mary's murderer. It was in vain that the good parish priest sought to divert her mind and lead her to better things; for, though she said but little and that quietly, he could see, like all who now came intimately near her, that her faculties were clouded and her control over her will and imagination almost totally destroyed.

How long she might have lived thus without becoming fully crazed was, fortunately, never tested. A letter came to her one evening, bearing a foreign post-mark, and dotted over with the many colored stamps which tell of journeys upon sea and land. It was the first letter she had ever received. No relative or friend, no acquaintance except Michael Herican, had she out of Easky, and she was sorely puzzled, as she broke the seal and turned the pages up and down and sideways, in the useless attempt to tell from whence it came. She called in a passing school-child to decipher it, and, as he blundered through its weary lines, she sat with her face buried in her hands, rocking her body ceaselessly to and fro. He reached the end and read the signature of "Bernard Davanagh." The widow's boy still lived. She lifted her worn face out of her hands and the tears chased each other down her cheeks. They eased her throbbing brain, and she bade the child go over it again, for of its first reading she had scarcely heard a word except the name. And now she learned that he was in America. He had been left sick on shore, at the last voyage of his ill-fated vessel, and escaped alive. Since then he had been tossed on every sea which bears a name, till, tired of the toil and danger, he had settled in the far-off mining regions of the western continent. He now sent for her and Mary to come out to him, enclosing money and passage certificates for each, and saying that in two month's time he hoped to have them both with him in his new home. It was a long time before the old woman could comprehend the message; but, when she once really understood

that Bernard was alive, she would have started on the instant to reach her boy. Her idea of the distance was, that America lay somewhere out beyond Dromore, as far, perhaps, as that was from Easky, and it was with difficulty that the neighbors, who came flocking in when the news went flitting up and down the street, could control her. Those who stayed with her through the night, and those who went back homeward, had settled it, however, before morning dawned, that, though the journey might be fearful and the chances few, it was better she should go and perish by the way, than stay at home to grieve, and craze, and die.

There was not much preparation. Her cottage sold, her furniture distributed among her friends, the other passage-paper given to a woman in Dromore, who eagerly grasped the chance of going out to seek her husband, and Bridget Davanagh left Easky and its graves for ever. The emigrant best knows the weariness and hardship of a steerage passage in a crowded ship, and this old and worn-out woman endured them as a thousand others, old and feeble, have done since then and before. But the long voyage had an end some time, and, in a day after the ship was moored at New York wharves, the mother had found her son. He had a cabin built and furnished, deep in the wild gorge of a mountain, out of whose sides the glittering anthracite was torn by hundreds of tons a day; and here he took her to live and care for him. Not a face around her that she ever saw before; the dialect of their language so differing from her own that she could only here and there make out a word; Bernard himself grown up into a tall, stout, burly man, black with dust and reeking with soot and oil, she longed almost fiercely for her home by the green sea, and wished herself back again a score of times a day. When her homesickness wore off, as it slowly did, and she formed new acquaintances, and grew familiar with the scenes around her; above all, when she began to realize the comforts which the new world gave beyond the old—she became reconciled to her strange life, and seemed almost herself again. Only when, now and then, her spite and hatred to the name of Herican broke out again did her mind reel with its fury; otherwise, she was more like Bridget Davanagh in her early days of second widowhood than she had been for years.

Meanwhile, of Michael Herican. He had married Kitty Moran, as the Easky story said. It was, on his part, an act of sheer despair. Not that he did not love her. His passion had grown stronger and more absorbing every hour, and she well returned it. But it was no calm conclusion of his judgment that led him to unite his life with hers. It was more like the suicide of a felon who sees his fate before him, but would rather die by his own free act, to-day, than anticipate inevitable death to-morrow. When the Widow Moran " went to her own place," her fortune fell to them. He opened a little store, and, for a while, life, cheered by business, seemed more bearable; but misfortune followed him and, by one loss and another, both his credit and his stock were sacrificed. Honest to the last farthing, he stripped himself of everything to pay his debts, and turned himself and his young wife, to whom privation had ever been a stranger, into the streets—to work, or beg, or starve. Then, for a time, he went to sea; but the lone hours of watchful idleness upon the deep gave him too many opportunities for recollec-

tion, and he could not endure it. As a common hireling he worked about the docks, and earned by this chance toil a meagre pittance for the bare necessities of life. But he could not settle permanently to anything. Of good abilities, with strong arms and a willing heart, it was this mental burden only which unmanned him, and this pursued him everywhere and always, like an avenging ghost. Then he began to wander. From Sligo they went to Ballina, and thence to Galway, and thence to Dublin, living awhile in each, but evermore a restless, wavering, aimless man. His poor wife suffered fearfully. Deprived of all the comforts she had ever known, and cut down sometimes to a mere apology for food and clothing, she rued the day when she was born; but she never blamed her husband. Through all, she clung to him faithfully; and when she found herself, at last, in the lowest portion of the capital, and living among those whose touch in other days would have been infection, however else she murmured, it was never against him. They stayed in Dublin for a year and more. A child was born there, but it soon died from exposure and insufficient food, and this made the mother's heart uneasy, and she longed to move. A berth fell in his way on board a homeward-bound Canadian timber-ship, and he agreed to go. He also paid the passage of his wife with labor, and, in due time, their weary feet were standing on the shores of a new world, ready for other journeys and, perhaps, better paths.

But it did not so eventuate. He was the same man still, though under other skies. There was a doom upon him. His family grew on his hands and opened in his heart new chambers of affection, but they could give no ballast to his brain. He could not anchor anywhere. The weird ship that sails up and down antarctic seas in an eternal voyage is no more harborless than was he. He fought the forests, axe in hand, and smote down many pillars of the olden fane. He toiled on board the river-craft that drift to and fro upon the broad St. Lawrence. He was a stevedore in Quebec, a laborer in Montreal. So he worked on from one town to another, fretting away his own existence, wearing out the health and strength of his devoted wife, until he reached the "States," and, by some mysterious fatality, came into the very village where Bernard Davanagh and his mother lived. Here he found work congenial to his tastes. The dark gloom of the long tunnels underground, the ghastly lamps, and, more than all, the exciting danger of the labor, kept his mind on the stretch and drowned his memory more effectually than it had ever been before. He did not know the nearness of Mary Carrol's mother. He would as soon have dreamed of meeting his dead children in the street as her, and his work late and early kept him out of sight, so that they did not hear of him.

But it happened on one Sunday morning, as he went to Mass in the great town, two miles away, that he heard the name of "Bernard" called by some one in the throng. He looked anxiously around him, and had no difficulty in recognizing, in the features of the man addressed, the son of the detested Bernard Davanagh of his youth. Had he not known the contrary, he might have thought it that very father stepped out of his grave. The recognition was not mutual, but the unquiet heart of Michael Herican recked little of the sacrifice that day, for thinking

where this new phase of his life would end. He feared no bodily injury. He had not lost his animal courage by his sufferings. But he felt like Orestes at the banquet, when he dispels with wine the knowledge of the ever-present furies, and then suddenly beholds the gorgon face pressed closely up to his. He saw in this an omen that, go where he would, the wrongs of Mary Carrol must live on outside him, as they did within.

How Bridget Davanagh and her son became aware that Michael Herican and his family were near them, it is of little consequence to know. When they did find it out, however, it was an evil greater in its results to them than to their enemy. Bernard had warmly espoused his mother's hatred, and added to it the natural fierceness of his own disposition. The discovery of her child's betrayer, and an occasional glimpse of him as he went by, revived all the old woman's vengefulness, and aggravated it beyond control. If Kathleen Herican had known all this, sick of her wandering life as she might be, she would not have stayed near them for a single hour. But she did not know it. Bernard and Bridget she had never seen in Easky, and Michael never told her they were here. Thus she, at least, lived on unconsciously, while vengeance sharpened its relentless sword for retribution, and hung it by an ever-weakening hair over the head of him she loved most of all.

Up to the morning of the fatal day no word or sign had passed between Michael Herican and either of the Davanaghs. But, as he went by to his work that morning, they both stood in their cabin door. The old woman could not resist the impulse to curse him as he passed her, and Bernard was as ready with his malison as she. Michael turned up the path that led toward them, and tried to speak in friendliness, but they would not hear him. At last, exasperated by their violence and abuse, he told the mother she was mad—mad as her daughter had been before her. It was a cruel word for him to speak, cruel for them to hear; but he did not mean it. It smote upon him as he hurried off to his work, and the image of the dead Mary came back and upbraided him many times that day. He left his work early, and went home. There was a strange look in his eye which made the timid heart of Kathleen beat faster when she saw it, and he was more than usually kind and tender to her and his child. His half-eaten supper over, he took his woodman's basket, and went out to gather fagots for the morning's fire. On his way home with others who had been on the like errand, as he came opposite the Davanagh cottage, the mother and the son came out and rushed upon him. One struck him with a stone, and felled him to the earth. The other smote him with an axe, and cleft his skull. It was all over in an instant. Not a word was said. The horror-stricken neighbors stood aghast a moment. When they came to their senses, Bernard Davanagh was climbing up the mountain on the further side of the ravine, and Bridget Davanagh, with bolted doors, kept ward in her devoted house alone.

They would have lifted Michael Herican from the roadside where he lay, but he was dead. The red blood oozed out of the gaping wound. It trickled on in narrow streamlets down the path. It clotted on the feet of men and women who came to gaze upon the mangled corpse. It stained the hands, and face, and garments of his wife and baby as they lay sobbing and shrieking on his pulseless breast. It dried up in the purple sunlight of the dying day, and soaked away into the dust and ashes of the trampled street.

I have little else to tell. The circumstances of the story, as I heard them, piece by piece, left on my mind an impression which would not let me stand by and do nothing. I was satisfied that, if not absolutely crazed, the murderess had acted in a moment of exceeding passion, no doubt resulting from the rankling words her victim spoke to her on the morning of that day; and, in her unsettled state of mind, the ordinary presumptions of the law, that passion cannot last, were not reliable. It seemed unjust, to me, that she should suffer the highest penalty known to our law, when probably her guilt was actually less than that of hundreds whom a few years in the state prison give their due. I therefore drew up a petition which the presiding judge and nearly all of the convicting jury signed, praying a commutation of her sentence to imprisonment for life. The prayer was granted, and Bridget Davanagh lives and will die an inmate of the Eastern Penitentiary of Pennsylvania.

HEREMORE-BRANDON; OR, THE FORTUNES OF A NEWSBOY.

"How'er it be, it seems to me
'Tis only noble to be good;
Kind hearts are more than coronets,
And simple faith than Norman blood."

CHAPTER I.

FOUR little boys: two of them had soft fair hair, and were dressed in the finest cloth; the other two had very bushy heads, and were dressed in whatever they could get. It was early Christmas morning, and the two rich boys were sitting by the window of a handsome brown-stone house, and they had each a stocking plump full of dainties; the two poor boys were calling the morning papers on the stone-cold sidewalk, and if they had any stockings at all, you may be very sure they were plump full of holes.

"An't he funny," remarked the smaller of the two in the house, looking at the larger of the two in the street; "an't he *too* funny!" And between laughing and eating, little Fred came near choking himself. "See his old coat, Josie, it trails like Aunt Ellie's blue dress! And such a queer old hat; don't it make you laugh, Josie?"

"I have seen so many of 'em," explained Josie.

"What are you laughing at, Fred," asked their sister Mary, coming up to them.

"Those newsboys," he answered, and imitated their "Times, 'Erald, Tribune! Here's the 'Erald, Times, Tribune!" so perfectly that their father thought it was a real newsboy calling, and cried out to them from another room to "hurry up and bring a Herald," at which command the children rushed eagerly into the

hall, and tugged with their united strength to open the doors, each anxious to be the first to speak to the odd-looking newsboys, and also to be the fortunate one to take the paper to their father. In the mean time, the two newsboys had not been unmindful of the faces behind the plated window.

"I say, Jim," said the big boy, who was about twelve or thirteen years old, "did you ever see the beat of that young 'un there? Don't you choke yerself, youngster, f'fear you'd cheat a friend from doing that same when you're growed up.—Ere's the 'Erald! Tribune! Times!—George! Jim, I wish to thunder there'd some new papers come up. An't yer tired allers a hollerin' out them same old tunes?—Times! 'Erald! Tribune!—How d'ye s'pose a feller'd feel to wake up some of these yere mornin's in one o' them big houses?"

"Heerd tell of stranger things 'n that, Dick," replied Jim, who read the weekly papers. "'Turn again, Whittington, Lord-Mayor of London,' as the cat said! Turned out true, too."

"*You'd* better get a cat, Jim, you're such a stunnin' feller; shouldn't wonder if you'd turn out alderman some of these days!" At which, for no apparent reason, Dick laughed until every rag was fluttering.

"They wants a paper; better 'tend to yer business," answered Jim, at which the other newsboy instantly grew grave, and, shuffling his old shoes across the street, mounted the steps where the children were waiting and calling for him.

"I want a New York Herald," said Fred very grandly.

"Han't got no 'Eralds," answered the newsboy.

Fred rushed into the house saying, "His Heralds are all gone."

"Tribune, then, and don't keep the door open," instructed the rough voice from some invisible spot. Mary shut the door all but a little crack. "Papa wanted a Herald," she said; "you ought to have one when my papa wants it."

"Thought I had, but couldn't help it; 'Erald's got a great speech to-day, and I've sold 'em all."

"Do you sell papers every day?" Mary asked.

The bushy head made a sort of bow, as the poor newsboy looked at the fair-haired little girl on the stoop, who condescended to question *him*.

"Yes, miss," he answered, "since ever I wasn't bigger'n a grasshopper."

"An't he funny?" said Fred.

"Don't you get tired?" asked Mary.

"Well, I can't say I doesn't, 'specially sometimes."

"An't you glad it's Christmas?" Josie asked, as questions seemed the fashion.

"I kinder am," replied the newsboy.

"Did you have many presents?" questioned Mary.

"Me? Bless you, who'd give 'em to me, miss?"

"Didn't you hang up your stocking last night?" Fred asked.

The newsboy seemed much amused at the question; for it was plain that he could hardly keep from laughing right out.

"Well, no, I didn't," he answered. "Don't think things would stick in one long, if I did!"

"Do you put your money in a savings bank? By and by you'd have enough to build a house may be, if you were careful," said Josie.

"Jim and me likes takin' it out in eatin' best," answered Dick.

"Why don't you bring me that paper?" cried their father's voice. And the two boys ran hastily into the house.

"You may have my candy," said Mary in a stately way. "I can have plenty more." And she put her store of dainty French candy into the boy's hand, and, while he was still looking at her in amazement, followed her brothers into the house and shut the door.

"Just you pinch me, Jim," Dick said, joining his companion. "Drive in hearty, now. An't I asleep?"

"Well, I dunno; what yer got there?"

"She give it to me."

"Who's that?"

"Her on the steps; didn't you see her?"

"You tell that to the marines! Guess you took it."

"No, I didn't," Dick said indignantly. "I never took nothin' as warn't mine yet."

"Let's have a look," said Jem, reaching out his hand for the package; but Dick would not let him touch it. "I'm going to keep it always to remember her," he said.

"Guess you want ter eat it yerself," Jem said. "I wouldn't be so mean."

"I an't gen'rally called mean," Dick answered with great dignity.

"Don't you wonder, Jim," said Dick, as they made friends and passed on—"don't it seem curious how some folks is rich and purty like them there, and others is poor and ugly like me and you, Jim?"

"George! speak for yerself, if ye like. Guess I'd pass in a crowd, if I'd the fine fixin's!"

"S'posin' me and you had dandified coats and yeller gloves, and the fixin's to match, s'pose anybody'd know we was newsboys ?" Dick asked thoughtfully.

"I *rayther* think," said Jim, "we'd be a deal sight handsomer'n some of them chaps as has 'em now."

"Let's save our money and try it, Jim."

"'Nuff said," answered Jim, laughing. And the newsboys in their queer garments, and with their light hearts, passed out of sight of Mr. Brandon's brown-stone house and fair-haired children.

But not out of all remembrance. The children had a party that Christmas afternoon ; and when they were tired of romping, and were seated around the room, the girls playing with their dolls ; the Catholic ones telling the others in low voices about the flowers and lights, and the wonderful manger which they had seen at Mass that morning ; and the boys eagerly listening to the stories of far-away lands, which one of the older people was telling, little Mary knelt in an arm-chair, and looked out of the window at the people hurrying through the driving rain and snow, and at the street-lamps glaring through the wet and cold. Her kind little heart had been very light, and a strange joyousness had surrounded her all day, making her more gentle than ever, so that she had not spoken one hasty word, or once hesitated to take the lowest part in any of the plays. Though she did not know it, the little infant Jesus had smiled on her that morning when she was kind to the poor, homeless newsboy ; and now she understood—for charity had enlarged her mind—more distinctly than she ever had before, that there were many cold and desolate children for whom there were no earthly glad tidings that day, yet who were as much God's own as the little ones grouped around her father's pleasant

parlors. Then, just as she did the best she could, and prayed in her heart for the children of the poor, she thought she saw the newsboy to whom she had spoken in the morning standing close to the railing by the window ; but before she could be sure of it, the servant lighted the gas ; she heard the children calling her for a new game, and she ran lightly away. But there was one crouched in the cold outside, who wondered at the sudden light and glow within ; and as the bewildered newsboy saw her dancing past the lighted windows, it seemed to him that it was not so far, after all, to the heaven and the angels of whom he had heard ; for the "glad tidings" had come to Dick, even Dick, and they woke up the good, the will to do right, which is in every heart, and which did not sleep again in him, even when the little, un-cared-for, outcast head rested on the stone steps that Christmas night.

CHAPTER II.

Very little idea had poor Dick of right or wrong. No fond mother took him to her heart when he was a toddling wee one, just big enough to half understand, and between her kisses told him of angels and saints, of heroes and martyrs, and of that Queen Mother up in heaven, dearer than them all, who never forgot those who once had loved her, and of the beautiful world with its flowers and fruits, its great rivers and high mountains, its delicious green and its glorious blue, which a good Father had given to men for their enjoyment. No loving sister, with bright eyes and tender voice, tossed him in her strong young arms, and sang to him how knights and warriors, the great and good of earth, and loved of heaven, had all been children once like him, only never half so sweet and dear.

No noble father, true in the midst of trials, ever watched with anxious care that those little feet should walk only in the straight and narrow path. So it was a hard thing for poor Dick, when he rubbed his brown hands through his bushy, uncombed hair the next morning, and pushed the worn old hat over his still sleepy eyes, to know just what to do to find the temple of Fortune. At times, though, he had followed the crowd of noisy boys and girls whom you may see around the doors of any Catholic church at about nine o'clock on Sunday mornings, and had listened with a critical air, and slightly supercilious, from some dark corner near the door, to the talking and the prayers which he did not wholly understand, but portions of which he did once or twice take into his "inner consciousness" and fully approve. In some way, he then seemed to feel that which made him less rough in all his answers, readier in all his responses to the call for papers, not always gently called for ; and, though he knew not why, there were fewer wicked words on his lips that day than for many a day before.

It happened that he kept his eyes open and grew thoughtful, and did not forget his wish to be better ; so that, from being a newsboy, he became an errand-boy in a book-store, where he learned to be honest and to tell the truth, which was a rapid advance in his education ; for you know it is more than some people have learned who have lived to be six times Dick's age. Sometimes a little lady came to that very store to choose her picture-books and Christmas stories ; and it was his place to open the door for her ; or perhaps some one would call out, "Dick, a chair for this lady," and then he was as happy as a prince. Sometimes he would be sent home with her pur-

chases, and mounted the steps, entered her father's house, and always felt "good" again ; for always the same picture of a little girl in blue, with fair hair, and her hands full of dainty French candy, and a ragged newsboy, dirty and amazed, would be there before him.

Christmas had come and gone more than once, and it was coming again, when Dick turned up the gas in a mere closet of a room very high up in a dingy boarding-house, and made a ghost of a fire in an old rusty stove. It wouldn't seem to us a very enlivening prospect ; for the room was but slightly furnished, and the stove smoked, while the wind beat at the not overclean windows, on which there were no curtains to shut out the dark and cold. But Dick seemed to think it something very luxurious ; for he rubbed his hands before the blue apology for a flame, and sat down on the broken wooden stool, with as much zest as that with which I have seen grand people sink into a great arm-chair after a walk.

"Christmas eve again," he said to the fire, for it was his only companion. "Let me look at you, Mr. Coals, and see what pictures you have for me to-night. How many nights, worse nights than this, I have been glad to crouch under an old shed, or in some alley, and now to think, thanks to the good God, I have a fire of my own ! Poor little bare feet on the icy pavement to-night, I wish I had you round my jolly old stove. When I am rich, I will !" Then he laughed at the idea. "But I won't wait until I am rich, or I would never deserve to have the chance."

"How are you, Dick?" said a cheery voice, though deep and rough, at the door. And a man came into the room, which either his figure, or his coat, or his voice, or the flute under his arm, seemed to fill to such an extent that the very corners were crowded.

"How are you, Dick ? It's blowing a hurricane outside, and you're as cold as Greenland here. It may do for you, but not for me ; old blood is thin, my boy, old blood is thin." At which Dick laughed heartily, while putting more coal on the fire ; for Carl Stoffs was in the prime of life, hale and hearty, weighing at least two hundred pounds, I am sure, and with a round face, very red, but also very solemn, for Carl Stoffs was a German every inch of him. The stove grew very red also under his vigorous hands ; but whether from anger or by reflection I will not attempt to say. "And now," he said, seating himself on the wooden chair, Dick having given it up to his guest, while he occupied a box instead —"and now, how are you, boy ? Ready for merry Christmas, eh ? You'll come to us to-morrow, so says my wife. In America, you all do mind your wives ; mine tells me to bring you."

"Then I must, I know," Dick said, looking at the other, who was near three times his size. "I would have a poor chance in opposing you !" But Carl Stoffs knew well how gratefully the friendless boy accepted the thoughtful invitation.

"Now, shall we have some music," said he, as he drew out his flute, and, without waiting an answer, put it to his mouth, and brought forth such rich, full tones from the instrument that Dick, as he stared at the now bright fire, seemed to be in a land of enchantment.

"You are the only man, from the queen of England down, whom I really envy," said Dick, in one of the pauses. "You can have music whenever you wish it ; I am only a beggar, grateful for every note thrown

in my way. Were you out, last night ?"

"Yes, all night in Fourteenth street, at the rich Brandons. Madam is very gay, this winter."

"I wish I were a musician," said Dick. "It must be jolly to see all the dancing and the bright dresses !"

"And the pretty ladies, eh ? who don't mind you no more than if you were a stick or a stone. Indeed, my boy, you'd soon get tired of it ; it seems so grand at first, the beautiful picture all in motion ; but your eyes —they ache after a little. Too much light, my boy, too much light." And the musician went long journeys up and down his wonderful flute before he spoke again. "They'll go music-mad over some fool at the piano ; but you play until your own music makes you wild, and never one thinks or cares about you. Last night, I played only for one. She was always dancing, and she seemed to go on the wings of the music just as it said to her *go.* I was not tired last night."

Awaiting no answer, he turned again to his flute, and all through the dingy, crowded house rang a joyous "*Gloria in excelsis.*" Rough captives of labor heard it, and answered to it, knowing well the glad tidings, the most glorious ever sung, and yet sung to kings and shepherds alike. The old sinners heard it, and thought of the strange days when even they were young and innocent.

"Finis," cried the German, rising slowly, and putting on his shaggy overcoat. "I promised my wife that I would be home at nine, and, as do all the people here, I mind my wife ; but it is one inconvenient thing. You will come to us after Mass, to-morrow?"

"You are too good to me. When I am rich, perhaps I shall know how to thank you."

"You should think yourself rich

low. You are young; there is no riches like that."

"I wish I were older, though," sighed Dick.

"Never say that, never, never. The poorest youth is better than the richest age," said the German earnestly. I shouldn't wonder if Mr. Stoffs had just found his first gray hair, and was speaking under its influence. At all events, he did not convince Dick, who said, with equal earnestness and more quickness:

"I must say it: every day seems too long, every hour goes too slowly, until I can get at my life's work. This waiting for it kills me."

"My friend, do you call this waiting?" laughed the German. "Was it waiting and doing nothing that changed you from—"

"But think," interrupted Dick, "of what ought to have been. Some day —some day I will get my hand to the plough, you'll see! At least," a little ashamed of the seeming conceit, "I hope you will."

"And what makes you care?"

"I think it's born in us all to like to be active—to be doing something. Indeed, it's about the only legacy my poor parents left me. It may be, for I know nothing of them, that they were just the same as other people, out of whom bitter poverty has taken all pride and ambition; but I can't think it, somehow."

"Do you really know nothing of them?"

"Nothing. I have a little sealed box, with an injunction on the outside of it that I am not to open it until I am of age. I don't know where I first got it, nor from whom it came. It may be some trick to tease me for years, and disappoint me at last, for all I know; and still I have always kept it, for it is all I have. And I think it came from them."

"It may tell you something wonderful," said his visitor, laughing For it was easy for *him* to understand that some young mother, who even in her poverty had found the means of reading and believing stories of princes in disguise, and countesses in cellars, disowned and disinherited, all for true love's sake, had made a mystery of leaving a lock of her hair, and perhaps a cheap wedding-ring, to her boy; and he could not forbear a little ridicule of the folly. "It may tell you something wonderful. If it gives you possession of half of New York, don't forget your friends, will you, Dick?" And then, buttoned up to his chin, and with his cap covering half his face, and looking just like Santa Claus, Carl Stoffs bundled his cherished flute under his arm, and obediently went home to his wife.

Dick lingered a moment, after he left, before closing the door. The room was not wholly his own; but his companion had a father and a mother in New Jersey, and he had gone home to them, with something in his pockets for the children's Christmas; so for that night Dick was in undisputed possession. The passages were dark and cold; the snow had got through some of the broken windows, and lay in several little hills on the entry floor; the sash rattled, and Dick shivered, as he stood irresolute at the door of his room. But the irresolution did not last long. He bundled up, as well as his scanty wardrobe permitted, closed the door firmly behind him, and went down the creaking, broken stairs, and through the dreary passages, where he could see the snow huddling up to the dark window-panes, as if it were a white bird trying to get in and beating its wings against the dirty glass. Dick had not far to walk, after leaving the house, before he found that which he had come out to find—somebody without a shelter from the storm. And I should not wonder if any night, however bitter and cold, that you or I should take a notion to go out on the same errand, we should not have to go far for equal success, and that even if we started from the most delightful dwelling-place in all New York.

Under the remains of some broken steps, or more truly by the side of them, for they were too broken to shelter a kitten, two dark figures were lying close together. In one of the pauses of the storm, when the street-lamp had a chance to shine a little, Dick could see that the figures were those of two boys asleep. He did not wait long to rouse them. One woke up at once, cross, and, if I must tell the truth, with some very wicked words on his lips.

"Get up, and come with me," said Dick.

"What yer want 'long o' me? I an't doing nothin'," he muttered.

"I know that; but I will give you a better place to sleep in. Come."

Bad words again. "I an't done nothin' to you. Le' me 'lone."

"I want you to come home with me. Did you ever hear of a newsboy called Big Dick? That's me."

"I an't afeard o' nothin'. Here goes!" And the poor little fellow, still believing the other was "chaffing," got on his feet. "Do you want t'other? He an't worth nothin', but he'll keep dark."

"Yes, both of you. Hurry him up; it is a terrible night."

"Come along, Joe. Where's yer spunk? I an't afeard o' nothin'."

"There's nothing to be afraid of," said Dick, as gently as the roaring storm would let him. "Don't talk now, but come on. I'll take you to a room with a fire in it," added Dick, in spite of himself feeling that he was *bon prince* to the little newsboys.

"Come on, Joe," urged the other, dragging and pushing the little newsboy, who was hardly more than a baby, but who seemed to whimper, sleepy and frightened, as no doubt he was, until, as quietly as the old stairs would permit, and almost holding their breath, they followed Dick to his room.

"An't this bully, now?" said Jack in an undertone, when he stood before the fire in the lighted room, and Joe, with round, staring eyes, but not a word of complaint or fear, had been put on the wooden chair. "I say, now, Joe an't much, but he'll never blab; but I'se all right. What yer want us to do, now, sir?"

"To get warm," answered Dick. "I was once a newsboy, and slept under stoops and sheds, like the rest of them; but now I've got a fire of my own, and I wanted company; so I went out and got you and Joe, and now make yourselves at home for to-night. Here's some crackers and cheese, and when you've had something to eat you can go to sleep here. It's better than out there, isn't it?"

The newsboy stared at Dick, and grunted something which sounded very much as if he did not believe a word that his host had said. The other sat silent, stolid, and seemingly ready to hear anything. He ate his share of the crackers and cheese greedily, but with a watchful eye on the giver. The warmth, however, soon proved too much for his vigilance, and, though his eyes were still fixed on Dick's face, they were heavy and expressionless. At last, Dick took him up, undressed him, and laid him in his bed in the corner; and then, for the first time, Joe's tongue was loosened. "There, now," he said, as he lay exactly as Dick had placed him, "I are dead and gone at last. 'Twasn't no lies about t'other world; they wasn't a foolin' on us after all. Here an't no more Heralds and Tribunes. I are dead and gone at last!" And so rejoicing, Joe's eyes closed securely, and it is likely he dreamt of angels, if he dreamt at all, until morning came.

"He an't much," said Jack, whom this act of Dick's, together with the fire and the food, had made less incredulous and more confidential. "He's a soft 'un; he an't got the right pluck. He'll never be nobody."

"Is he your brother?" asked Dick.

"Do yer think I'd have him for my brother? He's a youngster, come from nobody don't know where. He was fetching up in my quarters last winter, and didn't know his name nor nothin'; so we gives him a start, us fellers, and he's stuck on to me ever since."

Then Dick asked more about his new friend's life, and told him a little of his own, and a story or two that he thought suited to his understanding; and, having won the child to believe a little in his good intentions, had the satisfaction of seeing him at his ease, and willing to go to sleep with Joe in the corner.

When this was accomplished, Dick put out the fire and the light, and lay down on the floor to sleep soundly and well, until the joy-bells from the great city churches should wake his guests and himself to the glad tidings that Christmas had come again.

CHAPTER III.

And now I am sure you are satisfied that Dick was on the right road, acting religion as fast as he learned it; trying to be all he knew—to live a truthful, generous, self-respecting life. He had little help, you know, and, if he followed that crowd that I told you of oftener than before, and

heard much that enabled him to take whole books into his "inner consciousness" which would otherwise have been a dead letter to him, he was not one to make a flourish of trumpets about it, or to dream of complaining that the world would not stand still until he got up to it. He had but one intimate friend, it is true; but he was a friend you and I might be glad to win; a friend who never argued or lectured, but only quietly built his life on the only true foundation—the true faith—and then left it to show for itself. So, simply trusting in whatever was good, yet so fierce against whatever was evil, scornful of everything wrong and weak, practising as well as believing, you may be sure Carl Stoffs would never have held out his honest hand to Dick, if Dick were not worthy of it. And this makes me think great things of my hero, of whom scarcely anybody thought at all. He had his place in Ames & Harden's store, and he had his talks, too, now with one person, now with another, and perhaps thought of things he heard. He was only a boy yet, and had his follies, without doubt, fancying at times that there was something in him, if circumstances would only draw it out, which would prove him a great deal worthier of high places than those now occupying them. I am not sure but that, if he had had a country-home, he might sometimes have lain down under the trees, and, while watching in a dreamy way the clouds sailing down to the west, and the vigilant stars coming out to guard the earth in the sun's absence, and listening to the wind among the trees, the twittering of some wakeful bird, or the rustling of some grand old river, he might have had yearnings no one could explain, and not have felt the sky too far to climb or the river too deep to fathom ; for Dick's was only a boy's heart, that had still to learn that we cannot go from the Broadway pavement to Trinity spire in one step. Even in his city home, if home it could be called, it may be that, just after he had been to church with Carl, he had glowed with the thought that he—even he—might some day be a Loyola or a Francis Xavier, for "the thoughts of youth are long, long thoughts."

But as yet his life consciously held but one romance—one dream of earth. There were few to care for him ; but there was a little girl once who had made Christmas memorable to him, and Dick had not forgotten her. She had grown a beautiful young lady now, in Dick's eyes, though to all others she was merely a thin, dark school-girl. They still lived in the handsome house on Fourteenth street, and Carl Stoffs and his band played for many a dance there, although I am sorry to say that, even after a New Year's party, Dick had to be sent more than once to Mr. Brandon's office with a little bill, due to Ames & Harden, mostly for school-books, novels, and gilt annuals. But then that was no fault of Mary's, you know.

Mr. Brandon was not a pleasant man to go to with a bill, or for much of anything in the money line. "The deuce take it, my dear !" he often said to his wife. "Are you bent on ruining me ?"

"Don't be silly, Charley, love," the dauntless little woman would say, not in the least disturbed by the angry voice and black brow that were so terrible to Dick. "For people of our position, we live very shabbily."

"Hang our position ! I tell you, madam, we are going the road to beggary ; we are, indeed."

"O Charles ! do be quiet," was her

ready answer. "I am so sick of that sort of stuff."

"Then *be* sick of it," this dreadful man would exclaim ; "for I'll tell it to you every day and every hour, until it gets through your silly head. Money ! money ! money ! I never hear anything else in this house. I've sold myself for it, body and soul, and much good it has done me ! I'll not give you a penny, madam ; not a penny."

But that was all talk ; for, of course, he had to give his wife, who was a nice little body, very sweet and good-tempered, but rather fond of the good things of this world, whatever she had set her heart upon having.

"If papa should be right—" Mary would sometimes urge.

"Nonsense ! they all say the same thing ; why shouldn't they ? If I didn't spend your father's money in making things pleasant at home, he'd be spending it on clubs, or whatever it is which uses up their money when they have the spending of it all to themselves. You'll have a husband, likely enough, one of these days, who'll scold for every pocket-handkerchief you buy ; but you won't mind it. They must scold about something, you know, dear."

"O mamma ! I'd never live a day—if—." At which sentence, never completed, Mrs. Brandon would laugh, and the subject would be dropped for the present ; but, of course, after such scenes, Mr. Brandon wouldn't be very amiable to a boy like Dick with a bill in his hand. But Dick to him was a mere machine, belonging to a store over the way, and as such he treated him, with as little malice in his hard words as if he were swearing at a table or chair. To Dick, Mr. Brandon was Mary's father, and that meant a great deal ; Dick could never talk openly to him, nor stand in his presence quite as he did in the presence of other men.

For, though Dick had never been outside the city limits, and had never seen a hill, nor a field of corn, he was a trifle romantic, I am afraid, after all.

Yes, it is true that he grew to be almost a man without having ever climbed a hill or seen a field of grain. But there was a good time coming.

"Dick," said Carl Stoffs, that true and faithful friend—"Dick, would you like to go to the country?"

"Would I like to go to the country?" he repeated, finding no words of his own to say, so great was his bewilderment at such a question—"Would I like to go to the country?"

"Any time you're ready," said the German, seating himself. "Take your time to answer, my lad."

"What would I do in the country? I was never there in my life!"

"And you don't look more pleased than though I'd asked you to go to—to—the end of the world."

"I have often wished to see the country," returned Dick, in the tone in which we might wish to see China if we had nothing else to do; "but I don't see my way to doing so at present."

"I do believe, Dick, that you have lined the walls with gold pieces, you are so miserly of your time, and so stuck to this old place. Come now, we shall take you to the country, my wife and I. Now, to think there should be one on earth who never saw the green fields and the woods! It is to me a very odd thing! You are the blind man who never saw the sun, and does not think the sun worth seeing."

"Oh! no, indeed; not so bad as that: but—"

"Then you shall go. My sister has a house, with room for many, and we have taken half, keeping one room for you. Come and take your week with us."

"But, Mr. Stoffs, I intended during that week to read so much—to take long walks about the city—and Mrs. Stoffs—"

"My wife sent me; I would not of myself have such a blind man with me, to read, to study, to walk; how can you in the city now? You will be wild when you have been once with us. You will go to-day with me—I will be waiting for you at my place at five. Will you come?"

"Indeed—"

"You will come." And, in truth, Mr. Stoffs had previously said so much of that wonderful land in which he was now living that Dick could not resist his last appeal, and afraid and shy as he well might be, having never spent twenty-four hours in a home circle in his life, he gave his promise to be at the appointed place of meeting in good time for the train.

But when the magnetism of his friend's presence was taken from him, Dick's heart grew heavy in his breast. If it had been to go to another city, or on a matter of business, Dick's excitement would have been delightful; but "the country," of which he knew nothing, and of which he had such strange fancies, picked up he could not tell where, that was another thing. City boys always laughed at country people when they came to the city—they had such queer ways—and yet—and yet—he felt strange and shy about going among them. Perhaps he felt that the tables would be turned on him there, and that his ways would be as queer in their eyes as theirs had been in his; perhaps he felt the full force of the homely old saying that "a cock can crow best in his own farm-yard."

But, as the day wore on, Dick's spirits rose; he thought of all the stories he had read of fresh country life; a poem or two of cows and brooks came vaguely among his thoughts, and by the time he reached his little room, and began to pack his not abundant wardrobe, he was eager for the first glance at "the country."

"Then, may the Lord's blessing go with you," said his kind but very slovenly landlady. "I hope you'll come back as brown as a berry, sir. I was two year in the country once, and, though I won't say I'd like it for always, yet my heart do get to wishing these days for a sight o' the flowers and the fields. You'll mind the fruit, sir, and the dews o' night; there does be great dews fallin', and a deal of ague, I'm told. Good-by to you." And Dick said "good-by" to her with something like emotion; for it was his first "good-by" to any one, and the woman had been good to him, and if her hair was in a blouse, and her garments ill made and not clean, Dick was not startled, for he had never seen them otherwise.

Then he walked on to meet Mr. Stoffs, and found he was nearly an hour before the time. It seemed as if the moment of departure would never come; but it did, at last, and, as in a sort of dream, the dusty city youth was whirled by cottages nestling among proud, protecting trees, past the green hills, and through fields "all rich with ripening grain," until the panting train pulled up between a pile of stones and a little yellow station-house, with a narrow platform running beside it.

"Now, then, here we are!" said the German, and took up his bundles and basket; for who ever saw a Carl Stoffs in the cars tha, had not a bundle and basket, and a quantity of household furniture besides? This last Dick took in charge, and so laden the two made their way out of the cars. Around the little yellow station-house dodged two splendid bays with silver harness, that were being driven rapidly round a corner close to the narrow platform, and went out into the dusty road; for sidewalks there were none. Soon the sound of carriage-wheels made them turn aside, and Dick stumbled, as he walked for the first time on the soft green grass.

When you take a mountain lassie to Rome and show her St. Peter's, she is not enthusiastic; indeed, she is terribly disappointed. She expected something so much greater than her mountains, so much brighter than her green valleys. If Dick was disappointed when he put his foot on nature's velvet carpet and found it only caused him to stumble, I cannot say. I think he felt surprised that a brook beside the way and far blue hills before him wrought no emotion within him. Fortunately Carl asked no raptures.

"That was the Brandons' turn-out," he said in a prosaic way, as Dick recovered his footing, and returned to the road.

"Is that so?" asked Dick. "Do they live here?"

"Yes," said Carl, "and a fine place it is too; but I think the man's going too fast."

Then Dick was thoughtful for a minute or two, pitying the daughter, if it were so; but it is hard to think that a man's family are near to want when his stylish carriage has just turned you out of the road, and the pity soon seemed misplaced.

The walk seemed long to Dick; he did, indeed, enjoy the cool breeze. fresher and purer than any he had ever felt before ; but he had his own baggage and Carl's curtain-rods besides, and he was used to pavements. They had already passed many fine houses, with lawns and carriageways, shaded by great trees in front of them, and now and again a little house, with flowers and clustering vines, and groups on the porches ; but Carl's steps lingered at none. At last they turned out of the dusty road into a shaded lane, a veritable lane, as new to Dick as the Paris Boulevards would be to Mrs. Partington ; two or three more cottages, smaller and not so much gardenroom, and then Carl said :

" Eh! but I'm glad to get home! Come here, Will ! Come, boys !"

The last call seemed to fill the lane with children. They might have come down from the trees, or up from the earth, for all Dick could tell ; but at the sound of Carl's voice the place was alive—big boys and little boys, great girls and small girls, all round and fat, brown-eyed and yellow-haired, with all manner of greetings, gathered around the travellers, eagerly drew their baggage from their hands, and with baskets, bags, bundles, and curtain-rods, made a grand triumphal procession before them, shouting, laughing, pushing against each other, the big ones stumbling over the little ones, and yet nobody hurt.

A few steps more and a rustic gate was opened and some one came and stood under the archway of evergreen branches, intertwined with some drooping vines. She was facing the West, looking down the lane, shading her eyes with her hand, although the sun was almost down. Just for a moment she stood in the bright sunset glow, under the green archway, shading her brown eyes from the light, looking down the shadowy lane ; and, as she so stood, she

seemed a very fair and graceful girl indeed. An instant more and the children, in the importance of their mission as baggage-carriers, pushed past her, and she retreated with them toward the house.

" Come, Rose ! Here we are !" called Carl to her. And she turned and met them as they reached the gate.

" You are welcome," she said to Dick when he was introduced at the gate.

" You are welcome," said Mrs. Stoffs, coming toward them from the porch.

" You are welcome," repeated Mrs. Alaine, at the door. And Dick had not a word of answer to any one of them.

They were to him as grand as princesses and as gracious as queens, as they came forth to receive him and bid him welcome to their little cottage ; and Dick was not used to courts or to queens and princesses, so he could only bow and shake the hands so cordially extended to him.

I am afraid my hero was not at all happy for the first few minutes that he sat on the stoop between Mrs. Stoffs and Mrs. Alaine, not knowing what answer to make to even their simplest remark, and that he was much relieved when they joined their voices to the hubbub the children were making around Carl. Such shyness as Dick's is very painful to the spectators, as well as to the embarrassed one ; but, then, there's this to be said about it, when it is once entirely conquered it never can come back again, and I fancy there are some very nice people in the world, now very self-possessed and perfectly well-bred, who would give much to feel again the awkwardness and embarrassment which, once upon a time, caused them such keen annoyance. The women pitied Dick, but liked him none the less for the color that would come into his face and the hesitation of his replies ; but their feeling for the stranger was greater than any pleasure to themselves, and so it was not long before they went into the house with the declared intention of "getting tea." But going into the house was not going away altogether; for the room which served for parlor, library, sitting-room, dining-room, and all, had a low window opening on the stoop, and Carl and Dick could see them well, and speak, if they chose, without raising their voices, as they went back and forth from the table to the closet, and from the closet to the table, not to mention innumerable visits to Carl's basket, which seemed a pantry in itself. The children ran in and out, and one jolly little one, called Trot, who was as round as a dumpling, and was too young to be shy for very long, informed Dick she was glad he had come, for they were to have sweet-cakes for tea. Occasionally Rose would come and stand at the window and say something to tease "Uncle Carl," who was not slow to "give her as good as he got." Thus gradually Dick became more at ease, and began to distinguish a difference in the tones of the children's voices, and to take note of the strange Sunday-like stillness which, except for the merry noises in the house, was complete, and, to him, wonderful.

I think a tea-table is one of the nicest sights in the world. If there is a grain of poetry in a woman, and I believe that there is no woman without a grain of poetry in her, it will surely, mark my words, however rough and prosaic she may be, come out about tea-time. That was a very pretty tea-table at which Dick took his place that evening ; there was no

silver nor China, and there was, perhaps, too great an abundance of good things ; but it startled Dick, and I contend that it was nice and pretty, if only for the reason that it had a clean table-cloth, a bunch of flowers, and every dish in its proper place. Mrs. Alaine, who was only a feminine edition of her brother Carl, sat at the head of the table, in a clean calico dress, with a white collar and a blue ribbon. She had a child on each side of her, whose glee, at the prospect of sweet-cakes and peaches (out of Carl's basket) after they had eaten their bread and butter, she tried to moderate with a smiling, " Hush, children ! What will Mr. Heremore think of you ?" Mrs. Stoffs, who had also a round face, and was dressed in a clean calico, with white collar and a knot of pink ribbons, Dick had seen many times before, and dearly loved the good humor that bubbled all over her face whenever she spoke. She also had a child on each side of her, whose audible whispers about the good things coming she answered and mysteriously increased by promises of the same again another day. But opposite Dick was a face that was not round nor especially good-humored ; for the two children under charge of Rose were the least repressible of the whole flock, and they tried her slender stock of patience sorely ; especially, as she said afterward to her mother, with many blushes and half crying at the recollection, " as they would say *such* things right before the strange gentleman !" Rose had a pretty blue muslin, with a tiny bit of lace around the neck, for her raiment, and there was a something red, green, brown, blue, pink, or yellow, that fluttered here and there before Dick's eyes whenever she moved to help the children, or turned her young face, with its flitting colors, toward him. But whether it were a ribbon, or a blush, or the hue of her hair, or an aureole around her head, and whether it were no color at all, or all colors together, or a rainbow out of the clouds, I do not think Dick had, for one moment, a definite idea —at least, while it was flitting before his eyes.

After tea, Carl took out his pipe, and settled into his big chair on the porch; and the children, having got somewhat over their awe of the stranger, volunteered to take him down the lane, and show him where there had been a robin's nest last spring, an expedition, however, that was vetoed by Carl on the ground that you couldn't see even a robin's nest in the dark. Then Rose came out to tease Uncle Carl again; but, forgetting her purpose, stood where the light from within seemed to set her in glory, like the angels in pictures; and by and by, it came about, no one knew how, that her shrine was vacant, and she, a very nice little girl with her hands in the pockets—very impracticable pockets they were—of her muslin apron, was telling Dick, with the children as prompters and commentators, the full particulars of the finding of the robin's nest, and what work she had had to keep the children from bringing sorrow and dismay to the hearts of the parent robins by stealing away their little ones. Then, as the moon rose, there was no reason why the children should not take Dick down the lane to show to him the tree where the nest had

been; and then it was needful that he should know just how far it was from sister Rose's window, and yet how quickly, on hearing the shouts of rejoicing, she had come to Mrs. Robin's assistance. Then it was so funny to see a man who had never climbed a tree, that it was needful two or three should go up one to show how it is done. Then, too, there were lightning-bugs by the million around them, and as Dick had never seen anything like them unless it was fire-crackers on Fourth of July night, they had to catch several for his investigation. When Rose told how those little things are really the people of the forest, who are so timid they do not dare to come out in the daytime, but do all their praying by night, and have always been good friends to children, showing them their way home when lost, and driving away the ghosts that would frighten the wanderers, then the children opened their brown hands and let them fly away, promising never to make prisoners of them again.

And so, though Dick still felt strange and shy, it was not in such an unpleasant way as when he sat on the porch trying to answer Mrs. Alaine and Mrs. Stoffs when they spoke to him. When, at last, he closed his eyes that night, he was half ready to admit that "the country" might almost be the enchanted land some people had made it out to be.

CHAPTER IV.

In the beautiful dawn Dick awoke, hardly remembering where he was, and almost frightened at the wonderful absence of many noises which had never before failed to greet his waking. Not knowing whether it were very late or very early, Dick took the safest view of the subject, and hurriedly dressed himself; then, cautiously opening his door, he looked out to see if there was any sign to guide his further movements. All was silent around him; but the hall door stood wide open, letting in a square of golden sunshine at the foot of the stairs. He went carefully and noiselessly down, and found himself, when he reached the porch, in a flood of glorious light. The flowers that hung above the porch were sparkling in it, for the dew was yet fresh on all the world; a thousand birds were carolling songs of exultation from every tree, while the cool, fragrant morning air came to him in the freshest purest breezes that ever were known.

Even the pebbles, from which the sun had not yet kissed away a single dew-drop, were sparkling like jewels as Dick approached them on his way to the little rustic gate under the evergreen arch. He stood leaning over it a long time, looking down the cool, shadowy lane, his heart joining in the joyous morning hymn of nature, for the first time heard.

He was standing by the gate, enjoying all, when new voices reached his ears—human voices—and the children all at once came rushing from the garden at the back of the house, in a tumult of delight, surrounding him almost before they were aware of his presence, so intent were they upon their mission to the village.

" Me doing to the 'tore !" exclaimed little Trot, rubbing her hands. " Me dot a pocket."

Which double hint Dick took at once by putting pennies in the " pocket," much to her delight and the older ones' annoyance.

" For shame, Trot !" said Will, " that's as bad as asking ; and you can't go to the store either ; you'll get wet, the grass is all wet. 'Tan't no good for girls ; you stay home."

Whereupon Trot rubbed her brown little fists in her eyes, and loudly bewailed her misery in being only a girl, showing also that she had a will of her own that by no means acknowledged this big boy as its lord and master. Dick attempted to show him that whereas Trot's dress was already a finger deep with wet from the long grass through which she had been tramping all the morning so far, it couldn't make much difference if it got a little wetter. But Will was firm, and Trot inappeasable, until, much to our hero's relief, the noise brought out Rose, who was greatly ashamed of Trot for making "such a time before the strange gentleman," and very firmly decided for Will. In some magic way she sent the boy portion unencumbered by any of the weaker sex, on their way rejoicing, found something for the girls to do, and took Trot's hand so resolutely that not a sob was ventured by that small maiden, so that there was again peace in the land.

Then came breakfast, with a further display of clean calico, a great deal of laughing and merry talk, but in a less leisurely way than at tea, for the day's work was before not behind them. Breakfast finished, the children, our hero, Rose, and Rose's bosom friend, Clara Hays, were sent off to pick berries in the woods. Half the morning they were in getting started ; for everybody spoke at once, and everybody hurried and detained everybody else. There were at least a dozen false starts. As soon as seven got to the gate, Trot and Minnie were reported missing; no sooner were Trot and Minnie secured, than some one else was out of the way. But at last they got fairly off, and went down the lane in great glee ; the children swinging their pails and baskets in advance, and running back every two minutes to give some valuable information about the road or the woods or the berries, or something equally important. Rose, Clara, and Dick brought up the rear in a manner that showed they had a becoming sense of the responsibility thrown upon them as the elders of the party.

What they did all day in the woods, how many brooks they crossed, who fell in and was fished out with much laughter ; how little Trot got in everybody's way, and ate the others' berries as fast as they were picked ; how the children met other children on the road ; how often all parties rested, and teased each other, and compared the quantity each had picked ; and whether Dick, who had soon got over his awkwardness, put his berries into Clara's pail or into Rose's basket, I am not able to relate. I only know they returned at evening very noisy and very tired ; and that Rose had a larger stock than any other one of the whole party ; and that as she

took off her broad-brimmed straw hat, and pushed back the moist curls from her face, this young lady did not go up at once to wash off the purple berry stains from her hands, and to put on the pretty blue muslin with its tiny bit of lace around the neck, but lingered to hear the children, each interrupting the other, until they were nearly all talking at once, tell Mr. and Mrs. Stuffs and Mrs. Alaine the day's adventures. Dick, too, had somewhat to relate, and glanced at Rose while he told it, although it was only what the children had told twice over already, how Mr. Dick—it had come to that with the children—didn't know a turkey from a goose, and had called things by their wrong names all day ; whereat Rose laughed with the rest, and then ran up to bathe her glowing cheeks in time to help get tea.

When she came down, she found the children in the same eager excitement, following the two women from kitchen to cellar, from the closet to the table, still telling about the big snake they were sure they had seen run across the path just before them, and the rabbits, and what Minnie had said, and Will had done, and Charley had thought ; to all which the listeners gave an attentive ear, laughing when there was need, and surprised at the proper moment. At tea, the day in the woods continued to furnish food for animated discussion, and neither Rose nor Dick looked as if the subject were a tiresome one.

"And how did my little Trot get along ?" asked Uncle Carl ; but Trot, who was tired, and cross, and impatient for her piece of cake, made no answer.

"Trot tumbled into the water," said Will ; " she always tumbles in."

Then Trot who couldn't bear to be

teased, looked as if she were about to cry, but was appeased by a word or two from Rose, and Carl asked who pulled her out.

"Oh! I did," answered Will readily; " I and Mr. Dick."

" I see that Mr. Dick is very good to you," said Mrs. Stoffs, with a kind smile toward our hero, who colored and looked his delight.

" I don't think we can get along without Mr. Dick any more, can we?"

The children declared they could not, and Dick was as pleased as if he had just taken a degree; but Rose said nothing about the matter.

Well, that was a merry, merry week; there were so many things needed, and such long walks were required through the woods, and over the hills, and even down to the beach, in order to procure them, while every errand took all day to perform, that Dick learned to walk on the soft grass without stumbling; even to loiter slowly along by Rose's side, not often looking to see where he placed his feet; and the children were such good tutors that he learned the names of the birds and animals and insects that came in his way, and knew where there had been the best cherries in the spring, where there would be the best place for nutting in the fall, and when the grapes would be ripe, " If only he could be here!"

If only he could be here! But a week is only a week, and it will end, if it has a life-time in its seven days. The last day had come, and they all knew it; there had been a better dinner. "Mr. Dick's last dinner with us, you know," they had said to each other; and something more than sweet-cakes and peaches for tea, for "to-morrow Mr. Dick will not be here." But, for all their consideration, Mr. Dick hardly knew

that night if he were eating sweet-cakes or bitter bread.

It was a very quiet evening that followed the last tea at Carlton. The children were more silent than usual; even Trot was not proof against the indescribable feeling that settles over a group from which one is about to take his departure. She climbed into Dick's lap, and—an uncommon thing with that restless maiden—did not offer to leave her position all those long twilight hours. When Miss Brandon rode by—as I forgot to state she did at twilight every evening—her beautiful pony, her long dress, her hat with its drooping feather, her veil fluttering in the evening breeze, her buff gauntlets, and her silver-handled riding-whip — things which had set the whole flock in commotion before — were hardly commented upon. When Mr. Irving, so tall and princely, left her side for a moment, and, coming close to the gate, called after Will, it was found Rose had forgotten the usual bouquet of flowers for the ladies, and had to beg the gentleman to wait. Rose felt very guilty; but Dick endeavored to console her by saying that, without doubt, Mr. Irving was glad to have a little more time with such a beautiful young lady as Miss Brandon; and then fell to praising Miss Mary vehemently—how beautiful she was, how gracious and pleasant to all, and yet always remembering she was a grand young lady. Rose thought it very easy to be good and pleasant when people are rich and beautiful; and then Dick tried to comfort her again, and perhaps with better success than before; for her only answer was a silent act of contrition for the envious thought that had flitted across her mind. Then, still in silence, she cut the flowers that she could hardly more than guess at in the gathering twilight. Dick was silent, too; and yet there was a great deal he would like to have said, even though he little suspected that all he had so far made clear to her was that Miss Brandon was to him like an angel in a picture, or a heroine in some old romance, and that, beside her silent act of contrition, poor little Rose's heart had given one great throb, and had then made an act of resignation beside. But Dick found voice to ask for a good-by flower, which Rose gave; and it may be there were spoken then a few words of more solemn meaning, such as will come when two people, young and fresh, find their skies suddenly glowing above them, and their hearts full of grateful praise to God, who has made life so sweet. And it may be that little Rose, who said her prayers so regularly for all sinners and for all who are tempted, said a few broken, bashful words, exhorting Dick to goodness even in the midst of the "snares of the great city," and that he eagerly caught the words as they fell, promised her never to forget them, and inwardly made a quick cry for God's grace to let him die then rather than do aught to offend him who had showered such blessings upon him. It may be, too, that Rose—the simple-hearted maiden— was sure he would never break the promise, and that their good-by there was a request and a promise each to pray for the other. But if so, it was not said in long paragraphs, with flowing periods; for Rose was too conscientious to detain Mr. Irving a moment longer than needful.

But I am afraid Rose had to make another act of contrition that night; for when Will brought her the money for the flowers—the garden was her own—she would not take it, but told him to divide it among the children, himself, of course, included. Dick thought it very generous of her; but I have my own opinion about that. Too soon for all the last "good-nights" were said, and Dick knew he had spent out his last evening in Carlton for who could tell how long? Yet his dreams were not sad. If he did not actually believe he was riding on a splendid great horse, by the side of a fair damsel on a white pony, down the shadowy lane, into the broad road of the future; that he had given Carl a home for life, and a load of toys to the children, with, perhaps, an uplifting of his heart, and a readiness to bear whatever life should bring him worthy of a faithful Christian, I think it was something "very like it."

The next morning there was a hurried breakfast, after which they all went to the little yellow station-house to see him off, and waved their hats and handkerchiefs until the train was out of sight. A little longer, and they had returned in a rambling procession home, each with some remembrance of him to tell the other, while he was in the city at work once more, but as a different Dick Heremore from the one who had said good-by, not without emotion, to his slovenly landlady.

CHAPTER V.

WHEN Christmas came around again, and made the first break in the routine of his life after his ever-memorable visit to the country, Dick, now no longer a follower at a distance of that Sunday morning crowd, but a devout and well-instructed Catholic, to whom all the glory and grandeur of the Christmas lights and flowers, the music and the bells, were no longer mysteries; after hearing the grand high mass—not the only one he had heard that day —turned down Fourteenth street, ac cording to the custom of many years, in order that he might pass the Brandons' house, which had ever held a charm for him, since on its broad steps he had first seen the beauty and loveliness of charity. But he was not thinking just then of Miss Brandon, nor of his newsboy days, nor yet of the fast approaching hour when he should present himself at Carl Stoffs's table, in a quarter of the city very different from this, where he was to eat his piece of Christmas turkey. His thoughts, I am afraid, will seem wild ones; but he was young, it was Christmas-day, he had just come from that glorious mass, and the world seemed so small and easy to conquer to one who had heard the " glad tidings," so that he may be forgiven for dreaming, in a less prosaic and unspiritual manner than I can tell you, of a time when he would eat his Christmas dinner neither at a boarding-house nor at another man's board, but would carve his own Christmas turkey, at his own table. Of whatever he was thinking, he did not fail to notice the house, and to glance upward when he came to the stoop where he—was it really he, that rough, shaggy, ragged little newsboy, ignorant and dirty?— where he had, for the first time in his hard young life, heard a voice address him kindly; and his glance changed to a steady gaze of surprise when his eye caught a name on the door-plate that was not Brandon. He looked at the number—that was all right, but the old name was gone. He was perplexed, and walked absently backward and forward for several moments.

" Then Mr. Stoffs was right," he said, " and he " (meaning Mr. Brandon) " has had to come down a peg or two, or he would not have given up his house at this season. I wonder where they have gone now."

He remembered, at this moment, that none of the family had been at Ames & Harden's during the whole fall, and that he had not seen Miss Brandon since she and Mr. Irving had ridden down the lane for the flowers that Rose had forgotten to have ready at the usual hour. It so happened that, remembering the neglected flowers, why they had been forgotten, and how the negligence had been repaired, Dick's thoughts strayed from the graceful figure of the beautiful lady, who had seemed to him more magnificent and gentle than a vision, and turned to another figure, not tall nor stately—to another face, not grand nor graciously sweet.

But when he met Mr. and Mrs. Stoffs, almost the first words he said were,

" I went by the house on Fourteenth street to-day, and Mr. Brandon's name was off the door. I had not heard of their going away."

" It's long ago, though," said Mr. Stoffs.

" Is it any difficulty made them leave their old house?" asked Dick.

" There's been no end of difficulties," answered the German, puffing out great clouds of smoke between every sentence. " Things were bad enough last summer, and when Mrs. Brandon died—"

" Mrs. Brandon dead!" exclaimed Dick.

" Oh! I forgot that was after you left; it was quite an excitement. The horses ran away one night—those same stylish bays of which she was so proud—when she and her daughter were returning from some party, and she was dead before morning."

" And Miss Brandon?" Dick could hardly ask, his terror of the answer was so great.

" Miss Brandon," answered Mr.

Stoffs in a formal way, and puffing out greater clouds of smoke than ever, "Miss Brandon was ill for some days, and they were afraid would never get over the shock; your fine ladies are so nervous!"

"Miss Brandon is not that kind," said Dick hastily, vexed by the contemptuous tone of his friend's remark. "And I don't believe fine ladies are any more—more—fussy than others."

"I suppose you know them well enough to be a certain judge," said Carl, who seemed in a very ugly humor.

"Of course I don't know one in the world," answered Dick, with considerable animation and a deeper color in his face. "But I can't see the good of always running down people, just because they happen to be richer than ourselves."

"Hush! now," interposed Mrs. Stoffs, as her husband was about answering, "or no dinner shall you have this day. I will not let you two quarrel."

"You were going to tell me about Mr. Brandon's difficulties," suggested Dick very gently, after both he and Mr. Stoffs had assured their peacemaker that they were never in better humor toward each other. "You were going to tell me about Mr. Brandon's difficulties."

. "Yes. His wife she died, and it was found he had used all her money and had lost it, as he had his own; there was a failure and everything was sold out, and so—there's an end of him."

"Did he leave New-York?"

"I don't know. Who asks what has become of a one-time rich man after the bubble has burst?"

"I think I heard he wanted some situation to start life again," said Mrs. Stoffs. "Poor man!"

Mrs. Stoffs was right. Mr. Brandon had tried to start again; but he had been a hard man in his days of prosperity, and an unfaithful man, or he would not be as he was now; and so, many who heartily pitied him and his family for their fall, and who would willingly have given them assistance out of their own pockets, did not feel justified in giving him a position that could be better filled by some man in whom they could trust. Thus among all his rich friends, not one of whom felt unkindly toward him, there was none to push him a plank with which to save himself from drowning.

Dick had learned all that his hosts could tell, and knowing well how fearfully rapid is a man's fall when once he is over the precipice of failure, his heart was heavier than it had ever been for troubles of his own. He sought to sustain his part in the conversation, feeling that a silent guest seems selfish and ungrateful, and tried to laugh as heartily at his friend's jokes as ever; but it was not without an effort, and his friends were keen and saw that he was troubled.

"I do not like it," Carl grunted in his deepest tones, that Christmas night after Dick had gone and the children were asleep; "I do not like it."

"You must not think too hardly of him," answered Mrs. Stoffs, who, with that sort of perception women obtain when they become wives, knew her husband referred to Dick's troubled manner, the anxious way in which he had asked about Miss Brandon, and his hot resenting of Carl's careless words. "You are too hard on him," said Mrs. Stoffs, not because she did not equally dislike it all, but because there would be no conversation between them if old married folks were always to agree.

"Fine ladies, indeed!" muttered

Mr. Stoffs, puffing away harder than ever. "Miss Brandon—what for should he care if Miss Brandon was hurt, more than for any other lady?"

"She is poor enough now," said Mrs. Stoffs musingly. "It would not be so strange now;" and under her breath she sighed, "Poor Rose!"

"Not that he has one thought of such a thing," Carl went on consistently; "you women always get such ideas into your heads."

Mrs. Stoffs, being an experienced wife, raised no question about the ownership of the "ideas," whatever they were, but sat looking into the fire for a long time before she spoke again, and then it was to say, "After all, I am glad we were too poor to have Rose come up for Christmas."

"If she would not be satisfied with what we had, so am I," grumbled Mr. Stoffs.

"I was not thinking of that," answered his wife mildly.

"I know Heremore's never such a fool as to be thinking of one so much above him as Miss Brandon," remarked Mr. Stoffs.

"She is not above him now that they are poor," answered his wife.

"It isn't the money that made the difference," said Carl rather impatiently, "it's the habits that money gives. That's what is the matter. Miss Brandon may not be half worthy of him, and yet he would be mad to think of her; it is misery when people marry out of their rank, misery to both."

"But if they love each other?" suggested his wife.

"That only makes the matter worse; he knows not her ways. She has a language that is not his; if they did not care, they could go their own ways, and seek their own. I think Heremore is a great fool; I do!"

"I don't believe he has a thought of such a thing," said Mrs. Stoffs; but there was a manifest question in her voice.

"If he has, he'll rue the day he thought of it first," said her husband emphatically; and there the conversation ended; but when Mrs. Stoffs wrote again to Mrs. Alaine, which she did not do for some time—for to write a letter was an event in the honest woman's life—she thought proper to give her sister a hint of that which they had observed; and Mrs. Alaine, in her turn, thought proper to convey the hint, in the form of information, to Rose, who, however, answered readily,

"Love Miss Brandon? Well, mamma, and why shouldn't he?"

"Because Miss Brandon is not in the same class of life that he is, dear."

"I am sure Mr. Heremore is better off than her father is now," urged Rose; "for he has a regular salary, and Mr. Brandon has nothing left, and nobody will give him any place."

"No doubt, my child; but it is not money that makes the difference. Miss Brandon has her ideas of life now just as she had them when she was rich; and Mr. Heremore is what he is, and would not be different if he were suddenly made a millionaire."

So Rose said no more.

While Mr. and Mrs. Stoffs were thus disturbed about him, Dick, unconscious of any cause he had given for their disquietude, was walking slowly and thoughtfully home. "Where was that little Mary with her fair hair and gentle smile this cold Christmas night?" was the question he kept putting to himself. It was a clear, bright night, with the moon shining on the pavements and the frozen earth, not at all such a night as that during which he had slept by her father's steps, and there was no fear that her fair head was shelterless ; but still it was very sad to think of her, whose Christmas days had been such pleasant ones, in mourning for her mother, and perhaps in troubles such as those which men hear, but shudder to see, clouding the girlish youth that is so short, and should be so sunny.

"With God's help I'll find them out before to-morrow night if they are in this city," said Dick to himself, and then walked on more rapidly.

And he kept his word, though not without much trouble ; and within twenty-four hours he stood in front of the wretched boarding-house to which poverty and sickness had already reduced the family that, a few months before, had never dreamed of the meaning of want.

But though he had found them out and stood before their door, Dick had done and could do nothing to lessen their trouble. Mr. Brandon had not seemed more unapproachable when, a rich man, he scowled and said hard words to the ill-dressed errand-boy—than he now did to the simple clerk, though Dick himself was richer now than was the once rich merchant. Miss Brandon was, in his eyes, now no less a lady, belonging to a sphere far above him, than she had been when, in all the glory of wealth, youth, and beauty, he had seen her ride down to the Stoffs's cottage to buy flowers for her hair. It seemed to him greater presumption for him to think of approaching her now than it would have been then, so he passed and repassed her door, grieved for her trouble, but more grieved, if possible, that he, with his youth and strength, should be powerless to give her one grain of comfort. How often and often, as he had watched her—she all

unconscious of him and his grateful reverence—in her days of prosperity, had he dreamed of her as like some damsel of olden romance in sore distress, and thought that never had knight rushed more joyously or more potently to the rescue than he would to hers. Now his dream had come to pass—she was a damsel in sore distress ; but where was his prancing steed, his burnished armor, his ready lance ? Then, as he smiled in remembrance of his boyish fancy, he suddenly thought of Mr. Irving, the gentleman—just a boy's ideal of a gallant knight—whom he had seen so often with Miss Brandon in the country. He recollected well the manly bearing of that "perfect gentleman," whom he and Rose had looked upon as a veritable Sir Launcelot ; he had seen many an act of "gentle courtesy" shown in a grave, tender way, to the fair lady by whose side he always rode ; and where was he now that that fair lady needed her knight as never before ?

There was nothing morbid or bitter about Dick. When he asked himself that question, it was with no thought of the common judgment pronounced upon "summer friends." He recognized Mr. Irving's right to aid and comfort the family of his former host. He knew that he had wealth, position, character, and, of course, ample influence, and not for an instant doubted that he would use every means in his power to befriend Mr. Brandon, if only for the sake of that beautiful daughter whom he so evidently admired. Where, then, was Mr. Irving ? If he had been here, all this could not have happened. But as Dick asked himself this, it did not occur to him that Mary thought as he thought : if Mr. Irving had been here, all this would not have happened.

At last Dick, fully convinced that

he would be guilty of no presumption in speaking his mind to Mr. Irving on this subject, cheerfully turned
his steps homeward, and resolved
that the first moment he had of his
own should be spent in seeking Mr.
Irving, and informing him of what he
could not now be aware of, the down-
fall of the Brandons. For the fall of
the Brandons, as he heard from one or
two who knew, had been very great,
very rapid, and, it was feared, was not
yet completed. Mr. Brandon had
never held his head up since his
failure, but dragged around, shabbily dressed, querulous and half-
sick, dejected and clearly miserable.
His two sons had been given very
poor situations, on very niggardly
pay, by a relative in another city
who, having always been odiously
cringing to Mr. Brandon when he
had money, seemed to delight now
in heaping humiliations upon his
sons—so great a crime it was in his
eyes to be better bred, better educated, and more kindly cared for
than were his own rude, blustering,
ignorant boys. If only Fred and
Joe had been taught whence come
adversity and prosperity, doubtless
these humiliations would have been
crowns of glory for them; but theirs
had been only a vague, dreamy sort
of faith, which they never suspected had any application to their real
life. I dare say they were very idle,
useless, self-conceited, and aggrava-
ting boys; but I can't help feeling
sorry for them in their troubles.
Miss Brandon, Dick was told, had
not recovered her strength since
the accident, and however well she
might have been, with all her accomplishments, could not have done

more than she was now doing: giving music-lessons to a few persons
residing near her new home.

But all hope of seeing Mr. Irving
faded the first thing the next day;
for Dick's questions brought the
unwelcome information that he had
left home in October for two years'
travel in Europe, and Dick, of
course, could not presume to write
to him.

CHAPTER VI.

I could not tell you one-half the
projects Dick formed and rejected
as entirely hopeless before he at
last succeeded in inducing a gentleman who had been very kind to him
to make an offer to Mr. Brandon of
some place in his office, which,
while it would not be more than,
with his now broken energies and
failing health, he could easily perform, if he had the disposition,
would give him something to help
him live upon.

Soon after this offer was made
and (with much grumbling) finally
accepted, Dick, without really seeking it, found himself becoming
known to Mr. Brandon; and,
thanks to the patience with which
he listened to that gentleman's
railings against the world, and his
own hard fortunes in it, taken into
favor. It was a very sad sight
for a hopeful, self-respecting, God-
fearing Catholic like Dick to see
this querulous man, from whom
all vigorous spirit seemed to have
fled, brooding over his losses, instead of holding up his head and
bravely going forth to make the
most of what was left; a sad thing
to hear these miserable repinings in

which there was never a thought of gratitude for the long years of comfort and plenty with which God had blessed him. But Dick bore it patiently, and sought in every way which his simple experience could devise to draw him from his despondency; to inspire him with some trust in God. It was, however, without any apparent success, other than greater condescension from Mr. Brandon, who, at last, weak and nervous, would gladly avail himself of Dick's young strength in his walks home.

And so, in time, that which had seemed the impossible came to pass very naturally. Mr. Brandon urged Dick to enter the house, and he was received as a guest in Miss Brandon's home. Home it must be called, I suppose; though it was a dreary, desolate room, with "boarding-house" stamped in glaring letters all over the grey walls and badly-assorted furniture. Even Dick could realize that it must be a very different home from any which Miss Brandon had ever seen before; for it was far different from the only pretty rooms *he* had ever entered—those dear, clean, sweet rooms at Mrs. Alaine's.

"Mr. Heremore, Mary," was his introduction, accompanied by a patronizing wave of Mr. Brandon's hand. Do not be surprised; you know I have never said—not even in his days of prosperity—that he was a gentleman—"Mr. Heremore, Mary; a young man who has thought it not worth while to be unkind and disrespectful to an old man who has lost every thing."

"I have heard my father speak of you often," said Mary very quietly; but in such gentle tones that Dick wondered how any man could count himself poor—knowing *her.*

"I really felt very nervous," Mr. Brandon further explained, "about coming home alone. I have been so very uncomfortable to-day. But that's of no consequence, of course, *now.*"

"I am very glad you brought Mr. Heremore," Mary answered readily, and with more warmth than before; "and I am sure he was very careful of you."

After that, conversation became somewhat easier; although Dick felt half like an impostor, and could not do much to second Miss Brandon's efforts to make the hour go by pleasantly. She had several albums and scrap-books of engravings with which she tried to entertain him; but to do his best, he could think of little else than the languid, weary manner which had replaced the quick steps and stately sweetness he had known of old. When Mr. Brandon left them for a few minutes, she turned with animation and said:

"Mr. Heremore, I must thank you for your kindness to my father. I would not have him suppose I consider it kindness, but in my heart I know it is, and I know you mean it as such. Since things have gone wrong with him, he seems to have changed his whole nature; he does not appear to have any courage to stand against the tide. I suppose it would have been very different if Mrs. Brandon had lived; a wife would have kept his spirits up as no one else can."

"I know," stammered Dick, not knowing what to say under the gaze of her beautiful eyes, "I know—that the death of your mother last summer—"

"Mrs. Brandon, you mean," she interrupted in her quietest tones, "that is, my father's second wife. This Mrs. Brandon was not my mother; my own mother died long ago." This so coldly that, for some inexplicable reason, Dick fancied she was glad to correct him.

"You were in the carriage at the same time," said Dick, feeling that he must say something.

"Yes," answered Mary, "but I remember little about it; as soon as we found the horses were running away, Mrs. Brandon became very much alarmed, and almost before I could say a word to her, we were thrown out, and were both picked up senseless. She was not conscious of anything again. All these things together have completely unnerved poor papa, and I really feel very grateful to any one who is interested in him. His old friends have received but little encouragement to visit us here, although it is only a fancy of papa's, I am sure, that they feel any difference, and he is often quite lonely."

Mr. Brandon soon returned, and seeming to wish his daughter's undivided attention, Dick rose and said, "good-night."

It need hardly be said that he was after this more enthusiastically devoted to their fortunes than ever before. He spent a few hours there at different times during the winter and spring, and soon found himself at ease in that dreary room; but as he knew Mary better, his reverence for her, while it diminished not in the least, became a deep and fervent feeling, which kept her always in his thoughts. She, too, seemed to regard him with very kindly feelings, and the sympathy between them was so strong that it bore down many of their differences of association and education, and each was astonished to find an unexpectedly ready understanding in the other. But as yet Dick had said nothing of the little girl on the steps who gave him her candy one cold Christmas morning years ago.

Once at New-Year's, and again on the 22d of February, holidays on which he was free, Dick had been down to the cottage in the country, and had seen Rose and the boys skate and make snow-houses, and spent two of the coziest, happiest evenings of his life around the bright fire, talking pleasant talk with those dear people, among whom alone he realized the faintest idea of the word home. Now time had gone by so rapidly that he was to spend a whole week there as he had the year before. But not exactly the same; for the last time he had been there—a clear, bright day in February, when they were all coming home from the skating-pond together—it had chanced that he and Rose had fallen far in the rear of the children, who, having skated since one o'clock in the keen air, professed themselves "ever so hungry," and, as Dick would not hurry with them, walked off in disgust, each declaring to the other that they didn't like Mr. Dick half so much this time as before; he was "no good" at all.

"What a magnificent day!" Dick said, for about the tenth time, as he tramped by Rose's side through the crisp snow, just as the sun was going down in one great glow before them. "I think I never saw a more splendid winter day in all my life."

Not thinking of any addition to this speech, and not being able with truth to contradict it, Rose kept on her way, her neat little boots cutting the snow, and making, Dick thought, the most delicious music there ever was. Rose looked especially charming that afternoon; from the very crown of her head, with her wealth of golden hair, only half hidden by her felt hat, to the dainty little boots before mentioned, which her warm skating dress, looped up, did not even affect to conceal, Rose was charming. Dick thought that her very cloak seemed to nestle more lovingly to her plump figure than another's would; and as for the tiny muff, Uncle Carl's present, and the blue silk handkerchief knotted around her neck, Dick was certain that Stewart never sold anything half so pretty. So, if his lips talked about the weather, it is hardly surprising that his eyes embraced another subject; and I question if, when her demure glances met his gaze, Rose needed words to tell her its meaning; for, after all, are words, the dearest and sweetest that come from the lips, any dearer or sweeter than those the eyes speak?

But whatever she knew, Rose was a true little woman, and showed no sign.

"This is the place where Mrs. Brandon was thrown," she said, as they passed a broad street cutting across the narrow road they were following. "Just by those trees. They say the horses could have been managed only for her screams; a woman who screams at such a time must have very little sense."

"I think so," answered Dick, looking sadly toward the place Rose pointed out.

"Miss Mary behaved wonderfully well," continued Rose, with one quick look into Dick's face as they passed on. "She was perfectly calm, and tried to quiet Mrs. Brandon. She was very much hurt herself."

"Yes, so I have heard; she shows it, too; you would hardly recognize her now, she is so thin and altered."

"But, of course, she is more beautiful for that," said little, plump Rose. who had a great idea of delicate, fragile girls.

"Not more beautiful, exactly," answered Dick, who had not a great idea of delicate, fragile girls, "but it makes one feel for her more."

"I know you feel for her very much," said Rose.

"I have always honored her very much," answered Dick warmly. "It almost seems presumption for me to say I *feel* for her; but I do, indeed I do."

"I am sure of it," Rose responded with great warmth, and then there was silence for a long time.

Rose broke it with a little trembling in the first word or two at her own audacity, but gathering courage as she went on: "I knew you did when you were here last summer; then I heard of her father's failure, and then it seemed more natural; and—now—I am very glad for your sake. I hope you will be very happy. I do, indeed."

Now, Dick was no fool, and when the strangeness of this speech caused him to look harder than ever into the glowing but demure little face by the side of him, he felt for the moment a great inclination not to say a word; for provokingly innocent as she looked, he did not believe she was at all so ignorant of the real state of things. Rose felt the moment's hesitation, and, poor little thing, got frightened at her own conjuring, which fright so changed the expression of her face that Dick's hesitation vanished, and he answered:

"Of course I know what you mean, Rose, although it is so strange. I do not think of such a thing—it would be very strange if I did. You know better, don't you, Rose?"

Rose looked up with a careless answer, but thought better of it, and said nothing.

"You never did really think it, did you, Rose?" he added, pursuing his advantage, and repeating it until there was no escape for Rose, who had to answer truthfully, "No." She having made this concession, he made one, and told her the story of his boyish days, and of the Christmas day when he first saw Mary Brandon. He had not felt very easy about Rose's opinion of much he had to tell her, and was greatly relieved when he saw all her assumed carelessness depart, and that she listened to him with earnest sympathy. He was so encouraged by the gentle, womanly interest she gave him that he did not stop with the history of his boyish days, but went on to narrate a later experience; very few words sufficed for this. When he told it, Rose understood very well why, if Mary Brandon were a queen upon her throne, she would be no more than friend or sister to him.

After that, there seemed no more to be said; for they finished the walk in the still winter twilight almost in silence.

That was in February, when Dick went down to Carlton to spend Washington's birthday, and it inaugurated a new era for Will. Rose had a sudden interest in the post-office, which was a long walk from the cottage, and, in rainy weather or on very busy days, was beyond her reach. I believe all her spare pennies went into Will's coffers about that time, and I am sure all her cakes and apples went into his possession; but, for all that, he was an ungrateful page, and wished "there wasn't no post-offices in the world," which opinion Will may alter when his own time comes.

This was in February, and it was now August, and Dick was going down for a week, one whole week in the country. Rose was at the gate as she had been a year ago; but she did not say "you are welcome," as she had said before. The children took him into favor when they found he had not come empty-handed, but had brought the books for Will, the doll for Trot, and just such toys for

the rest as were most desired; and though many times in their rambles Will did have his patience sorely tried by "Mr. Dick's everlasting lagging," he was, on the whole, admitted to be an acquisition. I believe, though, that Rose's bosom-friend, Clara Hays, who was always urged to be of every party, and sadly neglected when she got there, was the greatest sufferer; it is not every day you see lovers who are perfectly well-bred and considerate for everybody. My excuse for Rose and Dick is, that they only had a week, and a week is such a short time when one is very happy!

Dick's week was nearly at its end when his birthday, his twenty-first birthday came, and his good friends made a little rejoicing for him in their homely way. It was a very beautiful August day, and was celebrated like a holiday by all the family. Yet it was not exactly a cloudless day for Dick, though it was the first birthday of his that had ever received the slightest notice from any one, and ought to have made him radiantly happy. He had received a present made for him with her own hands, with no one could tell how many loving thoughts of him worked in it, from his own dear Rose. His little table was covered with the first keepsakes he had ever received from any one, and still he was not happy. Among the treasures on his little table there stood one—which reminds me that I should not have called the others the first—from the mother whose face he could not remember, and what might it not contain? Hitherto he had thought but little of the box of which Carl spoke so slightingly years ago; but now that the day of opening it had come, he grew really afraid of it. He remembered stories of vengeance bequeathed from the grave, of crimes to be expiated by the children of the perpetrators years afterward, of fearful confessions of sin and sorrow and wrong in countless forms ; and Dick, in the first glow of his first joyous days, did not know how he could bear even a mist upon the rising sun of his happiness.

" Not until the last thing to-night," he said finally, laying down the box and turning away from the table. " I will be happy to the last minute," and he went down to ask Rose to walk with him in the beautiful twilight after tea. It was earlier than he had thought when he went down, and Rose was reading in the shadow of the porch, or seeming to read, for a book was in her hand, and not, as he supposed, engaged in getting tea.

" I did not suppose I should find you here," said Dick.

" Shall I go away ?" she asked, looking up and smiling.

" Yes, do," he replied, sitting by her, " you know there's nothing would please me better." But for all he tried to be gay, Rose saw that the shadow she had observed over him all day was deeper than before.

" Dear friend," she said, softened and made earnest at once, " something troubles you to-day."

" Yes, dear Rose, I am troubled to-day in spite of all the kindness shown me. My little box troubles me ; I am afraid to open it."

" Then the best thing is to do it at once, is it not ? One only makes such things worse by thinking about them."

" I know it. No, I will not open it now ; I will have every moment of happiness I can first."

" What happiness can it take from you ? You will be yourself still, let there be in it what there will. Our happiness is our own."

" O Rose !"

" O Dick ! if we are good, are we not happy ? And nobody can make us bad against our will."

" But, Rose, this may tell me something that you—there is my fear, Rose, it may take you away from me."

" Oh ! no, Dick, dear Dick, how can anything take me away from you ? But even if it did, you know we always said, ' *If it were for the best.*' If it were not for the best, we would not wish it, would we, dear ? Yes, we could help wishing it ; when the good God saw it was not best, he would give us strength to bear it."

" I never could bear it," said Dick.

" Yes, you would ; but I am not afraid. One should not be afraid of one's own parents. Come, there is a long time before tea. We will go up the hill where no one will interrupt us, and where we shall be within call if we are wanted. Won't you get the box, Dick, and we will open it up there ? that is, if you want me with you."

" You make me brave, dear Rose. Perhaps, after all, it is nothing."

So he did as she advised ; and, seated a little back of the house, the only spot in which there could be five minutes' reading possible, he broke the seal, undid the wrapping, now yellow with age, while Rose spoke a word or two of courage, then turned her head a little away from him, and you may be sure prayed hard and fast for strength and grace for both to hear whatever of good or of evil was in store for them. Inside the wrapper Dick found a tiny key with which he eagerly unlocked the little mahogany box which was, perhaps, to make great revelations to him.

Then Rose drew still further away from him, and with a more earnest gaze watched the sun going down to the west ; for they were young, and many things that you and I would count the merest trifles, were of great importance to them ; neither thought of anything worse than of something which should separate them. Poor little Rose trembled lest he should find a will therein—as she had read in story-books—that would make him too rich and great for her to think of him ; and Dick, to whom her love for him had always seemed a wonder—so great was his reverence for her and his own feeling of unworthiness—trembled lest he should find some legacy of disgrace that would make it impossible for him ever to see Rose again. So in silence and with wordless but earnest prayers, they sat together in the softening August sunlight, with hearts beating heavily for fear it might be for the last time.

CHAPTER VII.

AFTER all, there was not much in the mysterious box. A square package, looking like a letter, folded in the old style, and just fitting in the box, lay uppermost ; upon the outside of which, in a clear, round hand, was written the name *Richard Heremore.* Before breaking the seal of this, Dick took out two paper boxes, in each of which was a miniature, painted on ivory ; he glanced at one, then with an expression of intense relief, not unmingled with something of awe, he, for the first time, turned to Rose.

"Look, Rose," he said, in a low voice.

"Do you think this is your mother?" she asked, in a voice even lower and more reverential than his, after a long long look ; for it was a young and beautiful face, with clear eyes that looked frankly at you, and that bore in every feature the unmistakable stamp of true womanliness. 'Do you think this is your mother?'"

"I cannot tell yet," said Dick ; "but as *this* is here, it's all right ; there's nothing more to dread now !"

But Rose did not answer. Her quick eyes had seen more than the character ; they had placed the original of that portrait in her proper social sphere, and that—the highest.

The other miniature was of a man somewhat older, though not more than twenty-five or thirty, if so much ; but it was a face of less character and less culture. Dick showed it to Rose, but neither made any comment upon it. Dick then broke the seal of the letter, and again Rose turned away her face. A few slips of paper fell out as he unfolded the package ; these he gathered up without looking at them, and then, calling Rose's name once more, he read in a low voice, from the yellow paper, his mother's letter :

"MY DEAR CHILD : I have put aside a few little things that have been treasures to me, and as I may not live to see the day when I can give them to you, I write a few lines with them, which possibly may come to your eyes some day. A healthy, ruddy little fellow you are, creeping around my feet and trying to climb up my dress as I write, and I am so weak a woman that I may hardly stoop to raise my darling to my lap. It is hard for me, seeing you so to, to write to you as a man ; and what kind of a man I have no way to judge. I fear I shall not live long enough to leave any impression of your mother's face upon you ; and what will become of you, my own dear child, in this terrible world after I am gone, I dare not think. You are so tender and good now that I cannot realize that you will change ; but you will have no one to guide you. You put your arms up to me, your brown, hard little arms, as if to beg me not to speak of this, and I will try to believe that God will save you through everything; so that when you read this, you will be one whom I would be proud to own if I lived.

"You are my greatest comfort, and such a comfort! It seems as if you knew everything, and could console for everything; and often I think that for you I shall in some way find strength to struggle on for a few years more. Dear child, I know not how much or how little to tell you. I would like to write volumes for you, that you might know me in the future days when no father, mother, or brother will be near to help you in your troubles. But I can only write a little.

"I have been married five years, and you are my oldest but not my only child. You have a sweet little sister asleep on the bed. I say the words to you aloud, and you creep on tiptoe to look at her, turning and smiling at me as you go. Even if she should live after I am gone, which I cannot wish for, I cannot tell whether you will be kept together; if not, I know you will care for her if it is possible, if only because your dead mother asks it. I cannot believe the wonderful child-love you have for her and me will be permitted to die out, or that your heart can ever grow hard, your heart so tender now. There! kiss the dimpled hand ever so softly and come away, for you must not wake the darling now. Will you love her always, let what may be her fate? Remember always, she had no mother to guide her. Your father I have not seen for two years, since Mamie was a few months old. I have since heard that he is dead. I know none of his relatives; for he brought me an entire stranger to New York three years ago, and seemed unwilling that I should make many acquaintances. I have no relatives whom I have ever seen, in the world, except my father, who lives, or did live, at Wiltshire, in Maine. I do not know if he is living or not, I have written to him again and again, but I have heard nothing from him. He would have come to me if he were alive, for he was always devoted to me. I could write you a hundred letters about his love and devotion; and now, if I could only let him know where I am, he would come to me wherever he might be. I have named you for him. He saw you once when you were a month old; he came and took me home for the summer; he loved you dearly, as he loved me, and was proud enough of you. If only I could put you and Mamie in his hands now, how contentedly I could die! For this I toiled and struggled from the day I saw your father last, until this poverty and sickness have killed all hope. Not all hope; for I think every step I hear—and I hear thousands passing by—that my father has come to me to save me, to take my darlings under his care, and to let me die on my own white bed in my own dear room at home.

"There, darling, there's no more to tell. Why should I tell more? You come of good blood, my child, of a brave, upright race. My child, my darling, put your arms tight, tight around mamma's neck, and promise for the man that you will be worthy of your name and race. Be good, be true, be honest. How I should blush in my grave, it seems to me, if child of mine, if these dear children, so pure and innocent, who cling to me now, covering me with kisses, should soil their white souls with falsehood, deceit, or dishonesty. God knows what I would say. Fatherless, motherless, I must leave my little ones; no earthly help, no comfort, nothing, only the one hope that will not leave me to my latest breath, that my father lives, will find me out, save me, and take care of you.

"It has been hard for me to write this poor, childish letter; one poor apple-woman—poor, yet not so poor as I—has been my only friend; to her I have talked for hours of you, and she has listened earnestly, and will do her utmost for you two. God will aid her, I know. I will not put any 'good-byes' on paper so little likely ever to be seen by your eyes; but I will kiss you a thousand times, my darling, while I take one last look at these portraits of your father and me, you leaning against my knee looking at them too. You, pure, unsullied child, shall cling to me, and answer, though you cannot understand, the promises to be good I ask of you to fulfil through all your life. Your mother,

"MARY HEREMORE BRANDON."

"*Brandon!*" repeated Rose and Dick together, when he read the signature. Then Dick read the slips of paper that had fallen out of the letter; they were all the same, notices of her marriage from different papers:

"MARRIED.—At the residence of the bride's father, on Wednesday, May 5th, Charles Brandon, of New-York, to Mary, only daughter of Dr. Richard Heremore, of Wiltshire, Maine."

Rose looked at Dick almost with terror in her face. Dick knew not how to answer her.

"It may not be the same," she said at last.

"The letter does not seem sure of his death," suggested Dick.

"But you have met him—would he not have noticed your name?"

"I should think so. But it was long ago, and perhaps he has known others of the name. Besides, Miss Brandon—O Rose! if she should be that sister!—Miss Brandon told me

her mother died long ago; she seemed so proudly to disclaim this Mrs. Brandon, whom I called her mother."

"How could she be with your father, if Mr. Brandon is that, and he not know any thing about you?"

"I cannot understand it. I will go to see him to-morrow."

"O Dick!"

"Yes, dear Rose, I must. I have only two days of vacation left, and I must know all before I go back."

"And then you will not be here for so long?"

"Yes, I will, Rose; I'll be here if I have to walk all night, see your windows, and go back before daylight! Yes, I will see you. I will not bear all the long separation as I did before, it is too much! Now, may I go to-morrow?"

"Yes, Dick, you must go. O Dick! what a mother she was! I can just see her, so weak she could not lift little you in her arms; and yet, I am sure, giving you a thousand caresses, and crying over you as she wrote that letter! If she could only see you now!"

"I know she does see me; but she does not see me as I ought to be, having had such a mother."

"She is proud of you if she sees you."

"See how patient she was, Rose! She says she is poorer than the poor apple-woman, and yet no complaint; and she was not used to trouble, I am sure, from her face."

"So sweet and grave as she is! Really, Richard, look! Upon my word, Miss Brandon has just such eyes! It *is* so! See! the same blue-gray eyes, so clear, deep, and looking at you so frankly and graciously; not with the frankness of a question asked; but—I can't describe it—but that calm, straightforward way Miss Mary has when she listens to you; always as if she would encourage you, too, to go on. Indeed, you must go to-morrow!"

"It is so strange, Rose. I feel my head almost turning. Have we time to read it over once more?"

"I fear not, for it is already quite late; but you will tell mamma and Aunt Clara about it, and Uncle Carl?"

"Oh! at once; as soon as I can. I shall think of nothing else until to-morrow. Rose, he must have treated her badly, or she would have given me his name instead of her father's."

"I think, perhaps she meant *Brandon* to be added."

"She does not say a word against him; but she does not praise him. I will make him tell me, himself, if he is the man. Do you think he is?"

"I am sure of it! And Miss Brandon is your sister; perhaps that is why she spoke to you that Christmas day, and why you have always been so attracted to her."

"How strange it is! Will she be sorry to have me for a brother, I wonder?"

"Sorry! She will be very proud of you."

"I wonder how I should speak to her. O Rose, Rose! do say something to steady me; I feel so strange, and as if I were talking so foolishly!"

"You are not talking foolishly, dear Dick; and if you were, there is only Rose to hear you, and shall you not talk as you please to her?"

"Thank God, my darling! this has not separated us."

"No, not yet."

"Not yet!"

"What will your new father and your grand sister think of me?"

"Well, Rose, wait till I ask them!"

"Perhaps a grandfather, too," said Rose.

"I love him already. If he should

be living, that would be something grand, wouldn't it? You may be sure she loved him."

"And you may be sure she never let him know until perhaps the very last, that she was in trouble. Women and children never tell their sorrows to those who are entitled to help them."

"Why, Rose?"

"Oh! I cannot tell you that! I only know it's so. Here we are at home. Have patience; for though to-morrow you will have the news, to night is all *I* have!"

"And no matter what happens, Rose," said Dick, as they lingered a moment outside the house, "you will trust me just the same?"

"Of course I will," Rose answered readily. A question and answer that have been given—and falsified—I wonder how many times since the world began; falsified, for even a woman's faith is not without limit; though Rose thought it was, as many had thought before her. "Of course I will; why should you ask, Dick?"

"I don't know; only that everything seems whirling around with me to-night, and the only thing that seems clear to me is that I must not lose you."

"It will be your own fault if you do," said Rose. "But you must not try me too much; for things might get whirling around with me, too, some day, and I should not know faith from want of pride; so be good."

"And if it is possible, I must come down at once and tell you how it all ends. If it could only be that I could have you close at hand to tell you all!"

"Indeed! I am glad," exclaimed Rose, who, much as she loved Dick, could not endure to think of the time when she should have to leave her home. "Come in, now. What will Uncle Carl say to all this, I wonder?"

Uncle Carl did not say much, when, the children having been sent out to play, the elders drew their chairs closer around the still standing tea-table, and listened intently to Dick's story. The others received it with many exclamations and much wiping of eyes; but the stolid German smoked his big pipe and looked, or tried to, as if he had known it all before.

"I'll know before this time to-morrow if it's the same," said Dick, when the reading was finished, and many conjectures had been put forward and discussed.

"It is the strangest thing ever was heard of," exclaimed Mrs. Alaine, "that he should meet you so often and not know who you were!"

"With your mother's name, too," added Mrs. Stoffs.

"Perhaps, after all, he is not so ignorant," suggested Dick. "It may be that it was on account of my name he made so much of me."

"I think he must be devoured with remorse," Mrs. Alaine said forcibly, "whenever he thinks of his beautiful wife."

"This Mrs. Brandon couldn't hold a cándle to her," added Mrs. Stoffs.

"I never saw her," said Dick.

"She was very pretty," explained Carl, speaking unexpectedly.

"Pretty!" cried Mrs. Stoffs, in great surprise.

"Pretty!" repeated Mrs. Alaine, with great contempt.

"Pretty!" echoed Rose, with great incredulity. "Why, Uncle Carl, she was a little doll-baby!"

"She was very pretty," persisted Carl.

"Well, indeed, if you call such a baby pretty, I give up!" said Mrs. Stoffs. "Why, Mr. Dick, she did

not look as if she could say boo to a goose, and yet she ruled the whole house; it was her extravagance that ruined the poor man."

"I think it was his own dishonesty," said Carl.

"O Uncle Carl!" remonstrated Rose, "right before Mr. Richard."

"We don't know yet that he has anything to do with 'Mr. Richard,' as you call him; but I'd say it, if need were, to the man's own face. His wife may have been a little, tyrannical, extravagant fool; but the more fool he for letting her take other men's money out of his purse."

"Indeed, Carl, that's a thing they'll never say of *you*," responded his wife, laughing. "But now come away, and let Mr. Dick get some rest, for I suppose he'll be off by daylight."

"I shall, indeed," said Dick.

"Well, good-night! Mr. Dick, you must not let these things keep you awake; if you find your family out, it may be the last time you will sleep under our roof."

"If I thought that, Mrs. Stoffs, I should seek them with a heavy heart; but nothing can make that so but death, can it?"

"Go to bed, good people," grumbled Carl; "all your noise makes my head ache."

He went up with Dick and had a long conversation with him, after the rest were asleep.

"Go find Dr. Heremore, of Wiltshire, unless there comes to be no doubt that he is gone away, or dead," were his parting words; "he is better worth seeking than any other. You will need money, and you shall owe me for this." And he gave him a few gold pieces which Mrs. Stoffs, in the sanctuary of her own room, had hurriedly and gladly brought out from countless rags, all tied up in an old stocking, at her liege lord's command, for this purpose.

"But, Mr. Stoffs, I have, I think, enough for this."

"Then do not spend mine, but take it with you for fear of accident. Good-night ; do not be fooled by anything Mr. Brandon may say—he's an artful one—but find out all you can about your grandfather ; remember that."

So Dick was left to pass a sleepless, fevered night, filled with the strangest fancies, and perplexed by a thousand fruitless conjectures. At the first glimmering of daylight he was up, and, after making a show of eating the substantial breakfast his kind friends had prepared for him, turned, without being able to say more than a word or two, to leave.

"Dood-by," said Trot, sliding down from her chair, with her bib on, and her face not over clean, to get his parting kiss, as well as to put in a reminder for his return. "What 'oo bing Trot from the 'tore ?"

"What do you want, Trot ?" asked Dick, lifting her up.

"Me wants putty tat," she answered with animation ; "dear 'ittle titten !"

Dick promised to do his best, shook hands silently all around, tried to laugh at the old shoe Minnie had ready to throw after him, at last heard the gate close behind him, and was alone on his way to the little yellow station-house.

"He'd better be alone," Rose had said when something had been said privately about accompanying him. "He has a great deal to think about, and he can do that best while he is walking in this fresh morning air."

"O mamma !" she said, when Mrs. Alaine stood beside her, after Dick had passed out of sight, "O mamma ! if Mr. Brandon should take it angrily !"

"You may be sure he will not," replied Mrs. Alaine, "he is so broken down, he will be very thankful to find a son like our Dick who will be worth so much to him. He is the most selfish man ever lived, Mr. Brandon is."

"Well, I wish it were over," sighed Rose, turning back to the house and the day's round of household duties.

CHAPTER VIII.

As might have been supposed, Dick was at Mr. Brandon's office long before that gentleman made his appearance down-town. It was a sultry morning, with occasional snatches of rain to make the gloomy streets more gloomy, and the depressing atmosphere more depressing. Mr. Brandon was sensitive to heat; he had no cool summer retreat to go to in the evenings, and return from with a rose in his button-hole in the mornings; and as, instead of being grateful for the many years in which he had enjoyed this luxury, he was disposed to consider himself decidedly ill-used in not having it still, so soon as he found Dick waiting for him, he began his repinings in the most querulous of all his tones:

"Pretty hard on a man who has had his own country-place, and been his own lord and master, to come down to this blistering old hole every morning, isn't it, Mr. Heremore? Well, well, some people have no feeling! There are those old nabobs who were hand and glove with me, mighty glad of a dinner with me, and where are they now? Do they come around with ' *How are you, Brandon ?*' and invitations to *their* dinners? Indeed not!"

"Mr. Brandon, I have come to talk to you about some business," began Dick, who had prepared a dozen introductions, all forgotten at the needed moment; then abruptly, "Mr. Brandon, did you ever hear my name, the name of *Heremore* before?"

It would be false to say that Mr. Brandon showed any emotion beyond that of natural surprise at the abruptness of the question; but it is safe to add that the surprise was very great, almost exaggerated. He replied, coolly enough, as he hung up his hat and sat down, wiping his face with his handkerchief: "Heremore? It is not, so to say, a common name; and I may or may not have heard it before. One who has been in the world so long as I have, Mr. Heremore, can hardly be expected to know what names he has or has not heard in the course of his life. I suppose you ask for some especial reason."

"I do," said Dick, a little staggered by the other's unembarrassed reply. "Did you not once know a gentleman in Wiltshire, called Dr. Heremore?"

"This is close questioning from a young man in your position to an old gentleman in mine, and I am slightly curious to know your object in asking before I reply."

"I believe you were married twice, Mr. Brandon, and that your first wife's maiden name was Heremore?"

"Well—and then?"

"And that she died while you were away, believing you were dead; and that she had two children," said Dick, who began to feel uneasy under the steady, smiling gaze of the other —"and that she had two children, a son and a daughter."

"Almost any one can tell you that my family consists of my first wife's daughter, and two sons by my second wife. But that's of no consequence. Two children, a son and a daughter, you were saying."

"Yes, two; although you may have been able to trace only one. She died in great poverty, did she not?"

" I decline answering any questions. I am highly flattered—charmed, indeed—at the interest you show in my family by these remarks; and I can only regret that my fortunes are now so low that I know of no way in which to prove my grateful appreciation of the manner in which you must have labored in order to know so much. In happier times, I might have secured you a place in the police department; but unfortunately, I am a ruined man, unable to assist any one at present."

At this speech, which was delivered in the most languid manner, and in a tone that was infinitely more insulting than the words, Dick was on the point of thrusting his mother's letter before the man's eyes, to show by what means he had obtained his knowledge; but the cool words, the indifferent manner, had a great effect upon our hero, who found it every moment more difficult to believe in the theory that from the first had seemed so likely to be the real one, and so he answered respectfully :

" I assure you, I mean no rudeness to you, Mr. Brandon; but I am engaged in the most serious business in the world, for me. I may be mistaken in you, and shall not know how to atone for the mistake, should I come to know it; but I hope you will be sure of my respectful intention, however I may err."

Mr. Brandon bowed, smiled, and played with his pen, as if the conversation were drawing to a close. Dick, heated and more embarrassed than ever, was obliged to recommence it.

" But was not your first wife's name Heremore? I beg you to answer me this one question, for all depends upon it."

" A very sufficient reason why I should not answer it. But as you seem to have something very interesting to disclose, perhaps we had better imagine that her name was Heremore before it was Brandon. Permit me to ask if, in that case, I am to own a relation in you? I certainly cannot make such a connection as advantageous as I could a year or so ago; but though I cannot prove the rich uncle of the romances, I shall be glad to know what scion of my wife's noble house I have the honor of addressing."

It seems easy to have answered "*your son*," but the words would not come. More and more the whole thing seemed a dream. What! a man so hardened that he could sit before his own son, whom by this time he must have known to be his son, and talk after this fashion of his dead wife's house! Impossible! If, then, he should tell his tale, and tell it to an unconcerned listener, what a sacrilege he would commit !

" A very near relative," Dick said at last. " I know that Dr. Heremore's daughter married a Charles Brandon about twenty-five years ago."

"Ah! I see! And you thought there was but one Charles Brandon in the world! You see I shall have to learn a lesson in politeness from you; for I could conceive that there should be room in this world even for two Richard Heremores."

Poor Dick was silenced for the moment. He knew he was taking up Mr. Brandon's time, and so the time of his employer. He walked up and down the little office and thought it all over. Certain passages in his mother's letter came to his mind. In this way, perhaps, had her appeals been sneered at in the olden times !

" Mr. Brandon," he said, standing in front of his tormentor, his whole appearance changed from that of the hesitating, embarrassed boy to the resolute, high-spirited man — " Mr. Brandon, there has been enough trifling. I insist upon knowing if you were or were not the husband of Miss Heremore. If you were not, it is a very simple thing to say so. There are plenty of ways by which I can make myself certain of the fact without your assistance; but out of consideration for you, I came to you first."

"I am deeply grateful," with a mock ceremonious bow.

"But if you persist in this way of treating me, I shall have to go elsewhere."

"And then?"

"Heaven knows I do not ask anything of you, beyond the information I came to seek. I wondered yesterday why she should have given me her father's name instead of mine; now I can understand it. I had doubts while first speaking to you, but now they are gone. I believe it is so. If you will not tell me as much as you know of Dr. Heremore, I can go to his old home for it. It would have saved me time and expense if you had answered my questions; but as you please."

He was clearly in earnest. Mr. Brandon saw it, and stopped him at the door.

"My wife's name *was* Heremore," he said very indifferently, "and her father has been dead these twenty years. You have your answer. Permit• me to ask what you mean to do about it?"

"Dr. Heremore was my grandfather," said Dick, coming back and sitting down.

"Ah! indeed!" politely; "he was a very excellent old gentleman in his way; it is much to be regretted that he and you should have been unable to make each other's acquaintance."

"When my mother—your first wife —died, you knew she left two children."

"One—a daughter. I think you have met her."

"There were two. I was the other."

"Are you quite sure?" asked Mr. Brandon in the same languid tones; but, for the first time, it seemed to Dick that they faltered.

"I am quite sure. You would know her writing."

"Possibly. It was a great while ago, and my eyes are not as good as they were."

"You would recognize her portrait?"

"If one I had seen before, I might."

"I should say this was a portrait of the first Mrs. Brandon," he said, taking that which Dick handed him and looking at it, not without some signs of embarrassment, "or of some one very like her. And this is not unlike her writing, as I remember it." Oh! you wish me to read this?"

Dick signed assent, watching him while he read. Whatever Mr. Brandon felt while reading that letter, he kept it all in his own heart.

"This is all?" he asked when he had read and deliberately refolded it. "It is all at present," answered Dick.

Then Mr. Brandon arose, handed the paper back, and said very quietly but deliberately:

"My first wife is dead and gone; her daughter lives with me, and, as long as I had the means, received every luxury she could desire. The past is past, and I do not wish it revived. Understand me. I do not wish it revived. I want to hear nothing more, not a word more, on this subject. If I were rich as I once was, I could understand why you should persist in this thing. I am not yet so poor that the law cannot protect me from any further persecution about the matter. Your mother, you say, named you for your grandfather, not for me. If you wish paternal advice—all that my poverty would enable me to give, however I were disposed—I advise you to go for it to her father, for whom she showed her judgment in naming you. Good morning."

"You cannot mean this! You must have known me as a child, and known my name before, long, long ago, and surely consented to it, or she would not have so named me. Of course, it was by some mistake the Brandon was dropped at first, not by her, but by those who took care of me when she died; she could never have meant such a thing; it was undoubtedly an accident. You cannot mean to end all here—that I am not to know, to see, my sister!"

"I tell you I wish to hear not another word of this matter; do you hear me? Have I not troubles enough now without your coming to bring up the hateful past? You shall not add to your sister's, whatever you may do to mine."

"I insist upon seeing her."

"You shall not. I positively forbid you to go near her. Now leave me! I have borne enough."

"But I cannot let the matter rest here; you know I cannot. The idea of it is absurd! If you do not wish me for a son, I have no desire to force myself upon you. I do not know why you should refuse to own me; I am not conscious of any cause I have given you to so dislike me."

"I don't dislike you, nor do I like you particularly; I have no ill-feeling against you, but I don't want this old matter dragged up. I am not strong enough to bear persecution now."

"But I do not want to persecute you. I want—"

"Well, what *do* you want?"

"I hardly know. I may have had an idea that you would welcome your oldest child after so many years of loss, however unworthy of you he might be. I may have thought that if you once were not all you should have been to one who, likely, was at one time very dear to you, it might be a satisfaction to you, even at this late day, to retrieve— "

"You thought wrong, and it is not worth while wasting words on the matter. I have got over all that, and don't want it revived. I can't put you out, but I beg you to go; or, if you persist in forcing your words upon me, pray choose some other subject."

"I will go, since you so heartily desire it; but I warn you that I will not give up seeing Miss—my sister."

"As you please. You will get as little satisfaction there, I fancy; though it may not be quite as annoying to her as to me."

"I shall try, at all events."

"Try. Go to her; say anything to her; make any arrangement with her you choose; take her away altogether. I don't care a button what you do, so you only leave me."

"I will leave you willingly, and am indeed sorry to have put you to so much pain."

"Not a word, I pray you," answered Mr. Brandon, now polite and smiling. "You have performed a disagreeable duty in the least disagreeable way you could, I do not doubt. All I ask is, never to hear it mentioned again."

Dick stayed for no more ceremony. Glad to be released from such an atmosphere of selfishness and cowardice, he hardly waited for the answer to his good-morning before turning to the street.

In less than an hour he was in the dreary room, with *boarding-house* stamped all over its walls, saying good-morning to a stately young lady, very pale and weary-looking, who kindly rose to receive him. The lit tle room was hot and close; there were no shutters to the windows; the shades were too narrow at the sides; besides being so unevenly put up that the eyes ached every time one turned toward them, and the gleaming light was almost worse than the heat.

"I have been trying for the dozenth time to straighten them," said Mary, drawing one down somewhat lower, "but it's of no use."

"Are they crooked?" asked Dick innocently.

"Well, yes, rather," answered Mary, smiling. "I think I never saw anything before that was so near the perfection of crooked."

"I have seen your father this morning," Dick began, taking a chair near the table.

"There is nothing the matter, I hope?" she questioned nervously.

"Nothing that any one but myself need mind. I made some discoveries about myself last evening that I would like to tell you. Have you time?"

"I have nothing to do. I shall be very glad if my attentive listening can do you any service." She moved her chair, in a quiet way, a little farther from his, and looked at him in some surprise. She saw he was very earnest, excited, and greatly embarrassed. She could not help seeing that his eyes were anxiously following her every movement, eagerly trying to read her face.

"I am afraid I shall shock you very much, and you are not well; I am sorry I came. I thought only of my own eagerness to see you; not, until this moment, of the pain I may cause you."

"Do not think of that. I do not think, Mr. Heremore, you are likely to say anything that should pain me. I think you too sensible—I mean, too gentlemanly for that."

"I hope you really mean that. I am sure I must seem very rude and

unpolished in your eyes; but I would have been far more so, had it not been for you."

"For me?"

"Yes." And he told her about the Christmas morning in Fourteenth Street.

"And you remembered that little thing all this time!" Mary exclaimed. "And you were once a newsboy!"

"Yes; I was once a great, stupid, ragged newsboy. I do not mean to deny, to conceal anything. I am so very sorry, for your sake; but I hope you will like me in spite of it all. If just those few words and that one smile did so much for me, what is there your influence may not do?"

"Mr. Heremore, I do not in the least understand you."

"I don't know where to begin; this has excited me so that I do not know what I am saying, and now I wish almost that you might never know it; there is such a difference between us that I cannot tell how to begin."

"Is it necessary that you should begin?" asked Mary. "You told me you wished to speak to me of some discoveries you had made in regard to yourself. To anything about yourself I will listen with interest; but I do not care to have anything said about myself; there can be no connection between the two subjects that I can see; so pray do not waste words on so poor a subject as myself; but tell me the discovery, if you please."

"But it concerns you as much as it does me. Do you know much about your own mother? She died, you told me, long ago."

"I know very little about her. I presume her death was a great grief to papa; for he has never permitted a word to be said about her, and anything that pains papa in that way is never alluded to. The little I do know I have learned from my old nurse."

"You do not remember her?"

"Not in the least; she died when I was a mere baby."

"Did you ever see her portrait, or any of her writing, or hear her maiden name?"

"No, to all your questions. Does papa know you are here, this morning?"

"Yes; I went to him at once. At first he was very determined I should not see you; but in the end, he seemed glad to get me silenced at any price, and I was so anxious to see you that I did not wait for very cordial permission."

"You did not talk to papa about my mother?"

"Yes, that is what I went for."

"How did you dare to do it? Was he not very angry? I am sure you know something about mamma."

"Yes, I do. I have her portrait; this is it."

"Her portrait! My mamma's portrait! O what a beautiful face! Is this really my mamma? Did papa see it? Did he recognize it?"

"I showed it to him. He did not deny it was hers."

"*Deny it was hers!* What in the world do you mean, Mr. Heremore? Where did you get it?"

Then Dick, in the best way he could, told the whole story of the box, and gave her the letter to read. When Mary came to the part which said, "*Will you love your sister always, let what may be her fate? Remember, always, she had no mother to guide her,*" she turned her eyes, full of tears, to Dick, saying no words.

"She did not know that it would be the other way," Dick replied to her look, his own eyes hardly dry. "She would have begged for me if she had known that—" farther than this he could not get. Mary put

her hands in his, and said earnestly:

"No need for that; her pleading comes just as it should. Will you really be my brother—all wearied, sick, and worn-out as I am? Oh! if this had only come two years ago, I could have been something to you!"

But Dick could not answer a word. He could only keep his eyes upon her face; afraid, as it seemed, that it would suddenly prove all a dream.

But the day wore on and it did not prove less real. The heat and the glaring light were forgotten, or not heeded, while the two sat together and talked of this strange story, and tried to fill up the outlines of their mother's history.

"I feel as if our grandpapa were living, or, if not living, there must be somebody who knows something about him," she said.

"I think I ought to go and see. Mr. Stoffs was very particular in urging that."

"I think so; even if you learned nothing, it would be a good thing for you just to have tried."

"I know I can get permission to stay away for a few days longer; there's nothing doing at this season. Would it take long?"

"I don't know much about it; not more than two days each way, I should think. There is a steamer, too, that goes to Portland, and you can find out if Wiltshire is near there. The steamer trip would be splendid at this season. Are you a good sailor?"

"I don't know. You have got a great ignoramus for a brother. I have never been half a day's journey from New York in my life."

"Is that so? Well, you must go to Portland. How you will enjoy the strong, bracing sea-breezes; they make one feel a new life!"

Then suddenly Dick's face grew very red, but bright, and he said eagerly: "Would you trust me—I mean could your father be persuaded—would you be afraid to go with me?"

"Oh! I wish I could! I would enjoy it as I never did a journey before! Just to see the sea again, and with a brother! I can't tell you how I have all my life envied girls with great, grown-up brothers. Nobody else is ever like a brother. Fred and Joe are younger than I, and have been away so much that they never seemed like brothers. A journey with you on such a quest would be something never to be forgotten."

"It doesn't seem as if such a good thing could come to pass," answered Dick. "I don't know anything about travelling; you would have to train me; but if you will bear with me now, I will try hard to learn. Do you think your father would listen to the idea?"

"No; he would not listen to ten words about it. He hates to be troubled; he would never forgive me if I went into explanations about an affair that did not please him; but if I say, 'Papa, I am going away for a couple of weeks to New England, unless you want me for something,' he will know where I am going, what for, and will not mind, so he is not made to talk about it; that is his way."

"Will you really go, then, with me? You know I shall not know how to treat you gallantly, like your grand beaux."

"Ah! don't put on airs, Mr. Dick; you were not so very humble before you knew our relationship. Remember, I have known you long."

"I wonder what you thought of me."

"I thought a great deal of good of you; so did papa, so does Mr. Ames."

"You know Mr. Ames?"

"Ah! very well indeed; he comes to see us every New Year's day; he actually found us out this year, and I got to liking him more than ever; he has come quite often since, and we have talked of you; he says you are a good boy. I am going to be *grande dame* to-day, and have lunch brought up for us two, unless Madame the landlady is shocked."

"Does that mean I have staid too long?"

"No, indeed. Mrs. Grundy never interferes with people with clear consciences, at least in civilized communities; in provincial cities, and country towns she will not let you turn around except as she pleases; that's the difference. There are no bells in this establishment, or, if there are, nobody ever knew one to be answered, so I will start on a raid and see what I can discover."

In course of time she returned with a servant, who cleared the little rickety table, and then disappeared, returning at the end of half an hour with a very light lunch for two; but that was not her fault, poor thing!

Then hour after hour passed and still Dick could not leave her; he had gone out and bought a guide-book, which required them to go all over the route again, and there was so much of the past life of each to be told and wondered at, that it was late in the afternoon and Mr. Brandon's hand was on the door before Dick had thought of leaving. Of course he must remain to see Mr. Brandon, who, however, did not seem any too glad to see him. Nothing was said in regard to the matter which had been all day under discussion. Mr. Brandon talked of the news of the day, of the weather, and the last book he had read, accompanied him to the door, and shook hands with him quite cordially, to the surprise of the landlady, who was peeping over the banisters in expectation of high words between them. Mr. Brandon even went so far as to speak of him as a very near relative, as several of the boarders distinctly heard. Mr. Brandon hated to be talked to on disagreeable subjects, but he knew the world's ways all the same.

"Come very early to-morrow morning," Mary said in a low voice as they parted, "and I will let you know if I can go."

Dick did not forget this parting charge, and early the next morning had the happiness of hearing that her father had consented to let her go.

"Papa isn't as indifferent as he seems," she said. "When it is all fixed and settled, he will treat you just as he does the rest of us, only he hates a scene and explanations. I suppose he *was* unkind to poor mamma, and now hates to say a word about it; but you may be sure he feels it. And now you must take everything for granted, come and go just as if you had always been at home with us, and he will take it so."

"But what will people say?"

"Why, we will tell the truth, only as simply as possible—as if it were an everyday affair—that papa's first wife died while he was away from home, and that when he returned from Paris, where he says he was then, the people told him you were dead too. I don't know why that old woman should have told such a story."

"Nor I, but perhaps, poor, ignorant soul, she thought the boy was better under her charge than given over to a 'Protestant,' who had acted so like a heathen to the child's mother; but good as was her motive, and perhaps her judgment, I hope she did not really tell a lie about it, so peace to her soul. Who knows how much Dick owes to her pious prayers?"

A very proud and happy man was Dick in these days, when he journeyed to Maine with his newly-found sister. It is true that the change in Mr. Brandon's circumstances did not enable Mary to have a new travelling suit for the occasion, and that she was obliged to wear a last year's dress; but last year's dress was a very elegant one, and almost "as good as new;" for Mary, fine lady that she was, had the taste and grace of her station, and deft fingers, quick and willing servants of her will, that would do honor to any station; so her dress was all *à la mode*, and Dick had reason to be proud of escorting her. She had, however, something more than her dress of which to be proud, or Dick would not have been so grateful for finding her his sister; she had a kind heart, which enabled her always to answer readily all who addressed her, to make her constantly cheerful with Dick, and to keep everything smooth for the inexperienced traveller, who otherwise would have suffered many mortifications; she had, too, a womanly dignity, a sense of what was due to and from her, not as Miss Brandon, but as a woman, which secured her from any incivility and made her always gentle and considerate to every one. Dick could never enough delight in the quiet, composed way in which she received attentions which she never by a look suggested; for the gentle firmness, the self-possession, the quiet composure, the perfect courtesy of a refined and cultivated woman were new things to him; and to say he loved the very ground she walked on would be only a mild way of expressing the feeling of his heart toward her.

Added to all this, giving to everything else a greater charm, Mary's mind was always alive; she had been thoroughly educated, and had mingled all her life with intelligent and often intellectual people, whose influence had enabled her to seek at the proper fountains for entertainment and instruction. Whatever passed before her eyes, she saw; and whatever she saw, she thought about. In her turn, Mary already dearly loved her brother; although two years younger than he, she was, as generally happens at their age, much more mature, and she could see, as if with more experienced eyes, what a true, honest heart, what thorough desire to do right, what patience and what spirit, too, there was in him, and again and again said to herself, " What would he not have been under other circumstances !" But she forgot, when saying that, that God knows how to suit the circumstances to the character, and that Dick, not having neglected his opportunities, had put his talent out to as great interest as he could under other influences. There was much that had to be broadened in his mind, great worlds of art and literature for him to enter;

but there was time enough for that yet; he had a character formed to truth and earnestness, and had proved himself patient and energetic at the proper times. It now was time for new and refining influences to be brought to bear; it was time for gentleness and courtesy to teach him the value of pleasant manners and self-restraint; for the conversation of cultivated people to teach him the value of intelligent thoughts and suitable words in which to clothe them; for the knowledge of other lives and other aims to teach him the value or the mistake of his own. These things were unconsciously becoming clearer to him every day that he was with his sister, who, I need hardly say, never lectured, sermonized, or put essays into quotation marks, but whose conversation was simple, refined, and intelligent, whatever was its subject. Others greater than Mary would come after her when her work was done, we may be sure; but at the present time Dick was not in a state to be benefited by such.

CHAPTER IX.

WHEN they arrived at the Wilt-shire depot, Dick and Mary were still undecided what step to take next; for neither of them favored the idea of asking at once for Dr. Here-more, feeling certain that the proba-bilities of his being alive would van-ish the moment that such an inquiry was proposed.

It was a nice enough town, with fine breezes from the sea blowing through its streets, and a quaint look about the houses that made Dick, at least, feel as if they were in a foreign land. Dick and Mary stood on the depot platform together, undecided still.

"Let us walk a little way up and see what we can see," Mary pro-posed.

All that they found at first were a few lumber-wagons, a market-wagon, and now and then a group of boys playing; but finally they came upon a store, at the door of which several long-limbed countrymen were talking and chewing tobacco. I should have said "chewing and talking;" for the chewing was much more vigorously prosecuted than the talking. The presence of the strangers, one a lady in a plain but very stylish dress, attracted some attention; the men surveyed them in a leisurely, undaz-zled way, hardly making room for them to pass; for, having seen the sign POST-OFFICE in the window of this store, Dick and Mary concluded to enter and make inquiries. The afternoon sun streamed in upon the floor; the flies buzzed at the win-dows; and a man, with his hat on and his chair tilted back, was at the back of the store. He made no sign of changing his position when he first saw the strangers, not because Mr. Wilkes was any less well disposed toward "the ladies" than a city mer-chant would be, but because country people fancy it is more dignified to show indifference than politeness. In time, however, he tilted down his chair, freed his great mouth from its load of tobacco, and lounged up to the counter where Mary and Dick were standing.

"I want to ask you a question," Dick answered to the storekeeper's look; "I suppose you know this town pretty well?" Dick was so afraid of the answer that he did not know how to put a direct question in regard to Dr. Heremore.

"Rather," was the laconic reply, with no change of the speaker's coun-tenance.

"Do you know if a Dr. Heremore lived here once, twenty-five years or so ago?"

"I wasn't here in them days," for Mr. Wilkes was a young man who did not care to be old.

"I did not suppose you did know, of your own knowledge; I thought you might have heard."

"I suppose you have come to see him?"

"Or to hear of him," added Dick

"Come from Boston or York, I suppose?"

"From New York," answered Dick; "can you tell us who is likely to give us information?"

"About the old doctor?" asked

Mr. Wilkes in the same impassive manner.

"Yes," said Dick, rather impatiently.

"I suppose you are relations o' his ?"

"We came to get information, not to give it," Dick replied in a quiet tone but inwardly vexed.

"Well," answered the storekeeper, not in the least abashed by this rebuke, "there's an old fellow lives up yonder, who knows pretty much everything's been done here for the last forty years; you'd better go to him; if any one knows, he does. Better not be too techy with *him*, I can tell you, if you want to find out anything; people as wants to take must give too, you know. That there road will take you straight to the house; white house, first on the left after you come to the meeting-house."

"Thank you; and the name ?"

"Well, folks usually calls him 'The Governor' round here; you, being strangers, can call him what you please."

"Will he like a stranger's calling ?"

"Oh! tel him I sent you—Ben Wilkes—and you are all right."

"Thank you!" Mary and Dick replied and turned away. "Ben Wilkes," who, during this conversation, had seated himself on the counter, the better to show his ease in the strangers' society, which—Mary's especially—secretly impressed him very much, looked leisurely after them as they passed out of the store; then took out some fresh tobacco, and returned to his chair.

"I don't like to go," said Mary, "it may be some joke upon us."

"I am afraid it is," answered Dick; "but, after all, what can happen that we need mind ? If it is a gentleman to whom he has sent us, no matter how angry he is, he will see that you

are a lady, and you will know how to explain it; if he has sent us to one who is not, I guess I shall be able to reply to him."

Their walk was a very long one, but the meeting-house at last came in sight, and next it, though there was a goodly space between, was a large white house, irregular and rambling, with very nicely kept shrubbery around.

Dick opened the gate with a hand that was a little nervous; but Mary whispered as their feet crunched the neatly bordered gravel walk to the low porch, "It is all right, I am sure; there is an old gentleman by the window."

"Will you be spokesman this time ?" asked Dick.

Mary nodded, and as the path was narrow and they could not well walk side by side, she was in front, so that naturally she would be the first to meet the old gentleman.

A very fine old gentleman he was; a large man with a fine head, and, as his first words proved, a remarkably full, sweet voice. Seeing a lady coming toward him, he rose at once from his arm-chair, closed his book and advanced a step or two to greet her. Mary was one of those women toward whom courteous men are most courteous from the first glance; and this old gentleman, who moved toward her with all the grace and ease of a vigorous young man, was one of those men to whom gentle women are gentler, from the first, than to others.

"Good-evening," he said, as Mary looked up to him with a smile at at once pleasant and deferential. "Good-evening," and as she did not say more than these words, the gentleman continued, "I will not say, 'Come in,' for it is too pleasant out of doors for that; but let me give you chairs."

"Thank you, sir, we are strangers, but, we hope, not intruders," she replied.

"Certainly not," he answered. "It is a great pleasure for me to receive my old friends, and a pleasure to me to make new ones; and strangers, even if they remain strangers, bring with them great interest to the quiet lives of us old people." This he said in a tone not in the least formal, or as if " making a speech," and still looking more at Mary than at her brother. They were not yet seated, and no expression but that of kindly courtesy crossed his face while looking into the sweet, gravely smiling one before him; his tones were hardly altered when he added, "I have waited for you these many long years, Mary; but I never doubted you would come at last. You must not play tricks upon my old heart; it has suffered too much to be able to sustain its part as it did in old times."

Mary drew back a step, at this strange address, but she could not withdraw her eyes from his, as in tender, gentle tones he spoke the last words. Dick stood closer to her, but said nothing.

"Indeed, you mistake," Mary said, with great earnestness; "I have told you the truth, I am really a stranger, although you have called me by my name, Mary. I am Mary Brandon, and this—"

"Is your husband. Well, Mary, are you not my daughter? If you were changed, why come to see me? I heard you were changed. I spent four years in Paris and Rome, following up the trace given me in New York, and then I came back disappointed but not despairing. 'Mary will not die without sending for me or coming to me,' I said; and I have taken care always to be ready for

you. I never thought you could come to me with coldness or indifference. I was prepared for almost anything—to see you poor and broken-hearted; no shame, no sin, no sorrow that would part us. I did not think to see you come back beautiful, happy, rich," a glance at her dress, "and without a word of greeting."

"Dr. Heremore?" said Dick, not because he believed or thought it, but because the words came forced by some inward power greater than his knowledge.

"Well, Charles," answered the old gentleman, sadly but composedly, turning at this name, "can you explain it?"

And then Mary understood it all. The years were nothing to him who had waited for his child's return. She was in his arms before Dick had recovered from his first bewilderment, now, by this act of hers, trebly increased.

"Ah my child! if I spoke severely, it was only because I could not bear the waiting. I knew your jokes of old, darling; but when one has waited so long for the dear face one loves, the last moments seem longer than all the years. I will ask no questions. I see you two are together, and it is all right. You can tell me all at your leisure. Now, Mary, I must kill the fatted calf. Even though you and Charles have not returned as prodigals," he added as if he would not, even in play, risk hurting them.

"Not yet, please," said Mary. "Let us have it all to ourselves for a few minutes." And they seated themselves on the sunny porch, the old gentleman's delight now beginning to show itself in the nervous way he moved his hands, and his disjointed sentences. Mary took off her hat at once, and threw it, with rather more of gayety than was quite natural to her, upon one of the short branches, looking like pegs, which had been left in the pillars of the porch.

"You haven't forgotten the old ways—eh, Mary?" Dr. Heremore asked, as he saw the movement. "I remember well how proud you were the day you first found you could reach that very peg, and you are as much a child as you were that day, is she not, Charles?"

"Pretty nearly," answered Dick, who could not fulfil his part with Mary's readiness.

"How deliciously fresh everything looks!" exclaimed Mary.

"You should have seen it in June. I never saw the roses thicker. O pet, how I did wish for you, then! The time of roses was always your time."

"And I love them as much as ever!" exclaimed Mary, telling the truth of herself. "Next year, if I am alive, I will be here with them; we will have jolly times looking after them. I have learned a great deal about flowers lately, but I shall never love roses like yours." This indeed, Mary felt to be true.

"Flora has had to be replaced," said her grandfather observing her eyes resting on a statue in the garden in front. "I will show you the alterations I have made, and a few are improvements. But you must have something to eat now. I cannot let you go a minute longer. You came up by the boat, I presume?"

"Yes, and had a hearty dinner," Mary answered, having a dread of a servant's entering, and getting things all wrong again, "To eat now will only spoil our appetite for tea, and I want you to see what an appetite I have."

"Perhaps you are too tired to go around the garden?"

"Tired! No, indeed."

"I am afraid it will not interest you much, Charles," the old gentleman said to Dick. "You never did care much about the little place."

"Oh! I assure you, I would be delighted to see it all," Dick answered, eagerly; but Mary had noticed the constraint in her grandfather's voice whenever he addressed the supposed Charles, and said quickly:

"Oh! we don't want you, you don't know a rose from a sunflower; pick up a book and read till we come back."

"This way, dear; have you forgotten?" Dr. Heremore said, looking at her in a perplexed manner as naturally enough she turned away from the house. "This way, dear, you lose the whole effect if you go around. Come through the house. There, dear old Mary," he added, smilingly handing her a glass of wine which he poured out from a decanter on the sideboard in the dining-room. "Drink to 'The Elms' and no more jokes upon old hearts."

"To our happy meeting and no more parting," added Mary, drinking her wine with him. He poured out a glass for Dick, or Charles, as he thought him, and, rather formally, carried it to him. It was very clear that "Charles" was no favorite.

All through the trim garden, and then through the whole house, Mary followed her grandfather, her heart, as it may be believed, full of love for the tender father of her lost mother. She stood in the room which that mother had occupied, and could not speak a word as she gazed reverently around. It was a thorough New England bedroom—a high mahogany bedstead, a long narrow looking-glass with a landscape painted on the upper part, in a gilt frame, a great chintz-covered arm-chair by the bed, a round mahogany table, with a red cover and a Bible, a stiff, long-legged washstand in the corner, a prim chest of drawers under the looking-glass between the windows, composed the furniture of the room; a badly painted picture of a young girl in the dress of a shepherdess, and a pair of vases on the mantel, were the only ornaments; a crimson carpet and white window-curtains were plainly of a later date than the furniture.

"I have had to alter some things," said Dr. Heremore, as they came out of the room, "but I got them as much like the old ones as I could, that you might feel at home here. Your baggage should be here by this time, should it not? How did you send it?"

"We left it at the station," answered Mary. "You know we were not sure—not certain sure that we should find you."

"I suppose not, I suppose not. These have been long years, Mary, but they have not changed us, after all. But I must send for your trunks. I suppose Charles has the checks."

"We brought but very little with us," Mary said, considerably embarrassed, and, seeing the change in his countenance, she hastened to add, "But now that it is all right and we have found the way, we will stay with you until you turn us out; at least, I will."

"Then you will send for more things, and how about the children?" with the same perplexed look at her. Mary knew not what to say. Was it not better to tell him the real truth at once? How could she go on with this deception, as innocent as any deception can be, and yet how break down his joy in its very midst? Silently she stood beside him, at a hall window, looking upon the prospect he had pointed out to her, considering what answer to make him. He,

too, was silent; for a long time the two stood there, and then it was the doctor who spoke first.

"Mary, your children must be men and women now. I had forgotten how long it was; but I remember you were here last the year the meeting-house over there was put up, and I just was thinking that was over twenty years ago. Richard was a few months old, then. Mary, don't deceive me. Tell me the truth."

Mary turned sadly toward him, and laid her hands in his.

"*Grandpapa*, I will," was all she said.

It was a great blow to him, but something had been hovering confusedly before his mind ever since they came out together, and now it was clear. He turned abruptly away from her at the first shock, then came to her more kindly than ever. "Forgive me, dear," he apologized with mournful courtesy; "I did not mean to be rude, but it is a great shock. You are very like her, very like her, but I should have known at once that those years could not have left her a girl like you. I will not ask more—your mother—"

"My *father* is living," Mary said, with tears streaming down her face, as he stopped, "and that is my brother down-stairs."

"Is he your only brother? have you sisters?" he asked.

"We are your only grandchildren," she answered; and he understood that his child was dead, and another woman had filled her place.

"You are a noble girl," he said, with lingering tenderness in every word. "We will go down now. I will greet Richard, and then, dear, you will let me be alone for a little while. I shall have to send for your things, you know."

"If it is any trouble—" began Mary.

"None, I will see about it at once."

They went down, and he greeted Richard, then went away slowly, still begging them to excuse him for the inattention to them. Soon after, a barefooted boy of twelve or fourteen or so went whistling down the road past the house, staring at them as he went by; an hour after, the same boy returned with their bags; these were taken up-stairs by a thin, severe-looking, very neatly-dressed woman, who quickly and with only a word or two showed them their rooms, and told them that, as soon as they were dressed, tea would be ready.

Mary dressed in her mother's room with a sense of that mother's spirit around her. She fortunately had brought a dress with her, so that she was able to make a slight change. Then slowly and with great reverence she went down the stairs, meeting Dick in the hall, to whom she whispered, "O Dick! how I love him; but I am afraid it will kill him; the purpose for which he has lived these twenty years is taken from him. Can we give him another?"

"It may be that you can," Dick replied, looking tenderly into her sweet face, all aglow with the bright soul-life which had been kindled so actively in the last hours. "If you can, Mary, try it; do not think of anything else; stay with him, do anything you think right and good for him; he deserves more from us than—" Dick hesitated, not willing to speak unkindly of Mr. Brandon, who certainly had been a father to Mary—"than any other."

"I will try," Mary answered speaking quickly and in a low voice. "If it seems best that I should stay a little while, you will explain to papa? But perhaps, after all, it will be you who will be able to replace her best."

"We shall see," Dick said, and

then Dr. Heremore was seen coming toward them, with less lightness in his step than they had noticed before; otherwise there was but little change, except that his voice was more mournfully tender than at first.

"It is a long time since I saw that place filled," he said, arranging a chair for Mary before the tea-urn. "And it is very sweet to me to see your bright young face before me; a long time since I have had so strong an arm to help me," he added, as Dick eagerly offered him some little assistance, "and I am very grateful for it."

There were no explanations that night; he talked to Dick and Mary as to very dear and honored guests, of everything likely to interest them, and was won by their eager attention to tell them many little things about his house and grounds, which were his evident pride and pleasure, all in the same subdued, courteous way that had attracted them from the first. There seemed, in the beginning, a far greater sympathy between Mary and him than he had with Dick, which was the reason, undoubtedly, why he devoted his attention more especially to his grandson, whose modest replies, given with a heightened color and an evident desire to please, were very winningly made.

"I have two noble grandchildren," he said to them as they stood up to say good-night. "My daughter, short as her life was, did not come into the world for a small purpose; she did not live for little good; she has sent me two to love and esteem, and to win some love from them, I trust —yes, I *believe.*"

The next day, he set apart a time and then there were full explanations from both sides. Dick's story we know already. Dr. Heremore's can be told in a few words. His daughter married, when very young and on a short acquaintance, a gentleman who was spending his summer holidays in the vicinity of Wiltshire, and, immediately upon her marriage, had gone to N—— to reside; they remained there until Richard was a month old, when his daughter made him a long—her last—visit; from there to New York, whence a letter or two was all that came for some little time; then one written evidently in great depression of spirits. Dr Heremore, on receipt of this, went at once to New York to see her, only to hear that she had gone with her husband to Europe. A little further inquiry proved to his satisfaction that Mr. Brandon was in the South, and that his wife was not with him; his letters were unanswered, and his alarm was every day greater and more painful. At last, he followed a lady—described to be somewhat of his daughter's appearance, bearing the same name, who had joined a theatrical company, though of this last he was not aware for a long time—to Europe. As he had said before, he came back disappointed but not despairing, to hear of Mr. Brandon's death—the same false report, perhaps intentionally circulated, which his daughter had heard. Her letters to him, of which she spoke in her letter to Dick, were lost while he was away searching for her. He had not been rich, then; but coming home, he had resumed his practice, and lived patiently awaiting news of her, energetically laboring to secure a small fortune for her should she ever come to claim it. This little fortune he would divide at once, he said, between her two children; for " what," he argued with them, " what is the use of hoarding it to give to you later when, I trust, you will not need it half as much? A few hundreds in early youth are often worth as many thousands in after-years."

"That will do for Dick," Mary conceded, "because it *would* be a great thing for him to have a little start just now; and besides, there's Somebody Else for *him* to think of; but I will take my share in staying here. You will not drive me away?"

"Your father?"

"Papa would—it's a shabby thing to say—be very willing to have me away, in his present circumstances. He has been wishing and wishing for Fred and Joe constantly ever since they went; but for me—he thinks girls are a sort of nuisance, I know he does; and will be very grateful to you if you divide the burden with him."

"But if—just as I got used to loving you, there should be another Somebody Else besides Dick's? How about this out of civilization place, then?"

Mary grew very red indeed, but answered readily, " Oh! that's a long way off; and besides, he may not think this out of civilization, you know."

So it was settled. One of the clerks who had been from early boyhood in Ames and Narden's store had been long intending to start out on his own account, and Dick was very sure that they could fulfill their olden dream of partnership, now that Dr. Heremore was willing to give them a start. Dick went down to New York the day after this conversation, and there was a long talk between the members of the firm, and the two clerks, which culminated in a dinner and the agreement that all was to go on as it had been going, until the first of May, when there would be a new bookseller's firm in the New York Directory, to wit, BARNES AND HEREMORE.

After a brief conversation with Mr. Brandon, Dick hurried to Carlton, and was not long making his way to the shadowy lane. To her honor and glory be it said, Trot was the first to see him; and without waiting for a greeting, not even for the expected "dear 'ittle Titten," ran with all speed into the house, crying, "Thishter! Thishter! Mr. Dit itli toming!" at the top of her voice; and Rose, all blushing at being caught "just as she was," had no time to utter a word before "Mr. Dit," was beside her. There was great rejoicing over Dick; the children pulled him in every direction, to show him some new thing he had not yet seen, until he began to tell the story of his adventures, when they stood around in perfect silence. Mrs. Alaine and Mrs. Stoffs wiped their eyes between their smiles and their exclamations of delight; old Carl once held his pipe in one hand and forgot to fill it for nearly a minute, so absorbed was he; but Rose alone did not say a word of congratulation when Dick's good fortune and his brightened future were announced. I even think she had a good cry about it, after a little talk with Dick by herself, that evening, so hard it is to leave one's home.

"There's not a thing to wait for now," Dick had said, with beaming eyes; and poor Rose's ideas of "youth," and "time to get ready," and all that sort of remark, were put aside without the least consideration. "We will have a little house of our own," Dick continued, "we will not go to boarding, as some people do; you are too good a housekeeper for *that*, I am sure; and as New York has no houses for young people of moderate means, we will have a home of our own near the city. Shall we not, Rose?"

Dick was a very busy young man for a couple of months after this. One thing Dr. Heremore did that seemed hard, but not so very unnatural, and of whi· 'i no one who has never felt a wrong to some one dearly loved should judge. He begged that he might never see Mr. Brandon, nor be asked to hold any communication with him. He gave Mary a certain sum of money, which he wished her to use for her father and step-brothers; but beyond that, he left Mr. Brandon to help himself.

After attending to all his grandfather's requests and suggestions, Dick, as he had been invited to do, returned to Wiltshire to give an account of his management, and to take up some things for Mary's use. He was on his way to the boat when he suddenly started and exclaimed, "Mr. Irving!" for no less a person than his "Sir Launcelot" was standing beside him. Mr. Irving, not recognizing him, bowed slightly and passed on, and Dick began to be relieved that Mary was so far away; perhaps, after all, it was a great deal better.

But another surprise was in store for Dick, who—an inexperienced traveller even yet, and always in advance of time—had gone on and waited long before the boat prepared to leave; for at the last moment a carriage drove rapidly to the pier, and a gentleman sprang from it in time to catch the boat. It was "Sir Launcelot."

"Mr. Heremore, I believe," he said to Dick, when they met somewhat later on the boat. "I called on Mr. Brandon to-day, just after you met me, to pay my respects to him on my return from Europe. I found him in a different business from that in which I had left him, and very reserved. I asked after the ladies of his family, who, he told me, were at your grandfather's and his father-in-law's, in Maine, adding that there was a long story, which I had better come to you to hear, if you had not already left. I have business in Maine, so followed you up."

So they made acquaintance, and the new-found relationship with Mary was explained, as also the reverses Mr. Brandon had met with.

"His wife dead, too, you tell me!

How shocked he must have been at my questions of her! How like him not to give me a hint!" exclaimed Mr. Irving.

The new friendship progressed well, as it often will between two gentlemen, one of whom is in love with the other's sister, although there was a wide difference between their characters. Mr. Irving was many years older than Dick, as his finished manners and his manly presence attested, without the aid of a few gray hairs on his temples, not visible, and half a dozen or so in his heavy moustache, very visible and adding much to his good looks, in the eyes of most of the ladies who saw him. It seemed as natural to Dick that this travelled man, so polished, so princely as he was, should be just the one to please his high-bred sister, and he captivated by her, as that he himself should belong to Rose and she to him. Consequently he did not put on any of the airs in which brothers, especially when they are very young, delight to appear before their sister's admirers.

Dick had even tact enough, when they reached Dr. Heremore's house —for, of course, Mr. Irving's "business in Maine" did not interfere with his accompanying Dick to Wiltshire— to be very busy with the carriage and trunks, while Mr. Irving opened the little gate, and announced himself to the young lady on the porch. When Dick, a few minutes after, greeted his sister, he had no need, though Mary's color did not come as readily as Rose's, to say with Sir Lavaine:

" For fear our people call you lily maid,
   In earnest, let me bring your color back."

I think that Dr. Heremore, though the very soul of courtesy, looked rather sadly upon Mr. Irving; but he was not long left in any uncertainty in regard to that gentleman's wishes; for the very next day his story was told; how he had known and loved Mary from her very earliest girlhood, but that he was afraid of his greater age, and, anxious that she should not be influenced by their long acquaintance and the advantages his ripened years had given him over admirers more suited to her in age, he had gone to Europe, but lacked the courage to remain half the time he had allotted, and now was back, and—"

"And, ah! yes, I understand; I am to lose her," said her grandfather sadly. "I knew I could not keep her."

"Giving her to me will not be losing her. We talked about it last night, and we are both delighted with this place; and as I am bound to no especial spot, (Mr. Irving was an author,) and she loves none half so much as this, we can well pitch our tent here."

But when further acquaintance had enabled the man of "riper years" to take a place in Dr. Heremore's life which neither Mary nor Dick could fill, it was settled that the old house was large enough for the three; and as Mr. Irving was wealthy, healthy, and wise, the sun of Mary's happiness shone very brightly.

There's nothing more for me to say except that Dick went down to Carlton still once again, and that in its church there is a little altar of the Blessed Virgin, whereon Rose had the unspeakable delight—so precious to every pious heart — of laying a beautiful veil — Mary's gift to her "sweet little sister" — which Trot looks critically at every Sunday, and may be a little oftener, and puzzles her small head wondering if its delicate texture — the veil's — will stand the wear and tear of the years that must pass before she can replace it with hers; which always makes uncle Carl laugh. And Rose has persuaded Mary to dedicate her own in the same way, and Mary has laughingly complied, a little shame-faced, too, at her own secret pleasure in doing it, at the same time half wondering "what will come of it." Rose does not wonder; she thinks she knows.

As for Dick, there is every reason to believe that this coming Christmas there will be two or three glad hearts travelling around in company with two or three rough, ragged, shaggy boys; that he will carve his own Christmas turkey at his own, own table; and that there will be a *couleur de Rose* over all his future life.

PÈRE JACQUES AND MADEMOISELLE ADRIENNE.

A SKETCH AFTER THE BLOCUS.

IT was just five months since I had left it, the bright, proud Babylon, beautiful and brave and wicked, clothed in scarlet and feasting sumptuously. King Chanticleer, strutting on the Boulevards, was crowing loudly, and the myriad tribe of the Coq Gaulois, strutting up and down the city, crowed loud and shrill in responsive chorus—petits crévés, and petits mouchards, and petits gamins, and all that was *petit* in that grand, foolish cityful of humanity. Bedlam was abroad, singing and crowing and barking itself rabid, and scaring away from Babylon all that was not bedlam. But there were many in Babylon who were not afraid of the bedlam, who believed that crowing would by-and-by translate itself into action, into those seeds of desperate daring that none but madmen can accomplish, and that, when the bugle sounded, these bragging, swaggering maniacs would shoulder the musket, and, rushing to the fore, save France or die for her. No one saved her, but many did rush to the fore, and die for her. They were not lunatics, though, at least not many of them. The lunatics showed, as they have often done before, that there was method in their madness. They cheered on the sane, phlegmatic brethren to death and glory, while they stayed prudently at home to keep up the spirits of the capital; they were the spirit and soul of the defence, the others were but the bone and muscle of it. What is a body without a soul? The frail arm of the

flesh without the nerve and strength of the spirit? Pshaw! If it were not for the crowing of King Chanticleer, there would have been no siege at all; the whole concern would have collapsed in its cradle.

The story of that Blocus has yet to be written. Of its outward and visible story, many volumes, and scores of volumes, good and bad, true and false, have been already written. But the inward story, the arcana of the defence, the exposition of that huge, blundering machine that, with its springs and levers, and wheels within wheels, snapped and broke and collapsed in the driver's hand, all this is still untold. The great *Pourquoi?* is still unanswered. History will solve the riddle some day, no doubt, as it solves most riddles, but before that time comes, other, grander problems of greater import to us will have been solved too, and we shall care but little for the true story of the Blocus.

"Yes, monsieur," said my concierge, when we met and talked over the events that had passed since the first of September, when I fled and left my goods and chattels to her care and the tender mercies of the Prussians and the Reds—"yes, monsieur, it is very wonderful that one doesn't hear of anybody having died of cold, though the winter was so terrible, and the fuel so scarce. It ran short almost from the beginning. We had nothing but green sticks that couldn't be persuaded to burn and do our best. I used to sit shivering in my bed, while the petiots tried to warm themselves skipping in the porte-cochère, or running up and down from the *cintième* till their little legs were dead beat. O Mon Dieu! je me rapellerai de cette guerre en tous les sens, monsieur."

"Did many die from starvation," I asked—"many in this neighborhood that you knew?"

"Not one, monsieur! Not one of actual hunger, though my belief is, plenty of folks died of poison. The bread we ate was worse than the want of it. Such an abomination, made out of hay and bran and oats; why, monsieur, a chiffonier's dog wouldn't have touched it in Christian times. How it kept body and soul together for any of us is more than I can understand."

"And yet nobody died of want?" I repeated.

"Not that I heard of, monsieur; unless you count Père Jacques as dead from starvation. He disappeared one morning soon after he told Mlle. Adrienne, and nobody ever knew what became of him. They said in the quartier that he went over to the Prussians; but they said that of better men than Père Jacques, and besides, what would the Prussians do with a poor old *toqué* like Père Jacques, I ask it of monsieur?"

I was going to say that I fully agreed with her, when we were both startled by a sudden uproar in the street round the corner. We rushed out simultaneously from the porte-cochère, where we were holding our confabulation, to see what was the matter. A crowd was collected in the middle of the Rue Billault, and was vociferously cheering somebody or something. As a matter of course, the assembly being French, there were counter-cheers; hisses and cries of "renégat! Vendu aux Prussiens!

drôle," etc., intermingling with more friendly exclamations.

"Bon Dieu! ce n'est donc pas fini! Is the war going to begin again? Are we going to have a revolution?" demanded my concierge, throwing up her hands to heaven and then wringing them in despair. "Will the petiots never be able to eat their panade and build their little mud-pies in peace! Oh! monsieur, monsieur, you are happy not to be a Frenchman!"

Without in the least degree demurring to this last proposition, I suggested that before giving up France as an utterly hopeless case, we would do well to see what the row was about; if indeed it were a row, for the cheering, as the crowd grew, seemed to rise predominant above the hissing. Already reassured, I advanced boldly toward the centre of disturbance, my concierge following, and keeping a tight grip of the skirts of my coat for greater security.

"Vive Mlle. Adrienne! Donne la patte Mlle. Adrienne! Vive le Père Jacques!" The cries, capped by peals of laughter which were suddenly drowned in the uproarious braying of a donkey, reverberated through the street and deafened us as we drew near.

With a shout of laughter, my concierge dropped my skirts, and clapping her hands:

"Comment!" she cried, "she is alive, then! He did not eat her! He did not sell her! Vive le Père Jacques! Vive Mlle. Adrienne!"

Those of my readers who have lived any time in the quartier of the Champs Elysées will recognize Mlle. Adrienne as an old friend, and rejoice to learn that, thanks to the intelligent devotion of Père Jacques, she did not share the fate of her asinine sisterhood, but has actually gone through the horrors of the siege of

Paris and lived to tell the tale. Those who have not the pleasure of her acquaintance will perhaps be glad to make it, and to hear something of so remarkable a personage.

For years—I am afraid to say how many, but ten is certainly within the mark—Père Jacques's donkey has been a familiar object in the Rue Billault and the Rue de Berri, and that part of the Faubourg St. Honoré and the Champs Elysées which includes those streets. Why Père Jacques christened his ass Mlle. Adrienne nobody knows. Some say, out of vengeance against a certain blue-eyed Adrienne who won his heart and broke it; others say, only love for a faithful Adrienne who broke his heart by dying; but this is pure conjecture; Père Jacques himself is reticent on the subject; and, when questioned once by a curious, impertinent man, he refused to explain himself further than by remarking, " Que chacun avait son idée, et que son idée à lui, c'etait Mlle. Adrienne," and having said this he took a lump of sugar from his pocket and presented it affectionately to his *idée*, who munched it with evident satisfaction, and acknowledged her sense of the attention by a long and uproarious bray.

" Voyons, Mlle. Adrienne! Calmons-nous!" said Père Jacques in a tone of persuasive authority. " Calmons-nous, ma chérie!"—the braying grew louder and louder—"wilt thou be silent? Uplà, Mlle. Adrienne! Ah, les femmes, les femmes! Toujours bavardes! La-a-a-à, Mlle. Adrienne!"

This was the usual style of conversation between the two. Père Jacques presented lumps of sugar which were invariably recognized by a bray, or, more properly, a series of brays, such as no other donkey in France or Navarre but herself could send forth; and while it lasted Père Jacques kept up a running commentary of remonstrance.

" Voyons, Mlle. Adrienne! Sapristi, veux-tu te taire? A-t-on jamais vu! Lotte, veux-tu en fini-i-i-r!"

Though it was an old novelty in the quartier, it seemed never to have lost its savor, and as soon as Père Jacques and his little cart, full of apples, or oranges, or cauliflowers, as the case might be, were seen or heard at the further end of the street, the gamins left off marbles and pitch-and-toss to bully and chaff Père Jacques and greet his *idée* with a jocular " Bonjour, Mlle. Adrienne." The tradesmen looked up from their weights and measures, laughing, as the pair went by.

When provisions began to run short during the Blocus, Père Jacques grew uneasy, not for himself, but for Mlle. Adrienne. Hard-hearted jesters advised him to fatten her up for the market; ass-flesh was delicate and rarer than horse-flesh, and fetched six francs a pound; it was no small matter to turn six francs in these famine times, when there were no more apples or cauliflowers to sell; Mlle. Adrienne was a burden now instead of a help to her master; the little cart stood idle in the corner; there was nothing to trundle, and it was breaking his heart to see her growing thin for want of rations, and to watch her spirits drooping for want of exercise and lumps of sugar. For more than a fortnight Père Jacques deprived himself of a morsel of the favorite dainty, and doled out his last demikilog to her with miserly economy, hoping always that the gates would be opened before she came to the last lump.

" Voyons, ma fille!" Père Jacques would say, as she munched a bit half the usual size of the now precious bonbon. " Cheer up, ma bouriquette! Be reasonable, Mlle. Adrienne, be reasonable, and bear thy trials like an ass, patiently and bravely, not like a man, grumbling and despairing. Paperlotte, Mlle. Adrienne! if it were not for thee I should be out on the ramparts, and send those coqui.s to the right-abouts myself. Les gredins! they are not content with drilling our soldiers and starving our citizens, but they must rob thee of thy bit of sugar, my pretty one. Mille tonnerres! if I had but their necks under my arm for one squeeze!"

And, entering into the grief and indignation of her master, Mlle. Adrienne would set up an agonized bray.

Thus comforting one another, the pair bore up through their trials. But at last came the days of eating mice and rats, and bread that a dog in good circumstances would have turned up its nose at a month ago, and then Père Jacques shook in his sabots. He dared not show himself abroad with Mlle. Adrienne, and not only that, but he lived in chronic terror of a raid being made on her at home. The mischievous urchins who had amused themselves at the expense of his paternal feelings in days of comparative plenty, gave him no peace or rest now that the wolf was really at the door. Requisitions were being made in private houses to see that no stores were hoarded up while the people outside were famishing. One rich family, who had prudently bought a couple of cows at the beginning of the Blocus, after vainly endeavoring to keep the fact a secret, and surrounding the precious beasts with as much mystery and care as ever Egyptian worshippers bestowed on the sacred Isis, were forced to give them up to the commonwealth. This caused a great sensation in the quartier. Père Jacques was the first to hear it, and the *gamins* improved the opportunity by declaring to him

that the republic had issued a decree that all asses were to be seized next day, all such as could not speak, they added facetiously, and there was to be a general slaughter of them, a *massacre des innocents*, the little brutes called it, at the abattoir of the Rue Valois. The fact of its being at the Rue Valois was a small mercy for which they reminded Père Jacques to be duly grateful, inasmuch as, it being close at hand, he might accompany Mlle. Adrienne to the place of execution, give her a parting kiss, and hear her last bray of adieu. At this cynical climax, Père Jacques started up in a rage, and seizing his stick, set to vigorously belaboring the diabolical young torturers, who took to their heels, yelling and screaming like frightened guinea-pigs, while Mlle. Adrienne, who stood ruminating in a corner of the room, opened a rattling volley of brays on the fugitives.

All that night Père Jacques lay awake in terror. Every whistle of the wind, every creak in the door, every stir and sound, set his heart thumping violently against his ribs; every moment he was expecting the dreaded domiciliary visit. What was he to do? Where was he to fly? How was he to cheat the brigands and save Mlle. Adrienne? The night wore out, and the dawn broke, and the raid was still unaccomplished. As soon as it was light, Père Jacques rose and dressed himself, and sat down on a wooden stool close by Mlle. Adrienne, and pondered. Since her life had been in jeopardy, he had removed her from her out-house in the court to his own private room on the ground-floor close by.

" Que me conseilles-tu, Mlle. Adrienne?" murmured the distracted parent, speaking in a low tone, impelled by the instinct that drives hu nian beings to seek sympathy somewhere, from a cat or a dog if they have no fellow-creature to appeal to, Père Jacques had contracted a habit of talking out loud to his dumb companion when they were alone, and consulting her on any perplexing point. Suddenly a bright idea struck Père Jacques; he would go and consult Mère Richard.

Mère Richard lived in a neighboring court amidst a numerous family of birds of many species, bullfinches, canaries, and linnets. She had often suggested to Père Jacques to adopt a little songster by way of cheering his lonely den, and had once offered him a young German canary of her own bringing up.

" It's as good as a baby for tricks and company, and nothing so dear to keep," urged Mère Richard.

But Père Jacques had gratefully declined. " Mlle. Adrienne is company enough for me," he said, "and it might hurt her feelings if I took up with a bird now, thanks to you all the same, voisine."

To-day, as he neared the house, he looked in vain for the red and green cages that used to hang out au troisième on either side of Mère Richard's windows. The birds were gone. Where? Père Jacques felt a sympathetic thrill of horror, and with a heavy heart mounted the dark little stairs, no longer merry with the sound of chirping from the tidy little room au troisième. He refrained, through delicate consideration for Mère Richard's feelings, from asking questions, but, casting his eyes round the room, he beheld the empty cages ranged in a row behind the door.

But Mère Richard had a donkey. There was no comparison to be tolerated for a moment between it and Mlle. Adrienne, still their positions were identical, and Mère Richard,

who was a wise woman, would help him in his present difficulty, and if she could not help him she would, at any rate, sympathize with him, which was the next best thing to helping him. But Mère Richard, to his surprise, had heard nothing of the impending raid on donkeys. When he explained to her how the case stood, instead of breaking out into lamentations, she burst into a chuckling laugh.

" Pas possible! Bouriquette good to be eaten, and the republic going to buy her, and pay me six francs a pound for her! Père Jaques, it's too good to be true," declared the unnatural old Harpagon.

Père Jacques was unable to contain his indignation. He vowed that rather than let her fall into the hands of the cannibals, he would destroy Mlle. Adrienne with his own hand; he would kill any man in the republic, from Favre to Gambetta, who dared to lay a finger on her; aye, that he would, if he were to swing for it the next hour!

" Père Jacques, you are an imbecile," observed Mère Richard, taking a pinch of snuff; " you remind me of a story my bonhomme used to tell of two camarades of his that he met on their way to be hanged; one of them didn't mind it, and walked on quietly, holding his tongue; but the other didn't like it at all, and kept howling and whining, and making a tapage de diable. At last the quiet one lost patience, and turning round on the other, ' Eh grand bétat,' he cried, ' si tu n'en veux pas, n'en dégoute pas les autres!'"

Père Jaques saw the point of the story, and, taking the hint, stood up to go.

" What did you do with the birds?" he demanded sternly, as he was leaving the room.

" Sold four of them for three francs

apiece, and ate three of them, and uncommonly good they were," said the wretched woman, with unblushing heartlessness.

"Monster!" groaned Père Jacques, and hurried from her presence.

All that day he and Mlle. Adrienne stayed at home with their door and window barred and bolted; but night came, and the domiciliary visit was still a threat. Next day, however, the little door stood open as usual, and Père Jacques was to be seen hammering away at the dilapidated legs of a table that he was mending for a neighbor at the rate of twenty-five centimes a leg; but Mlle. Adrienne was not there. Had Père Jacques put an end to his agony by actually killing her, as he had threatened, and so saved her from the ignoble fate of the shambles? Or had he, haunted by the phantom of hunger which was now staring at him with its pale spectral eyes from the near background, yielded to the old man's love of life, and sold his friend to prolong it and escape himself from a ghastly death? Most people believed the latter alternative, but nobody knew for certain. When Mlle. Adrienne's name was mentioned, Père Jacques would frown, and give unmistakable signs of displeasure. If the subject was pressed, he would seize his stick, and, making a *moulinet* over his head with it, prepare an expletive that the boldest never waited to receive. One day he was caught crying bitterly in his now solitary home, and muttering to himself between the sobs, "Ma pauvre fille! Mlle. Adrienne! Je le suivrai bientôt—ah les coquins, les brigands, les monstres!" This was looked upon as conclusive. The monsters in question could only be the Shylocks of the abattoir who had tempted him with blood-money for Mlle. Adrienne. When curiosity was thus far satisfied,

the gamins ceased to worry Père Jacques; the lonely old man became an object of pity to everybody, even to the gamins themselves; when they met him now they touched their caps, with "Bonjour, Père Jacques!" and spared him the cruel jeer that had been their customary salutation of late: "Mlle. Adrienne à la casserole! Bon appétit, Père Jacques!"

The days wore on, and the weeks, and the months. Paris, wan and pale and hunger-stricken, still held out. Winter had come, and thrown its icy pall upon the city, hiding her guilty front "under innocent snow;" the nights were long and cold, the dawn was desolate, the tepid noon brought no warmth to the perishing, fire-bound multitude. No sign of succor came to them from without. In vain they watched and waited, persecuting time with hope. The cannon kept up its sobbing recitative through the black silence of the night; through the white stillness of the day. Hunger gnawed into their vitals, till even hope, weary with disappointment, grew sick and died.

One morning, the neighbors noticed Père Jacques's door and window closed long after the hour when he was wont to be up and busy. They knocked, and, getting no answer, turned the handle of the door; it was neither locked nor barred, merely closed, as if the master were within; but he was not; the little room was tenantless, and almost entirely stripped; the mattress and the scanty store of bed-clothes were gone; the iron bedstead, a table, a stool, and two cane chairs, were the only sticks of furniture that remained; the shelves were bare of the bright pewter tankards and platters that used to adorn them; the gilt clock with its abortion of a Pegasus bestrid by a grenadier, which had been the glory of the chimney-piece, had disappeared

What did it all mean? Had the enemy made a raid on Père Jacques and his property during the night, and carried away the lot in a balloon? Great was the consternation, and greater still the gossip of the little community, when the mysterious event became known through the quartier. What had become of Père Jacques? Had he been kidnapped, or had he been murdered, or had he taken flight of his own accord, and whither, and why? Nothing transpired to throw any light on the mystery, and the gossips, tired of guessing, soon ceased to think about it, and, like many another nine days' wonder, Père Jacques's disappearance died a natural death.

. A day came at last when the mitrailleuse hushed its hideous shriek, the cannon left off booming, the wild beasts of war were silent. Paris cried, " Merci!" and the gates were opened. The city, like a sick man healed of a palsy, rose up, and shook herself and rubbed her eyes, and ate plentifully after her long fast. Many came back from the outposts who were wept over as dead. There were strange meetings in many quartiers during those first days that followed the capitulation. But no one brought any news of Père Jacques. There were too many interests nearer and dearer to think of, and, in the universal excitement of shame and vengeance and rare flashes of joy, he and Mlle. Adrienne were forgotten as if they had never been. But when, on the day of my return to Paris, my conversation with my concierge was interrupted by the cheering of the crowd in the Rue Billault, and when the cause of the hubbub was made known, the fact that both Père Jacques and his *idée* were well remembered and, as the newspapers put it, universally esteemed by a large circle of friends and admirers,

was most emphatically attested. Nothing, indeed, could be more gratifying than the manner in which their resurrection was received. The pair looked very much the worse for their sojourn in the other world, wherever it was, to which they had emigrated. Mlle. Adrienne's appearance was particularly affecting. She was worn to skin and bone; and certainly, if Père Jacques, yielding to the pangs of hunger, had sacrificed his *idée* to his life, and taken her to the shambles, she would not have fetched more than a brace of good rats, or, at best, some ten francs, from the inhuman butchers of the Rue Valois. She dragged her legs, and shook and stumbled as if the weight of her attenuated person were too much for them. Even her old enemies, the gamins, were moved to pity, while Père Jacques, laughing and crying and apostrophizing Mlle. Adrienne in his old familiar way, cheered her on to their old home. How she ever got there is as great a marvel as how she lived to be led there to-day; for, what between physical exhaustion and mental anxiety—for the crowd kept overpowering her with questions and caresses—and what between the well-meant but injudicious attentions of sundry little boys who kept stuffing unintermitting bits of straw and lumps of sugar into her mouth, it is little short of a miracle that she did not choke and expire on the macadam of the Rue Billault.

Many an ass has been lionized before, and many a one will be so again. It is a common enough sight in these days, but never did hero or heroine of the tribe bear herself more becomingly on the trying occasion than Mlle. Adrienne. As to Père Jacques, he bore himself as well as he could, trying hard to look dignified and unconscious, while in his inmost heart he was bursting with pride. While he and Mlle. Adrienne ambled on side by side, some facetious person remarked that Père Jacques looked quite beside himself. This, indeed, was a great day for him and his ass. Yet, notwithstanding that his heart was moved within him and softened towards all men—nay, towards all boys—he could not be induced to say a word as to where he had been, or what he had done, or how he and Mlle. Adrienne had fared in the wilderness, or what manner of wilderness it was, or anything that could furnish the remotest clue to their existence since the day when they had separately disappeared off the horizon of the Rue Billault. Provisions were still too dear, during the first fortnight after the capitulation, to allow of Père Jacques resuming his old trade of apples or cauliflowers; besides, Mademoiselle Adrienne wanted rest.

"Pauvre chérie! il faut qu'elle se remette un peu de la vache enragée," he remarked tenderly, when his friends condoled with him on her forced inactivity. He would not hear of hiring her out for work, as some of them proposed. Mère Richard came and offered a fabulous price for the loan of her for three days, with a view to a stroke of business at the railway station, where food was pouring in from London. Père Jacques shook his fist at the carnivorous old woman, and warned her never to show her unnatural old face in his house again, or it might be worse for her.

THE THREE RULES OF RUSTIC GRAMMAR.

FROM THE SPANISH.

CHARACTERS.

Don José, a rich landed proprietor.

Doña Alfonsa, his wife.

Doña Concha, a rich widow, sister to Doña Alfonsa.

Calixto, the son of Don José and Doña Alfonsa.

Uncle Matias, the capataz * of the estate.

Maria, an old servant.

SCENE I.

Uncle Matias (entering).

The Lord be praised! (*Looks all around, and, seeing that the room is empty, adds*)—for ever! But what

* General overseer, in-doors and out.

are we coming to? The mason that built this house wouldn't know it. The master is not in his office; the mistress is not in the store-room; in this room there is nobody. Yesterday, I told the master, "Señor, the vineyard must be dug over, for the year comes in an ill-humor; and, if the stocks don't get what they're asking for, the vintage will be so bad that the holy father's blessing itself couldn't do it any good." For answer I got a growl. The mistress, when she meets me, doesn't say even so much as "Good-by, jackass!" The house has been upside down and inside out ever since young Master Calixto came home from the capital with his aunt—one of your furbelowed great ladies, with more airs than a pair of bellows, more trimmings and ornamental work than the top of a house, and more vaporings than those new ships that paddle themselves.* *Vamos!* Here comes the young master! What a fine fellow he has grown! and bearded and broad, too, and the sole heir to a property that is none of your dog-and-gun entails, but one of the right sort. The lad lacks nothing but the itch, that he might have the pleasure of scratching.†

SCENE II.

Enter Calixto, frantically.

Calixto. I've a mind to hang myself!

Uncle Matias. God keep you, young master! how exasperated your worship is! What vexes you so? Your worship seems to have got up, this morning, with your hackle ruffled.

Calixto. I could not get my eyelids together the whole night.

Uncle Matias. How should you, when your nose was between them?

Calixto (to himself). What course to follow—what to do!

Uncle Matias. Young master, your worship frightens me. What is it that has you so beside yourself?

Calixto. It is because I am the most unfortunate of men!

Uncle Matias. Oh! that. By the life of the wandering Jew!‡

Calixto. My perverse destiny assigns to me an avaricious father, an unenlightened, selfish mother, and a vain and tyrannic aunt. What an unhappy lot! What a fatal star is mine!

Uncle Matias. Oh leave off this high-flown talk, your worship, and tell me what is the matter. Uncle Ma-

tias has pulled you through more than one *scrape.*

Calixto. That is true; but the present one is not like those of "past and gone," as you would say. It isn't a matter of hiding some piece of child's mischief, nor of gaining for a boy the indulgence of his caprice. It is an affair of moment and affects my destiny—the felicity of my life.

Uncle Matias. All the better reason why your worship should take counsel. Because you see me here with my old spatterdashes and my furrowed face, and because I haven't book learning, it appears to you that I don't understand things. But let me tell you, young master, that it isn't from books one learns how to manage one's self in this unworthy world. It is by experience. Therefore, let him that wants to know much get an old fellow like me.

Calixto. I know that you people who don't read have for your guidance a rustic grammar, of which you, Uncle Matias, are a professor of the highest grade.

Uncle Matias. Call it what you please, your worship, but remember that length of days gives knowledge along with experience; and that the devil, even, don't know by hocus-pocus, but by reason of his years; and I, who am older than Dupon,* should know something. So, unbutton your waistcoat, and let us see the trouble.

Calixto. Well, you must know that my father wants to send me to Habana to recover an inheritance to which they are contesting his right. As if he had not enough property already!

---

* Steamboats.
† No le falta sino sarna que rascar.
‡ By all that is most unfortunate.

* Gen. Dupont, who commanded one of the armies sent by Napoleon I. into the peninsula. The Spaniards considered him the most cunning of their enemies. Hence, "*Mas viejo que Dupon*"—older than Dupont—said o persons who are very astute.

Uncle Matias (*aside*). Father, I accuse myself of being a carpenter, and of having many boards!* (*Aloud.*) Young master, because we have much is no reason why we shouldn't take what our lot portions to us. I've always heard say that it's good to have a loaf and a piece besides.

Calixto. Let somebody that wants the piece go after it; I will not. My aunt is determined that I shall return (with her) to Sevilla to marry her niece Diana—an empty bottle, all ruffles and flounces, with the face of one dug from the grave—and establish myself there in the capital. She will make me her heir on these conditions, but, if I do not comply with them, will disinherit me. Let her!

Uncle Matias. This ought to be taken into consideration, señorito!† It is true that the empty bottle, with more rufflings than the sea, and more wrigglings and squirmings than a rabbit under raffle, displeases and shocks one; but the inheritance is another thing, and deserves to be well weighed before it is let go. We sometimes make up our mind in haste to repent at leisure.

Calixto. I shall not repent of this. She may keep her niece and her money; let the loss go for the gain. Then my mother will not consent on any terms to the West India project, or to let me live in Sevilla, or that I shall leave home at all after my studies are concluded.

Uncle Matias. And where could you go, señorito, and find yourself better off than in your own native place, in your own house, at the head of your estate? Your worship surely doesn't want to go as agent to Madrid, like a notary's son?‡

Calixto. My worship proposes nothing of the kind. I want to travel in distant parts; go to Madrid, or wherever I please. My superiors are three, and each one is set in his own way, and determined to have it. I'll be hanged if this does not beat the family of the god Baco.*

Uncle Matias. Don't talk so, señorito. The family of the god Baco are the father, the son, and the devil. But your worship appears to be like the cricket, bound to jump somewhere.

Calixto. Is it just that my parents and aunt, who have no heir but me, should be my tyrants? They are very unfeeling!

Uncle Matias. Young master, all the more because yours is the only tongue to speak, it should never speak ill of your parents. To do that is like giving a blow to God on Good-Friday. How can you expect that they will be willing to let you go like a discontented bird, and live away from home, and country, and father, and mother, in their old age? If my son were of such mind, I should have to teach him his duty out of a wild-olive primer.†

Calixto. I have no such intention; I mean to establish myself here—in this place; for, though it is not pleasant, it is my own, and that of my family, in which the property that will one day be mine is located. But, since my circumstances permit it, what I want, before I settle down here for life, is to travel, become acquainted with the world, form opinions, acquire knowledge, in order to make myself an intelligent and cultivated gentleman.

---

* A sarcastic saying frequently used by Spaniards when a person absurdly complains of having too many good things.
† Young or little master.
‡ The Spanish landed proprietors, or *hidalgo*

(*hijo d'algo*, son of somebody) class, look with great contempt on notaries and clerks.
* Bacchus.
† Wild olive serves the Spanish parent instead of birch.

Uncle Matias. Well, if your worship has determined to see the world, like the young blades in stories of enchantment, there's nothing to do but get the master to agree to it, give you a lance, the best horse in the stable, and his blessing. I've nothing to say against it, so long as your worship don't mean, when you get home from strange parts, to go to experimenting with the plough and harrow they use off there.

Calixto. Set your mind at rest. I'm not going for the purpose of studying ploughs and harrows. But, instead of consenting to my reasonable desire, they all dispose of me without taking my ideas upon the subject into account. Ought one to submit to such oppression? And presently they'll begin to tell me how much they love me! What they all love is to rule me!

Uncle Matias. It is plain, señorito, that you are the poor rabbit at which they are all shooting. But a dutiful son takes the bad with the good. Have their honors told you their intentions?

Calixto. No, my *mae* * Maria has enlightened me. They talk freely before her. But I am going right away, now, to tell them that I am resolved not to go to Habana; not to marry my ill-brought up *eleganto-na* † of a cousin; and not to bury myself, in my twenty-third year, in a dull country-town! (*Goes toward the door.*)

Uncle Matias (detaining him). Stop, señorito! What are you going to do but ring the bell at the wrong time? Wait, señor. All the watching in the world won't hurry the dawn. Let's talk the matter over. You don't want to go to Habana; neither do you want to offend your father and lose your allowance; isn't that it?

Calixto. That's exactly it.

Uncle Matias. And the aunt's inheritance and goods wouldn't come amiss, if you came by them fairly, and without the empty bottle in starched frills, with name wrong end first? *

Calixto. You comprehend the case.

Uncle Matias. And, if it could be brought about so, you would like to have your mother consent to let you see foreign parts, and furnish your saddle-bags well besides?

Calixto. This is the very summit of my desires.

Uncle Matias. Well, to see if they can be accomplished, will your worship follow my advice?

Calixto. That depends upon what it is; tell me.

Uncle Matias. If it is not going to be followed, your worship must excuse me. I join this to this (*pressing his lips together with his fingers*). Promise to do as I tell you, and, if it don't turn out well, you can still do what you were going to.

Calixto. I promise. Let me hear how I am to act.

Uncle Matias. Keep easy and dark inside your jacket, without taking their honors beforehand. In such cases, the way is to *wait and see.*

Calixto (reflecting). Not attack, but be on the defensive to ward off with advantage. Very good tactics, Uncle Matias.

Uncle Matias. The best, señorito— the very best. In this world, if you wouldn't go wrong, there's nothing like them. Don't get into a fret, but wait and see.

Calixto. I hear my father and mother and my aunt approaching, disputing as they come.

Uncle Matias. All the better; but

---

* Mammy, said of nurse or foster-mother.
† Elegant with extreme affectation.

* Said of unusual or unpronounceable names.

make free with the way, your worship, and get out of sight.

Calixto runs out of the room.

Uncle Matias (alone). The master is a good man, but a bad tailor. The mistress hasn't quite as many lights as the age, and don't understand piquet. The aunt is as crazy as a bean-field. People of this kind take more turns than a key. There's nothing to do now but leave them alone, and let one ball push the other. As for the lad, he only wants his wits sharpened.

SCENE III.

Enter, in hot dispute, Doña Alfonsa, Doña Concha, and Don José.

Doña Concha. Send an only son to Habana, to incur the peril of the black-vomit, for the sake of a problematic inheritance! It's an unheard-of atrocity! It's unnatural! and nothing less!

Doña Alfonsa. Embark the son of my life on the deep seas, to be two long months at the mercy of the winds and waves; and all to get property that—God be thanked—he does not need! I will not consent! No!

Don José. He will go without your consent.

Doña Concha. He will refuse to go; and he will do right.

Don José. How! will refuse if his father commands him to go?

Doña Alfonsa. You are not going to command him! To take such responsibility would be to act as a bad father.

Don José. I shall have no occasion to do it. Calixto is not a child that does not understand what is for its own good. You ought to know that to recover an inheritance one

goes further than Habana—to China itself—and leaves on the trot, even if he is a grandee of Spain.

Doña Alfonsa. Only those do it who have nothing.

Doña Concha. Those who have no money to pay an agent.

Don José. Pay an agent! To take charge of both the saint and the alms?* The ideas of women! They do not have to act either as agents or principals in the management of business matters, and so never understand anything about them.

Doña Concha. Nevertheless, I wish you to understand that, if he goes in search of an inheritance that may dissolve into salt water, as those American properties are very apt to, he will lose mine, which is certain if he marries my niece, and takes up his residence in Sevilla.

Doña Alfonsa. Take up his residence in Sevilla! Leave his old father and mother! Abandon his house and lands of his forefathers! The Habana project is bad enough, but this is too much! And marry for interest besides! He will never do it, sister, never! and he will be right!

Doña Concha. He will not prefer the capital of a province to a miserable country village? will not accept the fortune I offer him, with a most elegant wife, who is my niece and his relative? We shall see if he will not!

Doña Alfonsa. He will not, because he does not love your niece, and because it is his duty to live with his parents in his own house, and on his own estate, as all his ancestors have before him. And is this, sister, a reason why you should disinherit him?

Don José. For this reason I wish him to secure the property in Ha-

* To appropriate both the estate and the pay.

bana, which I, whom you are pleased to call a bad father, will yield up to him at once, in order that he may live independently, and not be obliged to enslave himself by accepting an inheritance with conditions attached.

Doña Concha. He will enslave himself more if he exposes himself to become food for the fishes of the sea, the caimans and the crocodiles—may God defend us!—to obtain the one in Habana.

Don José. Foolish terrors of women! We will leave it to him to decide.

Doña Alfonsa. Blessed word!

Doña Concha. Immediately! This suits me.

Doña Alfonsa. For it is clear that no young man in his five senses will decide to go to sea, decide to marry a woman that another has chosen for him, and to establish himself away from his own native place.

Doña Concha. Sister, you live in Babia,* and are more than a century behind the age.

Don José. There is nobody in any age that refuses to go after an inheritance.

Doña Concha. What is said is said; let him decide.

Don José. Agreed. (*Goes out muttering.*) I'll talk to him.

Doña Alfonsa (*apart, as she goes out*). How you are going to be undeceived! To think that they know a son better than the mother who bore him! (*To Maria, who has been in the background during this scene.*) Maria, call Calixto, I wish to speak with him.

Doña Concha (*apart, as she leaves the room*). To suppose that a stylish young fellow like Calixto is going to bury himself in this forlorn hamlet! What blindness! And to imagine that

a man, already rich, is going out to America to defend a lawsuit! Paltry idea of a country-bred proprietor! It will, however, be well to give Calixto a hint of what is going on.

SCENE IV.

Calixto.

You hear what Maria says; all three are looking for me to propose their plans, each one in the belief that I shall be found compliant. This is the time, Uncle Matias, for me to speak out; now they will listen to me, and each one will carry away a well-inculcated no!

Uncle Matias. Nothing of the kind! You'll spoil all, señorito.

Calixto. Why, would you have me concede to each one what is asked?

Uncle Matias. Neither this nor the other.

Calixto. What then, old boy?

Uncle Matias. Neither flat nor high nosed.* *Don't commit yourself.* Say neither yes nor no. But here comes the master, and I'm off. Keep your jacket buttoned tight, señorito, and don't commit yourself; don't drop a word that he can hold you by.

Calixto. Perhaps the old fox is right. At any rate, we will try the rule of his grammar by being non-committal—neither exasperating them nor consenting to them.

SCENE V.

Enter Don José.

Son, I have already spoken to you on one occasion of the fat inheritance I have to contest in Habana.

Calixto. I recollect it, sir.

Don José. They write me that, in order to have my claim properly represented it will be necessary to send a confidentia person out there with the documents which are yet wanting. He must understand law, and be prepared to make the matter his business.

Calixto. It will be very proper to send such a person, father.

Don José. But it would not be easy to find a person as trustworthy as this affair requires, and, as you have just finished a course of law, does it not strike you that you are better qualified and more suitable than any one else can possibly be? One old Spanish saying is, "*For your own, you.*"

Calixto. Thank you, señor, for the proof you give me of your confidence.

Don José. I intend that the whole of this property shall be yours for your allowance and to reward your zeal.

Calixto. For this generosity on your part, I am—as I ought to be—truly grateful.

Don José. You are convinced, then, of the propriety of my decision?

Calixto. Your having made it, señor, is proof to me of its propriety.

SCENE VI.

The same and Doña Concha.

Doña Concha. Here, brother! For more than an hour, the overseer, the workman, the wheelwright, the guard, the foreman, and the chief shepherd have been waiting for you.

Don José (*hastening*). I'm going, I'll be there. I'll see you again presently, señora sister; in the meantime, convince yourself, to your disgust, that men understand affairs and one another better than women can understand them, however much Lycurgus-

like they may fancy themselves to be.

SCENE VII.

Doña Concha and Calixto.

Doña Concha. What is this that your father has just told me? Is it possible, you foolish boy, that you have pledged yourself to go to the focus of the yellow-fever to dispute an estate that you do not want?

Calixto. An increase of fortune is never to be despised, aunt.

Doña Concha. No; but you can have the increase without making a painful, fruitless, and dangerous voyage. Know that I have always loved you and continue to love you as a son, and that I propose immediately to declare you my sole heir if you promise to give up this mad undertaking.

Calixto. Aunt, so much goodness overpowers me.

Doña Concha. You will establish yourself in Sevilla, and marry Diana, who will bring you (for her wedding portion) my grange of *Los Almeses,* which yields sixty thousand reals annually. With as much more that your father ought to give, you could afford to wait with patience for our estates. What do you think of the plan?

Calixto. It exceeds my desires, aunt.

SCENE VIII.

Doña Alfonsa enters hastily.

Doña Alfonsa. Calixto, my son, where do you keep yourself? I have been looking for you for the last hour.

Doña Concha. He is attending to matters of sufficient importance, sister; discussing means by which to avoid exposing his life to gratify ava rice, and to escape also the death in life to which selfish affection would condemn him. (*Goes out.*)

Doña Alfonsa. That is it! That is it! So, then, my sister has been putting into your head the unnatural idea of abandoning your native place and your old parents?

Calixto. But, dear lady, at twenty-three a man cannot always remain shut up in one place, although it may be a very good place. You can be quite sure that the famous rat that turned hermit and lived in a cheese was an old rat.

Doña Alfonsa. I wish that those fire-ships and steam-carriages had never been thought of! They are what has turned the world upside down! they are what has brought in this wicked propensity to keep moving and to move all things, as if everything was not best in the place that God designed it for. My child, where can you be happier than with your father and mother; in your own house, where all love you; in your native town, where all know and respect you?

Calixto. If I went, it would be only to take a journey, see what is going on in the world, and return.

Doña Alfonsa. Changed and discontented, and a renegade to your country! Well—and your father, too, wants to send you off upon the raging ocean in one of those ships that it swallows at a gulp.

Calixto. But, mother, many people go to America and come back without any mischance.

Doña Alfonsa (*not attending*). Your aunt wants you to live in Sevilla, away from your old father and mother, who must remain alone with no one to care for them.

Calixto. She makes me her heir on that condition.

Doña Alfonsa. Yes, if you marry her niece, who knows how to talk

French, and don't know how to say the Rosary. Of course you said no?

Calixto. I said neither yes nor no

SCENE IX.

Enter Don José, Doña Concha, and Uncle Matias, who stations himself at one end of the stage, behind Calixto.

Don José (*rubbing his hands*). Come, now, we are ready to hear how Calixto has decided.

Doña Concha. And his decision is not that it will suit him better to become an adventurer, searching the world for inheritances, or to remain in your supper-without-lights * style here, in this paltry village, rather than live, as a gentleman ought, in the capital of his province. What do you say, Calixto?

Calixto (*with decision*). Well, señores, I say—

Uncle Matias (*pulling at Calixto's sleeve*). *Stop where you are.* For word escaped from the mouth or stone from the hand there's no return.†

Calixto (*somewhat confused, lowering his voice*). I have not made up my mind. (*Apart.*) He is right. Entrench yourself, and don't open a postern.

Uncle Matias. Just so; bless your little bill, señorito!

Don José. How is this, son? Did we not settle it that—

Calixto. We left it unsettled, señor.

Uncle Matias. Well answered!

Doña Concha. Calixto was talking with me afterward, and concluded, very judiciously, to gratify an aunt who proposes nothing but what is for his happiness, and most suitable in itself. Is it not so?

Calixto. I will do all that you desire, except—

---

* *Un cena á oscuras*—plenty without pleasure.
† *Palabra y piedra suelta no tienen vuelta.*

Uncle Matias (pulling his sleeve). Stop where you are !

Doña Concha. What do you say ?

Calixto. That perhaps I may comply with your wishes when I return from Habana, if I go, though I have not decided to make the voyage.

Uncle Matias. Good ! you understand it.

Doña Concha. And will not decide to go running after a fortune like some Don Nobody of a beggar's son. O señor brother-in-law, not all men have that " mutual understanding."

Don José (apart). The sly thing has circumvented me ; but I would rather my son lost her estate than that she should have the disposal of his future. (*To Calixto in an undertone.*) I will excuse you from the voyage to Habana, and double your allowance, if you will promise not to have that spoiled niece of your aunt. (*Aloud.*) Calixto does not think of changing his state at present. The gentlemen of our house have never married for interest.

Doña Concha (aside). He'll send the boy off to America yet. I have never seen a more obstinate man than this brother-in-law of mine. (*In a whisper to Calixto.*) My dear, I promise to secure my estate to you without conditions, if you will not go to Habana.

Doña Alfonsa. Both of them disposing of my son, and despatching him whither it suits them, as if the mother that bore him had nothing to say about it ! It would not be surprising if the one with her tongue, and the other with his saws and sentences, should succeed ; she in making him marry her shallow-pated niece, he in persuading him to go to America. May God forbid it ! (*Approaches Calixto hastily, and says in*

his ear.) Calixto, my son, if you will not sail for Habana nor go to live in Sevilla, I will not only permit you to travel on *terra firma*, but will also provide you with all the money you need for your expenses.

Calixto (apart to his mother). I shall conform to your wishes, mother.

Doña Alfonsa (triumphantly). Calixto will neither go to sea nor establish himself in Sevilla ! As if I did not know the son of my heart !

Don José (to his wife). Rib of my side, my son is not going to stay pinned to your petticoats like a pocket. He shall visit Madrid to see that the Cortes indemnify me for the privileges of which they have despoil ed my house.

Doña Concha. I rejoice, brother-in law, that you have desisted from your mad project, and that my sister has given up her childish, old-times no tion of condemning Calixto to the existence of an oyster.

Uncle Matias (apart to Calixto). Does your worship see, my señorito ? You have obtained all you wanted, and have your three superiors under your thumb, and grateful, into the bargain.

Calixto. So it appears ; for I am not going to Habana ; not going to marry ; not going to establish myself anywhere at present ; and I am going to travel. I owe this good result to you, Uncle Matias.

Don José. To Uncle Matias, did you say ?

Doña Concha. The capataz ? in what way ?

Calixto. The way of his *Three Rules of Rustic Grammar.*

Doña Concha. And what are his three rules ?

Calixto. Wait and see, Don't commit yourself, and *Stop where you are.*

Down in the pleasant west of England a river—the copious Brue—follows its course to Bridgewater Bay, between the Sedgemoors and other rising grounds. Somersetshire farmers now drive their ploughs and graze their cattle where I am going to describe water: thanks to those Benedictine monks whom they have so clean forgotten. But at Christmastide, some sixty years after the first Christmas the world ever saw, there were no monks at Glastonbury; for the simple reason, there were no Christians there. No one had banked out the waters of the Bristol Channel, and converted a brackish and unwholesome swamp into fine arable or pasture land. The Brue had it all its own way, to make islands, pools, and treacherous bogs with its unrestrained waters; until it had got so far west as to struggle with the advancing tide of the bay.

Glastonbury has the holiest memories of any place in England; and they date from the first moment when the faith was planted there. The sacred name of our Lord was brought to this marshy district in a far-off heathen land by one of his own disciples, Saint Joseph of Arimathea.

Who has not heard of the Glastonbury thorn? A history of Somerset would be incomplete which did not mention its blossoming every Christmas that comes round. It was fair and fragrant for fifteen hundred winters, while all around was sapless and dead. People try to account for this standing miracle by something peculiar in the soil, as they would explain away the freedom of Ireland from snakes and toads, or the healing virtues of St. Winifred's Well. There were probably Sadducees in Jerusalem who thought the Pool of Bethesda was all nonsense, or a mere chalybeate. Anything you like about the powers of nature, but nothing of the marvels of grace. Chemistry to any extent, but of miracle not one jot. Thorns blooming at Christmas? It is all a question of earth, soil, stratum, and the lay of the ground, with those who are "of the earth, earthy."

But we are now on our way to Glastonbury as Christian pilgrims, staff in hand. And it is very fit that we should regard the old thorn (or such suckers and cuttings of it as may be found) with reverence. For that thorn is a Christian tree, planted by Christian hands. More than this: it was planted by the hands whose unutterable privilege it was to unfasten and take down from the cross, and bear with adoring reverence to the tomb, the body of God, separated from his soul, united ever with his divinity.

We are accustomed, in our meditations on the passion, to contemplate the emaciated, agonized form of our Lord stretched and racked upon the cross; or, after the *Consummatum est,* when eventide was come, laid stark and bloodless in the arms of the Queen of martyrs, his most desolate Mother. Naturally we lose out of sight, by comparison, other agents and events in what followed his expiring cry. Yet look again. In the growing dusk of that first Good Friday, at the foot of the cross, and in the group of five or six persons to whom the eternal Father seems to commit the lifeless body of his Son, there is the saint of Glastonbury. With the dolorous Mother, and the beloved disciple, and the saintly, penitent Magdalene, and the other holy women, and Nicodemus, St. Joseph of Arimathea also bears his part.

To come back to Glastonbury; we must pass over some thirty years from that sacred paschal eve. Pentecost soon followed it, with its fiery tongues on the apostles' brows. They were illuminated and strengthened to preach the faith over the earth lying in darkness. So they separated on this worldwide mission, each on the path whereon the guidance of God's Spirit led him. "Their sound went over all the earth, and their words unto the ends of the whole world." St. Philip went into Phrygia, and, by some accounts, was martyred there. Others make him to have preached the gospel in what is now France, and that St. Joseph was one of his companions. A better supported tradition has it that St. Joseph, with St. Lazarus and his two holy sisters, Martha and Mary, landed at Marseilles from Judea. Anyhow, here comes St. Joseph of Arimathea to Britain, with a faithful band of eleven disciples. He has reached the distant region of tin-mines which the old Phœnicians had discovered and worked in Cornwall, Scilly, and, perhaps, the Mendip Hills. He is come not for precious metals, but to bring the priceless word of life.

So, rather more than sixty years after the Incarnation, and while Saints Peter and Paul are still alive in Rome, though the day of their martyrdom draws near, we find ourselves on the brow of Weary-All Hill, a mile or so south-west of the spot where Glastonbury Abbey will be built.

Weary-All Hill! the name it has been known by for generations back. But not a likely name to be given it by St. Joseph and his eleven companions, as they stood on it for the first time, eighteen centuries ago; as they looked on the marshy plain,

dotted with islands, in and out of which the glassy stream is winding. Weariness, at least lassitude of spirit, was unknown to those apostolic men. Had they not come all this way to bring the everlasting gospel? Had not their feet been "beautiful upon the mountains" as they crossed them, bearing this message of heavenly love?—mountains deep in snow, yawning with frightful clefts and precipices, gloomy with impenetrable forests, to which this Weary-All is scarcely a mole-hill?

"At length, then," said St. Joseph, when the twelve had paused on the brow of it to recover breath; for few of them were young, and it *was* rather a pull for a Somersetshire hill—"at length we have reached the end of our pilgrimage."

As he spoke, he pointed with his long staff to the little group of islands already noticed. A cheery December sun lingered on the scene, and, though it was evening, still cast a gleam upon the wide-spread water. The Brue was winding along, noiseless and limpid, sprinkled with its dark islets, as the shining coils of a snake are variegated with the spots upon its skin. There was no ice yet, though it was already the Christmas season. Perhaps the sea-water that mingled with the marsh from the Bristol Channel prevented its formation. The leafless thickets that fringed the slopes of West Sedgemoor, and clothed both islands and marshland in irregular clumps, allowed a more distinct view of the mirror of waters than when shaded with summer foliage. There was a kind of grave and sober animation over the whole scene.

A short distance further off, to the east, rose a solitary peaked hill, perhaps even *then* called the Tor. It has several scarped lines, or passes, drawn around it, denoting that the

Romans had fortified it as a stronghold, which they occupied from time to time. Years after, a little chapel in honor of St. Michael the archangel will be built on its summit. Years later, again, that little chapel will be enlarged into a stately church, the tower of which still remains. And nearly fifteen centuries after St. Joseph first stood on Weary-All, the last abbot of the stately Benedictine monastery, as Glastonbury had become, was martyred there with two of his monks. His crime was, that he rendered to Cæsar *only* those things that were Cæsar's, and refused to acknowledge the tyrant Henry VIII. as head of God's church in England.

Northward of where we stand, at the distance of five miles and more, the abrupt range of the Mendip Hills caught at that moment almost the last beams of the declining sun, as it sank, fiery red, toward the western ocean.

"The end of our pilgrimage," said St. Joseph again, slowly, and gazed down on the peaceful spot. "These are the islands of which the heathen king spoke :—how are we to name him ?"

"Arviragus," answered one of his companions, nay, it was the saint's own nephew, called Helaius.

"Permitting us to set up there a Christian altar, and to proclaim the names and the praises of Jesus and Mary."

"May the kindness be returned a hundred-fold into his own bosom," ejaculated Theotimus.

"Amen," answered St. Joseph fervently. And Joseph his son, and Simeon, and Avitus, and the rest, responded.

Then all knelt there on the brow of the hill ; all but Hoel, their poor pagan guide to the spot. And with Christian psalms, and the Gloria Patri, and invocations to the court of heaven to assist them in their praises, they poured out thanksgivings to him who had permitted their long wanderings to cease, and their missionary life in this heathen land to begin.

Hoel stood near, leaning on his shepherd's crook. He guessed in general what it was about ; but he understood neither Hebrew nor Greek.

He is a true Briton of that date, is Hoel ; and he might literally be called "true blue," for he is painted all over in blue patterns with the juice of the woad, like his northern cousins, the Picts. His scanty garments are dyed the same hue with the same plant, which yields its juice plentifully in this part of Britain.

He looks at the saint, and thinks he is inquiring the name of that principal island in the group to which his staff points.

"Iniswytryn," cries Hoel, in explanation. "You're Latin scholars, gentlemen ; so I suppose you know what that means—*Glassy island.*"[*]

Glass, in those days, imported by the Romans into Britain, sorry stuff as the best of it would now be reckoned in the Birmingham or St. Helen's foundries, was thought a wonder of rarity and beauty. So Glassy Island was a name equivalent to our calling *another* island that we love very dearly the

"First flower of the earth, and first gem of the sea."

, Hoel now spoke again in the same strange jargon as before, composed of British, or what we should call Welsh, and a little Latin. It was

* *Insula Vitrea*, the Roman and therefore the British name (by a slight corruption) of what was afterward called Glastonbury. *Glas* is the Celtic word for grayish blue, (γλαυκὸς,) and enters into numerous local names in Ireland, Wales, and the Highlands. Its affinity with our word *glass* is probably more than a coincidence of sound, the ancient glass being mostly of the same neutral tint. Others derive the name of the place from the woad-plant, *glais*, which grows abundantly in this watered district.

the dialect of those parts of Britain where the Romans had established their colonies and introduced their tongue. Be it noted, we are at this moment near the Roman colonies of Uxella, or Bridgewater, Ad Aquas, or Wells, and Ischalis, or Ilchester.

"So you are going to settle down there," remarked Hoel. "Won't you offer some sacrifice on first sighting the place?"

"We have no means of sacrificing this evening, friend," answered St. Joseph calmly, "nor to-morrow morning, I fear, unless we obtain materials, which at present we lack."

"Means!—materials!" said Hoel, musing with himself. "Well, every nation, I take it, has its own customs. But I know those who would not be long without providing the materials."

St. Joseph wished to ascertain what was passing in the man's mind. The zeal which urged St. Paul to become all things to all men, that he might save all, burned in the holy missionary's bosom. It made him seek out all that might serve the purpose of his coming. He had everything to learn: language, habits of thought, customs of social life, and the very observances of British heathenism.

"And how," he asked, "would you offer a sacrifice, good friend, when you had nothing to offer it with?"

"I? Nay, *I* could not. What good would a sacrifice be from a peasant like me?"

"To pray is to make an offering, is it not?"

"Yes; but I don't mean that. You know I mean something more; why, something really sacrificed — consumed, to make the gods favorable. Have you no such sacrifice in your religion? Then it can't be the true one, *I'm* sure!"

"Certainly," said St. Joseph, "we

have the one true and adorable Sacrifice, of which all others are mere shadows, and some of them very dark, distorted shadows. Every morning we offer to the true and living God that spotless Lamb who alone can take away sin, or be a worthy thank-offering to his majesty and his mercy."

"A lamb?" said Hoel, still musing; "why, that's not to be had at this season. But would nothing else do instead? For example, now, I've a nice—"

"Do not concern yourself," answered St. Joseph, and smiled again, kindly. "We shall be able to provide ourselves in a few days, when we have made acquaintance with the neighborhood. I suppose they grow wine in these parts?"

"Wine?" repeated the peasant, opening his eyes. "Oh! yes, to be sure." Then, after a pause: "You're fond of wine, then, after all, like our own Druids? Well, I should hardly have thought—"

Helaius could hardly repress a smile at his mistake.

Hoel looked at him; then, as if he had hit on the cause of his amusement, laughed his loud clownish laugh, too.

"Wine? Ah! the very best, if you can buy it of those gray-bearded gentlemen; and old mead, and metheglin; or cider from our apples hereabout. We grew a mortal sight of 'em.' *

Then he broke out into singing, and a kind of war-dance, to please his companions, as he deemed:

"All under yon oaks, and the mistletoe sprouting,
When victims have bled in the circle of stones,
We drink down the sunset with sword-play and
      shooting,
And he that refuses, we'll raddle his bones:
                        His bones!
And he that refuses, we'll raddle his bones!"

* Glastonbury was afterward called by the Saxons *Avalon*, or the Island of Apples.

It was difficult not to smile at his extravagant tones and gestures.

"Gently, gently," said St. Joseph to his companions, " or we shall be misleading him, and doing harm."

"Oh! never mind, ancient sir," remarked Hoel encouragingly, though he had not understood what was said. "All quite right—why shouldn't one ? Only, it strikes me, you've no place to lay in a stock of it at present. Now, our Druids burrow out caves 'tis thought, somewhere under their cromlechs—"

"Listen !" interrupted St. Joseph, laying his hand on the other's arm. He looked into Hoel's face, and gained his attention in a moment. " Listen, while I say a thing to you. Bread and wine, the ordinary food of man in our native land, have been appointed by him whom we serve, as the materials of that true sacrifice which he will accept. He requires, and will admit, no other. Animals were sacrificed to him of old, before he appointed this new and better way ; but now—"

"You spoke of a lamb," interrupted the peasant, growing rather sulky, "so I just took the liberty of informing you as we'd none at your service."

It was not the moment to pursue such high and mysterious truths with him any further. But Hoel himself would not be let off, nor would he let off St. Joseph. Something seemed to be working in his mind.

"A lamb is a lamb," persisted he doggedly, though he seemed to mean no disrespect ; "and a sacrifice is a sacrifice ; and bread is bread, I hope ; and wine, I'm sure, is wine."

"All things are what they have been created by God," answered St. Joseph very gently, "until it is his holy will and pleasure to change them in any way, or even to change them into other things."

Hoel looked at him, but said nothing. His look, though, meant inquiry, and this St. Joseph perceived.

"Is not a tree changed into something very different from what it was before," he went on, "when the warm air of spring breathes upon it, and the sap rises into it, and it puts forth green buds, and they swell, and burst, and afterward come leaves and fruit ?"

"True," answered he ; and then was silent, thinking.

"Did you ever see one of the trees down yonder blossom at this season ?"

For all answer, Hoel laughed, and pointed to the leafless boughs on the island, and the shores around them.

"Could the gods whom you worship cause them to do so ?"

"Not one of 'em all," answered he, with a somewhat scornful gesture.

"Then, *who* makes winter pass and spring return ; the bud burst forth, and the fruit ripen ?"

A pause. The poor pagan was not prepared to answer.

"Now," continued St. Joseph, "*my* God, the one living and true, not only has appointed the laws by which seasons come round with their produce, and the sun rises and sets. He sometimes, moreover, changes these things, according to his own all-perfect will, so that the sun stays motionless in the heavens above, and the tree blooms in midwinter on the earth below."

Hoel mused, and mused again, while his eyes wandered from the speaker to the rest, in whose looks he read confirmation of the words. Then he turned to take a sweep over the wintry scene that lay beneath and around. Woods and thickets skirting the slopes of Sedgemoor, the osiers lining the banks of the Brue, the few apple-trees that were even then on Iniswytryn—all without sign of a leaf.

He bent his eyes to the ground, knit his brows, seemed determined to hear no more, and to believe nothing of what he *had* heard.

Still the gentle, persuasive voice of the saint sounded in his ears:

"What is that, friend, you have in your hand?"

"My shepherd's crook," was the brief and surly answer.

"And see, my pilgrim-staff, that has aided my steps so far. Yours was cut from a British sapling, out of your moist soil, I dare say, no longer ago than last autumn. Mine, under a burning sky, long years since, in Judea, a land you never heard of. It came from a thorn-brake that had furnished thorns for a crown of which you know nothing. Which of these two staves would bud the quickest, if they were planted side by side?"

Hoel looked up, pleased to find something he understood. "Mine would, of course," he grinned out. "'Tis a right slip of mountain-ash, and would have leaves next spring, if I struck it into the ground."

"And what if mine now budded before you could count ten?"

"You jest with me where I see no jest," exclaimed the countryman, disposed now to be angry, "or you speak as one of the unwise."

"There is no jest here," answered St. Joseph with unruffled look. "You say truly. By no power of mine could the seasons alter, or the effects of them. My Master has said: 'All the days of the earth, seed-time and harvest, cold and heat, summer and winter, night and day, shall not cease!' But what if his power and his will unite to make some wonderful change in all this?"

"His power is great in the summer," answered Hoel, casting a look at the declining sun; "but in the winter time he seems further off, or feebler. He cannot melt the ice, nor draw up the dew, nor warm my fingers while I stand watching my sheep."

It was plain he was speaking of his deity, then sinking in the west, lower every moment.

"Ah!" said Avitus, "is it even such darkness as this into which the land is plunged? Would we had pushed on sooner from Gaul!"

"Courage, brother," whispered Simeon in answer. "There has been no time lost. Man can do but little, except pray and obey. If he does these well, he does good all around him. What says the holy text? 'Well done, good and faithful servant; because thou hast been *faithful in a little*.'"

Meanwhile St. Joseph had been in silent prayer. By some inspiration he felt moved to ask for power to work the first miracle ever wrought in Britain. Our Lord had promised: "These signs shall follow them that believe. In my name they shall cast out devils, they shall speak with new tongues, they shall take up serpents, and if they shall drink any deadly thing, it shall not hurt them: they shall lay hands on the sick, and they shall recover." "Amen, amen, I say to you, he that believeth in me, the works that I do, he shall do also; and greater than these shall he do, because I go to the Father. And whatsoever you shall ask the Father in my name, that will I do; that the Father may be glorified in the Son."

And even while St. Joseph prayed, it seemed as if witnesses of the miracle, and disciples of the truth, were being given him; for, stealing up the ascent from various directions, knots of the wild Britons, in threes and fours, converged on the summit of Weary-All Hill. I do not suspect

Hoel of treachery, or that he had meant to lead the foreigners into a snare. It is likely the rude inhabitants had perceived them from afar as they stood there, their forms traced on the hill-top against the red sunset sky. But these new-comers seemed to have no friendly intention. Most of them held in their hands the rude weapons of ancient British warfare. The bare arms of some were stained blue with the juice of the woad; others were tattooed; they had the wild and savage look we have seen in prints of the Sandwich Islanders. So, with threatening aspect and gestures, on they came, brandishing their lances and *celts*, or bronze hatchets, and beginning a sort of war-cry.

Yes; the moment was come, and the sovereignty of the true Lord both over nature and grace was to be manifested in one and the same moment.

St. Joseph told his companions how strongly the thought had come into his mind. It had, indeed, guided much that he had already said to Hoel. As by one impulse, they all knelt again, and besought our Lord to remember now his promise; so that the soul that had remained impervious to his word might see his work.

St. Joseph then approached the peasant, who by this time was surrounded by his countrymen. In a mild voice, yet with an authority not to be resisted, he said:

" Plant your staff here, upright in the ground."

Hoel was startled, looked at him, then slowly obeyed.

The multitude still gathered, their gestures more threatening every moment.

" Call now, if you will, on your gods, that the staff may bud and blossom."

The peasant turned by a kind of instinct to the setting sun; clouds were mantling round it; its form was veiled; nothing seen but a dull and rusty stain of sunset fast paling into twilight. Hoel shook his head.

" You will not call on it to hear, to help you?"

He was answered by a gesture which implied that the power of Hoel's god was set for that night.

Then St. Joseph, with another ejaculation of prayer, struck his thorny staff into the ground beside the other. He made over it the sign of the cross, saying:

" By the grace of him who for us men hung on the tree on Calvary, wearing the thorny crown, I bid thee be as thou wert wont to be in the bloom of spring!"

There was still light enough to see how, here and there on the length of the staff, the shrivelled rind began to swell and to break, how the green buds shot forth and lengthened into twigs; how these ramified out again, branch from branch, sucker after sucker; how the old staff expanded into a shapely trunk of thorn-tree, crowned with a pollard head of rustling leaves.

And then through the keen wintry air was wafted such a fragrance as had never saluted the senses of shepherd, or of dreaming bard, wandering through the brakes and thickets of leafy May. The seasons had been reversed at the strong prayer of the just. He who enabled Josue to command the greater and lesser light in the firmament, " Move not, O sun, toward Gabaon, nor thou, O moon, toward the valley of Ajalon," now honored the name of the true Josue, the Captain of salvation, by the " things that spring up in the earth,"[*] which obey their Lord as

---

[*] *Benedicite omnia germinantia in terrâ Domino.*
—Dan. iii. 76.

perfectly as sun, and moon, and stars.

What cries of astonishment broke from 'the rude men who crowded round I How they came trembling to the feet of St. Joseph; how they kissed the hem of his robe, and adored him as a god! They thought he was Baal himself; they shrieked out that the sun had set in clouds because Baal had come in person to take the place of his representative. And though St. Joseph and his companions testified by signs of abhorrence and earnest words how much the rude impiety disturbed them, yet, "Speaking these things, they scarce restrained the people from sacrificing to them."*

But this reverence, misguided and idolatrous at first, soon found its true channel, and was directed to the Giver of every best gift. And so the gospel was preached in Glastonbury, and grew, and flourished, and breathed out its fragrance like the thorn itself.

* Acts xiv. 17.

Then, after nearly fifteen hundred years, came a winter more killing than any Christmas during which the thorn had bloomed; and "a famine, not of bread, nor a thirst of water, but of hearing the word of the Lord." The decree of spoliation went forth; the royal commissioners, with a warrant from Henry VIII., thundered at the gates. The choir of Glastonbury, as of numerous other shrines in England, was desecrated; treasures of literature in the library and scriptorium were torn in shreds and scattered to the winds, with the relics of innumerable saints. The abbot, and two of his brethren, were drawn on a hurdle to the Tor, and martyred on its summit; the community dispersed, and the ruins, covering many acres, were given over to strangers, as a stable for their cattle.

But this was long after St. Joseph and his companions had been gathered to the saints.

THE STORY OF AN ALGERINE LOCKET.

I.

IN the sunshine of a May morning stood an old gray house, with a porch draped in woodbine and sweetbrier. A mass of wisteria climbed to the very chimneys, and on the lawn a bed of red and golden tulips swayed with the soft breeze. A wren was building in an acacia and singing, while a young girl watched his work and sang also, trying with her fresh soprano voice to catch his melody.

The old house was the homestead of Holly Farm, and the young girl was Sybil Vaughan, the heroine of a very short story.

"Sybil looks charming in white," thought Miss Mildred; sitting at the window of the green parlor with her mending-basket beside her; "and the locket is quite becoming."

It was before the day when every

one began to wear medallions, and the one that hung by a quaint twisted chain from Sybil's neck was a locket of rich enamel, brought to her from Algeria by a midshipman cousin, and quite unlike our gewgaw from the Palais Royal.

As we have said, Miss Mildred sat at the window of the green parlor, raising her eyes now and then from her work to watch her pretty niece, her adopted daughter. During the seventy years of her life, she had sat at that same window almost every morning since she was old enough to work a sampler, or to read a paper in the *Spectator* or a chapter of *Evelina* to her mother and younger sisters.

In her girlhood, Holly Farm had been a lonely place, remote from town and village. The trees, now rising luxuriantly around the house, were then, like her, in their youth, and revealed whatever might be passing in the lane below the lawn. At a period of life when young people gaze abroad in vague expectation of some wonderful arrival or event that shall alter the current of existence, Mildred Vaughan had turned longing eyes toward this lawn hour after hour, and she had thought her morning's watch well rewarded if the old doctor had trundled by in his high-topped chaise and nodded to her in friendly greeting.

With a capacity for painting that in these days of potichomania, decalcomania, and the rest would have passed for originality, if not genius, she had received one quarter's lessons in oil-painting, and by dint of studying a few beautiful family portraits had acquired a keenness of perception that made her hunger for the world of art. With an earnest love for books, she had been obliged to devote her time to the care of her younger brothers and sisters. And

so, out of her monotonous life, she had brought into old age an exaggerated idea of the value of learning and luxury, with a belief in possibilities and a regret for what might have been generally supposed to belong exclusively to youth.

This sounds more melancholy than it really was. Miss Mildred had kept her ideal of happiness fresh and vivid, and that is in itself a source of keen enjoyment. And, being a devout and trusting soul, she had framed for herself a prayer out of the thwarted aspiration of her heart and mind: " I thank thee, Lord, that there are joys so beautiful on earth, and I thank thee that they are not for me. Thy will is dearer to me than the realization of any dream."

Every one loved to come to Miss Mildred for sympathy. She believed in the reality and the durability of their joy, in the depth and in the cause of their grief. She did not say to the mother who had lost her little baby, " He is saved from sorrow and sin." She did not say to the young widow, " You have had the best part of life ; later come trial and vexation of spirit." She knew that in bereavement the balm often enters with the sting ; that the stainless beauty of the thing we lose is our only earthly consolation for its loss.

A great change had come to Holly Farm since the time when the doctor's visit was an important event. The sweep of meadow-land west of the house now served as camping-ground for the —th Regiment, Massachusetts Volunteers, in which young Henry Vaughan held a second lieutenancy. Drumming and fifing, the arrival of carriages full of gayly dressed people to visit the camp, the music of the regimental band on moonlight evenings, such was the ourse of daily life on green slopes which cattle and sheep had once possessed without dispute, nibbling the grass and drinking from the river in all contentment.

Indeed, Miss Mildred's standard of events had so naturally changed in that course of seventy years that, when the little white gate swung open, and a young man in uniform walked across the lawn, she merely said to herself: "That must be Captain Adair coming to see Harry. He walks better than any man I ever saw. The maid's hanging out clothes; I do hope Sybil will have sense enough to come and speak to him instead of letting him knock."

Sybil had the amount of sense requisite for the emergency. She led the way into the green parlor, and, leaving Captain Adair with her aunt, went to announce the arrival to her brother, who was trying on his new uniform, and blushed to be caught admiring the epaulettes before a mirror in the library. There was no need of apology. Sybil was in full sympathy with the occasion, and returned to the parlor feeling as proud of her brother's military outfit as he of the beauty of the sister leaning on his arm.

It was a pleasant meeting. Adair's frank and sympathetic manner had won its way through Miss Mildred's reserve; and his familiarity with the world and its ways secured him an easy victory over his young lieutenant. Sybil was less impressionable than the other two. Her manners were gentle and courteous to all, but it was not easy to penetrate her likes and dislikes, or to find out their cause. Just a trifle uninteresting, she was, poor Sybil, like many nicely poised young persons before they have enjoyed or suffered keenly. The very finish of her beauty, of her lovely manners, of her pleasant voice and accent, left nothing to be desired—no suggestion of anything be-

yond. But a soul so brave, so pure and honest as hers deserved to be developed, and the occasion for development came.

II.

ADAIR'S LETTERS TO HENRY ALLEYNE.

CAMP EVERETT, May, 1861.

I HAD an adventure yesterday that should have fallen to your lot, my dear Alleyne, not to that of a prosaic dog like me.

Hearing that my second lieutenant lived near the camp, and that he could not enter upon his duties for a day or two, I took it into my head to go and see what stuff he was made of, for, Alleyne, I am awfully interested in Company B, and in every creature connected with it. How could I ever have lived in that bore of a city, or slept within four walls, or used a silver fork! "Going off at half-cock, as usual," you say? Well, perhaps that is better than never going off at all. But to return to my story.

I went through a shady lane, leading from the camp to Vaughan's house. (Vaughan is the second lieutenant and owner of the camping-ground.) As I drew near the gate, I heard a woman's voice singing. A little further on came a gap in the trees, and I took a reconnoissance—such another I can never hope for during my military career. A low-spreading stone house, covered with vines, stood among fine old trees. Great bunches of blue blossoms draped the walls, and on the velvety lawn were clusters of brilliant flowers. Beneath a tree, honor bright, Alleyne, if ever angels do appear in white gowns with broad rose-colored sashes, it was an angel that stood beneath that tree, answering a bird with a voice as fresh, an expression as natural as his own. I stood there looking and listening—it was really very fascinating —until I suddenly remembered my errand. Then I pushed open the gate, and, walking across to the porch, lifted the bright brass knocker. But the rival of the wren, without letting me wait the coming of some creature of baser clay, came from among the trees, and asked if I wished to see Mr. Vaughan.

Now, I had wished to see Mr. Vaughan, and as it would not do to say on so short an acquaintance that my wishes were too completely satisfied by the vision before me to leave any want unfulfilled, I stoutly declared that I did wish to see Mr. Vaughan, and that I was Captain Adair.

And then she showed your too susceptible friend into a summer parlor, where the general effect was white and sea-green, and where there were hanging-baskets of flowers surrounded by vines and soft moss, and where an elderly lady in a lavender dress, with white lawn apron and kerchief, sat sewing, and where portraits of rosy-fingered dames and periwigged gentlemen gazed on us from the walls and read our destinies—mine must have been too plainly legible on my ingenuous countenance. And the old lady received me very courteously, and the maiden went to find her brother, and, when the brother came, he looked like his sister, and surely never before was lieutenant greeted by his superior officer with such ineffable tenderness. And we dined, so far as I could judge, off dishes of topaz and crystal, heaped high with ambrosia, and soon after dinner I returned to Camp Everett, and met the colonel going his rounds.

"You come from young Vaughan's, I see," he said. "What impression did he make upon you?"

"Charming, highly delightful, very promising," I replied, with a happy combination of diffidence and childlike openness of manner.

He gave me a look out of his shrewd old eyes. "So attractive a person will be an acquisition to the regiment," he remarked, and let me pass on to my tent.

I am half-asleep. Good-night!

ROBERT ADAIR.

CAMP EVERETT, June, 1861.

THINGS go on grandly at the camp, and between ourselves the colonel has just said that Company B is better disciplined than any other in the regiment—a compliment I'm very proud of, coming, as it does, from an old West Point martinet.

And now for the second part of my idyl. Every afternoon, Vaughan and I go up to his place and smoke awhile in the orchard. Then, by accident—it is wonderful, the unerring accuracy of accident at times— we appear at the east window of the green parlor, and there are Miss Vaughan and her niece, sewing or drawing, and sometimes Miss Sybil sings, to the accompaniment of a charming Pleyel piano, canzonets of Haydn in a style as fine, as pure, as exquisite as the composition. She —Sybil, I mean—has never danced a German or heard *Faust!* Duly shielded by the presence of aunt or brother, she is sometimes taken to hear the *Nozze di Figaro* or to see *Hamlet*, or to some other unexceptionable afternoon entertainment. I smile sometimes to see her absolute ignorance of life, and wonder that, in a village not twenty miles distant from a city where the world runs riot, this being has sprung into womanhood, unconscious of the existence of anything less spotless than herself.

This guarded life has given to her manners a certain high breeding that would keep one at a distance but for her kind, frank nature. No one can venture to fancy himself distinguished above others.

Do you know what this makes me feel? That hitherto, and I am nearly twenty-five years old, I have looked at women with a coxcomb's eyes. Any day, any hour, I feel ready to throw myself on her mercy, but an instinct tells me that her love must be won by something better than professions. When I have suffered in the cause she loves well enough to give her only brother to defend it, then I will speak.

Noblesse oblige—I see that in a certain lofty sense this is the motto of her life, and it shall be mine. Do you remember what our dear old philosopher used to say in the scientific school? "The better you begin, the harder is the work before you." And when we asked what he meant, he only said, "Noblesse oblige." It is true, whether the *noblesse* acts upon us in the form of intellectual strength or of spiritual gifts, or in the old material sense of inherited rank.

Except the hour spent at Vaughan's each day, and an occasional visit to my mother in town, I am wrapped up in the affairs of Company B. The life here is to me most fascinating. You would laugh to see me with a set of wooden soldiers before me on the little table in my tent, studying manœuvres, extricating my company from the most astounding and unheard-of perplexities. The progress of my lieutenants; the health, morals, and immorals of the company; the incapacity of our bugler to draw the faintest sound from his instrument—in short, everything that indicates growth or decay of discipline in Company B, seems to me a matter of national importance.

One word more about Miss Sybil

Vaughan. My mother has seen her, and sympathizes with me. When she came to visit the camp, I took her to Vaughan's house to rest. As we left Holly Farm, she gave a sigh of relief, and said: "Robert, I feel as though I had stepped back half a century. When I was a girl, young ladies were like Miss Sybil Vaughan."

One more last word. In your letter you said, with an air of superior wisdom, plainly expressed in the tails of your letters: "You are in love." Of course I am, and I should be a fool if I were not.

Your friend,
ROBERT ADAIR.

III.

IT was June still. The laburnum path was all aglow with blossoms, and the grape-walk, just beyond, made a shadowy retreat toward evening. Sybil was sitting there with her work lying on her lap. She had not sewed three stitches. Why had not Harry come as usual that afternoon to the east window to get his cup of black coffee? Why—O dear! there are so many whys in the case, and never an answer anywhere. Why was there an indefinite air of bustle in the camp as she looked down on it from her bower? Why was there an undefined sense of stir in everything?

She watched the sun drop nearer and nearer to the distant hills. The air was full of saffron light, and heavy with the perfume of flowers. Nature was so new and fresh in her June loveliness; and life was full of a promise of coming beauty, as it had never been before to Sybil in any other of her nineteen Junes. That sense of stir was in her own soul no less than in external nature.

There came the click of an iron heel upon the gravelled path. Sybil half-rose from the bench, and then sank back again. Adair stood before her. "We are ordered off," he said. "We go in an hour. I've but one moment to stay, for I promised Harry to leave him time to come and say good-by."

In the white, scared look on Sybil's face he read the right to speak.

But it had all been so hurried, she thought, when he was gone. Oh! for one of those minutes to return, that she might express to him a tenth part of the joy and pain, the hope and terror, that filled her heart. She could remember nothing clearly or in order, and yet she would have given all the other memories of her happy life to recall each word as it was spoken. He had asked her to give him something of her own, a ring, a glove, a ribbon, no matter what. And she had taken from her neck the medallion, and laid in it a little curl of her hair, and given it to him; and she had felt his hand upon her head, and heard him say, "God keep my sweet, innocent love!" And when she lifted her head he was gone, and she had told him nothing. It could not be a dream, for on her left hand was the ring he placed there—one that she had seen him wear, and thought too beautiful a jewel for a man to have, but now she felt so glad that he had worn it. He had said this was to be the guard of the wedding-ring that he would place there as soon as he could get a furlough to come home; and she had said—yes, thank God! she did remember saying that, at least—she had said that no one but himself should take off this ring or put another in its place; yes, thank God! she had said it.

Then Harry had come, too overjoyed at the news of her engagement to feel the pain of parting. That memory was full of turmoil; mixed,

too, with self-reproach that all other emotion was so lost in her new joy or pain, whichever it might be called, that Harry's going gave her no uneasiness.

The sun dropped behind the hills; star after star pierced through the darkening blue. Stillness lay on the valley below, so lately full of tramping horses, and shouting men, and shifting lights.

At last she heard her aunt's voice calling her, and roused herself to go and tell her beautiful story, old as the human race, new as that very June evening. She wondered that Aunt Mildred understood it all so well. Short-sighted Sybil! it was you who were beginning to understand Miss Mildred.

One August day, when a sultry fog held the earth in bondage, and scarlet geraniums blazed like red pools among the wilted grass, Miss Mildred pushed open the little white gate, and, with that hurried step that in old age so poorly simulates speed, hastened across the lawn. She gave a quick glance into the two parlors which were vacant, and then went up-stairs, grasping nervously the low hand-rail. In the upper hall she stopped, and leaned against the balustrade to take breath, and courage, too. Then, opening the door of Sybil's room, she stopped on the threshold to see her lying on the floor with a newspaper crushed in her hand. A bulletin in the village post-office had told her all: "Found dead on the field, Captain Robert Adair, —th Regt. Mass. Vols." They lifted Sybil up and laid her on her bed. She did not "strive nor cry," but in that first grief it pleased God to measure her power of endurance.

It was not in victory that Adair had fallen, but in one of those engagements where, humanly speaking, life seems thrown away. But such thoughts should not disturb the mourners cradled in the providence of God. He chooses the time and the occasion, and what is lost in the current of human events he gathers up and cherishes.

Weeks passed away. Letters came —precious in their recognition of Adair's high integrity, his courage, his compassion; letters, too, from his mother, far away in her summer home, acknowledging Sybil as one with her in love and bereavement. But she lay, white and listless, on her bed, taking little notice of anything except in the expression of gratitude. Harder than anything else for her aunt to bear was the pathos of Sybil's resignation.

There came a soft afternoon, early in September, when for the first time Sybil's easy-chair was placed in the open air, under a striped awning that made an out-door room on the west side of Holly Farmhouse. Here she could be sheltered from the direct rays of the sun, and yet enjoy the trees and flowers.

Great velvet bees hid their heads buzzing in the freshly-opened cups of the day-lilies; a humming-bird dipped his dainty beak into the sweet-peas, and then flashed away to hide himself among the nasturtiums pouring in a golden stream over a broken tree-trunk on the lawn.

Amid the glow of nature, Sybil looked very wan and frail. She had begun to think a little now, and her thoughts ran thus: "I am resigned to God's will. I've not the shadow of a doubt that this is all right. I am more than willing to die; I am willing to live, if only there is a thread to hold by—a stone, a stick, a straw to begin to build my life upon. Other women have borne this and lived. I've seen them going about among their fellow-creatures, talking, smil-ing, laughing, when others talked, and smiled, and laughed. I have no more sensibility than they. What I have lost was perfect; but what they had lost was perfect, perhaps, to them. I don't rebel, but I am dying of pain. It goes on, and on, and on; if it would stop but for ten minutes and let me take breath, I think I could catch hold of something on earth and begin to live again. There's that dear Aunt Mildred coming through the hall. Now, I *will* give her a free, happy smile, and lighten her burden if I cannot lighten my own."

Miss Mildred held in her two hands a great vase of spreading golden-rod, which she set down on the little garden-table. Just where she had placed it, against a background of dark-green leaves, it made so beautiful a picture that Sybil uttered an exclamation of surprise and pleasure. There was a delighted look on her aunt's sweet old face that made her think: " Here is something to hold on by; here is something to build on, if only I am generous enough to try."

Miss Mildred arranged the cushions in Sybil's chair, and then took her hand very gently.

" There is a man in the hall, dear, who brings you a little packet from Virginia. Can you see him ?"

" Yes; at once, if you like. Please let him come out here. I can talk to him better in the open air."

He came—a shy, elderly man, whom Sybil remembered seeing once at the camp. He stood awkwardly, shifting his military hat from hand to hand, till she asked him to sit down near her, and said a few reassuring words. Then, seeing that he was struggling to conquer his emotion, she fixed her eyes on the vase of flowers, trying to keep down the impatience struggling within her.

"My name is Abel, lady," he said, at length. "May be you've heard the cap'n say as how I couldn't play the bugle, at the camp below there. The folks all said I couldn't learn, I was so old and dull; but he allus believed everybody was good for something, he did."

Sybil was leaning forward, breathless to hear more.

"I remember you," she said. "Oh! do go on. Tell me everything—every little thing about it all."

"Wall, you see, lady, my two boys they was all I had, and they jined the regiment, and I couldn't live without 'em; and I was hale and strong, and so I made bold for to jine, too. There was one place left in the regiment then—the bugler's place, in Company B—and I pled so hard, the cap'n he said I might try. And, lady, the plaguy thing used to seem to shut right up when I wanted to make it blow, and the men used to laugh at me, right out afore my boys. And Abner and John Henry they felt kind o' cheap, and they kept sayin' to me, 'Father,' they says, 'it makes us feel kind o' bad to hear you tryin' so hard and not learnin'; don't you think you'd better give it up?' And says I, 'No, boys,' says I, 'while there's breath in my body, I won't give it up till I've conquered that crittur.' And, lady, when the cap'n see me tryin' so hard and allus comin' to grief, what does he do but he takes hold himself, and he learns all them signals, and he teaches on 'em to me. And so I went to the war with my boys, and I nursed John Henry through a fever, and I kept Abner from fallin' into bad company; and, lady, if I could have saved the cap'n's life by givin' my skin inch by inch, I'd have done it; but I couldn't. So I just held his head against this old heart, and let him breathe his life away.

And I laid him down on the sod as tender as if I'd been his mother."

"May God reward you! Did he suffer much?"

Tears, such as she had longed for, were pouring from her eyes.

"No, lady; he was gone before the surgeons came on to the field. He lay quite still, without a moan or sigh; and, now and then, he'd say a word to me. I was wounded, too, just below the knee. I dropped down about six feet off from him; and when the retreat came, and I saw as how I was left behind with the cap'n, didn't I praise the Lord!"

"What did he say to you?"

Abel took a little packet from his breast, and laid it in Sybil's hand. "He says to me, 'Abel,' says he, 'when you can get a furlough *honorable*,' says he—'for you mustn't go when the country needs you bad—you take this locket' (a-unhookin' it from his neck) 'to Miss Sybil Vaughan—her that lives in the stone farmhouse above our old camp at Holly Farm—and you tell her as how the poor thing tried to save my life; and she'll see it by the great dent in the gold made by a bullet. And you tell her as how she's to open it herself, and see what I put there. And you tell her'—I'm a Methodist, lady, but I'll tell you word for word what he said."

"Yes, word for word."

"'You tell her,' says he, 'how I pray that Christ and his Blessed Mother may be her comfort as they are mine; and tell her as how I've never let a thought enter my mind, since we parted, that she wouldn't have approved. And tell her,' says he, a-raisin' himself half-way up from the ground, 'you tell her I love her fond and true, and that we shall meet in heaven when she's done the work on earth she is so fit to do. And tell her to comfort my mother. Poor mother!' And then he put his arm round my neck, and kind o' stroked my cheek, and he says, soft and low, a few words, and all I heard was, 'Receive my soul,' and then I kissed him, and laid him down on the turf, and his face was like as I think it will be in heaven at the great day. And now I'm goin' to leave you, lady, 'cos I know as how you want to be alone. And, with your leave, I'll come again, and tell you how we loved him, and how we cried like babies round the ambulance that brought him to the camp; and how there was scarce anything left to send home to his mother, 'cos he used to give his things away to the sick boys—blankets, and money, and shirts, and all."

Then Abel took Sybil's delicate hand reverently on his broad, brown palm, and kissed it.

"Lady," he said, "you're the only thing ever I see that was fit to mate with him."

"You will come again," she said. "As you have no daughter, and there must be many things needed to make you comfortable during your convalescence, you will let me see to all that. And you will let me replace the many things you must have lost or worn out during these hard three months?"

She spoke beseechingly, looking up into his face like a child pleading for a toy.

"You shall just wind me round your finger like he did," said Abel. "I allus thought I'd got grit in me till I seen him, and then it seemed as though I hadn't no will but his'n."

Sybil was alone with the little packet. With trembling fingers she untied the string and removed the wrappings of paper. There lay the medallion with its twisted chain. She passionately kissed the battered enamel that had stood between him and death. Then she opened the locket. With the silky, yellow curl lay a little lock of dark-brown hair. She was touching it tenderly, wondering when he had placed it there for her consolation—whether just before the skirmish or soon after he left her—when a turn of the locket in the level rays of the sun showed two words scratched on the inner side with some rude instrument. She looked closer, and read : " Noblesse Oblige."

When Miss Mildred came to lead her into the house, there was a change in her face that filled the gentle lady's heart with gratitude. It was the look of courage that comes to those who recognize the claim of their high birth as the children of God.

THE SHAMROCK GONE WEST.

BY THE AUTHOR OF " ROMANCE OF THE CHARTER OAK."

ABOUT a generation ago, there might have been seen moving across the Wabash Valley, Indiana, one of those heavy-built wagons, with broad canvas tops, known in the West as prairie schooners. The wheels, which had not been greased since they left New Hampshire, were creaking dolefully, and the youth who urged on the jaded team declared that the sound reminded him of the frogs in his father's mill-pond. Attached to the rear of the wagon was a coop,

containing a rooster and half a dozen hens, evidently suffering from their long confinement ; while underneath the coop, swinging to and fro, as if keeping time to the music of the wheels, was a bucket.

Nat Putnam held the reins with a tight grip, his eyes were fixed straight in front of him, and his steeple crowned hat, which looked as if it might have been a legacy from one of his Puritan forefathers, was placed as far on the back of his head as possible·

so as not to obstruct the view. He was perhaps twenty-one or two years of age; but it would have been rash to gauge his wisdom by the date of his birth. If ever there was a Yankee hard to outwit, it was our friend, and his mother had often declared that her boy could see through a stone wall. The very shape of his nose, which was not unlike an eagle's beak, warned you to be on your guard when you were making a trade with him; while his face, spotted all over with freckles, could readily assume every expression from highest glee to deepest melancholy; thus enabling him to fill whatever post in life might be most congenial, were it circus clown or ruling elder.

"Mr. Putnam, when are we going to halt?" inquired a female voice, which seemed to come from the interior of the wagon. Before the youth answered, the speaker had placed herself at his side and was gazing at him with a woeful look. Poor thing! well might she ask the question. Ever since he had picked her up in the State of New York, he had kept travelling on and on, until Mary O'Brien thought he was never going to stop. Her father, who had been with them the first week of the journey, had died, and Nat had only tarried long enough to bury the old man, and let the daughter say a few prayers over his grave.

"Don't find fault," he replied. "The spirit moves me to keep pushing West; the further I go, the better I feel. This everlasting woods must come to an end by-and-by, and when we reach the open country you'll not grumble."

"But I'm quite worn out," pursued Mary; "and my shamrock is tired too. If you'd only rest and make a home, and let me plant it! The jolting of the wagon and the want of sunlight is killing it. Poor shamrock!" Here

she left the seat, but presently returned, carrying a box filled with earth, in which was a little three-leafed clover.

"See," she exclaimed, "how different it looks from a month ago. 'Tis drooping fast." As she spoke she gave the plant a kiss. Her companion glanced at her a moment, then with a smile of pity, "How old are you?" he asked.

"Eighteen."

"Humph! I guess you're out of your reckoning. If you were that old, you'd chuck that piece of grass away and take to something serious. There's my Bible, why don't you read a chapter now and then? 'Twould instruct you, and keep me from getting rusty—a thing I'd deeply regret, for I may take to exhorting if farming don't pay."

"Throw my shamrock out of the wagon! Why, Mr. Putnam, 'twas father's, and he brought it all the way from Tipperary. I'm going to keep it—as long as I live, I am. It may wither, but I'll never throw it away."

"Well, well, as you like. But I repeat—why can't you read the Bible once in a while, instead of wasting your time playing with a lot of dried peas? Do they come from Tipperary, too?"

"Oh! these are my beads," she replied, taking her Rosary from her pocket; "and it's praying I am, when you see me slipping these little round things through my fingers."

"Praying! Then you must have prayed a heap. Are you in earnest?"

"I am."

"Well, can't your spirit be moved without using them peas, or beads as you call them? It seems to me they must bother you."

"I use 'em, sir, to keep count, or I mightn't say all the Hail Marys and Our Fathers." Here Nat started, and lifting his sandy eyebrows, "Aha!"

he exclaimed. "So! Indeed! Then 'twas keeping a tally of your prayers? Well, now, there's something in that. I really didn't believe you were so 'cute. The devil couldn't say that you hadn't been square on your devotions when you'd kept a strict tally."

The girl smiled, then, bowing her head, seemed to be whispering something to the shamrock.

"Different from other gals!" thought Putnam, as he glanced at the pale face and long, raven hair, which without braid or ribbon flowed down until it rested on the bottom of the wagon. "Yes, different from other gals! Can't quite make her out. She ain't a child, yet seems like one. Keeping a tally of her prayers is the first sign of her being 'cute. But that's a beginning anyhow. I'll educate her little by little. Oh! if she'd only take to the Bible." Here he gave the reins a jerk, then asked Mary to read him a chapter from the Book of Proverbs.

"I can't read," she frankly replied.

"Can't read! Can't read! That I won't believe. Why, there's Jemima Hopkins, in Conway, where I come from, that not only reads, but has started on a lecturing tour; and she ain't—let me see; she was born the year of the comet—no she ain't a day over fourteen."

"Well, I'm not Jemima Hopkins."

"No, that you ain't; Jemima is a prodigy."

"And I'm a goose."

"But don't own it," said the youth. "Talk as little as possible, and then the world may not find it out. Why, I know a chap in Conway that passes for 'larned,' and all 'cause he has the toothache every time he's asked to make a speech. You see, he puts on a wise look, holds his tongue, and has so humbugged the folks that they call him Uncle Solomon."

"Well, I don't want to be taken for what I'm not," rejoined Mary, a tear trickling down her cheek.

"What ails you now?" exclaimed Nat. "Oh! how different you are from Jemima Hopkins!" The girl made no response, but sighed, "Father, father."

"The old man's underground," pursued the youth, in as soft a voice as he could assume. "Crying won't bring him back. Dry your eyes, and vow to smash to atoms every whiskey-bottle that ever comes within your reach. I suspect his constitution was undermined by habits of intemperance.

"Father didn't drink in Ireland," sobbed the girl. "'Twas at that horrid grog-shop in New York he got the habit."

"Pure fountain water," murmured Nat, rolling his eyes toward the heavens, "what a blessed thing thou art! Those who give thee up for alcohol make a poor swap." Then suddenly fixing his gaze on the young woman, "Mary," said he, "I never but once tasted liquor. 'Twas at a cattle show year afore last; and do you know what happened? I paid two hundred and fifty dollars for a horse that was foundered and kicked so bad I couldn't drive him home. Now that's something I'd never have done if my head had been clear; but 'twas a lesson—a good lesson, and I told Jemima Hopkins (who got wind of it—women find out everything) to make her first lecture on temperance."

The young woman, who seemed not to have been listening to this episode in his history, was now moaning piteously for her father, nor did she cease until her companion in an agitated tone bade her keep quiet. "Your lamentations," he said, "are horrible to listen to."

"Don't you love your father?"

spoke Mary, gazing at him through her tears. "Wouldn't you cry if he were dead?"

"Cry if he were dead!" repeated he youth with a shudder. "Oh! why did you ask me that question? You're a strange being. Who gave you power to look into my heart? Do you know that I quarrelled with the old man, and left without saying good-by, and every mile I've travelled his last look has haunted me? 'I am near the grave,' he said, 'don't abandon me. Attend the mill, 'twill soon belong to you.' But I laughed in his face. 'The mill,' said I, 'is out of repair, and only fit to shelter rats and swallows; while the soil won't yield more than fourteen bushels of corn to the acre.' And then I turned my back on him."

"When he's dead, you'll be sorry for that," said the girl. "Write home and ask his forgiveness. Do, before it's too late."

"Home!" murmured the youth as he drove along. "Home!" Oh! what memories were awakened at the sound of that word which spoke in a thousand magic whispers! He was again a little boy seated on his father's knee, in the old house at the foot of Mount Kearsarge, listening to stories of the Revolution. The wind was howling—the snow coming in through the key-hole and under the door—a fearful night to be out. But what did he care about the tempest? He was safe on his father's knee.

"Mary," said Putnam, just as they reached the foot of a hill, "I'll take your advice, and write home the first chance I get. And I'll tell the old man that I'm sorry for the hard words I used. I'll ask him, too, to follow me—for I'm going to halt by-and-by; and I'll make him as comfortable as if he were in New Hampshire."

"Do," said the young woman;

"'twill bring God's blessing on you."

Here he placed the reins in her hands, then, telling her that he was going to reconnoitre and find which was the best way to get over the hill, he left the wagon with a lighter heart than he had known in many a day.

A little climbing brought him to a spot where the ground was again level, but where the timber was thicker and the wagon would have hard work to get along; and he was wondering if the everlasting forest was never coming to an end, when he was startled by a rustling noise, and, looking round, saw a wild turkey dart off her nest, while at the same instant ever so many young ones, which appeared as if only just hatched, began scattering in every direction. "I'll catch this fellow," said Nat, running after the nearest bird, "and make him a present to Mary." But, young as it was, the little thing managed to reach a clump of hazel-bushes about thirty yards distant, into which its pursuer dashed only a step behind, and in his excitement Nat kept straight on, nor did he stop until he found himself clear of the thicket. But there he came to a sudden halt, and for almost a minute stood as if rooted to the earth. Was the scene which had burst upon him a vision of paradise? The forest had ended, the hill sloped gently to the west, and before him like a boundless sea, fired by the rays of the setting sun, lay the prairie of Illinois. Then he shouted for Mary, who with impatient step hastened up the hill, wondering what was the matter, and who arrived just as he was beginning to sing *Old Hundred.* The glorious view brought tears of joy to her eyes, for she felt sure Nat had at length found a spot where he would be willing to settle down and make a home, and, clasping her hands, she likewise offered up a prayer of thanksgiving.

"Isn't this ahead of anything you ever dreamed of ?" exclaimed the youth, when he had finished the hymn "I've heerd Parson Job at camp-meeting trying to picture heaven ; but, although I'd not have dared say it aloud, yet really I never felt as if I'd care a straw about such a place as he described—fellows with wings and harps skipping around, and singing hallelujahs for all eternity without ever getting out of breath. But here is a country I can imagine like the home of the blest."

"Heaven is more beautiful than this," rejoined his companion. "Yet 'tis a glorious country. Oh! settle here, do, and give my shamrock rest."

"As you say," continued Nat, patting her cheek, and at the same time piercing her through with his sharp gray eyes. "You're my 'Blessing.' I owe you more than I ever can pay. When you made me promise to write home and ask the old man's forgiveness, a load heavier than a millstone was taken off my heart. You ain't as larned as Jemima Hopkins, and you ain't 'cute—though keeping a tally of your prayers is something, and shows what you may become by proper education—but, ignorant as you are, there's still a great deal in you." Here he left her, and went back for the wagon, which, after not a little difficulty, he managed to bring across the hill ; then, having chosen a spot near a spring of water, he unhitched the horses, while Mary let out the fowls, who clapped their wings as if they were mad ; nor did the rooster stop crowing until the hens—anxious to make their nests—gathered round him. and forced him to hold his tongue and be serious.

As it was sunset, Putnam could do little more than reconnoitre the vici-

nity of the camping-ground, so, shouldering his rifle, he walked off, leaving the girl to prepare the evening meal.

But Mary had scarcely lit the fire when he came running back, and pointed out to her a figure on horseback, advancing along the prairie. "It may be an Indian," said he. "If he's peaceful, I'll read him a chapter in the Bible ; if he's ugly, I'll shoot."

In about a quarter of an hour the stranger had approached near enough for them to discover that he was a person of their own race, with long, white hair, and a cross hanging at his side ; so, throwing down the gun, Nat shouted welcome. The traveller, although astonished to hear a human voice, did not draw rein, but kept on up the hill, and in another moment the youth had grasped his hand and was giving it a hearty shake.

"So soon!" exclaimed the Jesuit missionary—for such was the character of the new-comer. "Already! Oh! you Americans are a great people. In a few years you will be across the continent."

"Well, I've fetched up here," said Putnam, grinning. "Not that the spirit didn't move me to push further West ; but yonder gal—my 'Blessing,' as I call her—urged me to stop."

Here the priest glanced at Mary, then remarked :

"Your sister, I suppose, or wife ?"

"I haven't any sister," replied the youth, "and ain't 'spliced' yet. She's a gal I picked up as I was coming through York State. Her father was with her, and I took him along too ; but he died in a few days, and I buried him on the roadside, and as she had no home I told her she'd better stick to me. She's awful green, but for all that she has her good points, and has made me happier than I've been in a long time."

With this Nat beckoned to Mary, who, as soon as she discovered in whose presence she was standing, fell on her knees, while the missionary gave her his blessing.

That evening the youth, true to his promise, wrote an affectionate letter to his father, which the Jesuit assured him he would deliver with his own hand. "And I will bring you an answer," said the latter, "for I shall pass this way on my return to the mission, which I hope to reach before winter sets in."

The next morning, when Putnam awoke, he found that the priest had already departed.

"That," said the youth, "is a point in his favor. The early bird catches the worms. So, Mary, he was one of your preachers? First I ever saw."

"I hope you liked him," rejoined the girl.

"Well, his coming so handy to take my letter did bend me toward him; yet I don't think I ever could sit still under his preaching."

"And why not?"

"'Cause he's a papist. I've heerd enough about 'em."

To this the young woman made no response, but gazed sorrowfully at her companion a moment, then turned her eyes toward the West. The scene was enchanting. The breeze, which had risen with the dawn, was coming joyously over the prairie, brushing aside the mist, gathering up the perfume of ten thousand flowers, and touched Mary's lips like a breath from the Garden of Eden. And as it played with her raven hair, and brought the roses to her cheeks, Nat could not help thinking she was as fair as any lass he had ever met in New Hampshire.

"Yet she don't seem to know it," he said. "She's very green about

her beauty." A herd of deer were feeding only a short distance away—in every direction the grouse dotted the plain—while circling round and round, in bold relief against the azure sky, was an eagle.

The whole of this day and the next, Putnam kept hard at work felling trees to build a log-house, while the girl remained near the wagon, plying her needle, watching her shamrock, which already showed signs of renewed life, and gathering the eggs, which the hens insisted on laying every hour, so as to make up for lost time.

At length, when he had cut down trees enough, he bade Mary follow him out on the plain, having first filled her apron with stakes—for what purpose she could not imagine.

"What on earth are you doing?" she exclaimed, after having walked by his side almost an hour.

"Can't you guess?" he said, halting abruptly. "Are you so green as all that?"

"Upon my word," replied the girl, "your conduct is distressing; yes, it frightens me to see you turning and twisting in every direction, driving these pieces of wood into the ground, and counting on your fingers. Oh! what'll become of me if you've gone mad?"

"Mad! Ha! Jemima Hopkins wouldn't have said that. Jemima—"

"Was born the year of the comet," interrupted his companion, laughing, "and I'm only a goose."

"Well, don't own it if you are; I'll educate you. And now here goes the first lesson." With this he lifted his forefinger, then shutting one eye, "You must know we won't be long in such a beautiful spot without company. My wagon-tracks will lead many to Illinois who wouldn't have stirred from the shadow of Mount Kearsarge if I hadn't set the example. Methinks even now I hear 'em cracking their whips and bidding good-by to the old folks in Conway. They'll come, too, from other parts of New Hampshire; ay, by the score and hundred they'll come. Now, such being the case, why not have a town laid out by the time they arrive? And right here where we stand shall be our mansion : 'cause, you perceive, it's a corner-lot. While yonder, on t'other corner—so as to be handy in case of rain—I'll get 'em to build the meeting-house; and oh I won't I be proud when it's finished I And what a fine rooster I'll put on the steeple !"

" No, put a cross," said the young woman, " or I'll not go inside of it."

"₊What I a cross, emblem of popery, on this virgin soil, where there's never been one seen, unless 'twas that which your preacher carried yesterday? No, indeed I I've heerd enough about popery."

" I'll pray God to enlighten you," said the girl, at the same time heaving a sigh.

" Well, the more light I get, the less I'll want a popish emblem on top of the meeting-house." Here Nat struck his forehead, then gazing at Mary with an expression of anger, " Have you come so far with me," he said, " to quarrel at last? Bah I you are a goose." With this he turned on his heel and walked off, muttering to himself and evidently very much excited.

Poor Mary did not open her lips again that day, but helped build the log-house with the greatest good-will. Nor did Putnam address her a single word. In fact, it was not until a week had gone by and the dwelling was almost finished that he so far recovered from his ill humor as to speak to her in a friendly way.

" Mary," said he, looking proudly up at the mud-plastered chimney, " this is a good beginning. The first

house is always the hardest to erect ; and you've worked like a beaver. Tell me, now, are you still of the same mind about the cross? Will you stay away from meeting unless I give up my point ?"

" I will," replied the girl firmly. " I want a Catholic Church, or none at all."

" Is my ' Blessing ' in earnest ?"

" Yes, and praying hard that God may open your eyes to the truth."

" Open my eyes ! Well, you're the first mortal ever insinuated that Nat Putnam wasn't wide-awake. But enough; there's a split between us nothing can mend. Alas !" Here he walked off to the hill muttering, " What a pity ! what a pity ! Ignorant as she is, there's yet something about her which goes to my heart. I love Mary O'Brien. I might even ask her to become my wife, if she hadn't such foolish notions about religion. But not content with making the sign of the cross afore every meal, she actually wants one put on top of the meeting-house. What an idea ! A cross ! A thing never seen on this virgin soil till that old preacher came along."

For more than an hour the youth wandered about the hillside, lamenting Mary's obstinacy and superstition, until at length he heard her blowing the horn for dinner.

" Let her blow," he said, " I'm in no humor to eat anything. I'll just lay down anu take a nap." With this he threw himself on the ground, and was about settling his head on a comfortable spot, which seemed as if intended by nature for a pillow, when he gave a start and rose to his feet. " As I live," he cried, " this is a grave ! And if there isn't a cross at one end of it !—and some thing carved upon the wood—what can it be ?" Here he stooped, and, after brushing away a little moss which partly covered the knife-cuts, spelt out the words,

" May his soul rest in peace ! "

" Well, now, this does beat all," he continued. " Who'd 'ave believed a cross had got to this place ahead of me ? And there's something about the epitaph which makes me feel solemn. I wonder how long since these words were cut. Perhaps for years and years only the deer and eagles have gazed upon them. Perhaps since the day the corpse was buried, no lips but mine have spoken over this lonely grave, ' May his soul rest in peace !' "

For a few minutes the youth lingered by the mound, wrestling with himself—for he was conscious that a change was coming over him—then wended his way back to the cabin, resolved to be frank with Mary, and confess that a cross had got here before Nat Putnam.

He had arrived within a couple of paces of the door, which was half-open, when, hearing her speaking, he stopped. "She is praying," he said. "What a fine voice she has ! Better than Jemima's." Then, softly advancing, he discovered her kneeling on the floor, her hands clasped, and her cheek wet with tears. In an earnest tone she was asking God to pardon her father his many sins of intemperance; then with equal fervor, she began to pray for the speedy return of the missionary, bringing Putnam a blessing and forgiveness from his aged parent.

At these words the youth trembled with emotion, and bursting into the room, "Mary, Mary," he cried, " I take back all I said. I laughed when you made the sign of the cross, and I called you ignorant. But you're more larned than Nat Putnam. Your prayer, a moment ago, stirred me up as I never was stirred

at camp-meeting. It made me feel as when through the dark clouds I see blue sky peeping out. Praying for the dead ! O God ! if your preacher comes back and tells me father is dead, I can do one act of reparation—pray for his soul. And but for you, I'd not have written home ; but for you, black remorse would have gone on eating deeper and deeper into my soul—and remorse is hell."

" Mr. Putnam," said the young woman, who, startled by his wild look, had risen to her feet, " my prayers have been heard."

" Yes, they have. I am a Catholic, and vow that our first meeting-house shall have a cross upon it, O my ' Blessing !' never can I be grateful enough to the Almighty for throwing you in my path !"

" It seemed an accident," pursued the girl, " yet it may indeed have been God's work. If it has proved for the good of your soul, it, perhaps, has saved mine. I cannot tell you how I was tempted when I lived in the city of New York. Why, one night, when I was out looking for father, somebody whispered in my ear that I might live in splendor if I chose. The tenement-house where we lodged seemed to hold as many people as there are in the whole of Tipperary. Father and I, with a score of others, slept in a damp room underground. Oh ! when I think of those days, it is like a horrid dream."

" Well, why don't them people follow my tracks ? There's land enough here, dear knows. Yes, let 'em all come ; only they must leave whiskey behind. I want this to be a temperance settlement." Then, after a pause, " But, Mary, I wonder if amongst them I'd find another like you, my ' Blessing ' ?" With this, he rose, and was about to throw his arms round her neck, when he checked himself; then, after fumbling a moment in his pocket, went out to where her shamrock was blooming, and, close by it, he put in the ground a pumpkin-seed. Happy were the June days which followed. With what a light heart did Mary watch the youth at work!

"He's a strange being," she would say; "different from any I ever met in the Old Country. But, for all that, he is good; and when Father De Smet returns I'll have him baptized, and then there'll be no firmer Catholic than Nat Putham."

And the young man—how shall we describe his feelings as, hour after hour, he follows the plough?

"I'm making a home," he would say, "for my 'Blessing.' How she leans upon me! If I were to die, what would become of her? She don't know enough to give lectures, like Miss Hopkins. Oh! if I could only mix her and Jemima together. Yet she's pretty handy at the needle, and since she's overhauled my things I ain't lost a button. And yet my suspenders, darn 'em, do give awful jerks once in a while."

One morning, while he was thus silently praising Mary's skill in the art of sewing, he stopped, gave a groan, then, letting go the handle of the plough, "Wrong!" he exclaimed. "There goes one! Rip! whew!" and, as he spoke, he grabbed a button out of the furrow. For more than a minute the youth examined it thoughtfully, turned it over and over, put it to his eye; then, with a grin, "No," he said, "Mary didn't sew this on; the thread sticking to it ain't the kind she uses. Ah! Jemima Hopkins! Jemima Hopkins! 'tis some of your work. Yes, I remember; 'twas just afore you started off lecturing, and when your head was full of big words. O Jemima Hopkins!"

And so the summer passed away.

The corn came up magnificently, and when it was in all its glory, with the west wind shaking the tassels, Putnam would call Mary out to admire it. "It looks," he would say, "like a regiment of militia on parade." The pumpkin-seed which he had planted was now well above ground, and creeping slowly but steadily round and round the shamrock. Once the girl was tempted to pull the vine up, but, on reflection, it occurred to her that she had better not. And she was right; for under its broad leaves her little plant found shelter from the scorching rays of the sun; and when the thunder-storms burst over the prairie, the shamrock would have been crushed by the great rain-drops, which fell thicker and faster than ever she had known them fall in Ireland, but for the same kindly protector.

One evening, toward the middle of September, Nat came home from work at an earlier hour than usual. He appeared troubled; there was evidently something on his mind; and, when the girl asked what was the matter, he scratched his head, devoured her a moment with his sharp, gray eyes, then, turning on his heel, walked off to a log near the door. There he seated himself, and, after musing awhile, beckoned her to approach.

The young woman obeyed, not, however, without some misgiving. "Mr. Putnam," she thought, "has got tired of living so long in one place, and is anxious to move further west. Alas!"

In another moment she was seated near him and gazing anxiously in his face. He returned her look only for an instant, then coughed, and, rolling up his eyes, "'Tis a solemn thing to do," he murmured. "But I can't help it, and wouldn't if I could. I've felt it coming over me ever since the day she persuaded me to write home to father. Jemima Hopkins would grab at me like a sunfish at a worm in April if I gave her a chance; but this girl is so innocent-like that really I don't know how to begin. And then her very dependence on me, the solitude of this spot, makes her kind of sacred, and I dread lest even words of purest love might give her offence."

"Well, Mr. Putnam," said Mary, interrupting his soliloquy, "you're not going to move away? Don't make my shamrock travel any further. Speak! Oh! I feel so anxious."

At these words, Nat cleared his throat, cracked his knuckles, then, in a voice singularly agitated for one of his temperament, "Mary," he began, "I am never going to move from this spot. You are fond of it, and that's enough." At this unexpected announcement the girl clapped her hands. "But," he went on, "I am not contented; there is yet something wanting to make me perfectly happy."

"And, pray, what is it, sir? I know I am very green, but tell me if the fault be mine; tell me, and I promise to do all I can to please you."

"Well," he pursued, raising his hand and pointing at the pumpkin-vine which circled round the shamrock, "do you see yonder plant almost hiding, and at the same time protecting, the smaller one?"

"I do."

"Well, now, Mary, suppose you be the shamrock, and let me be the vine?"

As he spoke, he gazed earnestly at her. A faint blush crimsoned the girl's cheek. She seemed a little startled; and when she replied, "Yes, I will be your shamrock!" it was in a voice low and scarce above a whisper.

"Well done!" cried Nat, tossing his hat in the air. "Well done! As soon as the priest comes, we'll have the knot tied."

That very evening, the missionary arrived, bringing Putnam news from home, which, although sad indeed, was yet not unmingled with consolation. His father was dead, but the last words he had spoken were words of forgiveness to the youth who had abandoned him in his old age. The Jesuit remained at the log-house almost a fortnight, instructing the convert in the faith, and, before he departed, the latter had the happiness of serving a Mass offered for the repose of his father's soul.

"This never would have happened but for you, my ' Blessing,'" said Nat, pressing Mary's hand. "Those who will follow me to this enchanting spot may laugh at my becoming a Catholic, but 'twill be because they are ignorant. Your religion has in it something sublime; it reaches across the grave, and, by our prayers, gives us a hold upon those who have gone before us. Father! father!" Here his voice failed, and for a minute or two he wept. At length, mastering his grief, he turned to the priest and signified that he was ready for the marriage ceremony to begin. It was short; but while it lasted, a song-sparrow (the first the youth had heard since he arrived in Illinois) alighted upon the window-sill and piped a joyous carol. Often had he heard the bird at his home near the foot of Mount Kearsarge, and now its sweet notes fell on his ear like the voice of a spirit come all the way from the Saco Valley to wish him happiness on his wedding-day.

That evening, he took his wife and the priest to visit the mound on the hillside, and around it they knelt and offered a prayer for the unknown whose dust lay beneath.

As they sauntered back to the cabin, Putnam expressed a lively hope that all his friends in New Hampshire would emigrate to the West. "And when Jemima arrives," he said, closing one eye and looking at his wife with the other, "you'll see something worth seeing; for she's awful smart, and when we get arguing together it's diamond cut diamond. But I'll convert her; oh! I will."

"No doubt," rejoined Mrs. Putnam, "the discussion will be animated and interesting, for you have a clear head and a ready tongue, while Miss Hopkins was born the year of the comet; but believe me, husband dear, it is praying, not arguing, brings into the fold those who are out of it."

"That must be so," he continued, "for you never argued with me, and yet now I'm a Catholic. O happy day when Nat Putnam met Mary O'Brien! And while I will strive by every honest means to improve my worldly condition, I will remain true to the faith. Illinois is a wilderness now, but they're coming, Mary, they're coming; and, before your raven hair turns gray, a city will stand on this prairie; and opposite our corner-lot shall be a church with a cross upon it—a Catholic church. And 'twill be thanks to you, my 'Blessing;' yes, thanks to the shamrock gone West."

GOD IS OUR AID.

A CHRISTMAS STORY OF '67.

In the dim twilight of an October evening, a rich man prepared to leave the vast treasures accumulated by a fruitless life. Fruitless, I say, for though his increasing millions ranked him a merchant prince of the great metropolis, yet the gold had hardened and crusted and metallized his heart—fusing a subtle poison that destroyed the softer instincts of his nature. Therefore, instead of bearing upward a Godward soul on prayerful incense, those last pulses concentrated in one bitter feeling against the daughter whose faith had won from him the intense hate of his life. The owner of millions each year increased his avarice, bowing him low before the god of the nineteenth century, and inciting the struggle, the sacrifice, the sin, for place and station and gold, literally proving the poet-king's cry,* " *Quoniam omnes dii Gentium dæmonia !* " So, while the stormy gusts swept up the avenue, and the lowering sky increased the night, the old man gathered his failing strength for the last great effort. " Hold me, William, support me ere it is too late. Quick ! give me the pen, I must sign while yet my hand has power." Then they put the pen in his trembling hand, his stalwart son supporting him, and all the fiercer passions played upon that cold face, and in those cruel eyes, as he wrote the signature disinheriting the child of the wife whose fair face looked in silent reproach from the portrait opposite. And William Stanfield folded the paper and locked it

* " For all the gods of the Gentiles are devils."

in the escritoire, and old Thomas of the iron heart " slept the last sleep." But this Stanfield, he of the stern Puritan stock, had not always been thus. First, he married his wife as a mere boy of twenty—a gentle New England girl—who had left William to him ; William, so staunch in his loyalty to the heritage left by the *Mayflower* stock. But Thomas laid his boyish love to rest within the quiet " God's-acre " of the village church, and then wandered to New York to build his fortune. Fate did not withhold her favors from this sturdy son, who met and conquered her ; for he was determined to succeed, and did !

And strange to say that at this time human softness yet lived amid the dross and corruption of the world, for Thomas Stanfield was by no means indifferent to certain influences. So, one bright Christmas morning, he found himself in New Orleans, and, stranger still to relate, his partner, Mons. Crécy, persuaded him to listen to the magnificent service at —— Church. The music was exquisitely appealing, thrilling the nobler attributes of man's better nature ; and so this worldly materialist forgot to speculate or dream of gold for two long hours, and sat rapt, while his soul absorbed its divine inspiration. If there is a season when the hardness of humanity dissolves and merges into its spiritual essence, it is when music gently lifts it to its higher affinities, and brings it *en rapport* with God. And thus the man of gold listened to the soft soprano, and far beyond the latticed grating caught a glimpse of dark eyes that haunted him long after the anthem ended. And when Etienne Crécy asked him to dine at the "Grove," his plantation near the city, he accepted, scarcely realizing what he did till he found himself behind a pair of splendid bays, with New Orleans far in the distance.

The balmy, bright-skied South always brought a pleasant Christmas, for oranges hung golden on the trees that formed the grove leading to the house, and the sweet breath of the blossoms perfumed the air. This to the Northerner, accustomed to ice and snow at this season, was a most enjoyable contrast; and his stroll over the beautiful grounds afforded real pleasure. Then they rested on the broad piazza, or gallery, as it is called in Louisiana, and talked of business details, when suddenly Mons. Crécy discovered that his guest was strangely distrait, for a clear, soft voice was sounding, to an accompanying harp, and Mr. Stanfield recognized the same silver tones that had absorbed him during the morning service. "*Qui tollis peccata mundi, suscipe deprecationem nostram,*" fell earnest and tender on his ear—it was, it must be, the same, and he turned to M. Crécy. "It is my daughter Madelaine," said the old man; and at dinner he saw the same fawn-eyes that had first glanced from behind the grating in the old church. And those shy, sweet eyes found a place in the heart of the cold New Englander, and in the spring he bore her a bride to his beautiful home in New York.

Three years passed, and only the step-son shared their household. Some trouble attended the marriage, for the parish priest, Father Jean, at first refused to unite her with such an obstinate heretic. But the maiden loved this son of the Puritans, so either her gentle influence or his pertinacious perseverance overcame the scruples of the good priest, and Thomas Stanfield finally triumphed, giving some vague promise in reference to the children. He fully intended evading the fulfilment of the promise, for soon after his marriage he acknowledged thus much to his wife, who, with tears in her dark eyes, said she would only pray for God's grace to change him. So, almost as a curse it seemed, for three years no child came to bless the marriage. True, the young wife was very dear to this stern husband, but the element which had strengthened his forefathers still waxed strong within him, and the self-asserting dogmatism heired from John Carver's band sounded in the stern words that answered his wife when, with quivering lips, she told him of his little daughter's advent. He kissed the pale young mother tenderly and lovingly, but even in that hour he did not restrain himself from replying, "She belongs to me!" and Madelaine understood too well what those words implied. So she only whispered, as her white face grew whiter, "*I will leave her to God.* May our Holy Mother care for her!"

Then the gentle soul departed with the cross upon her bosom, and those last words on her lips, and many, many years after Thomas Stanfield heard repeated in his dreams, "God shall help her."

And a judgment rested on the rich man's harvest, for this warm-hearted, earnest Southern wife was very dear to him. But the child grew in loveliness, and her impulsive nature felt the need of more than her cold father accorded. Firm as he had been in reference to the child, it seemed strange that he evinced so much indifference to her education, for though she had been baptized in his own church, and sent to Protestant schools, yet very little care was bestowed upon her religious instruction. When she grew old enough, she accompanied her father to church, and through the long sermons her weary little eyes would often close. She went merely from habit, because her father wished her with him, for there was nothing in the cold, formal ritual, if that bare service can be called a ritual, to attract or warm her heart; but it was part of her duty to go; and so she went. Thus her childhood passed, and so her girlhood opened. Children rarely exert the reasoning faculties, accepting with boundless trust what is proposed by their elders. Faith and confidence are largely developed, therefore a grave record is written of those intrusted with these young immortals. But when reason waked and the heart expanded, this warm loving nature asked for more than what was offered, and her soul felt starved, hungry for the food it found not. Thomas Stanfield was now devoted to his business, from nine in the morning, when his *coupé* drove him to his office, to six in the evening, when his key opened the massive door of his palace—his whole soul entered into the fascination, the strife for increasing millions. And at night, as he sat silent in his high carved chair, the closed eyes and set features told that the scheming still continued. Was it strange, then, that the young girl yearned for something more than her home offered? Well, one September evening, soon after their return from the country, the servant handed in a card, bearing the simple inscription, "Kenneth C. Arnaud." Then Mr. Stanfield, disturbed in the midst of some speculation, testified by a grunt his welcome to a distant relative of his wife. "This is Miss Stanfield, my daughter," he said, as he seemed to remember that another person occupied the room. The stranger was a courtly, handsome gentleman, and started as his eyes rested on the young girl. "How like my cousin Madelaine," he said, "as I remember her in my childhood." For the first time the old man seemed to realize the resemblance, and turned to examine the fair girl who was his daughter. "Yes," he faintly assented, and the conversation dragged through a half-hour's duration, when Mr. Arnaud rose to go. But this was not his last visit, for he passed the winter in the city; and many evenings found him at Mr. Stanfield's house, where Madelaine sang to him the songs he loved best. Then a new life opened to the young girl, and her heart felt a strange happiness it had never known before.

The Advent season came—a time of joy and gladness in the churches that celebrate this season, but scarcely remembered or noticed in dissenting congregations; and on the first Sunday that Mr. Arnaud formed one of the family party, he proposed that Madelaine should accompany him to St. ——'s church, as the music was always attractive there. Old Mr. Stanfield was half asleep, when the name of this Roman Catholic church startled him. "Only to listen to the music, papa!" she laughingly replied to his frown, and she went. The ritual was new to her, the service a strange mystery, but she patiently watched it all, listening to the exquisite bursts from the choir. Then sounded the "Alma" with its sweet cadence, and the heart of the young girl thrilled within her. She could not explain, but she felt a strange attraction that drew her against her will to this beautiful ritual. Then came the lovely benediction, and the devotion of the kneeling hundreds, the solemn censer's cloudlike offering, the elevation, and the echoing bell, at which a hush swept like an angel's presence over the rapt thousands. It was all a lovely dream to this young enthusiast, and, closing her eyes, troops of seraphim and cherubim seemed prolonging the words—

> " Tantum ergo Sacramentum
> Veneremur cernui."

She returned to her home filled with a new life, and for the first time her soul felt its thralls. She was very quiet that night, and even her father remarked the change. Poor child ! she had needed all that had been denied to her, and the starved spirit was just tasting of the food immortal. Is it not often thus in life, that a charm, a mere instinct, leads us to the path for which we have been vainly striving ? Give me thine heart ! was the cry of the Holy Mother to the footsore and weary, to all who sought consolation from that loving breast ; and the listening angels caught the echo of that cry, and bore it up to the great Pontiff, who sends the Comforter to spread the white-winged dove on the troubled soul that calls for peace !

The spring came, after the long, cold winter, and Kenneth Arnaud asked the old man for his gentle daughter. But Mr. Stanfield had always regarded Madelaine as a mere child, and seemed shocked and angry at the request. He had forgotten that eighteen years had passed since his soft-eyed wife had whispered, " I leave her to God " —and now a Catholic had asked his child in marriage ! He did not answer the young man for several weeks, not till the sweet eyes of his daughter had been dimmed with many tears, and her childish heart had felt, ay, painfully felt, the first great sorrow of her life.

" It seems strange that my faith should prove an objection, Mr. Stanfield, for not very many years have passed since you gave your own example."

The old man looked him steadily in the eyes, and replied :

" And the great unhappiness of that union was the education of the children that were to come. What say you of this ?"

" That, your daughter shall determine."

" You can speak this with safety, Mr. Arnaud, for my daughter has proved a quick pupil."

" I can scarcely comprehend you, Mr. Stanfield, and, as a gentleman, will not understand the accusation implied."

" I do not accuse you of influencing my daughter, but her bias in favor of the Romish Church is a subject that cannot afford me happiness."

The conversation was serious, and very painful to both, and at last Mr. Stanfield closed the interview with this remark : " As my daughter's happiness is concerned, I cannot withhold my consent, but I wish you to clearly understand that, when she renounces the church of her forefathers, she also relinquishes all right to her father's estate."

A proud smile curled the young man's lips as he replied, " I feel privileged to claim her, even though the conditions were far more capable of inflicting unhappiness."

And so they were married, and the old man and his son William bowed before the golden calf, and worshipped it, offering their souls as homage at its shrine.

For the young wife, one brief year of happiness passed, and yet there was unrest even then within her soul, for she craved with hungry longing the new life which she feared to taste, because the ties binding her to her father appealed to her heart, and she dreaded an anger which she knew would never forgive what he considered so fearful an error.

But one cold morning in the winter of '61, the telegraph bore to New York tidings of the secession of Louisiana, then the sons of the sunny South rallied to her standard, and for four long years a bloody war desolated that section. She, the young wife, had never given her thoughts to politics, nor did she understand why hate and bitterness waged with such deadly strife between the two portions of a country which she so dearly loved; but her husband decided for her, and, feeling that her life was only a part of his, she followed. And those were years fraught with agony—years that recorded suffering that aged more than time had power to accomplish; for over each battlefield brooded a great host of prayer —prayer born of love intensified, and of partings which would know only the meeting above; and the race schooled by those years grew, developed, lived, more than generations ordinarily experience in a whole lifetime.

Col. Arnaud won a soldier's reputation, and the autumn of '64 found him, with his fine regiment, encamped a few miles below the Confederate capital. Madelaine soon followed him to Richmond, bringing her little family, her boy Kenneth and a baby daughter. The winter was very trying to this delicate woman, for the city was crowded with refugees from all parts of the Confederacy; every square inch was occupied, and therefore comfortable accommodations were impossible to find. Then the depreciated currency rendered the price of necessities almost fabulous, so that barely to live required great sacrifice and control. But the cour-ageous wife and devoted mother gathered her little ones, and contentedly dwelt in one small room, happy to welcome her husband whenever his brief furloughs allowed him to spend a day with her. But the great culmination approached, and the troops that wore the tattered gray were soon to furl the cross of stars that had proudly waved over many a gallant fight; and on one cold wintry morning she heard the newsboys shout " Extra! extra!" and soon Franklin Street was echoing with news of the fierce battle below Richmond. Madelaine had not seen her husband for almost four weeks, and her heart sank as she listened. " I will get a paper," she said, and, leaving her nurse with the children, she descended to the street to purchase one.

Poor young thing—she little realized how literally she had followed the Scriptures, for she had forsaken all things, and he, her brave husband, was all she had to cling to; and now —but she was too truly a woman for control, and she fainted when she read the cruel words that told of her husband's fate. A night of horror followed, and the roll of the ambulance in the early gray of the next morning startled her from her troubled sleep. They, those of his brigade, in their faded gray bore him to the small chamber where his young wife waited, and pale and ghastly she saw him laid upon the bed, where he was soon to sleep the long pulseless sleep. All that glory could render to sweeten the pain of dying was offered, for the journals rang with the grand charge he had led, and his deeds of daring were as household words in the crowded Confederate capital. But the great edict had gone forth, and the priest of his church came to offer the last consolations.

"My own true wife," and he summoned the bowed figure, the frail girl-woman who knelt beside him. The sweet eyes were dim with tears, and the voice was tremulous with passionate grief. His left arm drew her to him, for the right was crushed and powerless. "I am about to ask a brave act from you, my darling; do you think that you can please me?"

"Ask me anything, Kenneth, only stay with me. Oh! do not leave me yet," and burning tears blinded her.

"'My ways are not thy ways, nor my thoughts thy thoughts': do you remember these words, my own wife? And then—only a little while, when we shall meet where the for evermore will indeed be eternal! But not of this did I wish to speak, Elaine, but "—and he hesitated—"if my faith could be taught to my little ones?"

She did not reply at first, but, with one gaze of devoted, earnest love, she turned, and kneeling by his side, with the weak precious hand clasped within her own, she repeated: "And receive, O Lord, thy servant into thy holy church, for which her heart hungers." And he answered, "Amen!"

But this was no sudden desire influenced by her devotion to her husband; for, six years before, when she had listened to the sweet vesper service, the latent life had wakened, and the slumber had seen sleep no more, but the message, "Wake to thy salvation!" electrified her soul, and her whole nature thrilled its amen there; since then she had been peculiarly situated, and shrank from provoking anger in her father, as she realized how very stern he could be when he felt himself aggrieved. But now her heart told her she must no longer hesitate, the great crisis asked for action, and she felt that all worldly considerations must be forgotten when her husband, and her own

heart also, called for a decision which shaped her life. So she was baptized by the holy father beside the bed where her husband lay dying; and the priest's voice was very tender as he welcomed this stricken daughter Christ had given to his fold.

Only a few days after, she laid her husband to rest beneath the poplars at "Holleywood," where many of his comrades were lying; and then came the gloomy, stormy March, and the sad April when the snowy flag was folded, and it was during this season that the widowed mother was received into her husband's church.

The war had closed, and we all remember the fearful wreck that followed when Madelaine Arnaud found herself battling with the grim wolf whose shadow darkened her door. Her husband's fortune was all gone, and the delicate, dependent woman felt that she had but little to hope for from her father; still she would not believe that he could entirely forsake her, even though she had become a member of the church his soul abhorred. So she wrote in her extremity and asked for advice. Many anxious days and nights passed, and no letter came; a fortnight intervened, when, one morning, she opened the envelope handed to her by the postman, and read:

"You have chosen your way in life, and, when you forsook your father's faith, he also separated from one who had joined herself to idols. I enclose all that you may ever claim from me.

"THOMAS STANFIELD."

She found enclosed the last note written by her mother, only a few hours before her death, and a silver crucifix, with the name "Madelaine Crécy, La.," inscribed on the back or flat side of the cross.

She was very young to be left so entirely alone, for she was not yet

twenty-five, and two children depended on her for support. What could
she do, and how must she act? In
her agony, she cried, "Save me, O
Father, for without thine aid I am
lost!" Then the crucifix fell from
her letter, and, clasping it, she drew
her boy to her, and, kneeling, prayed:
"Lord, thy enemies and mine have
risen up against me: I therefore cast
myself at thy feet to implore thy
succor."

The soft eyes of the little one gazed
into her own, and, nestling closer, he
asked:

"What makes mamma so sad?"

There are seasons in life when
suffering is too great for expression,
when tears refuse relief, and the over-
charged heart, paralyzed by pain,
seems incapable of pulsation. Then
even speech fails; and the poor, desolate woman only pressed her child
closer, and appealed to her God for
protection.

Thus days passed, and she seemed
unable to act, for at the South all was
poverty and desolation, while she
dared not anticipate what awaited
her in New York. But the few dollars were growing less, and her children required food, so she decided
to try the great city, and thither with
her faithful nurse she journeyed.
Her mother's note gave her strength,
and she often re-read the faint trace-
ry on the faded paper.

"For, my darling child" (the note
read), "should you ever wander into
the dear fold of your mother's church,
feel always that my blessing will rest
upon you, and though I may not live
to guard you, yet my prayer will be
then as it is now for God to be with
you.

"MADELAINE CRECY STANFIELD."

And though she did feel crushed
and desolate on that stormy September
evening which found her in the great
city, still a strength came to her
which she had never known, and she
felt that God would protect her.
Through the crowd at the depot she
wended her way, and thence in the
midst of a pouring rain to a cheap
boarding-house, where she passed the
night. The next morning she met
an old servant who had known her
as a child, and, with tears streaming
from the old eyes, she took her to a
small but respectable house in the
town-part of the city, where she rent-
ed two rooms, and commenced her
new life. A touching sight it was to
see her in her sad mourning dress,
she so fair and fragile, yet feeling
that three depended upon her exer-
tions, she rose to the emergency, and
determined to succeed, or die in the
service. She had brought a letter to
a priest of her church, and to him
she applied. He was very kind, and
promised to do all that he could, but
at the same time told her that pupils
were not easily obtained, and recommended her to watch the newspapers.
And she did search the journals, de-
voting herself to answering advertise-
ments, but, save a few questionable
replies, nothing came of this attempt.
Meantime she began to feel the
pinchings of want, and ventured to
try sewing, but how was she to obtain work? "Go yourself, my dear
young mistress," said the good old
negress—"go yourself; and may de
kind Lord bless you!" And, shrinking
and nervous, she applied to a merchant down-town. She could scarcely find words for her request, but her
pale face appealed, and she bore
away her parcel. Tireless were her
continued efforts, and all through
snow and ice she persevered in her
work. "God will help her!" the
dying mother had said, and through
the darkness of her life's storm she
tried to comfort herself with this assurance.

It was very hard to realize that her father accumulated useless thousands and lived in princely style at the other end of the city, while, only because she believed in her mother's faith, she must suffer and toil with her little ones, needing comfort, and often even bread. Then the old man died, and, ere he died, the scene with which this story opens shamed his last hours.

But the exposure of three winters told on this delicate woman, and, when she felt her strength waning, all the horrors of starvation frightened her; for she knew that there were none to help her. She had moved still lower down-town, and into a smaller room, and there, with · her faithful nurse, she endured life. But then there came a time when, though the will is strong to do, the physique fails to support, and the brave heart, struggling to conquer, feels despair steeling its vitals, and thus it was with Madelaine. The autumn of 1867 set in early, and November was cold and cruel to the poor. She, weaker than she had been, felt her slight unheeded cough increase, and, when December came, was too ill for any exertion. Bitterly the winter opened, snow covered the city, the wind keen and merciless swept the island, and thus the Christmas week found her with the little ones dependent, and she utterly helpless. The last penny had been expended, and the children were wailing with hunger.   ·

Kenneth had looked into her own tearful eyes, and whispered, "Darling mamma, I will pray to Our Lady, and she will ask God to help you." She only kissed her brave, trustful child, but had no strength for utterance. So, when the chill night wrapped the city and darkened the gloomy chamber, the child picked up his mother's rosary, and, throwing it around his throat, held the crucifix in his infant hands, and, kneeling beside his mother's low, poor bed, pleaded that the blessed Virgin would be kind to his dear mamma; and then the sweet child went to sleep murmuring Our Lady's name.

The dawn was fast breaking over the city when the child kissed her, and said, "She has heard my prayer, mamma, for I dreamed that a beautiful angel like the picture in your prayer-book came to me, and said, 'God will help her!'—and does not that mean you, mamma?"

"I hope that our kind Father will help us, my darling; therefore we must try to deserve his help."

"Oh! he will help you, mamma, and I will help you, too."

The day wore away, the last slice had been divided, and there was literally nothing else in the house. Hunger, starvation, was before them, and God, only God, could help them.

The snow fell heavily, the wind blew, and even the elements seemed warring against her, for she had not even fuel to keep off the cold.

Two o'clock chimed from Trinity and, turning, she missed Kenneth. He was now eight years old, and often went out alone, but, with an instinct plainer than words, her heart rose to warn her of danger.

Three, four, five o'clock came, but still the child did not return. The lamps glared in the dark streets, and the night seemed too cold for human life—when—crash! a shriek, and a pair of horses dashed madly down the streets, throwing the occupants of the coach senseless upon the sidewalk. A crowd soon gathered, and bore the crushed and suffering man into the gloomy room where the sick woman lay. Her room opened on the street, and so they laid him on the small bed where the nurse slept.

"Bring a light," sounded a gruff voice.

"Don't you see dat de poor chile has no light for herself? Stonishing de fools dat libs in dese parts!"

A kind voice asked, "Is there no money? Take this and buy a candle." The speaker was a shabbily-dressed man, but the whole aspect showed that he had known better days. He remained with the injured man, and while they go to find a light I leave them. . . .

The snow was falling in great white feathery flakes, covering the dark alleys and darker tenements with its soft downy covering, and the little ragged, barefooted gamins of the great city were shrieking and screaming with delight; but not to build mimic forts or to join the army of snow-ballers did our little wanderer pause. "Mamma shall have some money," he said, "and I will begin to work for it, so I will go to the streets where the fine houses are, and there the men will give me work." Only eight years old was this little soldier in the grand army, but his noble face was radiant with the workings of his soul, which no poverty could injure. His little clothes were patched and scanty, and his poor little frozen toes came through the holes in his worn shoes; but the eyes shone with a light that could not be dimmed, and the firmly-set lips told that he was quite determined to do his best on that afternoon. At first he shrank from the cutting wind that swept from the East River, but, with hands in his pockets and cap pulled down, he ran on till he came to Broadway. Crowded with the happy crowd of the vast metropolis, the great highway was gay with bright faces on this eve of the feast of joy. Windows bright with presents for the favored children of fortune, shops thronged by smiling mothers eager to gratify their pampered darlings. and child-infant as he was, the little one paused to look at the pretty toys; but tears filled the large blue eyes, and he said, "Oh! I can't look at these things, for poor mamma is sick and wants food." At that moment, a gentleman passed, and the child went up and pulled his warm overcoat, "Will you give me some work, sir?" But the creature, a fashionable young fop in tights, shook him off, and passed on. Then came another, this time a respectable gray-haired worthy, and, running in front, the same appealing voice asked the same question. But the successful merchant, hurrying home, was intent upon some new speculation, and, suddenly disturbed, was not very amiable, as he replied, "Be off, you little vagabond!"

This time the policeman came up, and taking him by the arm gruffly ordered him to move on. And thus, on the eve of this blessed festival, when the great city joyed in each household, there was no grain for this wee waif, no crumb for the little estray, who was struggling against the power of the ebb which fate had sent to test his strength for the hereafter. On, on past the Fifth Avenue. Hotel, through Madison Square, glancing at the glittering icicles or gleaming snow-drifts, shivering over the frozen pavements, on he travelled, faintly trying for that which seemed for ever denied to him.

"*I will* find it for her," he said, "for the beautiful angel, our Holy Mother, told me that she should be taken care of. I see her now far up in the clouds." And up in the leaden sky, far beyond the pure, beautiful flakes, he gazed, half-hoping that the Mother of Christ would smile on him again. And did she not even then hover over the young boy-warrior? Did she not pray that he, too, might be strengthened in this hard fight which his infant powers essayed? *Adjuvabit eam Deus!* * the dying mother had prayed, and his promises would not fail. At last, far up the avenue, when the cold, shadowy twilight stole on the great city, he paused before a stately mansion. Curtains of silk and costly lace draped the windows, and liveried servants were sitting on the box of the handsome coach awaiting the master's coming. Then the heavy door of massive bronze opened, and the master slowly descended the broad steps. "Oh! you will help me, won't you? Please give me some work, for I want to earn money for my mother!"

"Send that little beggar away," was the irritable rebuff, and the footman flung him aside, not heeding where he fell. The carriage rolled away, and no thought was given to the small human bundle, roughly hurled from the rich man's path. Then night darkened over the city, and the stars, God's eternal sentinels, guarded earth as they had done eighteen centuries before when they watched the birth of the incarnate God. And beneath the same shimmering light the boy-warrior lay, all worsted in the strife, as thousands had sunk before, and all unconscious of the cruel hearts that still pulsed on. The torn little cap had fallen off, and the fair golden curls shaded the pale, childish face, turned upward as if in appeal to the Blessed Mother he had seen in his dreams. Was she watching still, and did her kind eyes see the crucifix clutched in the poor cold hands—the crucifix with the dead Christ, whose birth the morrow would celebrate? But the soft feathery flakes fell steadily on, covering the sweet face of the little one. Ah! God of

* "God shall help her."

infinite love and goodness, will the great army with the ranks of sin, and greed, and lust, prosper and thrive and live, while this young soldier, this infant of purest soul and lion heart, lies all unheeded, dying, the victim of cruelty and selfish forgetfulness?

But see—a policeman tramps near, and he comes with stalwart tread, swinging his burly arms, and clapping his gigantic hands to keep the fingers from freezing, for verily death seems to breathe out in the stealthy, deadening cold. Bravely he glances with searching look up and down the broad avenue, then pauses suddenly by the side of the obstruction just without the pavement.

"God and his holy saints forsake me, if this same bundle ain't a child! Ugh! but it's an ugly night for this small specimen to be left here! But come, let's see, my little man," and he tried to move him. "St. Patrick save me! if I ain't afraid that he'll never feel again!" And he dropped the little arm he held, and the crucifix, falling, lay dark against the glittering snow. The sight of the cross at once touched the stout Irishman, and this sturdy six footed son of the Green Isle, this huge guardian of the great city, gathered the stray lamb to his bosom tenderly, pityingly, as its own mother, and bore it to the station-house. And, full of the warm impulse of his race, he chafed the poor little hands, and lingered by the pallet on which he lay, till great tears fell from eyes that had not seldom looked unmoved on the misery of the metropolis. He raised the child's crucifix to his lips, and though he hurriedly summoned a physician, he muttered, "Poor little lamb, if he does come back to life, it will only keep an angel longer from Our Lady's home!"

The man returned to his duty, and hours passed before he was relieved, but ere he returned to his own home, and the young wife waiting him, he went back to the station-house to look after "the pretty young one" who had died with the cross in his hand; for he fully expected to find him dead on his return.

"We have had hard work to bring him back, Murphy," said the doctor, as the man walked up to the child. "Only five minutes more, and the cold would have reached the little heart, which was losing all sensation. We have had a time of it, and he has just fallen asleep. These are what we found on him. The card was fastened to his worn jacket, and the crucifix has also a name engraved." And picking up the card from the table the policeman read, "Kenneth Arnaud, 312 East —— Street." On the back of the silver cross was the name, "Madelaine Crécy, August 15, 18—."

"Poor little child! said the policeman. "I'll take him home, for his house is near my own."

So he wrapped the sleeping child in an old blanket, and carried him through the storm. A light glimmered on the first-floor front room as he approached the house, and the man stepped in to inquire about his young charge. As he opened the rickety door, the wailing voice of a woman smote him with the agonizing pain it expressed. "The gentleman may remain," she said, "but for God's sake find my child. O sir! bring me back my child!" and her sobs and moans were heart-rending. The negress rocked to and fro with the little girl, trying to keep her warm and still her feeble cries for bread, chanting the while in dull monotone, a habit peculiar to her race, and which at this time increased the oppressive gloom of the place, not at all relieved by the flickering tallow-candle, nearly burned out—on the small bed in the corner the wounded gentleman lay groaning in agony, and impatiently awaiting a messenger he had summoned—a sad eve truly that announced the blessed festival!

At this time the policeman tapped with his club, but receiving no answer, and not caring to wait in the cold, he once more opened the door. Standing mute on the threshold, for the scene at first deprived him of speech, then walking to the centre of the room, he asked, "Is the mother of Kenneth Arnaud here? For I have found a child of that name, who wore a crucifix on which was engraved 'Madelaine Crécy.'"

With one wild scream the mother answered, "He is mine!" and, as she clasped him to her heart, the soft eyes unclosed, and the feeble little voice whispered, "Darling mamma, I asked them all for work that I might buy you bread, but—oh! my head hurts, for a wicked man flung me away from a gentleman who rode in his carriage. But, mamma, don't cry, for she—the one with the angels —will care for us. Oh! I have just seen her, and I waked to find your own eyes where hers had been. Dear mamma, keep me with you, away from the cruel man, and the ice, oh! the cold snow!" And his little frame shivered with the recollection.

"Madelaine Crécy!" the sick man muttered on his couch in the corner. And the policeman approached. "Yes, sir, that was the name on the crucifix, and I thought the little fellow was dead when I picked him up in front of the millionaire's house on Fifth Avenue."

"My God! and it was my servant who cast him from me! Will you take a message to that house, my good man? Do not refuse me, for gold shall pay you well. I—I am that millionaire, and an avenging God has crushed me." With his uninjured arm, he drew out a card from his pocket, and said, " Take this to my residence, and tell my housekeeper to come to me at once." Then, placing an eagle, his own valued pocket-piece, in the policeman's hands, he prayed him to hasten his errand.

But the mother's weak voice also called the kind Irishman. She had heard nothing of the conversation, for she was absorbed with her darling, who in broken words had told his little story.

" I have nothing to give you, sir," she said with tears streaming down her pale cheeks. " The rosary was my mother's, and besides this I have not even food for my children. But I will pray for you, and God will bless and reward you, sir; he will grant what I cannot give."

She clasped his rough hand, which her tears fell upon, and he hurriedly left the room, for his own eyes were very dim.

Many and varied are the phases which the great city presents to these her guardians, but in his fifteen years' experience none had touched him more than this.

He closed the door after him, and the solitary candle burned to its socket. It was now past midnight, and a long silence ensued, broken only by the snores of the negress, for the starved infant had cried itself to sleep. The bruised stranger forgot his own suffering as he contemplated the surrounding misery, and for some time the stillness was profound. At last he muttered, " Madelaine Crécy! Madelaine Crécy! can it be the same! Then God have mercy on my soul!"

" Who calls my mother's name ?" asked the sick woman.

" I, your father's son, Madelaine Arnaud. I, your brother, who despoiled you, and sold his life for gold, but," and his voice trembled with emotion—" but who will devote that life to you now, if you will allow it, to atone for the cold selfishness of the past."

" I should be no daughter of the church, which you despise, William Stanfield, if I bore anger to my father's son. I teach my little children to pray, ' Forgive us, as we forgive those who sin against us,' therefore must my heart refuse all malice against God's creatures, else would my own prayers avail not."

He could not answer then, for he, the bigot, the scorner of that church which he had ridiculed, felt now the beauty of her teaching when, even in the midst of her sufferings, this desolate woman could forgive one who knew that he was responsible for so much that might have been alleviated.

" Elaine !"—ay, it was the first time that she had listened to her old name since the night when her brave husband had spoken his farewell, and the sound thrilled her with strange memories—" Elaine, your roof has sheltered me to-night, and saved from destruction one who claims as a proof of your forgiveness acceptance of the home which he will share with yourself and little ones."

And, ere she answered, the chimes of Trinity heralded the dawn of that thrice-blessed morning when the angels sang, " Glory to God in the highest, and on earth peace to men of good-will." And that message of the Incarnation brooded with its holy evangel on the troubled hearts within, as, when the Christmas sun shone over the snow-covered city, the carriage of the rich merchant bore its precious freight to his home, and light, and life, and joy succeeded the gloomy night. And she, when her prayer ascended on that night of shelter and rest, realized the fulfilment of her mother's benediction: " Adjuvabit eam Deu !"

THE SACRIFICE AND THE RANSOM.

AMONG the various manifestations of Christian charity in the middle ages—charity sometimes ill-understood perhaps, but always sincere and enthusiastic—there are few that show more expressively to what a degree the love of our fellow-creature can suppress all egotistical instincts, than the Order of Mercy for the redemption of captives. Sustained and encouraged by holy charity, the Father of Mercy embarked each year at Marseilles, braving plague, martyrdom, and slavery. In the name of that heavenly King, of whom he considered himself the ambassador, he demanded from the astonished tyrant of Algiers the liberty of the Christian captives, until then apparently condemned never to see again their homes. The savage Dey, awed by the heroic confidence of the unarmed pilgrim—moved, perhaps, by some secret compassion, accepted the gold offered as ransom ; and the obscure and humble father recrossed the sea, and returned again on foot to his distant monastery.

And what was the origin of this institution ? No legislative assembly, no council of ministers is entitled to the honor of having conceived the idea of this pious enterprise. The loving heart of a man who had devoted himself from his childhood to the service of suffering humanity was the first to devise a plan of carrying relief and consolation to misfortunes which, until then, had seemed beyond the ordinary action of Christian charity. Peter Nolasque, the founder of the Order of Mercy, was born In 1189, near Castelnaudari, in Languedoc, France. His learning was as remarkable as his piety, so that at the age of twenty-five, the education of the son of Peter of Aragon was confided to him by the celebrated Simon of Montfort. It was while at the court of Barcelona, in this high and responsible position, that Peter Nolasque resolved to devote his life and fortune to the ransom of the Christian slaves who languished hopelessly under the burning sun of Africa.

For this purpose he determined to establish a religious order for the deliverance of captives. Several noblemen contributed large sums of money toward the good work ; the court of Rome gave its supreme approbation, and on St. Lawrence's day, 1223, Peter Nolasque was declared the first general of the new institution, and invested with the monastic habit. He lived far from courts during the rest of his life, travelling painfully on foot to carry consolation and freedom to the wretched beings he pitied so truly. More than four hundred Christians were delivered from the hands of the Mussulman by his efforts alone.

He died on Christmas-day, 1256, leaving behind him the memory of a pure and generous life, and an institution which soon numbered among its members many of the bravest and noblest chevaliers of France.

THE SACRIFICE.

IT was in the year of our Lord 1363. The curfew bell had just been rung, the doors of the village houses were all fast shut, and within the castle wall the measured tread of the sentinel on the battlements was the only sound that met the ear. If, perchance, some belated traveller was still abroad, he hung his rosary around his neck, and hurried onward muttering pious ejaculations ; for a heavy mist deepened the shades of night, and the sad wailings of the wind and the hootings of the owl mingling together, sounded ominously in his terrified ears.

The only light visible was in the chapel of the monastery, where the monks of the Order of Mercy were reciting their evening prayers. They had just ended the last and solemn petition for "*all Christians, captive and suffering in the hands of the infidel*," when the bell at the great gate of the holy house rang loudly, and the brother-porter, rising from his knees, hastened to reconnoitre by the wicket who it was demanded admittance at such an unusual hour.

Three persons were at the gate ; one, a young man, wore a rich emblazoned coat of arms ; his head was uncovered save by the long clustering curls of dark hair, now heavy with the night-damp, that descended to his shoulders ; a youth, apparently his page, bore in his arms the knight's helmet. The third individual was an old man, who kept himself in the background, and who appeared by his plain steel cuirass to be an humble squire, grown gray in harness. The page's youthful face was sad and timid ; the elder man's showed the traces of violent passions in the deep lines that furrowed it, and his eyes even now seemed to flash in the light of the torch that the monk carried. The chevalier's noble countenance was pale and grave, and he stood leaning pensively on his sword.

"What wish you, Messire ?" asked the brother-porter of the knight, when,

after a deep but sharp scrutiny, his doubts were removed as to the quality of the strangers.

"May it please the Reverend Father Prior to grant me a short interview ?" ·

"May it be as you desire, Messire. I will seek the reverend Father when you have entered with your followers."

The heavy iron-bound gate of the convent turned on its massive hinges, and closed the instant that the travellers were within.

The golden spurs of the chevalier resounded on the cloister's marble flags as he followed the monk, and he murmured to himself the words of the Psalm, "*Hæc requies mea in seculum seculi*"— but his page and his squire knew no Latin, and his conductor heard him not.

They were introduced into a spacious ancient parlor lined with high black oaken wainscot ; the brother placed the torch he carried in an iron claw that was fixed in the wall for that purpose, and invited the strangers to seat themselves on the bench that ran round the chamber, then bowing profoundly, left them.

The squire immediately drew nearer to his young lord who appeared to be absorbed in thought.

"How, my lord," cried he, "is it possible that you believe that these monks can forward your plans? Why thus retard our journey? A few days more and we should have reached our goal, and many a good man and true would have made your quarrel his own. The brave free companies would have served you as never a hooded priest in France !"

"Banish all such thoughts for the future, Michel," replied the knight, "it is better to pardon than to revenge."

"Good Saint Denis ! do I hear the Lord of Montorgueil aright ! My lord, pardon the frank speech of an old soldier, but never was the escutcheon of your house dimmed without being washed in blood—and would you be the first to let it lie soiled in the dust?"

"Alas! Michel, it is indeed true that too much blood has been shed in the quarrels of our house!"

"Holy Virgin! can it be possible that my liege lord has forgotten the duties of a valiant knight?"

"Friend," replied the young warrior sternly while his pale cheek reddened with the emotion awakened by the squire's reproach, "I have remembered that I was a Christian before I was made a knight!"

Michel drew back in silence, gazing on his master with a countenance in which astonishment and grief were nearly equally portrayed, while the Lord of Montorgueil silently proceeded to take off his shoulder-belt and untie his silken scarf.

The heavy oaken door at length opened and the venerable prior entered. Quick as thought, the knight threw the sword he held in his hands at the monk's feet; then, falling on his knees, exclaimed in a loud, firm voice, "Reverend Father, in the name of God and of the holy Virgin Mary, I, Raoul de Montorgueil, chevalier, pray and conjure you to admit me into the religious and devout observance of our Lady of Mercy, for the deliverance of captives!"

"Amen, my son, so be it, if it be God who sends thee," replied the Prior.

"My lord, my lord," cried Michel, "remember the Sire of Valeri! Proud will he be, and loud his boast that fear of him has moved you to this. You know his *outre-cuidance!*"

"O my worshipful lord!" exclaimed the timid page, bursting into tears, "think of your lady-mother!"

"I think of the salvation of my soul more than of all else," replied the chevalier.

"Silence, good friend!" said the prior, as Michel appeared about to attempt another remonstrance; "and you, my son, seat yourself here by my side, and tell me what has induced you to seek this peaceful sanctuary."

The young knight arose and placed himself on the wooden bench by the monk; then, keeping his eyes steadfastly bent to the ground as if to avoid the sight of his two weeping retainers, "Reverend Father," he said, "most bitter is the remembrance of the past; for the last time will I recount the evil thoughts and deeds that once seemed so natural to me. For many a year all Brittany has resounded with the feuds of the Lords of Montorgueil and the Sires of Valeri; bitter has been the hatred and bloody the strife between these two proud houses; but I will not recall past outrages—let me relate only the last deadly wrong that filled my heart with unspeakable thirst of vengeance.

"Twelve days have not yet expired since the passage of arms at Rennes; the Sire of Valeri was there at the head of a numerous company of his partisans, and defied me to single combat, with many a vain and bragging word. I accepted his challenge, resolved to be the victor or die. The onslaught was terrible, for we were equal in strength and skill, and we long parried each other's thrusts. Forced at last to pause to take breath, the Sire o. Valeri proposed a truce.

"'Let us meet a month hence,' he cried, 'with twenty good men each, and end our quarrel.'

"'Why should we adjourn till another day what can be so well ended now?' I replied; 'our swords will be no sharper and our hate no hotter. No, may my spurs be hacked off my heels by your basest varlet, ere I consent to sheathe again my sword before one of us fall !' Then again fast and furious fell our blows until the traitor knight making a feint, struck me before I had time to cover and I fell. ' Yield !' cried my exulting foe. ' Never ! Never !' I replied. ' Then die the death !' and he raised his weapon.

" At that moment my young brother—alas ! alas ! why did my lady-mother bring him to those fatal lists !—my young brother leapt over the barriers and sprang to the rescue —the heavy blade descended on his fair head ! Father, I saw the long hair of the noble child red with his young life's blood, and I saw no more. When I awoke from my deadly swoon, I found that my good squire and gentle page had carried me from the lists and were weeping over me while they swore vengeance on the enemy of our house.

" I, too, thirsted for vengeance, for vengeance on all the kith and kin of the house of Valeri, and I resolved to seek fifty lances and attack the miscreant in his stronghold. Vainly my lady-mother prayed me to lay aside my sword and live for her. ' Leave vengeance to heaven,' she said, ' I have seen too much blood —O my son ! let me not weep over the mangled corpse of my last child !' Vainly she prayed ; I left her, reverend father, to mourn over the grave of my brother, while I carried death to the homestead of our enemy.

" But as I journeyed toward the quarters of the Free Companions, fol-lowed by these, my squire and page, intending to enlist some good lances under my banner, the remembrance of my mother's grief returned again and again, and my heart softened each time that I thought of her, child-

less and alone in her sorrow. I was meditating sadly this very day, when the sound of a bell ringing the *An-gelus* reminded me that it was the hour of prayer, and I alighted from my horse to repeat an Ave Maria. When I said, ' *Pray for us in the hour of our death*,' I asked myself for the first time, if in that supreme hour remembrance of my revenge would be sweet to me, and if, when in the presence of him who is the suzerain of the lord as well as of the vassal, I should dare to vaunt me of the blood I had shed. Thus I continued to re-flect as I resumed my journey, until at last I found myself before the gate of this holy house, and I heard echo-ing beneath the arched cloisters the strains of that sweet *Salve Regina*, that pilgrims say the angels sing at night beside the fountains.

" All the bitterness and anguish of my heart melted away as I listened ; '.O Mother of Mercy !' I cried, ' it is then here that thou art awaiting me ? Yes, I will henceforth be thy knight ; it is better, I feel, to wipe tears away, than to cause them to flow.' I threw myself on my knees, and when again the holy strains repeated ' *O cle-mens ! O pia ! O dulcis Virgo Maria!*' my resolution was firmly taken, and I had vowed myself to the service of the blessed Virgin. Receive me then, Father, as her servant."

Raoul threw himself once more on his knees before the venerable priest, who raising his arms toward heaven silently gave thanks for this miracu-lous conversion ; then turning to-ward the knight, blessed him and gave him the kiss of peace. " How admirable are the ways of God, my son," said he ; " how little did my brethren and I think while we were praying this night for all captives, that there was one so near us being freed at that moment from his bonds ! Thou wast smitten on the road, my son, like Saint Paul ; like him thou art, perhaps, destined to become a chosen vessel of grace. In the name of God and of the blessed Virgin, I receive thee into our holy order, and admit thee to the ordeal of our novitiate."

The sobs of the two retainers had been the only sign of their presence that they had given while the knight was speaking ; but now the old squire cast himself at his feet, and in broken accents besought him to have pity on his poor vassals, and not abandon them to the scoffs and outrages of the enemy of his house.

"Have pity on us," repeated the page, wringing his hands.

"My friends, weep not like women," replied their master, "I have thought of everything. God will comfort my lady-mother, and she will rejoice to have her son a knight of the holy Virgin. My kinsman Gaston will be your lord ; he is worthy of the inheritance I leave him, for he has a noble and generous heart. He is young, it is true, but I will place him under the tutelage of Messire Bertrand du Guesclin, and foolhardy will he be who shall then attack our house or harm its vassals. Reverend Father, I crave your hospitality for my two retainers, and I entreat you to permit me now to seek peace and strength in prayer."

The prior took his hand and conducted him in silence to the chapel. A single lamp burnt before the sanctuary, and shed a faint, solemn light upon the image of our Lady of Mercy. Raoul prostrated himself at the foot of the altar and poured forth his ardent soul in supplication. When he arose, the marble steps were wet with tears.

"Father," he said to the prior, "I am strong now—the sacrifice is accomplished."

The young convert passed that night in writing. He addressed a long and loving letter to his mother, relating to her all his struggle—his burning wish for vengeance, his fear of shame, the tender mercy that had touched his heart : the parchment on which he wrote was stained with many a tear. "I could not remain in the secular world without revenging our injuries," said he in conclusion, "I have left it that I may pardon. Honored lady and dear mother, bless your son and pray for him."

To Messire Bertrand du Guesclin he gave a rapid sketch of the facts, and besought his protection for his young kinsman, now Lord of Montorgueil.

A third letter still remained to be written ; how much it cost him to break this last link with the outward world, was revealed by the sobs that burst from his quivering lips, by the tears that dropped heavily on the oaken table on which he leaned. "No," cried he at last, "this tie *cannot* be broken," and taking his pen he traced some hurried words: they were addressed to his brother-in-arms, his friend, his playmate in happy childhood, his rival in his first feats of arms.

"Dear Aymar," were his concluding words, "my heart can never change toward you—oh ! believe that it beats the same under the monk's frock as under the knight's armor ! *For love of me*, Aymar, *avenge not my quarrel.*"

The ancient squire, who had passed the night in lamentations, interrupted only by exclamations of indignant surprise at the peaceful slumbers of his young companion, looked very sad and weary when Raoul entered his chamber at break of day.

"Michel," said the knight, "spare me your reproaches and tears ; they can avail nothing to change my purpose, but I have need of all my fortitude. Here are divers messages; be heedful of them, that they may reach their destination speedily."

He put into the squire's hands the letters he had prepared, each fastened with a silken string, and impressed with his seal.

"Give this rosary of golden beads to my lady mother," he continued, "she hung it on my neck when we parted; henceforth when she tells it, the remembrance of her Raoul will be mingled with every prayer. This ring, that I won in my first tournament, is for Aymar de Boncourt; beg him also to take my armor and my war-horse. And now farewell, Michel, the matin-bell is ringing, and I belong no longer to the world, but to God. Farewell, old friend, farewell; be as faithful to Gaston as you have been to me." He threw himself on the old man's breast and pressed him to his heart, then tearing himself from his arms, he gazed an instant tenderly on the still sleeping page. "Recommend this poor child to the new Lord of Montorgueil, Michel, and be ever his friend." He stooped and kissed the boy's smooth brow, then turned softly away—the door closed, and the squire and the page never looked on him again.

When the morning prayers were ended, the prior summoned the disconsolate retainers to his presence, and, after a discourse full of consolation and good counsel, dismissed them with a handsome largess from their beloved master. We will not follow them on their journey; suffice it to say that when the lady of Montorgueil received her son's unexpected letter, the first pang of sorrow and regret was excruciating, but the Christian mother was soon able to accept the sacrifice. She ceased to grieve, and in a few months retired to a convent, where she passed the rest of her peaceful and honored life.

Du Guesclin, whose noble heart was full of generous sympathy, loudly proclaimed his affection for Raoul, and his determination to protect the house of Montorgueil. This was sufficient to prevent all attempts of the Sire of Valeri against the vassals and lands of the new lord; and he contented himself with whispering accusations of cowardice against the knight who had left the death of his brother unavenged, and his own quarrel unvoided.

Aymar alone could not be comforted for the loss of his brother-in-arms, and it was long before he was seen to take his wonted place in the feasts and tournaments that formed the greater part of the occupations of the young chevaliers of his time and country.

Raoul meantime consummated his sacrifice; his long curls were cropped close, and the monk's white woolen robe replaced the knight's brocade and velvet. After a novitiate of a year and a day, he pronounced the three vows of his order in the Chapel of our Lady of Mercy, with an especial promise to give his life for the ransom of captives. From this time forward he was only known as the Brother Sainte Foi.

THE RANSOM.

TIME passed away, and France was once more at peace with England for a brief space; at peace, but far from tranquil, for the Free Companies, which at first consisted only of nobles, younger sons of powerful lords, had been terribly augmented by the disbanded soldiers of both countries, who found inaction intolerable, and who now ravaged her defenceless provinces. In vain the outraged people cried for help and pro tection; the state, without money or men, was unable either to prevent or punish. At length the brave du Guesclin imagined a means to employ these fiery spirits. He sought the formidable band, then encamped on the plains of Chalon, at the head of two hundred chevaliers, and addressed them: "Most of you," said he, "were once my companions-in-arms, you are all my friends. Your vocation is not to ravage and destroy, but to conquer and save. Necessity, only, I know, has forced you to such extremities. I come now to offer you the means of living honorably and of fighting gloriously. Spain groans beneath the yoke of the Saracen: would you not rather choose to be the deliverers of a great nation than the ruin of this fair country?"

At these words the Free Companions surrounded the chief, and with enthusiastic acclamations swore as one man to follow him whithersoever he should lead. The noblest of the French chivalry joined the enterprise, and Spain soon reëchoed with the well-known war-cry of "Notre-Dame Guesclin!"

The Sire of Valeri and young Aymar of Boncourt were among the bravest of du Guesclin's gallant band, and their exploits soon became the favorite themes of the troubadours and trouvères of tuneful, glory-loving France. But when the chief and his victorious warriors returned to their native land, Aymar and the Sire of Valeri were not among them. Had they fallen in the last bloody encounter? Had they been traitorously ensnared and were they now languishing in some Moorish dungeon? Several of the adventurers affirmed that the two knights had embarked for France, but no vessel from Gallicia had reached a port of Brittany.

The Fathers of the Order of Mercy were soon aware of the rumors that circulated concerning the fate of the two bravest chevaliers of the age; their continual efforts to collect funds for the ransom of captives placed them in communication with all parts of Christendom, and the news of the disappearance of the Sire of Valeri quickly reached the ears of Brother Sainte Foi. The mysterious fate of him who was Raoul's enemy saddened him, but terrible indeed was the pang he felt when he learnt that his friend Aymar was also lost. All his fortitude, all his resignation, suddenly forsook him, and he wept bitterly.

"My son," said the prior reproachfully, "I thought thou wast dead to all earthly things."

"O reverend father!" replied he, "earthly things are perishable, but holy friendship comes from Heaven and dieth not. Let me weep for my friend. David wept for Jonathan; their souls were one; mine also was one with Aymar's."

From this time forward the young monk seemed to waste away, his cheek grew thinner and paler, his eyes were dim and tear-worn. In vain, hoping to arouse him, his superior sent him without, to seek funds for their work of charity; no change of scene could dispel the melancholy languor that had taken possession of him, and the whole fraternity deplored that so pious and ardent a spirit would, in all probability, be so soon taken from among them. After much anxious deliberation the chapter at last resolved to invest him with the title and functions of Redemptorist, and, on account of his youth and inexperience, to associate him with an aged monk who had been several times sent on the errand of love and mercy.

Brother Sainte Foi was accordingly summoned one day before the assembled fathers.

"Brother," said the prior, "don thy sandals, take thy staff, and be ready to depart."

"I am ready, reverend father."

"Thou dost not enquire whither?"

"Obedience questioneth not, reverend father."

"It is well, my son; depart, then, and may God be with thee! Go to the land of the infidel—go ransom the captives!"

Brother Sainte Foi, transported with joy, threw himself at the prior's feet, unable to speak his thanks, while his dim eyes flashed, and his faded cheek reddened; youth, and health and strength came back, as if by a miracle, and the good prior, delighted to see the effect he had produced, entered into full details for the guidance of the young Redemptorist during his mission. The whole community assembled to pray for the happy issue of his journey; and after receiving the blessing of the elders, he set forth laden with the rich alms destined to relieve so much misery.

A long and wearisome journey on foot brought the Redemptorist father to the port where he was to take ship for Algiers, and here he was joined by the venerable monk who had been appointed his guide and counsellor in the holy work. They embarked together on a Genoese vessel they found ready to sail, and a favorable wind soon carried them across the Mediterranean. The young father's heart beat hard when he heard the cry of "land!" and saw the cruel coast of Africa, where so many fellow-Christians were groaning hopelessly beneath the yoke of the bigot Mussulman.

"It is there that our brethren suffer. O father!" cried he to his companion, "but we are going to succor, we are going to save!"

And when, at last, the vessel entered the port of Algiers, the Redemptorist knight knelt and kissed the soil of the wished-for land, where he was about to make his first trial of arms in the holy lists of charity.

The two monks, whose errand was well known, were immediately surrounded by a crowd of slave-merchants, who scoffingly taunted them, "Have you plenty of gold, Christians? for we have plenty of slaves; you may have a shipload of them." Father Antoine had learned prudence and replied as guardedly and as briefly as he could to the miscreants that pressed upon him. He hastily directed his steps, followed by his companion, toward the hospital which the Order of Mercy had with much difficulty obtained permission to build at the entrance of the port. Arrived there, without tarrying to rest, he commenced ringing the great bell that never tolled but to announce the joyful tidings that charity, holy charity that suffereth long and is kind, that beareth all things, that believeth all things, hopeth all things, endureth all things; charity that never faileth, had landed again on those burning sands, to bring hope and aid to the followers of the cross.

At that signal a crowd of disheveled, ragged men, many wearing chains at their wrists and ankles, were seen hurrying toward the chapel. Alas! who would have recognized in those emaciated, tear-worn spectres, the stalwart soldiers, the valiant chevaliers, whose deeds the silver-tongued minstrels of France were singing even then?

Sobs and joyous cries, prayers and ejaculations, burst from them as they threw themselves on their knees before their deliverers, and kissed their garments.

"Brethren," said the venerable father, his voice troubled and trem bling, "we have come hither in the first place for the salvation of your souls : during eight days we shall be here waiting to listen to your confessions, and to give you ghostly consolation, to preach to you the word of life, and to bestow on you the sacraments of our holy mother church. In the second place, we have come to work for your deliverance from captivity. Pray for us, brethren, that we may worthily acquit ourselves of our sacred tasks."

The unhappy slaves, whose hopes and fears could be read in their agitated features, gave a great cry when the good father ceased speaking. It seemed as if despair was calling on heaven for mercy, and then slowly withdrew.

The next, and the following days, slaves and masters besieged the hospital gate, and the two monks knew not a moment's rest while daylight lasted. Each evening, when they were once more alone, Father Sainte Foi would enquire eagerly of his aged companion if he thought that they would be able to ransom all the captives.

"We shall be able to save them all, father, shall we not?" he would say with trembling anxiety ; "I have so raised their hopes to-day that I could not leave one now to despair."

Father Antoine returned no answer to these enquiries ; he seemed rather to avoid the pleading eyes that tried to read his thoughts. So passed the eight days allowed them by the infidel. At length, on the eve of that fixed for their departure, a little before the solemn hour, when all the slaves that the alms of the faithful had been able to ransom were to be surrendered into the hands of the Redemptorists, the old man sought his young coadjutor.

"There are two hundred and twenty, dear brother," cried he, with a ra-

diant look of triumph; "and we have ransomed them all!"

"All, father! oh! I thank God and our Lady;" and the monk cast himself on his knees, and prayed silently ; then rising, clasped the good old father in his arms, in an ecstasy of joy.

That night Father Antoine repeated the evening prayer, as usual, with the captives, but his voice trembled, while Father Sainte Foi could scarcely restrain his tears. All hearts beat hard, and every face was pale and anxious. In the midst of the solemn silence that followed the repetition of the last supplication to the throne of grace, the priest arose slowly, and cast upon the woe-begone crowd a look so pitiful and so loving, that consolation seemed to fall like heavenly dew upon even the most despondent.

"Brethren," said he, "dear brethren! dear children! this is the twelfth time that the honored title of Redemptorist has been conferred on me; sometimes it has been the cause of much pain and disappointment to me, sometimes too of great joy."

Here the slaves stretched their trembling hands toward him, but their lips uttered no sound.

"My children, my dear children! at this moment my heart overflows with joy!"

A cry, a terrible, unearthly cry escaped from every mouth, as, moved by one and the same impulse, the liberated slaves flung themselves on their knees.

"In the name of our omnipotent God and of the Mother of our Redeemer, the Blessed Lady of Mercy, I, an unworthy priest, and my companion here present, declare you to be all free! The alms of the faithful have been sufficient to ransom you all. All of you, Christian brethren, will see your native land again !"

Bursts of frantic joy, rapturous embraces again and again repeated, succeeded to the silent anguish with which they had awaited their doom. The venerable father endeavored to calm this exhausting excitement, and then left to go pay the Moors the sum stipulated. Father Sainte Foi remained behind to help remove the fetters whose iron verily entered into his soul.

"To-morrow !" he cried, as he knocked off the heavy chains, "to-morrow, we shall quit this land of slavery and death !"

"To-morrow !" echoed the pale victims, "to-morrow ! Thanks, O Lord God ! Thanks, O well-named Lady of Mercy ! Thanks Redemptorist Fathers ! We are going home to-morrow !"

"Retire now, dear brethren," said Father Antoine, returning, "the Moors are satisfied, and to-morrow at break of day we shall meet again !"

The now happy crowd left the chapel to seek repose in the dormitories of the hospital until the wished-for morning light, and the two monks prostrated themselves before the altar in humble, hearty thanksgiving.

At dawn, the next day, the ransomed slaves were already marshalled on the open space before the hospital gate, waiting the signal for embarking. Father Sainte Foi was in the midst of them, full of ardor and energy, and as impatient for the happy moment when they should quit the land of the infidel as the unfortunate men he had saved. Father Antoine was there also, but, more reserved in the expression of his joy, he could scarcely repress a smile as he remarked the excitement and triumph of his young companion.

"But I was also once young," said he, "nay, to-day I could almost fancy myself so again ! And now, my son, see that all is ready, that no one is missing ; it is time to begin our march to the ship."

At this moment a cry arose from the assembled Christians. "Slaves ! more slaves ! O God ! they come too late—they have just arrived from the desert with their master—there are two of them—they are too late !"

"There are two of them," repeated Father Sainte Foi, and his cheek turned pale, "oh ! if there had been but one !"

"Alas ! they arrive too late," cried the good old priest, "our purse is empty. Go to them, my son. I cannot comfort them ; promise them that next year—but oh ! hide from them, if possible, the joy of the others !" Father Sainte Foi forced a passage through the assembled multitude, and found himself before the two unfortunate captives who had already learned their fate, and were bewailing it in heartrending accents. One, a man already past the prime of life, was wringing his hands and sobbing with a choking voice, "My children, my children, shall I then never see you again ?" Overcome by his emotion he fell fainting to the ground ; the father rushed to his assistance, but started back as he caught sight of his features. One moment, one single moment he hesitated, then cast himself on his knees by the side of the prostrate man, raised and supported the sinking head, and impressed a kiss on the pale brow. "Thus do I seal my pardon !" said he ; "Sire of Valeri, you shall see your children again !"

The other slave whom he had not yet remarked, at this instant uttered a joyful cry, and threw himself into his arms, exclaiming, "Friend, brother, dear Raoul !"

"Aymar—Sire de Valeri—O Blessed Virgin !" stammered the monk, with a stifled voice as he fell back insensible.

"Help! help!" exclaimed Aymar, for it was indeed he, "I have killed my friend!"

The unconscious father was carried into the hospital chapel, Aymar supporting him in his arms, while tears of mingled joy and grief coursed down his thin cheeks. Father Antoine desired him to retire, but not until his friend gave signs of returning life would Aymar leave him, to await in silence at the other end of the chapel the effect of the aged monk's consolations and admonitions.

"Father Antoine," spoke the young priest at length, raising himself on the bench on which he had been laid, "you know the vow I made on the day of my profession? If gold I had none, to give my body for the ransom of Christian captives. That time is come, father, but I cannot choose between these two. One is— no, *was* my enemy, and the other is my dearest friend! O reverend father, I fear to fail in my duty toward God if I refuse to return good for evil, if I leave the Sire of Valeri in captivity. And yet—how can I prefer him to my dear Aymar?—to Aymar for whom I would gladly give my life! Venerable father, help me in this terrible struggle and choose for me!"

"Hold!" cried Aymar, coming forward; "there is no choice needful here! Can you believe, Raoul, that I will accept your sacrifice? What, you a slave in my place! *I* return again to France at the cost of *your* freedom! Raoul, Raoul, do you know me so little? If your noble heart prompts you to ransom the Sire of Valeri at such a cost, let it be so, but never will Aymar consent to it for himself!"

"Generous friend!" exclaimed the young monk, seizing his hand.

"Nay, Raoul, we have been brothers-in-arms, we will now be brothers-in-chains; it is but a change of harness!" The two friends threw themselves into each other's arms, and Father Antoine blessed them while he wept.

"I cannot prevent you from making this sacrifice, my son," said he, at length, "it is according to our holy rules; but if God grant me life, next spring will see me here again to deliver you both. And now go, tell the Sire of Valeri what your charity has inspired you to do for him."

"No, no, father; I must not see him again. He is too proud—I know him well—to receive a gift from the hands of Raoul de Montorgueil; he would rather die a slave than be delivered by me. Let him never learn, I entreat you, by what means he recovered his freedom."

"It is well, my brother; it shall be as you desire."

Father Antoine hastened to the beach, where he found the Sire of Valeri recovered from his swoon. Without further explanation the good father told him simply that he was free, and invited the Mussulman, his master, to accompany him back to the hospital, where Father Sainte Foi, with a calm, clear voice, proposed to the astonished unbeliever to take him, a strong, young man—and he showed his muscular, nervous arm—in exchange for the broken-down and aged slave on the strand.

The avaricious master willingly accepted an offer so advantageous to himself, and Father Sainte Foi put on with a smile of ineffable happiness, the chains that had weighed so heavily on the once stalwart limbs of the enemy of his name and race. Father Antoine pressed his lips reverentially to those chains, and then seizing his cross, hastened to take his place at the head of the long line of ransomed Christians. But no chant of joy and triumph resounded as they bent their way toward the ship that was to bear them to their homes—they embarked silently, almost sadly—the sails spread, and the swift vessel was soon lost to sight.

The Moor took possession of his slaves. But we will pass over in silence their toils and their sufferings : his living faith sustained the Redemptorist father ; hope was the life-spring of Aymar ; their mutual friendship was the consolation of both. Aymar found his chains light to bear, since his friend was near him, and the monk feared that he had received his reward in this world, so sweet did their daily intercourse appear to him.

The young knight related to his younger brother-in-arms, how, on his return from du Guesclin's victorious expedition, the vessel in which he and the Sire of Valeri were embarked, had fallen into the hands of Moorish pirates, and how they had been sold together in the slave-market at Algiers. He loved, too, to recount to his sympathizing listener his feats of arms in Spain, until his friend, reproaching himself for giving ear to such worldly matters, would talk, in his turn, of heavenly things, of the peaceful joys and aspirations of his convent life, and would repeat the history of the Son of Man, who loved us so that he had willed to bear poverty, hunger, and death for us. When he told how he had not where to lay his head, "Oh ! never more shall I complain," cried Aymar, " for mine rests on the bosom of a friend !"

Thus the long days of slavery passed over the two captives, and when at last the hour of deliverance

arrived ; when Father Antoine, true to his word, came with the first days of the next spring to unloose their chains, Aymar looked tenderly in his friend's face, while Father Sainte Foi endeavored to hide a tear.

" Can you believe that I will ever leave you again ?" said Aymar, replying to his friend's thoughts. " No, death alone shall separate us henceforth ! I will accompany you to your monastery. The world smiled on me, but gave me pain and slavery ; Heaven has given me a true friend, and to Heaven I devote myself for ever !"

Then turning toward Father Antoine, " Father," said he, " receive me here, in the land of our cruel taskmasters, here, where we have suffered together, as a novice of the Order of Mercy !"

Father Antoine in answer threw his white mantle on the young knight's shoulders, and the two friends, hand in hand, climbed the side of the ship that was waiting to carry them back to France.

Here we will bid them farewell, in the full enjoyment of that perfect friendship ; we will not seek to know if other vicissitudes came to try it ; let us lose sight of them now, and believe, that, retired from the strife and noise of the world, they passed together the remainder of their quiet lives, busied in the acquirement of heavenly wisdom, and in the practice of those pure, simple, but sublime virtues which find in themselves their own reward and glory.

Can we doubt that Father Sainte Foi experienced that charity l ke mercy, " is twice blessed," .

" It blesseth him that gives, and him that takes "?

A BRIDEMAID! I had become a necessity. A sense of such importance was novel to me. It was a pleasant awakening to a consciousness that I had attained womanhood. To have been a bride would not have filled me with such unmingled joy; for then I might have been thinking over the possibilities of the future. Now I had only to play my part in the bright and bewildering present.

That there had been bridemaids before my time, of the loftiest and of the lowliest degree, from the jewelled princess to the humble dairy-maid, rendered my position none the less novel and refreshing. Then, too, the circumstances of the case were not to be lightly passed over—I had been chosen from among so many whose claims to consideration were far above mine.

An imaginative child always seeks and finds some object in which to concentrate its thoughts and its loves; something real to serve as an embodiment of its ideal fancies. Hence, all the wealth of my fervent nature had centred on Marian Howard.

From earliest childhood I had watched and wondered at her rare and high-born beauty. Every feature in her face seemed to have a distinct and separate fascination, while every adornment of dress that could enhance her varied charms was brought into requisition. To look upon her was a feast of pleasure to my eyes.

The quiet dignity of her manner kept a distance between us, so that she was a sort of far-off idol, after all. In her company we never gave way to our outgushing school-girl nature. I sometimes thought she would be happier if she were only more like us, or if we should welcome her with a girl's free and fervent greeting. But who dared try the experiment?

As we grew older, our paths in life diverged. Soon after leaving school, Marian went to live and to love in a foreign land, while I returned to the quiet pleasures of a rural home.

Four years passed, and then the fine old house which had so long remained silent again showed signs of life. They had returned—the widowed aunt and her beautiful niece.

The preparations for the wedding were immediately commenced, and Marian repaid my early devotion by offering me the highest mark of her confidence and regard.

The old tenderness came rushing back when I again beheld her more stately and more beautiful than ever. She told me it would be a quiet wedding—only a few friends, and I her only bridemaid. My arrangements were soon completed, and I awaited anxiously the appointed time. Soon it was the day before the marriage. I went over to assist in the final preparations, and was to spend the night with Marian. The morrow would witness, in the case of my friend, the great event of a woman's life—to be given away in marriage. I say of a woman's life, because marriage can hardly have the same significance for men; they are not given away.

The distinguished stranger who was so soon to call Marian his wife was certainly unlike any of the men I had ever known; but I had known so few, and my knowledge of the world was so limited, that I did not feel competent to pass judgment on him. Then there were such method, such calmness and system about the man, about the unbending aunt, about Marian, and about the whole house, that I felt cold with a chilling sense of not being able to get warm again, though it was a lovely summer afternoon. More of nature and less of art, I thought, might have warmed the approaching festivities.

The evening shadows were falling. We had just finished arranging and rearranging the costly bridal gifts, when Marian was summoned to attend her aunt.

Among the other presents was that grand conception, Gustave Doré's *Wandering Jew.* This work of human genius seemed a strange companion for the rare articles of luxury that surrounded it.

I took up the book and went out upon the balcony. The softly-fading twilight, the subdued spirit of the house, the reflective turn my own mind had taken, prepared me for impressions of the awful and sublime. It is said that " real genius always rises, and in rising it finds God." Surely the force and truth of this thought were here exemplified; for who could look upon these scenes, so truthful and intense, without a feeling of awe and reverence ?

I was thus occupied, I know not how long, when suddenly Mr. Gaston recalled me to myself. " How absorbed you are, Miss Heartly! I have been watching you with much interest. Pray, has the book any bearing upon the coming events of to-morrow ? Court beauties, I suppose," he continued carelessly, as he came toward me.

" Why !" said I, " you have returned early, Mr. Gaston. You cannot have taken that delightful drive Marian proposed to you ?"

" No," he answered; " I have no inclination for solitude; but you ladies are so occupied with these time-killing nothings, these endless little ar-rangements so indispensable to your happiness, that we lonely mortals are entirely ignored and forgotten."

" I think, sir, that calamity seldom befalls you," I replied, thus adding, perhaps, to vanity already sufficiently great.

" But the book ?" he continued, opening it listlessly. " Oh! the old fable in a new dress. It is strange how women cling to the marvellous and impossible. They seem to have but two absorbing ideas—love and religion. Extremes in either usually lead to the same pernicious result. I suppose an idol is a necessity to them, and it matters little in which they find it."

" I do not understand you," I replied. " Are you in jest, or are you seriously denouncing revealed religion ?"

" Revealed religion !" he repeated. " Is it possible that, at this stage of the world's advancement, *you* still cling to that antiquated idea of Christianity ?"

The modern methods of fashioning a god to suit the impious desires of vain and conceited mortals was then unknown to me. I looked at the man with wonder and distrust. He read my confusion and hastened to explain himself.

" Religion," he said, " as you accept it, makes us cowards instead of men. My reason is *my* religion; I acknowledge no other guide."

" Ah ! then," I exclaimed, " how often must you stumble by the way." I turned to the most effective picture in the book. " Here is an instance of the vanity of human pride. Here we can see the end of man's boasted strength—the anguish of a lost soul hopelessly looking for repose and peace."

" An imposing fable," he replied, " wanting only a woman's faith to give it substance and reality."

I was rising to put an end to this

unprofitable and distasteful conversation, when Marian joined us. My disturbed manner plainly annoyed her, and she evidently suspected its cause; for she addressed Mr. Gaston in German quite earnestly. Soon turning to me he said, "Pray, excuse me, Miss Heartly; I was not aware that you were a Catholic. I know your people feel most keenly what they profess. Of course you have already stamped me a condemned heretic."

"It is not for me to pass judgment on you," I replied; "and if I did, my opinion could be of very little value."

"Come, come!" said Marian, "this is a most unapt and gloomy subject for my marriage eve; and the sun, too, has gone down sullenly. I hope there is nothing prophetic in all this."

"What! growing serious now?" I said, as I drew her arm within mine, and we went to look for the fiftieth time at the final arrangements for the morrow's festivities.

I could not, however, throw off the feeling of uneasiness that my interview with Mr. Gaston had left. He had a way of cheapening one, so that, without knowing why, you fell immeasurably in your own estimation. This is never a comfortable condition to find one's self in, and it takes a good deal of nice logic to bring one back to one's normal state.

Perhaps it was the loftiness of his style that awed me; for he had a magnificent way of carelessly throwing the world behind him and walking forth in a sort of solitary dignity. "His manners are courtly," Marian's aunt said, and certainly they possessed all the cold stiffness that characterized her particular circle; still, I felt I had no real grounds for this feeling of distrust and aversion to Mr. Gaston, and I began to think it was rather ungenerous to hold him in so unfavorable a light. I could not shake off, however, an undefined dread of the approach-

'ing marriage. The apathy and indifference which had always been peculiar to my young friend did not forsake her even now, when apparently on the very threshold of happiness. I thought that intensity of feeling perhaps kept her thus silent, for overpowering happiness has this effect sometimes. The delusion was, however, speedily dispelled.

That night a sealed chapter in Marian's life was laid open to me, and I saw her as I had never seen or thought of her before.

After locking the chamber-door, she seated herself by my side, and said, "This is the first time in my life that I have known perfect freedom; I mean a liberty to do and say what I like with a feeling of security.

"You remember the 'Greek Slave.' Well, I am not unlike that delicate girl chained in the market-place. Every inclination of my heart has been chained down and locked, and my aunt has kept the key.

"I was an uncomplaining, passionless child. In my cradle I received my first lessons in self-control. As I grew older, I learned another lesson, too unnatural for even a thoughtful child like me to understand. I was not needed here; I was considered only as a desirable ornament for this great house. I might as well have been placed upon a pinnacle and petrified at once, for all the childhood that was allowed to take root within me.

"My aunt's domestic misfortunes had embittered her, and she had no children to soften the natural austerity of her soul. My mother, who was her only sister, had, contrary to my aunt's wishes, married where her heart inclined. This was never forgiven or forgotten until she lay dead, and I was a wailing infant at her side.

"My father soon afterward perished at sea, and my aunt took me to her home.

"She was not designedly cruel; but she knew nothing of a child's requirements. The freezing system seemed to her the most effectual method of crushing out a young, impulsive nature. There was danger I might become rebellious, and hence she required the utmost meekness and submission.

"As soon as I came to understand the power of beauty, I saw that it was to mine I owed food and raiment; for it fed the exhaustless vanity of my aunt, with whom display was then, and still is, the moving spring of her existence.

"I was a drawing-room child, kept for exhibition at stated intervals. The tiny jewels on my neck and arms were hateful to me. My embroidered robe was a costly thing. I had given a young life for it.

"I had a mortal fear of losing my beauty. Our gardener's daughter—a comely, cheerful-looking girl, whom I was always glad to see, for she made the morning brighter with her fresh young face—had caught that loathsome disease, the small-pox. When she recovered, the change that had come upon her so terrified me, that I was seized with a sensation as of coming danger. I shrank from the girl, as if she would be the cause of some future misery to me.

"She had a mother to whom she seemed infinitely more dear now than she had ever been. But I, a lonely waif, what would become of me if I should be transformed like her?

"It was not altogether for my own gratification that I desired to retain this beauty. It was not my own beauty. It belonged to my aunt, and was all I had to give her in return for what she gave me.

"I was not a child that saw angels in the skies, or that expected manna to come down from heaven to feed me.

"Artificial and unsatisfying as my life has always been, I have a clinging desire to remain with it.

"At times I have had a vaguely conceived notion of one day getting away from it and of being free; but the bending and breaking system has so subdued me that I might lose myself if left to the guidance of my own free-will.

"Marriage is a solemn thing. Would you like to change places with me to-night, Mary?"

I could not say yes, and I dared not say no; for I saw that she was losing courage, and beginning to hesitate about the important event so soon to transpire.

"That is a strange question, Marian dear," I replied. "To-morrow ought to be, and I hope will be, the happiest day of your life. Surely you must love this man when you have promised to be his wife?"

"Oh! yes," said she, "as well as I understand what it is to love. I sometimes tremble for fear I have not the qualities that make woman lovable and attractive. You forget how little I know of Edward Gaston.

"Our acquaintance began in a little German town, where he was stopping, for the purpose of establishing his claims to a disputed inheritance. He is an American by birth and education. He soon became a constant visitor with us. My aunt and he were on the best of terms. My own interest in him had never passed beyond the civilities of an ordinary acquaintance until he again joined us at Naples, where he lost no time in making known the state of his feelings.

"My aunt seemed to have had some previous knowledge of his preference; but its announcement was to me a complete surprise.

"She was proud of her nice dis

crimination in the selection of her friends, and Mr. Gaston had come into our circle labelled and indorsed a gentleman.

"Her gracious consideration, however, of his offer, in no wise obscured her caution. Satisfied as to his worldly affairs, and well assured of his position at home, there was nothing wanting but my consent, which was really the most trifling part of the arrangement. I accepted this marriage engagement as I would have accepted any other condition so mapped out for me.

"Business of a pressing nature which could be delayed no longer, called Mr. Gaston to America, and I did not see him again until our return a month ago.

"You see how little I know of him. Can you wonder that I am constrained in his presence? Of course, every thing will be different when I come to know him better.

"But I have one cause of feverish anxiety. I am not above the petty subterfuges almost incidental to a life like mine. A desire to hide mistakes committed through childish ignorance made me unscrupulous, as any member of a household who is watched and suspected must naturally be. Habit may have made these little irregularities almost a second nature, but my blood recoils from a wilful and deliberate deception. I am afraid Edward is misled with regard to my aunt's pecuniary condition.

"This life of seeming affluence, which has become as necessary to her as the air she breathes, drains heavily on her slender resources. Such portion of her time as is not spent in her handsome carriage, or in drawing-room entertainments, is passed in a most frugal and even parsimonious mode of living, and it is only by an economy painful to contemplate that she has kept things floating thus far.

"I cannot acquaint Edward with my aunt's existing embarrassments. She is my only kinswoman; and misguided as she is, I have a tender affection for her. I hope to be able to offer her a home with us, when, as soon must be the case, the last act in this miserable farce shall have been played.

"Now, perhaps, you can understand why I thus passively submit to a marriage that I would turn from if I could. I cannot openly say to Mr. Gaston, 'I have no fortune, I hope you expect none;' even to covertly approach the subject would be to impugn his motives, and I certainly have no right to suspect him of harboring mercenary ones. Still, I wish he were acquainted with the truth; for the world, you know, looks upon me as sole heiress of my rich aunt.

"I have no knowledge of what passed between Edward and my aunt at Naples, when our marriage was agreed upon; but I have a constant dread least he may have been deceived. I once mentioned to him, in conversation, that he would claim a portionless bride; but he seemed to take no notice of what I said, and I fear he still thinks my aunt's circumstances to be in reality what they seem."

"In giving way," I replied, "to such groundless fears, dear Marian, you underrate your own worth. Think how many noble and honorable men would be proud to call you wife, and in giving you a life of happiness make amends for the past." Yet as I looked in the silver starlight upon that lovely face, which had so attracted me in my childhood, I could not but regret deeply and sadly that she was not of my faith; for then she might receive wiser counsel than I could give from one of those whom Christ in his mercy has ordained to be a guide and a staff to weak and wavering souls.

The wedding breakfast was all that

even Marian's fastidious aunt could have desired. The few favored guests were of the most approved type. It would seem as if a judicious instructor had given each of them a select number of words, which they used with exemplary caution, and then retired to the contemplation of their own individual greatness.

As to Marian, the despondency of the night before had quite left her, and there was a high and noble resolve in her manner that made me truly happy to behold, while it calmed, if it did not entirely dispel, my own gloomy forebodings. The serene expression of her sweet face would have drawn me nearer to her, if that were possible.

How I loved her, as she stood before me, beautiful in the purity of her white robe, and infinitely more beautiful in the chastened security of her firm and lofty purpose—to be a true and honorable wife to Edward Gaston; to meet the conditions of her new life, whatever they might be, with a woman's trust and confidence, and better still, with a woman's hope in the never-failing reward of duty faithfully performed.

I could have been positively gay through desire to sustain Marian, and to let her know, without telling her in words, how thoroughly I appreciated and how heartily I approved her noble intentions, her courage and confidence; but as measured words and actions alone were allowed, I had to restrain myself. Still, the cooling process did not diminish my ardor, and when I got Marian all to myself, in her room, I kissed her so approvingly, and was so extravagant in the expression of all that I felt, that she folded me with loving tenderness to her breast, and kept me there so long that I felt with the quick beating of her warm heart she was giving me some of her own newly-found courage.

" Whatever happens to me, Mary dear, in the extremity of any darkness that may come upon me, I shall always know that you are true to me, that you are still my friend."

The tears that fell upon her hand as she gently raised my head, were my only answer, and she accepted them in the spirit in which they were shed.

In returning to my ordinary duties, I had much to reflect upon, much that made me still uneasy for Marian and her future, where so many doubts and fears seemed hanging on the will of one human being.

Vague rumors of Mr. Gaston had reached us, that he was a man wholly without fortune, drifting on the surface of events; darker things, too, were whispered with an indirectness which gave them an uncertain coloring. In my love for Marian, and in my fear for her, I could not credit these suspicions; yet my anxiety to again see her, and discover for myself the truth or fallacy of these reports, was intense. Indeed, my state of anxious doubt was becoming intolerable when I received a letter from Marian, telling me she was already tired of travelling, and would return soon to make a last visit to her old home before leaving for her future and distant one.

It was agreed that they should spend the day after their arrival with us. I was so happy and so occupied in preparing for their reception, that I had almost forgotten my previous anxiety in my present desire to have every thing ready and in perfect order. The pleasure I felt in the prospect of having my darling with me so soon was dreadfully toned down by the consciousness of my own inability to satisfy her aunt's critical taste. I trembled as I thought of her scrutinizing glance; but I had a never-failing source of hope in my mother. Her good-natured hospitality was of such a melting kind that I dared hope that even the rigid aunt might thaw under it, which she really did, greatly to my relief and comfort.

The dinner passed off creditably. My tranquillity was now entirely restored, and I had time to devote to Marian.

Up to this moment I had viewed her through the medium of my excited condition; now I was calmed, and, so far as the affairs of the day went, contented.

Marian's manner was restless and uneasy. My perception was keenly alive to the slightest difference between what she did and said now and to what she did and said formerly. So solicitous was I, that I think the most trifling modulation in her voice had a significance for me.

Much as I had looked forward to this reunion, much as I had desired it, now that Marian was with me, I shrank from being alone with her. I think if we had been that summer evening even in the solitude of a mountain fastness, an intuitive delicacy would have kept both of us from speaking one word upon the only subject that filled our hearts.

My mother's humanizing influence was having its effect on the stately old lady. She was captured without knowing it. Mr. Gaston had gone out for a walk; so Marian and I were left alone. I tried to talk about her new home, and repeated some things Mr. Gaston had told me before the wedding.

"Edward has changed his mind," said Marian, "and has found it necessary to make some different arrangements; so I really cannot tell much about our home. It is very far away; don't you think so, Mary?" I saw that her feelings were beginning to get the upper hand, and I did not dare trust myself to reply. I turned from her immediately on the pretext

of having forgotten some household duty. She strolled out to the garden in a spiritless way.

Every thing was revolving itself in my mind, and I was beginning to reproach myself; perhaps if I had encouraged her to speak, it might have lifted the load from her heart; another opportunity might not be permitted us; and yet, bowed down as the poor girl was, it would not have raised her in my esteem had she even with me disparaged her husband. To cover him with a wife's forbearance was now one of her hard but imperative duties, and I knew she would not shrink from it. This must be a check to our confidence, a bridge over which my kindliest sympathy must never pass.

Unmistakable evidences of a storm close at hand made me run to the arbor where I had last seen Marian. She was not there. While deliberating where I should next go, I heard Mr. Gaston's impatient tread. He stopped by a clump of trees near me, and in tones of suppressed anger commenced upbraiding his defenceless wife.

"What did you mean by suggesting such a thing as that?" he began; "have you any right to dispense hospitalities, to propose or consider them in that grand style of yours?"

"In expressing the wish," replied Marian, "that my aunt would be able to spend the winter with us, I had no intention of doing any thing beyond a natural act of gratitude; and I was not aware, Edward, that your feelings had so changed toward her. I am sure she has done nothing to merit your displeasure."

"Nothing to merit my displeasure? You are a most creditable disciple! She has made you like herself, truly. Is it nothing in your eyes that she has always lived a life of nicely-arranged deception? Your accomplished aunt has conducted a forlorn hope with a woman's tact, and the victims of her trickery are expected to bow to her superior sagacity. In a burst of universal sympathy you propose to take this wreck of decayed grandeur to my house. This was a part of the plot, I suppose."

" Edward," interrupted Marian, " how dare you speak in this way of my aunt, who has shown you so many marks of sincere regard? That she has not husbanded her resources, I grant; but that misfortune rests entirely with her, she is the only sufferer. She made you no promises, gave you no reason to expect a fortune with me; this I have learned since our marriage. Have no fear of the incumbrance. Dear as she is to me, I would rather let her beg from door to door than see her a recipient of your bounty !"

" Oh! you are proud now," he replied in a voice of withering scorn. " Take care," he continued; " you have not seen the end yet. Make yourself ready to depart. I want to leave this house instantly."

." Edward," she said, "however you choose to afflict me, whatever tortures you have in store for me, do not, I beseech you, subject me just yet to the pity of those I love, of those who love me. These people are my truest friends. I would not make them sharers of my misery. Spare me a little longer."

" Your fine speeches and these people are alike objects of indifference to me. Make yourself ready; I am going."

She made a movement to obey him; but turning round again, she said, " Edward"—the voice and tone I shall never forget; it was as if all she had ever valued in life had whispered a last farewell—" Edward, as I had hoped to give you a wife's unfailing duty, to be trustful, loving, and

true; so I had hoped you would give me a husband's protection, and perhaps a husband's love."

" I am not fond of scenes," he interrupted ; " your requirements are of so nice and delicate a nature that I would be quite incapable of gratifying them; so I shall not trouble myself to make the attempt; and for the future, spare yourself any unnecessary display of sentiment."

I could not have left the arbor without being seen. Marian passed by slowly, not to the house, but in an opposite direction, and Mr. Gaston started for the lower end of the garden. I caught a glimpse of him as he turned an angle of the walk. A wicked look had settled on his handsome face, as if dark spirits were urging him on.

A peal of thunder, prolonged and terrible, startled me. I ran to the house. The lightning was truly awful, and peal following peal of thunder made one shudder and long for human companionship. I had lost Marian in the gloom and darkness. She was not in the house; I did not see her in the garden. I went out into the storm in search of her.

I found her standing quite alone in sad and listless silence. Can it be, I thought, that death has no terrors for one so gifted and so young ? She seemed imploring that doom which the most abject and miserable would flee from if they could. I knew then, as well as I knew afterward, that she would have welcomed death that night without one single regret.

" Marian, dear," I said, approaching her, " how can you remain alone, and exposed in this manner, when every thing about you is quaking with fear ?"

" I do not heed the storm," she answered ; " I like it, it is so wonderful."

" Come, come, darling ! Why, the rain has drenched you," I replied, putting my arm about her and leading her to the house.

The storm had set in furiously. There was no leaving the house that night. I resolved that Marian should sleep with me; so I went to Mr. Gaston and told him I regretted our limited accommodations obliged me to offer him a temporary bed in the parlor.

When I told Marian of this arrangement, she seemed relieved. "I am glad to spend the night here and with you, Mary," she said. "All is so quiet and peaceful."

Quiet and peaceful! The greater storm in her own breast made her forget the contending elements without.

My aversion to Mr. Gaston was, I believe, heartily reciprocated, and he must have chafed at my influence over Marian. He took her away from her home, never to return, on the very next day. They sailed for Cuba shortly afterward.

The crisis Marian had feared for her aunt soon came, and she went, with the remnant of her fortune, to live in some western town.

Seven years had rolled by since all this, and Marian was fast passing into the shadows we like to call up when the world is hushed around us and, we are thinking—thinking.

I was married, and laughing children were crowding out these earlier remembrances.

An affection of the throat, from which my husband was suffering, rendered the best medical advice necessary. I accompanied him to New-York, where I found—let me pause in telling it, to do reverence to the unseen hand that led me there—Marian.

In this lonely stranger how little do I behold of my childhood's earliest pride!

"From Clifton?" said the physician thoughtfully, after examining my husband's case. "I have a patient, a strange case; she is paralyzed, and her mental faculties are stunned. A Cuban family brought her here and placed her under my care. Her husband had committed a forgery, and had fled the country to escape arrest. She is an accomplished lady, I should judge. She was left in Havana quite poor and friendless. I have been led to speak to you about her because she is always writing two words—Mary and Clifton. The Spanish lady who brought her here knew nothing of her former history."

I was silent during this recital, and so white that the doctor offered me water. I thanked him, and expressed a wish to go to my friend immediately.

"I cannot return to the hospital this morning," he said; "but I will give you my card, which will admit you to the lady at once."

There I found her, a silent, faded figure, sitting still, and for all purposes of life quite dead.

I was awed as I stood before her. I sat down and took her poor, neglected hand in mine. She looked at me and made a feeble attempt to gather back her hair which had fallen in great disorder about her shoulders. I rose to do this for her. It was still glossy and beautiful as ever. I began to arrange it in the fashion she had worn it seven years before. She took my hand from her head, laid it in her lap, chafed it, then reverently raised it to her lips. I could restrain my tears no longer, and I hid my face in the folds of her faded dress. She turned me toward her and wiped the tears from my cheek.

"You are going home with me, Marian darling," I said; "to live always in our own old home."

"I know it," she whispered; "I have been waiting for you so long, so very long."

This was the first time she had

spoken to me. The nurse had told me that she spoke occasionally, but always in an absent and incoherent manner.

Sea-bathing was recommended; but the doctor was of the opinion that her mind would never recover its original vigor.

I would like him to see her as she left me this morning, calm and beau-tiful, when the bell of the convent, where she is teaching German, summoned attendance.

My religion is no longer strange to her. She has accepted it as the crowning blessing of her life, and with a thankful spirit she speaks of the chastening hand that led her to this security and peace.

TRANSLATED FROM THE FRENCH OF SOUVESTRE.

THE INSIDE OF A STAGE-COACH.

ONE of the last days of September the rain had fallen all day in torrents, but finally, having ceased, left the sky so enveloped in fog that, though scarcely four o'clock, night seemed already to have overspread the earth.

A heavy diligence, with its relay of horses, ascended with difficulty one of the hills which separate Belleville from Lyons, while the postilions walked on each side of the team, pausing about every fifty steps to breathe and recover themselves. The wearied passengers had descended by invitation of the conductor, and were trudging along in no amiable mood, scolding the horses, the rain, and the miserable roads. Two of them, who came last, stopped suddenly at the turning of the ascent. One was a man nearly fifty years old, with a mild and smiling countenance; but the other, much younger, had an air of gloom and dissatisfaction. Throwing his eyes over the surrounding country, half enveloped in fog, he said to his companion:

"What weather and what a year, Cousin Grugel! The Saône has hardly entered its bed, and the valleys are again inundated."

"God preserve us, Gontran!" replied the man with the mild countenance; "the rainbow can appear any moment above the deluge."

"Yes," replied the other traveller, with slight irony; "I know your mania of hope, Jacques."

"And I yours of discouragement, Darvon."

"Well, I am right when I examine how this world goes. Where do you see peace, order, or prosperity? I only hear of incendiaries, contagion, deluge, and murder. What man's wickedness spares, the wickedness of nature annihilates, for even brute matter seems to possess the instinct of destruction; and the elements, like kings, cannot remain neighbors without warring against each other."

"That is only one side of things, my cousin—the sad side; but of the other you never speak. Your eyes are riveted on the volcano which dims the horizon, but you cannot lower them to the fields of ripe corn undulating at your feet. There is happiness in the world, if you can make up your mind to believe it."

"Well, I know nothing of it," replied Darvon, in a tone of vexation.

"But, yourself considered, may you not be placed among the most favored?"

"True, Jacques, and yet I have not been able to find, in all the good accorded me, either peace or contentment."

"What have you to wish for? You are rich, honored, and have a family who love you."

"Yes," replied Gontran; "but this same fortune has cost me the lawsuit for which I have just made the third voyage to Macon; my good reputation has not deterred the opposing lawyer from slander; and as to my family—"

"Well?" inquired Jacques.

"Well! my sister, with whom I always lived so affectionately, has just quarrelled with me."

"It will be a short quarrel."

"No, no; I am tired of working

without profit to establish order in her affairs. I have been too much annoyed by her want of system and reason."

" Think of her excellent heart and you will forgive her."

" Oh ! I know that you will always find a good reason for me to bear my sorrows patiently ; you have a recipe for every wound of the soul, and if I press you a little, you will prove me in the wrong to complain, and that all is quite right here below."

" Pardon me," replied Grugel ; "in the government of this world I find much to wound me, but I am not sure I am the best judge. Life is a great mystery, of which we comprehend so little. Must I own it to you, there are hours when I persuade myself that God has not afflicted men with so many scourges without intention. Happy and invulnerable, they could be endured ; each one would count on his individual strength, delight in his own isolation, and refuse all sympathy to his fellow-being. But weakness has no such resource ; on the contrary, it forces men to be friendly, to aid and love one another. Grief has become a bond of sympathy, and we owe to it our noblest and best sentiments, gratitude, devotion, and piety."

" Well done," said Darvon, smiling ; " not being able to sustain the good in all things, you give me the bright side of evil."

" Perhaps so," said Grugel ; " only be sure that evil itself is not absolute. Science borrows its remedies from the sap of venomous plants ; why, then, may we not from passion, misfortune, or inequality draw much that is good ? Believe me, Darvon, there is no human dross, however poor, without its particles of gold."

" In good faith, then, I would like to know what could be found in our travelling companions," cried Gon-

tran. " Let us see, cousin ; suppose we put to the test these curious patterns of our race, as we proclaim it so intelligent."

" It is very certain," said Jacques, smiling, " fate has not favored us."

" Never mind, never mind," replied Darvon, whose misanthropy was niggardly in its character ; " disengage the gold from the dross, as you say. But first, how many grains do you expect to find in this cattle-merchant before us ?"

Grugel raised his head and saw, a few steps in advance, the traveller who had called him cousin. A coarse man in a blue blouse, following with heavy steps the side of the road, while finishing his well-picked chicken-bone.

" I declare, that is the seventh repast I have seen him make to-day," continued Darvon, " and the coach-pockets are still laden with his provisions. When he has eaten enough, he goes to sleep, then he eats again, then goes to sleep in order to recommence his programme. He is a mere digesting machine, too imbecile to draw from him either response or information."

" Our companion with the felt hat can sufficiently acquit himself in that respect."

" Ah ! yes, let us consider him and try also to extract his gold. He joined our party only this morning, and already the conductor has sent him from the *impériale* to the travellers in the *coupé*, who again have sent him to the *intérieur*. We have had him but two hours, and he has already given us his own and his family history to the fifth degree. I know his name is Peter Lepré, that for twenty years he has been commissioner of colonial produce in the departments of the Saône and Loire, of Ain, Isère, and of the Rhone, and he has been married three times.

Then if you did not have to bear his questioning; but he is equally talkative and curious, and when his confession is finished, he awaits yours. If you are reflecting, he speaks to you; if you speak, he interrupts you. His voice is like a rattle in constant motion, the noise of which ends in making you nervous."

"Poor Lepré!" said Grugel; "at heart, after all he is a worthy man."

"He has one merit," replied Darvon, "that of annoying Mademoiselle Athénaïs de Locherais; for we almost forgot this amiable fellow-traveller, who, after recommending us all to get out to lighten the coach, remained in herself so as not to dampen her feet."

"You must forgive her," observed Jacques; "isolation has made her forget all ease of others; her heart is contracted."

"Contracted!" repeated Gontran, "you are deceived, cousin; Mademoiselle Athénaïs has a great deal of love for herself. The whole world seems to have been made for her special ease, and she can imagine nothing in it that does not bear upon her in some way or other. She is one of those sweet creatures who, hearing the cry of the midnight assassin, returns to her pillow complaining of having been awakened."

Grugel was going to reply, but they had arrived at the top of the hill. The conductor, calling the passengers, urged them to remount, as a courier had just appeared with an announcement, that, owing to the overflow of the Saône, the passage by Villefranche would be impossible, and that in order to reach Anse they would be obliged to turn more to the right, passing the Niseran higher up and taking another road. The coach which had just preceded them, not having taken this precaution, had been surprised

by the waters, and some of the passengers were reported to be drowned. Happily this last intelligence was not communicated to the travellers, but they vociferated loudly when apprised of the by-road they were obliged to take.

"There is a malediction on us," said Gontran, already peevish with the length of the journey.

"I knew it would be so, sir," cried Pierre Lepré, with volubility. The two postilions had just escaped from him, so he fell back on his travelling companions. "I was told on my way that the Ardiere and Vauzarme had risen considerably; indeed, we cannot tell if we can pass to Anse, where we may encounter the waters of the Azergnes and the Brevanne. Where in the world are you taking us, conductor? Shall we pass the woods of Orrigt? Well, I know the mayor, a thin man, always smoking. But, speaking of this, can we not stop again before we come to Anse?"

"Impossible," replied the conductor brusquely; "I am now eight hours behind time."

"Gracious! where will we sup, then?" cried the fat cattle-merchant.

"We won't sup at all, sir."

"I declare, I wish I had some broth," interrupted Mademoiselle Athénaïs, in a shrill voice, with her head out of the coach door; "I always take my broth at five o'clock."

"We have had nothing since morning," cried all the travellers.

"Get in, gentlemen," called out the conductor; "one hour's delay may prevent us from reaching there. You can't joke with an overflow, and I don't want my coach drowned."

"Drowned!" cried Mademoiselle Athénaïs. "Why, this is horrible. You shall be informed against, conductor! I demand that you leave the valley. Why don't you answer me, conductor? I will complain to your chief."

The diligence starting, cut the old lady's sentence in two, so she fell back in her corner with an exclamation of dissatisfaction.

Jacques Grugel felt himself obliged to tell her that the route they were taking would lead them away from the Saône and avoid the danger.

" But where will I get my soup?" inquired she, slightly reassured.

"We will not stop till we reach Anse," resumed Lepré ; "the conductor has said so, and God only knows what kind of roads we will meet with. Roads of the department ; that says everything. And then I know the engineer, a talented man ; his son was married the same day as my eldest. But we won't arrive till to-morrow, mark my words."

There was a general cry from the passengers. They had eaten nothing since morning, calculating on the lunch usually obtained at Villefranche, and Gontran had already proposed, with his usual vivacity, to make a descent on the first village and force them to serve up a supper, when the cattle-merchant cried out :

" A supper ! I have one at your service."

" What ! for everybody ?" asked Lepré.

" For everybody, citizen. I can offer you three courses, with your dessert, and something for a heeltap."

While speaking he drew from the pockets of the carriage a half-dozen packets, and, rolling his tongue around his mouth, proceeded to open them ; they contained provisions of every kind, properly enveloped and tied with care.

" Won't we have a feast ?" said Lepré, who had asked the cattle-merchant, in his inventory, " my friend, what *is* your name ?"

" Barnau."

" Good, Mr. Barnau ; but what good care you take of yourself."

" How can a man be at his ease," said the fat merchant, with a certain pride, " if he can't eat the best of everything ? However, these gentlemen and mademoiselle can judge of my victuals."

Grugel turned to Gontran, and gave him a significant look.

" Truly," said he smiling, and in an under-voice, " here are the *grains of gold* you looked for."

" *Grains of gold !*" repeated Barnau, who did not understand him ; " why, man, that's a sausage with truffles."

" And these gentlemen would have us believe grains of gold are good for famished people," resumed Pierre Lepré, laughing ; " that is a figure of speech, Monsieur Barnau. " I have a son who studied these figures in rhetoric. He explained it all to me ; but, pardon me, let us first help mademoiselle."

They presented the food to Mademoiselle de Locherais, who returned each piece, but finally ended by choosing the most delicate, complaining, as she ate, of the privations of travellers. To console her, Barnau offered her some old brandy ; but mademoiselle cried out with horror :

" Brandy to me ! What do you take me for, sir ?"

" You like sherry better, perhaps," said the cattle-merchant, in a careless way.

" I drink neither sherry nor brandy," cried Mademoiselle Athénaïs fiercely. " I take water only," she said, turning toward Grugel. " Did you ever hear anything like this rustic ?" she murmured ; " offer me cognac, as if the spices he has given us were not sufficient to burn one's blood. I shall surely be ill from it."

Finishing what she had to say, she arranged herself in her corner, so as to turn her back on the cattle-mer-chant, picked up a pillow she had with her, leaned her head on it, and fell asleep.

The diligence continued its tedious route. Though humid, the air was cold, and not a star was to be seen. Relieved by the repast which the gastronomical foresight of Barnau had permitted him to make, Lepré resumed his loquacity, and, although his fellow-travellers had long since ceased to answer him, he continued to talk on without being in the least concerned to know if he was listened to.

This noise of words, the slowness of their progress, the darkness, and the cold combined to render the pas-sengers nervously impatient, and every few moments might be heard yawns, shudderings, or subdued com-plaints. Darvon, particularly, seem-ed more and more excitable ; a prey to nervous irritation. He had al-ready opened and shut for the tenth time the blind of the coach-door, leaned his head to the right, to the left, and back on the cushion, fixed his legs in every possible position that the narrow space of which he could dispose allowed him ; and, finally, at the break of day, his pa-tience was entirely exhausted.

" I would give ten of the days which remain of my life to be at the end of this journey," cried he.

" Here we are at Anse," replied Grugel.

" True, upon my word," said Lepré, who had been asleep an in-stant. " Hallo, conductor, how long do you remain here ?"

" Five minutes."

" Open the door ; I am just going to say good day to the post-mas-ter."

The door was opened, and Barnau got down with Lepré to renew his pro-visions. Nearly at the same moment the clerk came forward to see if there were any vacant places.

" Only one," replied Grugel.

" How !" cried Mademoiselle de Locherais, who had just awakened with a start ; " would monsieur by any chance ask any one to come in here ?"

" A traveller for Lyons."

" But it is quite impossible," re-sumed the old maid ; " we are alrea-dy frightfully crowded. Monsieur, your coaches are too small ; I will complain to the administration."

" Ah ! without doubt here is our new companion," said Grugel, who was looking out of the door. " M. Lepré has already seized upon him."

" He is a military man," cried mademoiselle.

" A non-commissioned officer of the Chasseurs."

" Oh ! is he coming in here ? Why don't they make soldiers go on foot ?"

" In such a time as this it would be hard and fatiguing for them, made-moiselle."

" Is it not their trade ? Such peo-ple are never fatigued. These pub-lic conveyances do give you such dis-agreeable neighbors ! . . . . The de-rangement of your usual habits, to have nothing warm, pass the night without any sleep, be crowded, chok-ed ! . . . . I don't see why one of these gentlemen don't get up in the imperial."

" Notwithstanding the fog ?"

" What does that signify, for men ?"

" Mademoiselle would be less in-commoded," added Darvon ironical-ly. " She had better make the pro-position herself to our companion."

" What ! I speak to a soldier !" said Mademoiselle Athénaïs fiercely ; " I prefer being incommoded, sir !"

" Well, here he is," said Jacques.

The non-commissioned officer had indeed just appeared before the door, followed by the clerk with whom he was quarrelling. He was a spruce, dapper-looking young man, but his bragging and soldierly manners disgusted Darvon at first sight. He complained of the delay of the coach, having waited for it since the night preceding, and with words abused the clerk of the office, whose responses were timid and embarrassed. At last, the conductor declaring they must start, he came to the coach-door and looked inside.

"Magnificent collection," murmured he, after having cast an impertinent look on the travellers ; "I wonder if the *coupé* and the *rotonde* are as well furnished. Have you no women aboard, conductor?"

"The insolent creature !" murmured Mademoiselle.

"Well," resumed the soldier, "one must not be too particular in the country." And he took his place.

Gontran leaned toward Grugel, and said, in a low voice, "This one completes our collection of absurdities."

"Take care he don't hear you," replied Jacques.

Darvon shrugged his shoulders.

"Bragging people inspire more disgust than fear," said he, "and this one certainly needs a lesson in politeness."

Meanwhile, Barnau returned without Lepré. After having looked for the latter at the inn, and waited for him some minutes, the diligence started without him, to the great joy of mademoiselle, who hoped to be more at her ease. But her joy was of short duration, for the non-commissioned officer, who had located himself at first on the other bench, got up and took the seat next to her. The angry old maid adjusted herself brusquely, and pulled down her veil. The military man turned toward her.

"Ah !" said he, in a mocking tone,

"madame seems afraid of being looked at."

"Perhaps so, sir," said she, dryly.

"I quite understand the reason," resumed the soldier. "But she can calm her nerves. I can deprive myself of the pleasure." And as he noticed the movement of indignation of Mademoiselle de Locherais, continued, "I speak solely for the interest of her health ; and to allow her to breathe with her face uncovered, as we want air in this box, I think I had better lower the window."

"I object to it," said mademoiselle quickly ; "my doctor has forbidden any exposure to the morning air."

"And mine has forbidden me to smother," replied the young man, putting out his hand to open the sash.

But the old maid cried out. The window was on her side, she had a right to have it closed, and appealed to the other travellers.

However little disposed Darvon had been in favor of Mademoiselle de Locherais, he considered it right to defend her, and the result was a sharp discussion between him and the soldier, which would have ended in trouble had not Grugel ceded his place at the other window.

The soldier accepted it with a bad grace, preserving a strong feeling against Darvon.

Now, the reader has already perceived that Gontran's predominant qualities were neither resignation nor patience. The contrarieties of the journey had excited his sickly inability, therefore the disagreement which had already broken out between them was renewed several times, and only awaited a favorable opportunity to become a later quarrel.

Some of the smaller baggage had been placed by Darvon in a net suspended from the top of the diligence ;

the soldier pretended that it incommoded him, and wished it removed. Gontran refused to do it.

"You have decided it shall remain where it is?" cried the soldier, after a discussion in which he had grown more and more animated.

"Decidedly!" replied Darvon.

"Very well. I will get rid of it by the coach-door," replied the young man, while extending his hand toward the net.

Gontran seized the hand, and said, "Take care what you do, sir," in a changed voice. "Ever since you came in here, you have tried to make me lose my patience; your whole course has been one of abuse and tyranny, but you may as well understand I am not the man to put up with your tyranny."

"Is this a challenge?" asked the soldier, throwing on Gontran a disdainful look.

"By no means," interrupted Grugel, annoyed by the turn affairs had taken; "my cousin merely wished you to observe—"

"I don't accept the observations of snarlers."

"And snarlers don't accept your insolence," replied Gontran.

At this word insolence the soldier shuddered, a deep redness suffused his features.

"Where do you stop, sir?" asked he of Darvon, in a voice trembling with anger.

"At Lyons," replied the latter.

"Very well, we will finish our explanation there."

"So be it."

Jacques, alarmed, wished to interpose, but his cousin and the soldier spoke at the same time, and repeated they would terminate this affair at Lyons.

At the same instant great cries were heard, and the diligence was overtaken by a wagon entirely covered with mud. Mademoiselle de Locherais put her head out of the coach-door.

"O Lord! what a misfortune," said she; "Monsieur Pierre Lepré has overtaken us. Now we will be completely filled up."

As soon as they reached the public conveyance, the commissioner of colonial produce jumped out of the wagon, and presented himself at the coach-door, which the conductor had just opened.

"Is this the way you go off without waiting for the passengers?" cried he, furious.

"I warned you three times," interposed the conductor.

"Six times is customary, sir, or even a dozen; you are very miserly with your words. Does it cost anything to speak? I could not leave the post-master while he was telling me what happened to the diligence yesterday; for you did not know, gentlemen, that the one that preceded this was drowned."

"Drowned!" repeated every one.

"Very good," interrupted the conductor; "but get in."

"Anything but good," responded Pierre Lepré; "everybody is frightened enough."

"I beg of you to get up immediately."

"And what will our families think when they learn this disaster?"

"Be quick, then."

"Again, there was I trying to obtain these details, when they came to tell me you had gone on without me."

"And we are going to do the same thing again," said the impatient conductor.

"Bless me," cried Lepré, who hastened to get up. "I have had enough of wagons; here I am, conductor, lift me up."

The commissioner of provisions

was overwhelmed with questions, and he soon related all he had heard; then, interrupting himself, according to his usual habit, and recognizing the young officer, he cried out:

"Oh! this is the gentleman I had the honor of seeing at Anse."

"The same," replied the soldier.

"Delighted to meet you again," said Lepré. "Whatever you may think of me, I am the born friend of all the military. I should have had to serve myself if they had not found a substitute for me."

He was interrupted by Mademoiselle Athénaïs, who just perceived that he was quite wet.

"It is this abominable fog," said he, while wiping the water off with his handkerchief.

"But people don't come into a carriage in such a condition," replied mademoiselle, in a discontented way. "When you are covered with fog, you might as well remain out."

"To dry one's self?" asked Lepré, laughing. "Great goodness, I had enough of it; then my coachman was drunk, and just missed turning the wagon over into the river."

"The deuce!" said Gontran.

"We would have been added to the diligence of yesterday, unless we had found some good soul brave enough to fish for us. But such things have been. Three years ago, after a great inundation, a workman alone saved five persons who were drowning near the Guillotière."

"We knew of him particularly," said Grugel, "as my cousin's best friend was one of the saved."

"True?" asked the soldier.

"And he owed his safety to the devotion of that young man."

"Oh! all the details of that action were admirable," said Darvon, with great warmth; "the frightened horse had pulled the carriage into the strongest of the current; on the shore the crowd looked on, without daring to go to their relief; there seemed to be no hope for the five persons in the carriage."

"Bah!" interrupted the soldier, "perhaps some of them could swim, and have got nicely out of the scrape."

Gontran disdained a reply.

"The carriage commenced to sink," continued he, "when a workman appeared with a small boat, which with difficulty he guided into the midst of the Rhone. Three times it was on the point of upsetting. The people who looked on from the shore cried out, 'Do not go any further; come ashore; you are going to perish.' But he did not listen to them—still advancing toward the carriage, which by dint of skill and courage, he finally reached."

"And most happily," the military man replied.

"Without doubt," replied Grugel, who remarked Gontran's movement of impatience, "but only goodhearted people find happiness in such acts."

"It was a beautiful incident," interrupted Mademoiselle de Locherais, "and one that should have benefited its author."

"Pardon me, madame," said Darvon. "The workman no doubt considered that the true recompense for any generous action is in ourselves; for, after having saved these people, he retired without wishing to receive either reward or praise."

"Humph! perhaps he thought it useless to demand payment," said the officer.

"And is his name unknown?" said Pierre Lepré.

"Pardon me, he was called Louis Duroc."

"What! what do you say, Louis—"

"Duroc."

Lepré turned towards the officer.

"Why, that is your name?" cried he.

"This gentleman's name!" repeated all the travellers.

"Louis Duroc, called the African; I asked him his name at Anse, while we were talking at the inn, and I have seen it, besides, on his portmanteau."

"Well, what next?" asked the officer, laughing. "It certainly is my name."

"Can it be!" interrupted Gontran; "and you are—"

"The workman in question; yes, gentlemen. There would have been no use in telling it, but now there is no use in concealing it. I entered the service a week after the accident, and my regiment had to leave for Algeria, so that I never again met my friends of the carriage; however, I hope to see them again at Lyons."

"I will take you to them," said Darvon quickly, while offering his hand to the officer; "for I wish we may be friends, Monsieur Louis."

"What, we!" replied the military man, regarding Gontran with hesitation.

"Oh! please forget all that has passed," replied the latter; "I am ready, if necessary, to acknowledge I have been wrong—"

"No!" interrupted Duroc, "no, indeed; I was the wrong-headed one, and .I regret it, I give you my word of honor. Bad habits of the regiment, you see. Because we have no fear, we like to show it on all occasions, and to each new-comer, and so play the bully, but at heart good children; so without malice, monsieur."

He had cordially pressed Gontran's hand, Lepré seizing his at the same time.

"Good!" cried he; "you are a true Frenchmen, and so is Monsieur.

Between Frenchmen, people should always agree. I am delighted to have made your acquaintance, M. Louis Duroc. But, *à propos*, do you know it was a most happy coincidence that I obliged you to tell me your name, that you did not want to give me? Without me, no one would have known what you were worth."

"It is true," replied Grugel. "If this gentleman had talked less, this explanation would not have taken place, and my cousin would have mistaken the true character of Monsieur Louis. You see, chance seems to have taken the task of supporting my theory, and all the honor of the journey is mine."

As he finished these words, the coach stopped; they had arrived.

The travellers found the diligence-yard crowded with relations or friends awaiting their arrival. The misfortune of the day before was known, and had awakened all possible anguish.

Darvon no sooner stepped down, than he heard his name pronounced, and, turning, saw his sister hastening to him with cries of joy. Her anxiety on his account had caused her to forget their quarrel.

They embraced over and over again; their eyes moistened with tears as they looked at each other, smiling. They were reconciled.

As they went together from the diligence-yard Gontran met his travelling companions. Barnau and Lepré saluted them; Louis Duroc renewed his promise to visit them; Mademoiselle Athénaïs de Locherais alone passed without any sign of recognition. She was too much occupied watching her baggage. Jacques Grugel turned then to Gontran.

"There is the only objection to my doctrine," said he, pointing to the old maid. "All our other companions have more or less redeemed themselves in our eyes : the *gourmand* procured us a supper ; the babbler revealed a useful secret ; the quarrelsome one gave proof of his generous bravery ; but of what use has been to us the selfish egotism of Mademoiselle de Locherais ?"

" To make me realize the value of true devotion and tenderness," replied Gontran, who pressed his sister's arm more closely to his heart. " Yes, from to-day, cousin, I will adopt your system. I firmly believe there is a good side to everything, and that it is only necessary to know where to look for the *vein of gold*."

www.ingramcontent.com/pod-product-compliance
Lightning Source LLC
Chambersburg PA
CBHW030131030726
47498CB00007B/2651